Pachamama

Pachamama

Mother Earth
Three Generations of a Bolivian Family

An Autobiographical Novel

Mariana Swann

ISBN: 1533304580
ISBN 13: 9781533304582
Library of Congress Control Number: 2016908130
CreateSpace Independent Publishing Platform
North Charleston, South Carolina

In memory of
my mother and grandmother
and the courageous people of Bolivia

To Jim, my best friend,
our children, Christopher and Olivia, our daughter-in-law, Emma,
and my sisters Carolina and Teresa.

Contents

Acknowledgements

My very special thanks to
Richard and Anjali Barber
Jean Jennings
Alix Latchford
Heather Mascie-Taylor
Anna Morris
for their unwavering encouragement and friendship

Many thanks also to
Myra Cottingham
Karen Jay
Tom Jensen
Peggie Penrose

Muchas gracias to Señor Gustavo Rodríguez Ostria
for writing so movingly about Teoponte

Love and thanks to my husband, Jim, for his patience and continuous
support.

My Journey of Discovery into My Family's Past

My grandfather haunted me from my earliest years. Because of him, my sisters and I were not dark-skinned like our grandmother and the majority of Bolivians. Because of him, I spent my childhood wondering who we were and where we came from. He died several years before I was born but stayed behind, his ghost hiding in secret corners of every single house we inhabited. He was a German immigrant who arrived in Bolivia around 1918 under mysterious circumstances, married a local beauty, fathered children, and was murdered in the darkness of a lonely night train, leaving a trail of grief and betrayal behind him.

For decades I searched for answers to the mysteries of my family's history. As a young girl, I started asking questions. The adults gave me evasive answers, changed the subject, told me half-truths. Like medieval armour, secrecy and silence enveloped our story. When I was twenty, I came to Europe, went to university, married a British man, and settled in England. But the beautiful country where I was born—and my family's phantoms—would not leave me. So I kept on digging into the past every time I went back home and whenever my mother came to see me in England.

I grew up in the midst of social, political, and family upheavals, surrounded by my country's spectacular landscapes and protected by my mother's and grandmother's love. The Aymara and the Quechua—the native people and the majority of the population—lived in poverty, while the "white" minority controlled the economy and the running of the country.

My family was an interesting mix of German, Quechua, and Spanish blood. As we had pale skin and belonged to the middle class, we were luckier than most, but as my father had abandoned us, destitution lurked just behind the door. My grandmother's life was shrouded in mystery; I could not understand why she lived in a prison of her own choosing and why she spent her time praying and asking God to forgive her. In the 1970s, when I was a teenager, three of my cousins became involved in the guerrilla uprising that followed the death of Che Guevara, and their tragic lives also became encircled by a wall of silence.

It was only decades later, after my mother's death, that the truth started to emerge, and I realised that I could not allow my family's story to disappear into the void. If that were to happen, a part of me would disappear, too. So I started digging deeper into our past.

In 2010 I visited my country of birth again and once more bombarded my acquaintances and relations with questions. At the public library in La Paz, I read copies of old newspapers to learn more about a chapter of my family's narrative. A local historian also helped me, as did a former guerrilla fighter. Finally, I returned to the city where I was born: Tarija. There, a few words handwritten in dark ink, buried for nearly nine decades in a heavy leather-bound book of entries, confirmed what I had suspected for many years.

This is our story.

Part I

The Valleys

In December 1962 I celebrated my eighth birthday. That summer my mother decided to take me on a short holiday to Tarija, the city in the south of Bolivia where I was born and had lived for my first eighteen months. I have a vivid image of myself playing at the main town square with the local girls on that brilliant December afternoon, sitting by the edge of the tiled fountain, our bodies slightly twisted to one side, splashing water at one another, droplets running down our laughing faces and soaking our sundresses, my mother nowhere in sight to tell me to be careful and behave myself.

I was eight—the best, the perfect age to be—and it seemed to me that nobody else could be as happy and as proud as I was then. I was staying in this magical, charming town where I could ride my bicycle in the leafy parks and, hardly supervised by adults, play and run around under the cool shade of ancient trees. What a different place this was from La Paz, the capital of my country, where we lived surrounded by snowy Andean peaks nearly touching the sky at 3600 metres above sea level. There, my mother's eagle eye ensured I did not get into scrapes, and I was never allowed to play out in the streets, for fear of traffic. I was pleased and amazed; in Tarija my mother had become a more relaxed and less vigilant parent, and I was reaping the benefits.

She soon noticed how exhilarated I was, and when I told her—at the dining-room table later that evening—that being eight in Tarija was the best thing ever, she agreed with me.

"I know exactly what you mean," she said as she caressed my cheek. "Remember, I grew up and went to school here."

Of course she did! Curious to hear all about it, I asked her to tell me *everything* about her life.

"Everything?" She raised her eyebrows. "It's a very, very long story."

3

"Por favoooooor, Mami."

She smiled and winked at me. "Fine, but first you have to get ready for bed. I'll tell you a little before you go to sleep."

That night she started by telling me about what had happened to her when she herself had been an eight-year-old schoolgirl. Slowly, over several years, I would learn about her life and our extended family.

Time passed slowly and sweetly in Tarija, the Andalusia of Bolivia, in the fertile valleys in the south of my country. At the main plaza, on Sunday mornings after Mass, elegant señoras and señores strolled and chatted underneath tall palm and orange trees while a band played. In the early evening, people liked taking chairs outside their homes to sit and watch the world go by. The houses were red-roofed, built in the traditional Spanish-Moorish style, with courtyards filled with flowerpots and sometimes hanging vines. Some houses also had a chicken coop and an orchard in the back. At the weekends people enjoyed swimming in the warm, clear waters of the Guadalquivir River and picnicking on the riverbank.

Life in Tarija was indeed pleasant, as even the poor peasants who slept in crowded adobe huts on the outskirts of the town and scratched a living tilling the land for their wealthy masters did not go hungry; fruit and bread were cheap and abundant.

Richer houses had balconies with terracotta pots full of flowers. My father had one of those houses, just four hundred metres from the main square, Plaza Luis de Fuentes. Two big statues adorned the square: one of Luis de Fuentes, the Spanish conquistador who founded Tarija in the 1500s, and the other of a stocky statesman, Aniceto Arce, one of my father's illustrious forebears and president of Bolivia in the 1880s. There President Arce still stands, severe and unsmiling, wearing a double-breasted suit, one hand inside his lapel, haughtily looking down from his pedestal.

My mother, Emma, was born in 1928. As an eight-year-old she was the leader of her group of friends, running around the school playground in her white cotton tunic and knee-length white socks, her plaits tied with white ribbons, her face scrubbed. She excelled in arithmetic and soon was dividing and multiplying long figures in her head, to the great annoyance of her teacher, Señorita Ramallo, a forty-year-old spinster with a permanent frown on her face. One day the teacher ordered Emma to stay behind in class while the rest of the girls went out to lunch.

"It's time you learnt some manners," Señorita Ramallo said. "Maybe you haven't been taught properly at home, but here we will teach you how to behave."

Emma looked at the teacher, mystified.

"For a start, you have the terrible habit of showing off when doing your sums," Señorita Ramallo said, "and also—"

"But I'm not showing off. I like playing with numbers," Emma interrupted.

"You impudent girl! How dare you answer back like that!" The teacher raised her hand, held it above Emma's head for a couple of seconds, and put it down again. She then went to her desk, took out two peach stones from the top drawer, and set them on the floor. "Kneel on top of these."

Emma obeyed the teacher's order. Immediately, a searing pain shot up her legs.

"Aii!"

"That'll teach you to respect your elders. You'll kneel here for five minutes."

The girl stood up defiantly. "No. I won't!"

Señorita Ramallo grabbed Emma firmly by the collar of her uniform and stormed into the headmistress's office, demanding in an agitated voice that this rebellious child be punished.

A kind, plump and grey-haired matron, Señora Trigo, the headmistress, calmly asked a few questions. Why was Emma in trouble, and why was Señorita Ramallo so angry with her? Had Emma been rude to the teacher? No. Had she hit a classmate? Stolen food or lunch money? Used bad language? Disturbed the lessons in any way? Come to school unkempt? The answers to all these questions were in the negative.

"What, then, is the matter, Señorita Ramallo?" the headmistress asked.

"Well, she...she's too quick to speak," the teacher replied. "And... she's always jumping in with the answer. She needs to learn some manners, señora."

Señora Trigo nodded. "Let me have a word with Emma, Señorita Ramallo."

In private, the headmistress spoke in a soft voice to the nervous girl. "Emma, you must always show the greatest respect for your teachers. You can do sums in your head, but please do them silently." She smiled and added, "And you won't be kneeling on the peach stones."

From that day on, no child was ever punished that way again. However, for the rest of that year, Emma was given detention for the smallest mistakes, such as forgetting to erase the blackboard—but mainly just for being Emma.

Throughout her school career, despite being noisy and playful and attending every single party, Emma was a top student. She was pretty and healthy, and life was full of promise.

Emma and her sisters lived with their mother, Filomena, in a big house in the centre of Tarija. The house had a courtyard with hanging vines and an orchard with apple and apricot trees at the back. Emma was the middle child, her sister Alcira was two years older than her, and Eugenia was two years younger. Filomena did her best to raise her children as obedient girls and devout Catholics. As a widow, however, she found it hard to enforce her strict rules and to restrain the girls' boisterous personalities. Emma, especially, was well known in the town for being a tomboy. But Filomena could not bring herself to reprimand her too severely, as she had a soft spot for her.

One of the many things Filomena had forbidden the girls to do was eat at the market. "God only knows how that food is prepared," she would say, her nose twitching as if sniffing something foul. "You are never to go there. Is that clear?"

One Saturday Emma told her mother that she was having lunch at a friend's house, kissed her on the cheek, and left just before noon. Then she walked towards the main plaza, where she met up with her classmates. The central market was their destination.

At the market the air was vibrating with laughter and banter. Proud of their mixed Quechua and Spanish blood, the *cholas*, in their wide, colourful skirts, embroidered blouses, and shawls with tassels, vied for the customers' attention.

"*Cacerita*, buy from me these cute little apricots!"

"I'll give you a special price, just for you, Cacerita!"

"*Niñita!* Won't you try a slice of mango?"

"You can't go home without tasting my chicken soup!"

Luscious pomegranates, peaches, oranges and apples threatened to spill over the stalls. Ripe cherimoyas—dark green and ugly but tasting like vanilla ice cream—had pride of place. Emma touched the cherimoyas. Their rough skin reminded her of the flannelette nightgown that made her shiver every time she put it on. Such an ugly fruit and yet such a delicacy.

At the restaurant the cholas were cooking their stews in huge clay pots, dispensing the food in enamel bowls. Emma's mouth watered when she caught a whiff of steam coming from a cauldron with spicy pork stew and lentils. She and her friends sat at a corner table. A chola with a gold tooth took their order. "Niñitas, would you like to try the peach juice?" she asked. Of course they wanted to try the cloudy peach-and-cinnamon juice, which had been made the night before by soaking and boiling dried peaches until all the sweetness of the fruit had become heavenly nectar.

As soon as they finished their lunch, one of the girls suggested they go to the park and hire bicycles. But Emma couldn't go, as she had promised to help her mother finish embroidering a new tablecloth.

As she walked home, Emma's thoughts turned to her unusual home life. Under Filomena's strict instructions, the maid always went to the market to shop for food. When it came to buying other items, such as clothes, Filomena would send one of her daughters to the shops, also under strict guidelines. Emma loved her mother and never wanted to upset her, but talking to Filomena could be difficult. Filomena lived a life of nearly total isolation and dedicated most of her time to praying and reading the Bible. Emma had often wondered why her mother, a devout Catholic, never went to church and, apart from a couple of close friends and her two older brothers, never had any visitors. Instead, the local priest came to the house after morning Mass on Sundays, and Filomena received communion and confessed her sins in the privacy of her drawing-room. As far as Emma could remember, her mother had always been a prisoner inside her own four walls. However, Emma, Alcira and Eugenia were made to attend Mass every Sunday without fail. Emma did not pay much attention to what went on inside the church; she was too busy thinking about what she wanted to do in the future.

Sometimes it seemed to Emma that people looked at her with pity and, occasionally, disdain. She and her sisters were "the unfortunate daughters of that weird recluse and that German gringo." Emma's foreign father was a mysterious presence—or, rather, absence—in her life. She knew that when she was a baby her father had been murdered and that Filomena, suddenly widowed and with three little girls to bring up, had, for some reason, become a recluse. Apart from that, Emma knew very little about this tragedy. She had many questions she wanted to ask her mother, but she sensed that her father's story was something that could never be discussed. People sometimes asked Emma how her mother was doing and sent their regards, but most of the time it seemed as if Filomena did not exist. Slowly, she was being erased from the town's memory.

Alcira had told Emma that most of the savings their father had put aside for them had been lost soon after his murder. Their main means of support seemed to come from an old leather trunk that their mother kept beside her bed. The trunk, with bronze feet in the shape of a lion's paws, contained Filomena's inheritance from her wealthy mine-owning father: gold and silver coins, doubloons, and "pieces of eight" from the fabulous Potosi[1] in the highlands of Bolivia. Tucked inside her brassiere, Filomena kept a silk pouch. A silver key to the old trunk was inside that pouch, and Emma had caught a glimpse of it once or twice. Filomena would not talk

---

1 In 1545, the biggest silver deposit in the world was discovered in Potosi, Bolivia. The wealth of Potosi permitted Spain to become an empire and build its mighty Armada. The Spanish dollar, or piece of eight, a silver coin worth eight *reales* that was minted in Potosi, was widely used as international currency.

about money with her daughters and asked them to leave her alone every time she opened the trunk. "There's enough for me and the three of you" was all she would say before removing the silver key and closing the door.

When she arrived home, Emma was surprised not to find her mother in the sewing-room. The maid informed her that Filomena was indisposed. Alarmed, Emma rushed to her mother's bedroom.

"*Buenas tardes, Mamá*," Emma said but received no answer.

Filomena was lying in her bed, clothed in black from head to toe, reclining on two satin cushions, staring at the ceiling, her legs covered by a thin silk shawl. On her bedside table lay a black leather Bible with encrusted gold lettering and a black rosary.

"Is anything the matter, Mamá?"

Filomena looked at her daughter and, holding back her tears, said, "You have deceived me."

Emma's heart missed a beat. "Whatever do you mean, Mami?"

"Don't lie, child. Each and every one of your lies makes the tender heart of Jesus bleed."

"Mami, I—"

"Enough!" Filomena said. "Our maid saw you eating at the market with those silly girls you call your friends."

Emma was weeping. "Oh, Mami, forgive me."

"You will go to your room and stay there for the rest of the day, praying to the Virgin Mary and asking Jesus to forgive your sins," Filomena said. "Ten Hail Marys and ten Lord's Prayers."

"I'm so sorry, Mami. Forgive me." Before opening the door, her eyes cast down, Emma asked, "Could I at least help you with the embroidery?"

"No. Your hands are tainted by sin."

Emma entered her room and threw herself on top of her bed. Her pillow was soon wet with tears. She had hurt her mother's feelings; she was a bad girl. She was selfish, vain, silly. She needed to improve herself.

Filomena was aware that she could neither control her three daughters' every move nor keep them imprisoned in the house. Besides, she wanted her girls to be happy. So the next time the local priest, Padre Alberto, came to see her, she decided to confide in him.

They sat at a table in the courtyard under the shade of hanging vines. She poured two glasses of fresh lemonade and told the priest how miserable she was about Emma's behaviour.

"Dear Filomena," Padre Alberto said, "Emma has always been a devoted and loving daughter. Yes, she disobeyed your orders, but she hasn't actually committed a crime."

"But I don't want her eating with those Indians, Padre."

"Now, now, Filomena. You know very well that the Indians and the cholos are God's children, too. Why you dislike them so much, I do not know. The sin of arrogance is abhorrent to our creator."

Filomena looked down at the floor. "Yes, Padre. I'll do penance to expiate my pride."

As the priest put his hand on Filomena's head to bless her, he said, "Filomena, remember that you yourself have Indian blood."

She did not say anything. But what the priest was saying was true. She was the daughter of a wealthy Quechua miner and a Spanish señora; her skin was the colour of copper. She was pretty but did not care about her looks. Her big dark eyes were for reading the Bible and admiring the beauty of God's creation; her delicate hands were for praying and carrying out her household duties; her long black hair was tied into a severe bun at the back of her head. In her daily prayers, she thanked God for giving her three healthy, intelligent and pale-skinned daughters.

"About Emma," Padre Alberto said, smiling, "don't be so hard on the child. You don't want to alienate her."

"Oh no, Padre! She's my treasure."

"I know, I know. She's your favourite."

"No, no! I treat all my daughters the same."

"I'm sure you do, but anybody with a pair of eyes can see that you have a soft spot for your middle daughter."

Filomena didn't reply. She looked at her hands and twisted the end of her sleeve.

"Well, then, why not allow Emma to go and see her classmates after she says a couple of prayers? Young people need to be with their friends."

The priest got up to leave. Just before the maid opened the front door, Padre Alberto turned towards Filomena and said, "By the way, I often eat at the market. The food is delicious, you know. You should try it some time."

From that day on, Emma and her sisters were allowed to go to the market and participate more fully in their classmates' activities. However, socialising with boys was not encouraged. "Don't ever forget, dear girls, that all men, with the exception of our beloved priest and possibly my two brothers, are full of sin, and they will do their best to force you to sin, too," Filomena warned. "The best way to spend your time is in prayer and penitence. Repent of all your sins, and ask for God's forgiveness."

Emma did not understand what her mother meant. She did not believe that the occasional swearword, or her fierce arguments with Alcira, or the pencil she once stole from school would condemn her to eternal damnation.

One Sunday morning when Emma was sixteen, she and her friends organised a picnic on the banks of the Guadalquivir River. Their mothers had prepared corn on the cob, spicy *llajua* sauce with chillies and tomatoes, and potatoes with melted cheese on top. One hundred metres away from the girls, a group of *campesinos*,[2] or farm labourers, had just finished eating their lunch and started dancing the *cueca*, a popular traditional dance, to the tune of two violins and a guitar. Emma watched the danc-

---

2 Poor, mixed-race cholos and Quechua Indians often worked as campesinos. In Tarija, unlike in the rest of the country, some campesinos were white descendants of Spaniards who had fallen on hard times and adopted the clothes and customs of the indigenous people.

ing couples attentively. She wanted to learn the steps of this seduction dance, in which the man tried to woo the woman while she played hard to get. Men and women stomped their feet to the rhythm of the music and waved handkerchiefs above their heads. The women danced in their wide, colourful skirts, their puffy short-sleeved blouses gathered tightly at the waist, a carnation behind their ears, their long, plaited black hair bouncing as they danced. The men, in their white shirts and black mid-calf trousers, both of rough cotton, flirted with the women, encircling their partners' shoulders with their handkerchiefs.

Emma was becoming a striking beauty, with wide almond eyes, full lips, and long, wavy black hair. She looked radiant that afternoon, in her plain straw hat and white cotton dress with pink flowers. She wanted to practise the steps she had just seen, so she got up and asked her friends to join her. Soon the fiddlers were playing their instruments with renewed energy. All eyes were on the girls. "Well done, *niñas!*" The campesinos applauded. Emma was at the centre of the group of dancers, beaming from ear to ear. Everyone was clapping and cheering.

"*Muchas gracias, señores,*" Emma said to the labourers and curtsied.

They looked at her in amazement. No white person had ever addressed them as *señores.*

Emma sat down for a rest. While her friends were still practising the dance steps, an open-top red truck arrived and parked itself next to where the peasants were dancing. Emma watched as a plump, good-looking, and well-dressed man in his late thirties descended from the truck's cabin and joined the campesinos. She guessed he was their *patrón*, the rich landowner for whom the peasants worked. He must have felt hot in his dark three-piece suit, starched white shirt and tie, but Emma guessed that the clothing was necessary to keep up appearances.

The man ordered the driver to unload some boxes. Soon several bottles of homemade wine and baskets of sweet, powdery *alfajores* biscuits were unloaded as a gift to the party. "Buenas tardes, patrón," and, "Muchas gracias, Don José," the campesinos said as they received the refreshments, looking down at the ground as a sign of respect.

The campesinos offered the man a chair and a glass of wine. He removed his jacket, stretched his arms, and yawned before fixing his eyes on the teenage schoolgirls. Emma noticed that he was watching her friends with what seemed like hungry eyes, and she felt uncomfortable. Then the man looked at her and smiled. She averted her gaze, blushing deeply. Fortunately, after drinking half a bottle of wine and yawning some more, the man ordered his driver to take him home.

The girls and the campesinos soon resumed their dancing, each keeping to his or her own party. The air smelled of new grass and fresh earth. As the afternoon sun started its descent into the western sky, the noise of the roaring river was drowned by the music and the laughter of the fiesta.

To celebrate the beginning of the summer holidays, Emma and her classmates decided to organise an end-of-year party and invited teenagers from other schools. They rented a hall and decorated the place, hired musicians, and bought the food. Alcohol was, of course, forbidden to the schoolgirls, but Emma thought it was high time they tried it. She persuaded a couple of older boys to buy some bottles of wine for the party. "And you might as well buy a bottle of whisky too," she added. "This party will be the best ever!"

Dozens of printed invitations were sent to the young people of Tarija: "The fifth-form señoritas of San Luis School request the pleasure of your company at the end-of-year celebration." The party was a success. Unfortunately, the teachers were not as pleased by it as the teenagers, and when the girls went back to school the following Monday, they were severely reprimanded for using the school's name without permission, serving alcoholic drinks, and jeopardising the school's reputation. Señora Trigo, the headmistress, asked the fifth form to assemble in the main hall.

"Young ladies, your actions have brought shame to our school," the headmistress said, a severe frown on her face instead of her usual kindly expression. "I am particularly shocked that decent girls like you drank alcohol and smoked cigarettes at that party. I need to know who was behind this outrage; otherwise, the whole class will be expelled."

Without any hesitation, Emma got up. "It was me, Señora Directora."

Señora Trigo sighed. "Oh, Emma! Why did it have to be you?" After a pause she added, "I'm afraid we'll have to expel you from school. Do you understand the seriousness of your actions?"

Emma looked at the floor and nodded. "*Sí*, señora."

"Very good, then. You can collect your things and go home."

Two other girls got up. "If Emma is to be expelled, so should we." One by one the rest of the class stood up. "We are guilty, too," they all said.

Señora Trigo was impressed by this show of solidarity. "Very well, girls. Sit down. I shall go and discuss the matter with my colleagues."

Hardly a whisper was heard when the headmistress was gone.

When she came back, the girls stood up. "We have reached a decision," she said.

The girls looked at her with worry in their eyes. Was every one of them going to be expelled?

"We appreciate your honesty and your courage," the headmistress continued. "But let it be clear that this behaviour will not be tolerated a second time."

The girls held their breath.

"Do you solemnly promise never to take the name of our school in vain? Never to give the school reason to be ashamed of you?"

"*Prometemos*, señora."

"Instead of expulsion, you will help at the hospital for the next four weekends."

"Gracias, Señora Directora!"

Loud cheers and clapping were heard in the classroom.

In the 1940s parents did not encourage their daughters to continue their education after secondary school, as most girls' destiny was to marry and have children. But Emma wanted something else. Her dream was to go to university in either Sucre or La Paz. She needed wings to explore the world, to escape the constraints of her home and her small town, at least for a while. So when she finished high school, she decided to study economics in Sucre.[3]

Together with two other young women from her school, Emma arrived in Sucre in 1948 and immediately fell in love with the town. The city's colonial-style houses near the main plaza were white with thick dark wood-sculpted front doors and balconies; the climate was mild. Emma and her friends lodged at the house where her sister Alcira had lived while at the Teacher Training School, an elegant two-storey residence with a heavy carved front door. The house was furnished with imported furniture in the Louis XIV style, and uniformed and gloved servants looked after the household. The landlady, Señora Argandoña, a widow, wore starched white lace collars and embroidered gloves, even inside the house. Her white hair was tied into a bun held together with a silver comb. She smiled rarely, and her nose pointed upwards constantly.

Thanks to Señora Argandoña's social position, Emma was able to mix with the high society of Sucre. One afternoon, Señora Argandoña and her three young lodgers received an invitation to a ball at the Universidad de San Francisco Javier, where the president of the republic, Don Enrique Hertzog, and several government ministers were to be the guests of honour.

On the night of the ball, women in flowing evening gowns and gentlemen in dark suits filled the big hall. There was an orchestra playing Viennese waltzes, and the waiters wore tail-coats and white gloves. Emma was nervous. She had never been to such a prestigious event and with such important people. She wore a full-length embroidered evening dress of thin blue velvet and a white lace shawl. A blue tiara highlighted her face; her big dark eyes shone with excitement. As the names of the young women were announced, Emma's friends entered the ballroom; she, however, was feeling more and more insecure and was hoping her turn wouldn't come.

---

3 La Paz is the seat of government and the administrative, or de facto, capital of Bolivia. Sucre, the official capital, is named after Antonio José de Sucre, who fought alongside Simón Bolívar in the war of independence against Spain, obtaining the country's freedom in 1825.

Finally, her turn did come, and she stepped inside the room. All heads turned towards her, and there was a moment of absolute silence.

When the time came for dancing, several young men asked Emma to dance with them, but she spent most of the evening in the company of a dashing young stranger who only had eyes for her, a European foreigner called Yerko.

In February the yearly carnival celebrations took place, with parades, floats, street dances and bands. The whole town participated in this three-day event, from Saturday to Monday. The main streets were decorated with paper streamers and flowers. As was the tradition, children and teenagers filled small balloons with water, ready to throw them at one another. Craftsmen and trade unions each elected a queen to ride on their floats. The taxi drivers' union asked Emma to be their queen, and she accepted. When Señora Argandoña heard of Emma's plans, she was horrified. This was scandalous! How could a young lady belonging to one of the best families of Tarija sully her name by representing common taxi drivers? "No, Emma. You cannot mix with those dirty Indians. I forbid you to participate in such an outrage," the landlady said. However, Emma wouldn't break her promise to the taxi drivers. At the Saturday parade, she rode on their float, which was decorated with toy taxis and flower arrangements in the shape of cars, all in the colours of the Bolivian flag: red, yellow and green.

That evening Señora Argandoña was livid. "How dare you disobey me! Now I'm the laughing stock of Sucre. I've a good mind to put your things out on the street, and it's only because of my friendship with your mother that I don't."

The thought of being thrown out—or worse, going back to Tarija as a failure—was too horrible to contemplate. Emma apologised immediately and assured Her Ladyship that she wouldn't embarrass her again.

Several suitors vied for Emma's favours, but she was interested only in Yerko, the young blond foreigner she had met at the ball a few weeks before. Tall and slim, he was a successful businessman from Yugoslavia who imported machinery for the Bolivian mines.

One afternoon Yerko and Emma went to the Casa de la Libertad, the historic house where Simón Bolívar had signed the proclamation of independence. After visiting the museum, they ambled along the shaded corridors lined with pillars that surrounded the central courtyard and sat by the purplish-grey stone fountain.

The water trickled down from several spouts, spraying droplets that relieved the afternoon's heat. Emma dipped her hands in the water and splashed it on the violets and begonias in the terracotta pots.

Yerko took Emma's hand in his and kissed it. "Will you marry me, dearest Emma?"

Emma blushed. She had dreamt of the moment when Yerko would declare his love, but now that he had proposed, she panicked. "Dear, dear Yerko," she said and looked deeply into his eyes, "I cannot give you an answer yet."

"Why not, my princess?"

"My mother. She's frail and old and alone. And as you know, my two sisters have recently left Tarija with their new husbands."

Yerko nodded. Emma had told him about her family situation. She had also told him that a faithful seventy-year-old servant was looking after Filomena while she was in Sucre. "But what would happen to my mother if the servant suddenly died?" Emma said. "She'd die, too, of loneliness and neglect. No, I cannot bear the thought." Because of his work, marrying Yerko would mean going to live in La Paz and also travelling abroad for several months at a time.

"My plan has always been to finish my studies and return to Tarija to work and look after my mother," Emma continued. "I couldn't possibly abandon her."

"Dear Emma, you are a devoted daughter. We shall look for a solution."

Soon Yerko suggested that Filomena could also come with them to live in La Paz. Letters went from Sucre to Tarija and back again, discussing this possibility. But Filomena was adamant. She did not want to leave her home. She was too frail for new adventures, and she had heard that the altitude of La Paz didn't always agree with old people like her, but she did not object to Emma's marriage.

"Your mother is giving us her blessing," Yerko said.

"Yes, but I am not going to abandon her."

"Don't you love me, Emma?"

"More than life itself. But I cannot leave her."

"I will wait, my princess."

Emma had just started her third year of economics studies when worrying news reached her: Filomena was gravely ill with pneumonia. Without delay Emma prepared her bags and left for Tarija to be at her mother's side.

Filomena managed to pull through after several weeks of intensive care. Emma could not now contemplate going back to Sucre. She decided to remain in Tarija and become a teacher instead.

Yerko came to Tarija. "You have four weeks to decide," he said. "I cannot live in limbo forever."

Emma was torn; whichever way she decided, she'd end up losing someone she loved. But she never made up her mind. Soon after the deadline, and with no solution in sight, Yerko left Emma, my mother, for good. Before the year was over, he had married somebody else and was living in La Paz and travelling to Europe and back with his new wife. Emma was inconsolable, but she understood Yerko's decision. Decades later she would meet, by chance and only once, a much older and gaunt Yerko, and he would tell her that his wife had died of cancer and that they had never had any children.

And so my mother's destiny took a different path. Who knows what her life would have been had she stayed with Yerko—whether she would have been happier or at least endured less suffering.

Emma went back to the usual Sunday morning *paseo* in the main square of Tarija, when people walked at a leisurely pace and chatted to friends and neighbours, circulating in opposite directions so as to have a chance to see and be seen. Since Emma's return from Sucre, a plump and annoying older man had been pestering her during the Sunday promenade, trying to get her attention or speak to her, inviting her to visit his ice cream parlour. He was José Arce, the man who years before had admired her while she'd danced the cueca with her friends on the banks of the Guadalquivir. Week after week Emma hardly noticed him and barely bothered to reply to his greetings. Finally, one Sunday after Mass, with my distinguished ancestor Aniceto Arce staring down disapprovingly from his cold stone pedestal, Emma said, "*Buenos días, José,*" and that was the start of their courtship.

The rich and influential people in Tarija all came from traditional families with Spanish surnames, such as Trigo, Arce, Argandoña, Mendoza, Navajas. My father, José, was proud of his Spanish ancestry and even prouder of being a descendant of Doctor Aniceto Arce, who, as president of Bolivia from 1888 to 1892, brought the railways to my country. José was also proud of being related to the then-current president of the republic, Victor Paz Estenssoro, a social reformer who played a major role in the history of Bolivia.

I hardly remember my father, and all that remains of him now is an old sepia photograph. He's wearing a brown double-breasted suit with matching waistcoat and bow tie, his double chin underneath a slight smile on his thin lips. Although verging on obesity, he was a tall handsome man with a face of delicate features. People say I've inherited his features as well as his slender hands, but his physical attributes are all he ever gave me. He was a rich landowner, and he also had an ice cream parlour and a bakery. Unfortunately, his business acumen was nearly zero, and it was his older sister, Antonia, who ran the household. I never fully understood why my mother married him, but I guess she was hoping to mend her broken heart. She was clever, educated, and full of laughter and energy. He was more than twenty years older than her, hardly read a book, and seemed to live mainly for sensual pleasures.

The wedding night, in November 1953, was a disaster. Emma knew nothing about sex, which was not uncommon in those days. My grandmother had been too prudish and religious to explain this subject to her children. The morning after her wedding, Emma fled her house in tears and ran to her mother, saying that José was a beast who had hurt her and made her bleed. The young bride was comforted and told that now she was a real woman and that she needed to go back immediately to her husband and master.

Very soon more cracks appeared in the marriage. José was absent for weeks at a time, either on visits to his farm or little escapades in the neighbouring Argentinean towns. Even when in Tarija, he ate most of his meals outside and spent his evenings in the bars around the plaza. Emma wondered why he had worked so hard to win her hand, only to throw it all away now that she was his wife.

From the very first day of their marriage, Antonia lived with the newly-weds. José needed his sister's support, as she was an astute woman and took care of all his affairs. Stern and unsmiling, she liked telling Emma what to do. "Didn't you see your mother yesterday?" she would say. "Why are you going there again?"

"I'll see my mother as often as I want," Emma would reply, indignant.

"You're a married woman now. What if José comes home and you're not in?"

Antonia also controlled the household budget, and Emma had to ask her for money, which she found intolerable. One lunchtime, the two women had an argument.

"I am José's wife. I am the lady of the house," Emma said. "I will not take orders from you or from anybody else."

"I'll have you know that I've been running this house for longer than you've been alive. I shall tell José about your ingratitude and rudeness," Antonia said as she walked out of the dining-room, her face red, her food untouched.

One morning Emma was about to go out to see her girlfriends. Without knocking, Antonia entered her bedroom. "I forbid you to go out again! Your friends can visit you here, at home. You're a married woman now."

"Mind your own business," Emma said. "You're not my keeper."

"Actually, José has asked me to keep an eye on you. You, with your coquettish and flirty ways."

"Go to hell!" Emma stormed out of the house, slamming the front door.

In December 1954 Emma gave birth to her first child. I was a big baby, weighing in at four and a half kilograms (ten pounds). My mother always maintained that childbirth was not too painful and that she was more scared of going to the dentist.

Emma attended Sunday services at San Roque Catholic Church. The church was at the top of a hill from which one could admire the red roofs of the town and the verdant valley below. Three months after my birth, I was baptised at San Roque; afterwards, my family held a party at home to celebrate the event, and my mother and grandmother prepared the traditional *empanadas de lacayote*—pastries iced with egg white and sugar and filled with lacayote, a type of squash that grows in the Americas—and served them with sweet wine.

The week before Easter, the street leading to San Roque from the main plaza was decorated with flower arches. On Sunday a procession of people praying and singing hymns came down from the church, asking God to forgive their faults. Following the Spanish tradition, penitent men who wanted to atone for their sins or their families' shortcomings volunteered to carry on their shoulders the statues of Jesus, Mary, and several saints on wooden poles. Most, if not all, men would participate in this ritual sooner or later. Women covered their hair with black lace veils and walked slowly behind the penitents, fingering their rosary beads, reciting over and over the Hail Mary and the Lord's Prayer. People also carried ornate flower arrangements and shimmering candles of different sizes, shapes, and colours and banners with the name of their association or group. It was a beautiful sight and an emotional ceremony. Everybody sang hymns, a few people cried, and others sighed deeply. After passing through a few streets and swapping penitents—the wooden poles and statues were heavy—the procession turned around and went back up the hill to San Roque, cleansed of sin and relieved of worry, at least for that day. The smells of incense and fresh flowers followed the procession, drifting slowly in the afternoon air. A feast of wine and homemade pastries awaited the participants. Now was the time for laughter and dancing, and the revelry continued until late at night.

A year and a half after my birth, a country woman came to the house with a little girl and a baby boy and said that she needed money from my father—that these were José's children and that she was his common-law wife. Apparently these were not the only children that my father had sired (before and after his wedding to Emma), but these were the only ones he acknowledged as his. My mother took pity on the thin woman and her undernourished children. She gave them money, some clothes and food. But this really was the last straw.

That afternoon my mother filled a tin tub with lukewarm water and set it in a sunny corner of the backyard full of geraniums and carnations in pots. While I splashed and played with my yellow rubber duck, my mother contemplated her future, wiping angry tears with the back of her hand. On a three-legged stool by her side, a glass of homemade lemonade and a bowl of grapes lay neglected. A new baby was silently growing inside her womb, but she didn't know it yet. She had put up with so much already. She was a qualified teacher; she would work and raise her daughter herself. Hopefully, Filomena would agree to go away with her this time.

Just as the sun was disappearing behind the hills, Emma went to see her mother.

"Mamá, I have decided to leave José," she said, her face puffy from crying.

Filomena was shocked. "Emma, marriage is a holy sacrament."

"But I refuse to accept this fate, Mamá!" Emma protested. "Did you know that he has fathered yet another illegitimate child?"

"Oh, my poor, poor Emma."

Emma took a deep breath. "I need to get far away from here. Will you please, please come with me to La Paz?"

Filomena was silent for a couple of minutes. "I need to ask our Holy Mother Mary for advice. I will see you in the morning." She then got up, kissed Emma on the cheek, and retreated to her bedroom. There she remained for the rest of the evening, kneeling on her blue satin cushion, praying by the side of her bed. The following day Filomena's loyal old servant told Emma that Filomena did not wish to be disturbed, that she needed more time.

For two more days, Emma went to her mother's house to be told that Filomena was still praying. *She won't want to come with me*, Emma thought. *She's afraid of the altitude, and who can blame her? She's not used to strangers or big cities. But how can I go away without her?*

On the third evening, Filomena was ready to see her daughter. As the last rays of the sun coloured the sky purple, my grandmother opened her bedroom door and asked my mother in.

Filomena was sitting on her bed, her rosary and Bible on her lap. "Come in, come in, dear child," she said. "Last night I begged the Mother of God once again to guide me, and she came to me in my sleep."

Emma held her breath.

Filomena's expression was serene. "The Holy Virgin blessed me and told me to do what's best for us and our little girl." She then looked at the crucifix above her bed and crossed herself, got up slowly, and, stretching her arms towards her daughter, said, "I will go with you to La Paz."

Emma's face lit up. "Oh, Mamá, gracias!"

"But in the eyes of God, you will always be a married woman."

Filomena then reached inside her blouse and removed her silk pouch. After so many years against her skin, the pouch was worn and greying. "Go on, my daughter. Open the trunk. It's all that's left of my inheritance."

Inside the trunk were a few gold and silver coins. It wasn't a lot, but it would be of great help during their first days in La Paz.

The preparations for departure started immediately, in secret. Filomena left her house and affairs in the hands of her two older brothers. Emma packed some of her clothes, her two favourite books, and a few items for me. In the early hours of a July morning, my grandmother, my mother and I boarded a plane bound for the capital.

From the Valleys to the High Andes

La Paz, July 1956

The Lloyd Aéreo Boliviano plane from Tarija landed in El Alto Airport safely. As the doors of the aircraft opened, the icy air of the Altiplano high plateau touched my mother's face, and she shivered. Although the brilliant sun was now high in the sky, the temperature was barely above freezing. My mother descended the steps of the aircraft with extreme care, carrying me, eighteen months old, in her arms. As she reached the bottom of the steps, panic rose inside her, so she bit her lip to control herself. Earlier that morning, in search of a better life, she had left her hometown with me and my grandmother, unaware that she was pregnant with a second child. Friends, family, and a comfortable home had stayed behind, but nothing mattered more than getting away. Now we were here, in the middle of a harsh winter, in this strange environment thirteen thousand feet above sea level, finding it hard to breathe.

At this altitude the air seemed to vibrate and shimmer; the light was much brighter than in the valleys. Just outside the airport, white Andean peaks against a perfect blue sky greeted us. *They are a good omen; they are beautiful*, my mother thought, and she tried hard to cheer herself up. *I will make something of myself in this place; the future is mine.*

Many times I have imagined this and other scenes from stories that my mother—or Mami, as my sisters and I called her—told me about her life. My mother, the survivor, the fighter who would not allow life to defeat her. Twenty-eight years old, loud and exuberant, she would carry heavy burdens and endure deep sorrows. The previous week she had made a decision that would change all our lives. Now she would be the mistress of her own destiny; she would work and make new friends. There would be no more tears, or so she hoped.

"Don't worry," my mother said to my grandmother, holding her hand. "Everything will be all right."

My *abuelita*, my grandmother, Filomena, dressed in black from head to toe, said nothing. She seemed full of apprehension.

We boarded a taxi and headed towards the town. As the car went down the narrow, winding road to the centre of the city, three-peaked Mount Illimani, the city's sentinel, came into view in its bluish-white robe. "Look, Mamá! Isn't it magnificent?" my mother said. "Things will work out well. You'll see." My grandmother nodded but still said nothing.

The taxi took us to Aunt Alcira's house. My mother's older sister was allowing us to stay at a reduced price in the spare room in the attic of her four-bedroom house in Pasaje Alborta, in the elegant Sopocachi neighbourhood. My mother was grateful that at least we had a roof over our heads and she could devote her energies to finding a job.

Soon my mother realised that she was expecting a baby. Finding employment would now be extremely hard, as no school would want to employ a pregnant young teacher from the provinces. Three months after our arrival, in desperation, my mother sold some of her jewellery and borrowed money from Alcira.

"Well, Emma, it looks as if you'll have to go back to your husband," my aunt said one morning. "I can't keep you here. I've my own problems."

"Nobody is asking you to keep me," my mother said, gritting her teeth. "You know I can't go back to José."

Tired, anxious, unable to sleep, my mother pondered her future. Going back to Tarija was out of the question. How would she now manage to support herself and her dependants?

One Friday morning in early December, my mother attended yet another job interview. She felt that it had gone well, but she didn't want to raise her hopes too much. The following Monday she was informed that she had been successful and that she would be starting her new job as morning kindergarten teacher in February, at the beginning of the new school year. Elated with the news, Mami immediately made plans to re-build her life in this new city of better opportunities. In the meantime she would have to put up with living in the attic—and with Alcira's temper.

My sister was born just before the New Year and a few days after my second birthday. I don't remember anything about those early days, of course, but in years to come I would hear a lot about my childhood pranks. The adults in my family had been preparing me for the new baby's arrival. "You'll soon have a little brother or sister to play with," my mother had been saying to me. "And it'll be *your* baby, too," Abuelita Filomena would add, "and you'll be able to help us look after it." The much-awaited baby arrived purple, wrinkled, and premature, meowing like a sick cat and horribly skinny. The grown-ups, however, were enamoured of this little in-truder. Every time she made a noise, my mother and grandmother rushed to her side to attend to her. Worse, my mother had taken to holding the baby to her breast several times a day. Sometimes Abuelita also gave her a bottle of milk. Soon, the snivelling creature was given a name: Carolina. And then it was Carolina this and Carolina that, all day long.

One morning Carolina cried louder than usual, and when the adults came to see what was the matter, they saw me drinking greedily from her bottle while the baby complained of hunger.

"You naughty girl!" Abuelita reprimanded me. "No wonder the little mite has been unable to put on weight."

After that I started snatching and hiding my sister's soft toys and com-forters. My mother and grandmother never suspected a thing.

Aunt Alcira had also left her husband. She had three children: two older girls, Cecilia and Silvia, and a one-year-old boy, Gerardo.

One morning while Abuelita and we children were in the kitchen having breakfast, the sound of angry voices reached our ears. Aunt Alcira was arguing with my mother in the dining-room next door, screaming and no doubt get-ting red in the face as she often did. I stopped eating my buttered bread roll and tried to disappear under the table. Baby Carolina also stopped drinking her milk and burst into tears and then little hiccups. Immediately, I came to my sister's side to comfort her. Nobody, apart from me, had the right to upset my little baby. As I grew up, I took it upon myself to be Carolina's defender, and she and I became very close. Oh, but I did enjoy ordering her about.

Soon after our arrival in La Paz, my mother started divorce[4] proceedings, but my father never answered any of her solicitor's letters. I sometimes wondered why he never came to see us and never sent us birthday or Christmas presents. Did he not love us at all? As a result, I hardly knew anything about him and his side of the family. Slowly, I became aware that in our male-dominated, Catholic society, a divorced woman was the object of both scorn and pity. My mother, however, refused to behave like a victim.

Two years after our arrival in La Paz, my father had still not signed the divorce papers, sent any maintenance money, or acknowledged Carolina's birth. Filomena's brothers, who had been left in charge of her affairs in Tarija, hadn't answered my mother's letters, either. Clearly the time had come for my mother to pay a visit to all these people to put things in order.

Emma flew to Tarija with me, leaving Carolina with my grandmother. We stayed at the house of one of my mother's friends, an older white-haired woman called Brunilda. Together with her friend, my mother consulted with lawyers and visited the town hall to obtain documents, taking me with them everywhere. One morning my mother and Brunilda decided to leave me at home with the maids, as they had a long and busy day ahead. When they returned, to their horror, they found that I was no longer there. José and one of his employees had been to Brunilda's house and, tempting me with sweets, had taken me away. It didn't occur to the maids to object, since he was my father. He was a rich and influential man and had paid hefty bribes to the relevant people. The police and other authorities said there was nothing they could do to help my mother.

---

4   In the 1950s, Bolivia was one of the first Latin American countries where divorce was permitted.

I was just four when my father kidnapped me. One moment I was playing with my dolls, and the next moment I was in a dark room, crying and calling for my mother, smelling of pee, snot running down my nose. Where was Mami, and when was she coming? I missed my toys, especially Blancaflor, my life-size baby doll. I also needed my mother's nightie. I wanted to hold it, inhale its perfume, and think of Mami.

My father had said that I'd be happy here and that I shouldn't cry. I only saw him the first day, when he'd told me to come with him to a place where there would be cute little animals to play with. Instead, I was in this dank house with peeling brown paint on the walls and bare floors, and I slept in a tiny windowless room on a rickety bed with a lumpy and smelly mattress.

There was a skinny old woman at the house who wore her hair in long silvery plaits. Her spotty hands were bony and gnarled. She smelled of onions, and except for her long white apron, all her clothes were black. Apart from her I never saw anybody else. She spoke to me in gentle tones but never hugged me or comforted me, and when I asked where Mami was or when she was coming, she couldn't say. Still, I knew—I was certain—that my mother would come to get me.

I don't remember much about the house, but I do recall a floor-level cupboard in the kitchen. Once, while the woman was taking out the plates for lunch, I was able to look inside the cupboard. There, like dark-orange Play-Doh cubes, lay cut pieces of homemade quince jelly inside a glass container with a lid. Mami also made quince jelly. After that first glimpse of the goodies, I was determined to steal some jelly next time the old woman was busy with her chores. I'd feel much closer to Mami then.

My memory of the days after that fades again. The next thing I can remember, I was sitting in the small central courtyard of the house, playing with some pebbles. The front door opened slowly, and a gentle voice whispered, "Marianita! Marianita! I've some lollipops for you. Don't make any noise!"

"Mami! Mami!" I ran to my mother's arms. I didn't care about the sweets. She had come to rescue me, as I knew she would.

My mother and her friends had been desperately searching for me, enquiring everywhere, asking everybody. I was not at my father's big house in Tarija. I was not at his ice cream parlour, or at his bakery, or at his country house.

"Where is my Marianita? Where?" my mother had cried. "I've been all over the place, but José's servants refuse to open the door and talk to me."

This was my father's way of teaching Emma a lesson.

A few days later, Brunilda had news. "Emma, my maid's friend says Marianita is staying at the foreman's house in the country. All the servants have been bribed and sworn to secrecy, but the woman feels sorry for your child—apparently she keeps on crying and asking for you. Tomorrow afternoon she will leave the front door unlocked."

The servant in question was the same one who, two years earlier, had knocked on my mother's door asking for help for her little girl and baby boy, José's children. And that is how, thanks to this woman's compassion, my mother found me and came to my rescue.

That morning we boarded a plane that took us back to La Paz. I would never see my father again, and he would make no effort to contact me. He would neither contribute to my upkeep nor send a Christmas card or birthday present. Ever.

My recollections of the next few years at my aunt's house are thin and fuzzy. In the background, through the fine veil of memory, I sense the warm and constant presence of Abuelita Filomena, sitting me on her knee, singing lullabies, and caressing my cheeks, looking after me and my little sister while our mother worked. Then there was my mother, working, working, entering and leaving the rooms like a fast wind, hugging us, laughing with us. I see myself as a five-year-old, giggling and playing with my cousin Gerardo and my sister, Carolina, followed by silly arguments and tears, reconciliation and hugs. And then there was Aunt Alcira looming over us, ready to explode at any minute.

My days were filled with sunshine and blue skies, or so it seemed to me at that age. My mother and grandmother often reprimanded me for not being more generous with my sister. "You have to learn to share, you bossy-boots," they used to tell me. Carolina was shy, thin and prone to tears, and she often hid behind Abuelita's skirts, sucking her thumb. In years to come, my mother would insist that my sister's nervousness was caused by the stress she had endured during her pregnancy. Cousin Gerardo was a year younger than me and a year older than Carolina; he had rabbit teeth and chapped red cheeks, with straight black hair hanging over his eyes, and his knees were nearly always grazed. When we children played, Gerardo and I usually took the main roles. Little Carolina had to wait her turn, over and over. I was, of course, very happy to boss my sister around. This situation would last for several years, until she—at age twelve or thirteen—rebelled, to my total shock. She would, however, become my best friend and a source of great comfort in times of distress.

I liked living in my aunt's home. My playmates and I seemed to have endless energy, running up the stairs all the way to the attic on the third floor and then sliding down the banisters. The windows in the house had thick dark wooden frames; the shiny wood floor smelled of polish. In the middle of the lounge there was a patterned rug made of thick wool, and I liked sitting there with my dolls—provided Aunt Alcira was not around to shoo me away. When nobody was looking, I enjoyed running my fingers along the edge of the crystal fruit bowl on the coffee table and stroking the smooth surface of the porcelain elephant my mother had recently bought. I also loved watching and helping Abuelita bake biscuits in the white-tiled kitchen. But the best thing of all was the backyard, where we children played while Abuelita hung the laundry and sat to enjoy the afternoon sun.

Gerardo's older sisters, Cecilia and Silvia, didn't have much to do with us little ones. They were both at school and had their own set of friends.

Twelve-year-old Cecilia had a lovely pale complexion and was tall and pretty with long black hair in plaits. Silvia was two years younger than Cecilia; she was short, plump, and dark-skinned and looked like a younger version of Abuelita.

Often Gerardo and I would stand on tiptoe by the attic window to gaze at the view: the wide and deep valley of La Paz was surrounded by Andean peaks of the Cordillera Real. To the right of my window, I could see the imposing white-and-grey mass of three-peaked Mount Illimani; other snow-capped peaks rose to the left; and in front of me, below the snow line, the mountains were brown and reddish-black. I knew the outline of all these mountains by heart and liked drawing them in my colouring book. I often imagined that I was a condor soaring above the magnificent view, swooping over the peaks.

The attic was cramped: Mami and I shared a single bed, Abuelita slept on a fold-out couch—a chest of drawers was jammed between both beds—and Carolina's cot was at the foot of Abuelita's couch. A slim wardrobe in a corner next to the window completed the furniture, leaving hardly any room to move. But I loved living in this wonderful house in Pasaje Alborta, perching high up in the attic, admiring the magnificent view from my window.

The branches of the broom tree from next door overhung the wall of our yard, spilling delicate blossoms and forming a soft, thin yellow mattress on the ground. Mini-cacti in pots cheered up the grey concrete patio. We children played with tin soldiers, marbles, trucks, dolls and tea-sets. Our favourite toys were my doll Blancaflor—in her blue dress and black satin ribbon belt—and a red tricycle in the shape of a truck with a trailer, which we rode every day. Gerardo and I often pushed and shoved each other before taking turns to pedal, gripping the red steering wheel, our knuckles white, going round in circles, faster and faster, while little Carolina held on to the bar of the trailer with both hands, the doll on her lap. "Not so fast, not so fast!" my sister would plead. "Blancaflor will get hurt!" Often the three of us slept in the same big bed. Gerardo thought up disgusting games such as who could fart the loudest and the smelliest. When playing house, Carolina was usually the maid and my cousin and I the masters.

One morning we were playing restaurant. Gerardo and I were to be the cooks and later would be the customers. We had stolen biscuits, fruit slices and chunks of cheese from the kitchen and were preparing the menu.

Carolina complained, "I want to be the cook, not the waitress again."

"No," Gerardo said as he mixed biscuit crumbs with shredded apple that was going brown. "Tomorrow."

"But you said that yesterday..." Carolina whimpered.

Gerardo and I ignored her. She burst into tears. "I want to be the cook..."

What a nuisance she was. I didn't want Abuelita to come out of the kitchen as she had done last time to pull Gerardo's and my ears for upsetting my sister.

"Fine, fine," I said. "Be the cook today, you cry-baby."

Carolina beamed with delight. Soon the newly appointed chef presented us with a mushy grey-and-brown delicacy: crumbs, cheese shavings, stale shredded apple and tangerine slices were mixed together by unwashed hands and served in red plastic bowls from the dolls' tea-set. We always ate everything we prepared in our backyard restaurant, and I don't recall any of us ever complaining of an upset stomach.

Although Gerardo and I usually bullied Carolina into being the maid, occasionally I too was the loser in those power games and cried bitterly when this happened, to the total indifference of the other two. But being the odd one out never lasted long, and we got over our grievances quickly. Gerardo, as the only male in a house full of women, never endured the indignity of playing a secondary role in any games.

Carolina was a fussy eater; in fact, she didn't really like food at all and drove our mother and grandmother to despair. Whenever Carolina saw the spoon approaching, she would turn her head in the opposite direction.

Our mother was sometimes in tears. "She's so thin. I fear she'll become malnourished."

Abuelita comforted her. "She won't starve. She'll eat well enough when she's hungry."

To ensure that my sister got all her vitamins and minerals, our mother brought home an expensive packet of Manzarina, an imported ground cereal that tasted of apple, specially formulated for toddlers. Our mother also bought a big tin of sweet Toddy, a milk-and-chocolate powder. Carolina's appetite improved a little with these new foods, but they didn't last long, as I adored them, especially Manzarina. "That food is for Carolina and is very expensive," Abuelita would say as she combed my black hair, put bows on my pigtails, and rubbed my chubby cheeks with a flannel. "Your sister needs to put on weight. You don't."

One day at lunchtime, my mother brought home a jar containing a semi-liquid yellow substance. I liked trying new foods, so I spread a little on my roast chicken. The tangy flavour of this mild American mustard was something new and wonderful to me. I spread some more and then more. "Careful not to get an upset stomach," my mother said.

As I adored the yellow food so much, my mother brought home two extra jars. The following Saturday, while my mother and grandmother were in the yard hanging out the laundry, they heard Gerardo scream, "Help! Help!" They rushed inside and found me on the kitchen floor, semi-conscious, an empty jar of mustard by my side, my shirt stained yellow. My mother immediately mixed a spoonful of bicarbonate of soda in a glass of water and made me drink it. I soon threw up, and this relieved my indigestion a little. After that they put me to bed. For the next few hours, I saw pink hippopotamuses with enormous teeth and menacing purple elephants floating about the room, just like the ones in my Walt Disney comics. I whimpered and shivered until I fell asleep, exhausted. When I woke up later that day, I vowed never to eat mustard again.

In years to come, these monsters of my childhood would twice come back to haunt me, altered into more vicious, nightmarish beasts.

People often said that my mother and Aunt Alcira, with their delicate features and soft, pale skin, looked like glamorous movie stars. Alcira's friends used to compare her to Brigitte Bardot, probably because of her peroxide-blond hair tied into a bun and her nearly constant pout. My mother, with her dark hair, wide eyes, and full lips, was told she had something of Sophia Loren.

On a wall in the living-room hung a big black-and-white photo of my aunt's face in semi-profile. A trick of the camera showed cigarette smoke coming out of her left eye. She looked stunning. My aunt thought that my mother should do something about her appearance, too. "You need to look more stylish, Emma—make more of your beauty," she used to say to my mother.

But my mother had other priorities. "I don't have any money to waste on clothes or hairdressers," she would reply, annoyed.

Aunt Alcira, a clever teacher and a shrewd businesswoman, was also divorced. Her ex-husband, Uncle Eitel, lived in Santa Cruz, a city far away from La Paz, in the tropical area of Bolivia. Alcira had trouble controlling her fierce temper, and we children were afraid of her. She wrote books for primary schools to teach children how to read and write, and her papers were all over her study.

"Listen, children," Aunt Alcira said one day to Gerardo, Carolina and me. "You will never, *ever* touch my papers. Is that clear?" She looked at us with her big dark eyes, a cigarette between her lips, a pen in her ink-stained hand.

In awe, we shifted uncomfortably from one foot to the other, not daring to look at her.

"Is that clear?" she repeated. "Answer me!"

"*Sí, Tía.*"

"*Sí, Mami.*"

"Good. You cannot say I didn't warn you." She then gave us each a chocolate lollipop. "This is to keep you out of mischief."

My grandmother was a constant source of irritation to my aunt. Abuelita steadfastly clung to her decision to live like a recluse. When I was a little girl, my grandmother's odd behaviour did not worry me at all, but as I grew up, I started noticing that Abuelita was not like other grannies. "Ah, Mamá, I haven't got the time to listen to all your problems," Aunt Alcira would say. "If you don't even want to go out to the park, that's your own fault." My mother was more affectionate and more patient with Abuelita, although this didn't stop them arguing from time to time.

My aunt and my mother were ahead of their time. The term hadn't been invented yet, but they were both liberated women. They had both been to university; they both had careers. They had failed utterly at being submissive wives and at putting up with the demands of their macho husbands. Not in a million years would either of them ask permission before going out to see a friend or accept their husband's word as law. Their marriages didn't last—and it was the women who walked out. Because the two sisters were so alike, they tolerated each other with difficulty, and when they argued, their clashes were titanic.

To make ends meet, my mother found a second part-time job three evenings a week as a secretary at the Spanish embassy's cultural section. She was very pleased about this. But for me this was not such a good thing, as I missed her very much on those long, dark, and cold nights. On those evenings I sometimes felt like crying, especially if Aunt Alcira was shouting. Where was my mother to kiss my forehead and caress my cheeks before I went to sleep? Where was she to tell me that she loved me all the way to the moon and back? To console myself, I often slept in her bed, burrowing under the itchy red blanket, hugging her nightie and breathing in its faint perfume, pressing my cheek against the soft, silky material.

Before going to her school in the mornings, my mother would wake Carolina and me by "attacking" us. She tickled our feet, blew raspberries on our tummies, and kissed our cheeks.

"I'm leaving for work now, *mis angelitas*," she would say in her singsong voice. "Don't forget to tidy your toys and do as Abuelita says." She kissed us again while putting on her coat.

When she smiled, her big brown eyes smiled also, and her laughter sounded like water bubbling in the saucepan.

One afternoon, my cousin, my sister and I were playing in Aunt Alcira's bedroom—it was allowed—sitting cross-legged on the fluffy brown-and-white alpaca-fur covering on her double bed. Suddenly, we heard frightening shouts coming from her study downstairs.

"Who the hell damaged my book?" Alcira screamed. "I'll pull your ears out when I find you."

She summoned her son. "Gerardo! Come here immediately!"

Gerardo went downstairs, trembling. "It wasn't me, Mami. It was Mariana," he said.

No! That wasn't true! Horrified, I heard my aunt rushing upstairs. Quickly, I hid inside the wardrobe behind some thick, long coats, my heart beating through my chest.

Aunt Alcira was looking for me under the bed, under the desk, behind the doors. Then my mother arrived.

Alcira shouted, "Your damned children have touched my things again!"

"How can you be so sure?" my mother shouted back. "You always blame them. It could've been your kids, too."

"You're always defending them! I'm fed up with the lot of you!"

Abuelita came into the room. "Daughters, daughters! Please don't argue. You're scaring the children."

"That's OK, Mamá. We'll soon be moving out anyway."

"And who the hell is kicking you out?" Alcira yelled. "All I ask from these brats is that they don't touch my papers!" She stormed out of her bedroom, slamming the door.

A few seconds later, I whispered, "Can I come out?" and ran to my mother's arms. "I didn't do it, Mami. I didn't."

"Hmm…" my mother said as she wiped my tears. "Just make sure you never go near your aunt's things."

I knew it was Gerardo who had scribbled on my aunt's book, but he never admitted doing it. Years later, I would come to understand his behaviour. I too would have done anything to avoid being in Aunt Alcira's bad books. We were all scared of her booming voice, her quick temper and her hard stares. Once or twice she gave me a swift slap on the bottom—without my mother's knowledge, of course. But in her more relaxed moments, Aunt Alcira was often kind to us. "Here, children, I've bought you this book of fairy stories. Abuelita will read them to you." Or she would give us strawberry chocolates to eat after dinner. In those early years of childhood, I could not have guessed that my aunt was destined to endure the deepest suffering a human being can bear.

Empanadas—small dough parcels that look like Cornish pasties, filled with cheese or meat—were among our favourite foods. Early one evening Abuelita Filomena called us to the table: "Niños! I've made empanadas. Wash your hands!"

Abuelita sprinkled the hot cheese empanadas with sugar. We devoured the pastries and watched her prepare some more while she sang her religious hymns in her soft, sweet voice. A widow for several decades now, our grandmother was short, plump and dark-skinned, unlike my mother, my sister and me, who were pale. Her black rosary was always in her skirt pocket, and her small black Bible, with its gold lettering on the front cover, was always at hand. We children referred to her attire as the abuelita uniform: a black dress and shawl, black tights and thick dark-brown slippers. She let us caress her soft grey hair bun, sat us on her knees, and hugged us. She recited poems, sang traditional songs and lullabies, and told us Bible stories and fairy tales. The tales I heard on my grandmother's lap would be the types of stories I'd later read in the magic realism literature that came out of Latin America.

"Children are gifts sent by God from heaven," Abuelita told us after we'd finished eating. "But Lucifer, the devil, is forever trying to lead the little children astray."

Gerardo, Carolina and I looked at one another.

Seeing the concern in our eyes, Abuelita patted our heads and continued, "Don't you worry, *mis amores*. Ghosts and devils cannot hurt you."

"How's that, Abuelita?"

"Jesus has given a guardian angel to each and every child—remember?"

"Sí, Abuelita."

"Well, your guardian angels are much, much stronger and cleverer than the little devils."

"But, Abuelita, aren't the bad spirits hiding under our beds?"

"No, mis amores. Your guardian angels are always beside you, even when you are asleep. And our sweet Lord Jesus and his Holy Mother also look after you. You are not alone."

Thus reassured, we were able to listen to all sorts of magical and scary ghost stories about good always triumphing over evil.

Our grandmother filled the house with tenderness. "Come here, my little ones," she would say to us. "I've a surprise for you." She would then produce a ripe pomegranate, a mango, or a luscious tangerine from deep inside her apron pocket. "Would you like to try it?" she would ask. We would nod our heads, eagerly awaiting the pleasure of the sweet, juicy fruit while she carefully peeled and cut each piece into little cubes. She caressed our heads while we ate and called us her angels.

Abuelita smelled of soap, was obsessed with cleanliness and order, and washed and polished everything meticulously. She also prayed all the time, asking God to forgive her. To her, most thoughts and actions were sinful, and she told us to keep our minds and bodies pure. I tried hard to grasp the meaning of the word *sin*, without much success. I understood that it was wrong to tell lies, hit my sister, or steal coins from my mother's purse, but I could not imagine my grandmother doing any of those things. Once or twice I overheard her talking with my mother and my aunt, reminding them to keep well away from men, as they were all wicked and dangerous beings—with the exception of our holy priests and Gerardo, still an innocent child. What was she talking about?

Aunt Alcira's house was in a residential neighbourhood, Sopocachi, two minutes' walk from Plaza Abaroa. The square was peaceful, with pretty flowerbeds and a wide fountain in the centre. Inside the fountain was a monument to Eduardo Abaroa, the hero of the War of the Pacific, which Bolivia had fought against Chile in 1879. The adults said Chile had stolen the sea from us. I pictured the Chileans making countless journeys carrying the salty water away in enormous trucks, and it was only when my mother explained that what they had actually stolen was our seacoast that everything made sense. Gerardo, Carolina and I liked splashing in the fountain and climbing the slippery surface of the huge grey statue. I hated admitting it, but Carolina was the best climber. Climbing Abaroa's statue was forbidden, but we kept on doing it despite reprimands from passing adults. When we tired of climbing, we bought ice cream from the street vendors and then ran up the little slope of grass all the way to the top and rolled down the hill, staining our clothes green and brown.

Often grandparents came to the park with their grandchildren, but our grandmother never came with us. It was our older cousins, Cecilia and Silvia, or Aunt Alcira's maid who supervised us.

"Abuelita, can you take us to the park today?" I asked my grandmother one morning.

"No, mi amor. I cannot."

"But, Abuelita, we'd like to go with you."

Abuelita shook her head. "I've lots of socks to darn, and I need to prepare dinner."

She then put an end to the conversation by crossing herself and saying a little prayer.

The houses around the plaza belonged to wealthy people; there was also the US embassy, with armed guards at the door. A few intrepid beggars ventured into the plaza. Abuelita always gave us a few coins or some biscuits to give to mothers with babies. Occasionally, a toothless old man in rags stretched out his bony brown hand. He got a coin, too.

The church of the Carmelites was two blocks down the road, and Abuelita went there twice a week to pray and also for Sunday Mass. Apart from going to church, she hardly ever left the house. Sometimes the church handed out free tickets to the different activities and children's plays that it organised—that was the only time I enjoyed going there—but if there was a shortage of tickets, Abuelita chose Gerardo and left my sister and me at home.

"Why won't you come out to the park?" my mother would say. "You're being ridiculous. You didn't murder anybody!"

But Abuelita did not change; all she wanted to do was to be left alone to pray, bake and embroider. Why had my grandmother chosen to live like a recluse? What did she mean about "washing the stain"? Why did she hate men? I pondered these questions occasionally but was too young to spend time worrying about them. My grandmother's behaviour was annoying, but she was my abuelita, and I loved her. Occasionally, she would have afternoon tea with my mother and her friends at home but, apart from saying *buenos días* and *hasta luego*, did not participate in the conversation. Once or twice a year, after much coaxing and pleading from us, she would go on a family picnic to the countryside. But she was reluctant to go to the market, a restaurant, or any place where there might be a crowd. Many years would pass after her death before I discovered her painful secrets.

A New Daddy

1961–1962

My mother enjoyed her job as a morning kindergarten teacher at Colegio Bancario, a school for the children of bank employees. Once a year the school held a summer party. At that year's celebration, my mother met Pablo, a tall and handsome bank manager, and made a strong impression on him. "You are the prettiest and most interesting woman I know," he told her. "You light up every room." Very soon they were courting, and after three months he proposed.

One Sunday, while Abuelita was at Mass, Pablo came to the house. I thought he looked very handsome with his black hair and dark eyebrows against his pale complexion. He had wide shoulders and big hands with long fingers. "*Hola, chicas!*" he said as he lifted me high up in the air and then did the same to Carolina. My sister and I giggled, delighted.

My mother offered him a cup of coffee. As he sipped his drink, he gave us each a small, soft stuffed toy: a duck for me and a lamb for Carolina.

The following Sunday he brought sweets and tickets for the Argentinean circus that was visiting the town. Carolina and I were enchanted. He told us that our mother's Italian beauty would be the envy of all his friends. I wondered what that meant.

My mother must have been nervous about introducing her fiancé to Abuelita, but it had to be done. One evening Pablo came to the house with a bouquet of white carnations for my grandmother. She shook hands with him but did not smile or utter a word. My mother thanked Pablo for the flowers and then served coffee and almond cakes. Like a Russian empress, Abuelita sat in her armchair and stared blankly into space. Pablo and my mother did not hold hands or sit next to each other. He restated his honourable intentions and said that he wanted to get married as soon as possible. Again, my grandmother said nothing. After he finished his coffee, Pablo got up, kissed my mother's hand, gently pinched Carolina's and my cheeks, and said, "It has been an honour to meet you, Señora Filomena. Hasta luego." The visit had lasted less than fifteen minutes. I can imagine how mortified my mother must have felt, but she did not reprimand Abuelita. Silently, my grandmother had reminded her daughter that she did not approve of second marriages and of men in general.

My mother did not want to miss this new chance of finding happiness, so she chose a date for the wedding. She did not have to worry about my grandmother living alone, as Abuelita would be staying with Aunt Alcira and we would visit her often. My grandmother mumbled and grumbled quietly, but dependent on her daughters, away from her hometown, and carrying a huge burden of guilt that threatened to crush her spirit, she chose not to express her opinions forcefully.

"The one who behaved immorally is José," my mother said to Abuelita. "And you know he has completely forgotten about his daughters and has never even sent them a Christmas present."

"In the eyes of God, José is still your husband," Abuelita restated.

But my mother was determined. So, reluctantly, my grandmother agreed that life for a divorced woman with two young daughters was hard and that we girls needed a father. At the beginning of 1961, my mother and Pablo got married in a quiet registry-office ceremony.

La Paz was a magical place. At sunset the mountains seemed to catch fire, the snow glinting with the last rays of the sun. The lights in the streets and buildings came on swiftly, as night arrived suddenly, any time between six-thirty and seven. The evenings could be extremely cold, but that iciness added to the city's charm. In the darkness the city was a brilliant, gigantic open bowl, its sides encrusted with jewels that sparkled against the night sky. A city of steep hills, some steeper than others, La Paz was a sprawling, vibrant and chaotic combination of prosperous and poor neighbourhoods.

There were Spanish colonial churches, little museums, elegant plazas and tall office buildings. But there was also poverty and suffering: shoeshine boys trying to scratch a living, threadbare peasant Indians who had come to the capital in hope of finding employment and had only found despair, street vendors, beggars, and the occasional amputee—usually a former miner in a makeshift wheelchair.

The climate was peculiar. On winter nights the temperature fell to below freezing, but during the day the thermometer sometimes reached twenty-five degrees centigrade. On sunny days children had to be careful when playing outdoors, as the sun's rays here were much stronger than at lower altitudes.

We moved in with Pablo to a rented house on Nicolás Acosta Street in the San Pedro neighbourhood, an area very different from rich and residential Sopocachi, where Aunt Alcira lived. Lower middle-class families, as well as poorer ones, lived in San Pedro. The Coca-Cola and Pepsi-Cola bottling plants were there, too. Our home was three blocks up from Plaza San Pedro, a pretty square with a bandstand in the middle—the farther away we went from the plaza, the poorer the houses became. The streets were cobbled; some houses had only a thin coat of peeling paint on the outside walls, but others, like the one opposite ours, had balconies and patterned brickwork. On the street I sometimes saw poor, unwashed children whose Indian parents worked as street vendors, as road sweepers, or at the market. As a young child, I didn't really notice the deep social inequalities that riddled Bolivian society. In San Pedro, my eyes started opening up to our realities.

We did not bring any furniture to this new home, as we had not owned any while living at Aunt Alcira's. But the porcelain elephant that had sat on the lounge coffee table, one of my mother's favourite possessions, came with us to San Pedro.

Our new two-storey house was unique; it stood on a corner, orangey pink and shaped like the prow of a ship. The two streets surrounding the house were at different levels, which meant that the ground floor of the house was somewhat sunken in relation to the street on the right-hand side. The three bedrooms were small, but to us this house was our own little palace. My mother was especially pleased with the kitchen, with its pantry with metal-mesh doors to keep the flies out, the shiny black stone on the worktop for grinding chillies and chopping onions, and the dark wooden table where she kneaded and cut pastries at the weekends.

On the first floor, just outside the bedroom I shared with Carolina, was a small enclosed yard full of potted daisies, geraniums, and mini-cacti and stairs that led to the roof terrace. The terrace covered the length of the house and provided us with a magnificent all-around view; apart from a clothesline, it was kept empty. Its orangey-pink walls were about one and a half metres tall, which ensured we children could not lean over them. There I played with my sister and cousin for hours under a glorious sky, surrounded by Andean peaks that huddled together like loving siblings.

On Friday afternoons Gerardo would come to play. My sister, my cousin and I would spend hours on the roof terrace riding our bicycles, playing cops and robbers, and inventing and interpreting stories. When night-time arrived, Gerardo would say to my mother, "Tía Emma, can I please stay the night?" to which my mother always replied yes. Often, he had not brought pyjamas or a change of clothes, but it didn't matter. On Saturday he would again ask to stay the night, and on Sunday, and Monday. In fact, Gerardo would only go back to his house when he could no longer borrow clothes from us.

Gerardo's older sisters, Cecilia and Silvia, came to see us from time to time. They hardly ever played with us and spent their time chatting with Mami and Abuelita.

The garage on the ground floor had been empty when we'd moved in, but the homeowner soon rented it to an Aymara couple who used it as a butcher's shop. As my bedroom on the first floor was on top of it, for years I would be woken up at four every morning by the sound of the butcher's family getting things ready for the day. They would listen to their radio programmes, in Aymara, at full volume. They chopped the meat, cut the bones, and shouted orders at one another. The first few times I heard this racket, I had trouble going back to sleep. Furious, I punched my mattress and covered my head with my pillow. However, after two or three disrupted nights, self-preservation ensured that I slept despite the noise, only faintly hearing the din until it was time to get up for breakfast.

The butcher, his wife, and their three children lived and worked in the tiny shop surrounded by their tools, animal corpses, and the smell of blood. Late in the evening, a delivery lorry brought one or two fresh carcasses to be prepared the following morning at dawn. They didn't have a refrigerator, but the meat was usually all sold by mid-morning. My mother did not think these practices were hygienic, so she bought meat from another butcher who did have a fridge.

Outside our house, in the evenings, a woman would set up her small table and prepare kebabs and sandwiches. Early in the morning, other street vendors sold hot *api*—a thick, sweet drink made of purple corn, cloves and cinnamon—and *llauchas*, big semi-circular pastries filled with spicy melted cheese. This was the staple breakfast of the Indian workers who could afford it; those who couldn't had coffee and *marraquetas* (small French baguettes). The containers for these hot drinks were usually chipped enamel mugs. Plates and cups were rinsed quickly in a bucket and reused.

The food and drink looked and smelled delicious, but my mother allowed us to buy llauchas only from a woman she trusted at the big market. Other than fruit and wrapped sweets, we never bought anything from the vendors outside our home. On the corner opposite, a fruit seller would sit on the floor on top of her colourful striped cloth, displaying big red apples, juicy tangerines, melons, avocados, *pacays* (long green fingers like flattened cucumbers), prickly pears from cacti, and ugly dark-green cherimoyas with velvety vanilla ice cream flesh. Luckily for the poor, bananas and bread were cheap, and even beggars managed to eat something most days.

My mother, Carolina and I walked to school nearly every day, about forty minutes each way. There were buses that went near our school, but usually they were packed with people, some hanging out of the doors. On our way back from school, we would climb up from El Prado, a main artery of the town, until we reached Plaza San Pedro, where we sometimes sat down on one of the benches for a few minutes. On one side of the square was the men's jail, El Panóptico, and on another side the old San Pedro church, where we attended Sunday Mass. We often stopped at Helados Splendid, the ice cream parlour, and treated ourselves to a cone. Farther up the hill were two shops that we visited frequently—the *revisterías*—where we could buy, sell, hire and exchange comic books and magazines. One of these shops was owned by an unkempt fat old woman with a big mole on her nose and wild grey hair. We were afraid of her and thought that she was a witch. I could never bring myself to go alone into her shop and would wait until Carolina or Gerardo was available to go with me.

I was now six years old, ready to start school. As my mother was a teacher at Colegio Bancario, I was accepted there as a pupil. This school catered to the children of all bank employees. Kids from different racial and social backgrounds came here: the sons and daughters of cleaners and maintenance personnel shared a classroom with the children of bank executives. Although there was no official discrimination, we white kids knew that we should not play with the brown ones, as it would have been unseemly to make friends with cholo children.

At that time and for many decades to come, people refused to admit to having any Quechua or Aymara blood, despite the overwhelming majority of Bolivians being mestizo, or mixed-race. Being called an Indian or a cholo was a grave insult. Some people did their best to deny their ethnicity, even if their brown faces betrayed their indigenous origins. Having European ancestors was something to boast about. Germans were considered especially outstanding among white people and were much admired for their discipline, hard work and civilized manners. Many Bolivians suffered from an inferiority complex and felt that we should be eternally grateful to these Europeans who had chosen to come to live here to improve our race. But my mother, although proud of her German father, never considered herself anything other than Bolivian.

Colegio Bancario, a two-storey grey-and-green building, stood at the end of a short passage grandiosely named Calle del Aviador, just off Avenida Arce, one of the busiest roads of our capital. We children wore the standard plain white gown uniforms that all schools had, made of light cotton. The idea behind these tunics was that all children, rich and poor alike, would look the same. Pupils could wear anything they wanted underneath the uniform. The problem was how to keep these gowns clean, what with them being white and children being children.

My classroom, with long wooden planks on the uncarpeted floor, was on the left-hand side of the green-and-white tiled central hall. The desks were engraved deeply with names and drawings from past and present pupils; chalk dust seemed to be everywhere and was not easy to erase from the greying blackboards.

The first day of lessons was traumatic for many of my classmates. Not for me. How silly they were, those crying children, whimpering and sniffling, their fingers clutching their mothers' hands, hanging on to their skirts. I waved goodbye to my mother and watched her walk down the long corridor to her classroom. I could not wait for the bell to announce the beginning of the school day.

I would often see my mother through her classroom window, smiling, surrounded by her little ones, handing out Play-Doh and coloured chalk. The children would sit on their tiny chairs, listening to her every word. They all wanted to be her favourite. "Me, me, Miss Emma!" they would cry. My mother would pat the boys and girls on the head, sing with them, clap hands with them, and hug the ones who were feeling shy. Her smile and laughter filled the room.

I was proud that my mother was a teacher at the school but was under strict instructions from her not to make too much of this fact. "You'll be treated like any other pupil," she said.

I soon made friends with two girls in my class, Miriam and Beatriz.

One day I heard them boasting about the important jobs their parents had.

"My papá is a bank manager," Miriam said.

"My mami is an executive secretary," Beatriz added.

I did not want to be left behind. "My mamá is the Spanish ambassador." I didn't know what an ambassador was, but I knew it was an important job. I was not absolutely sure that what I was saying was true, but maybe my mother was a part-time ambassador? After all, she spent three evenings a week at the Spanish embassy.

"Really?" They opened their eyes wide, impressed.

"And where is Spain?" they both asked.

"In South America, of course." I was surprised at their ignorance. Didn't they know that Spaniards also spoke Spanish?

The teachers told us we were lucky to have a nice school with proper classrooms, desks and blackboards. They said many children in Bolivia, especially in the countryside, were unable to go to school. Because of shortages of both teachers and buildings, Colegio Bancario, like all other schools, had three shifts: morning, afternoon and evening. I attended the morning session, the most popular. The evening session was for the adults and teenagers who worked in factories or as domestic servants.

To learn how to read and write, we used Aunt Alcira's textbooks from her *Marcelino* collection. In her long academic career, my aunt would produce school texts that covered all the years of primary education. Her name was on the book covers, and I was very proud of her, but I never boasted about it, since my aunt was the source of so much work for my classmates.

I loved the smell of the freshly printed textbooks and the smooth feel of the virgin lined paper, awaiting our first attempts at forming letters and words. As far as I remember, corporal punishment was not used in primary schools. Teachers had full authority over their pupils and the support of colleagues and parents. Señor Arias, our music teacher, with a dour expression and a handlebar moustache, always addressed us by our surnames and commanded respect merely by looking at us. "González! Stop fidgeting and sing in tune!"

Homework was given from the first day of lessons, and I promised my mother to do it every day, without fail. I quickly learnt how to read. One of the first proper books I read was the Spanish translation of *Little Women*, by Louisa May Alcott. I remember a teacher asking me what the book was about and me freezing, unable to give a sensible answer. "Well…it's about some people…" Oh, the shame of it. I got over it quickly, though, and started a lifelong love affair with books and magazines. My favourite children's magazines were *Billiken*, published in Argentina, and *Condorito*, a Chilean publication about the adventures of a mischievous little condor and his friends. I also devoured Walt Disney comics in Spanish, imported from Mexico.

One day Mami brought home a book of Spanish paintings that the ambassador had given her. Curious, I sat on my bed and leafed through page after page of beautiful works of art. One of them struck me as the most exquisite painting I had ever seen: *Las Meninas*, by Diego Velázquez. I fell in love with the little princess and her attendants depicted in the canvas. In quiet afternoons I would often imagine myself living in a Spanish palace, wearing luxurious long robes, and being bathed in everyone's love and admiration.

A few weeks after I'd started school, my class teacher, plump and short Señora Loayza, told us about a powerful country called the United States, where people spoke English. I had of course already heard about that country and had informed Miriam and Beatriz that it was in a mysterious, faraway land in Europe. That day, my friends and I had a big shock. Señora Loayza showed us a map of the world, and we discovered that Spain was not in America but that the United States was. It didn't make sense. They didn't speak Spanish there!

Carolina and I were so excited! Our mother had given birth to a baby girl, and we were all going to visit them in the afternoon. Pablo said the baby was premature, whatever that meant, and that she'd be called Teresa. Carolina and I prepared a small basket with presents for the baby: our favourite comic books, our doll Blancaflor, and some biscuits.

"What shall we talk about with the baby?" Carolina wondered.

"School? No, that'd be boring."

"We'll talk about our toys, then."

Pablo, Carolina and I caught a taxi. The clinic smelled of disinfectant, and its interminable corridors were covered in shiny grey linoleum. I struggled hard to contain my desire to slide on those smooth floors. Finally, we saw the sign above a wide-open door: Maternity.

I ran to our mother, who was looking well although a bit tired. A nurse brought the baby, wrapped in a long white knitted shawl that nearly reached the floor. "Come and meet your new sister," the nurse said. Carolina and I looked in disbelief at this strange, scrawny new creature and said, "Hello, baby," out of politeness. She was definitely not pretty like Blancaflor. Her skin was wrinkly, yellow-grey and blotchy.

Back at home Carolina said, "I think she's ugly."

"Yeah. She looks like a rat."

Although we hadn't expected our baby sister to talk, we were saddened that she hadn't even acknowledged us or shown any interest in our presents, and she made the most pitiful whimpering noises. We felt extremely let-down.

But soon after baby Teresa came home, Carolina and I fell in love with her. We liked helping our mother to feed and bathe her. We loved playing with her and singing her to sleep. She put on weight quickly and became our very own adorable, plump baby.

My mother didn't want to give up work. Like all middle-class families, we had a live-in maid, Pancha, a matronly and affectionate chola with long black hair in plaits. Pancha often said that she would never allow anything bad to happen to her mistress, not knowing that soon her loyalty would be put to the test. But my mother could not leave Teresa in the care of a maid, so she asked Abuelita to move in with us to look after the baby.

A pleasant image comes to my mind: my stepfather is shaving in the bathroom. His face is full of foam, and he has a white-and-green striped towel around his shoulders. The sun is streaming through the bathroom window, and the sky is deep blue on this warm Saturday morning. Pablo says I can watch and learn, in case I ever need to do it. We both laugh. I sit on the edge of the bath. He brings the razor to his left cheek and carefully removes hair and foam from his skin. He looks very handsome this morning; I like his dark-brown eyes and thick eyebrows.

The local radio station is playing tangos. Every Saturday morning before lunch there is an hour devoted exclusively to tangos, the *mañana tanguera*. I love this sensual, romantic and melancholic music. My mother is in the bedroom next door, humming to the melody while making the bed. Carlos Gardel, the most famous of all tango singers, charms us with his beautiful voice. But why are tangos so sad? Pablo fiddles with his thin moustache and explains that it is because they are full of longing, of unrequited love, broken promises and shattered dreams. I'm not sure what all that means, but I don't ask.

"Aii!" Pablo says.

"What's the matter?"

A small, thin red line appears on Pablo's cheek. "Pass me some toilet paper, Marianita," he says.

I give him the roll, and he pulls out two sheets, folds them in four, and sticks them onto his wet skin. The bleeding stops.

"Gracias," he says.

I smile at him. On my lap sits the new doll he gave me last week.

"You like your doll?" my stepfather asks.

"I love it, Pablo."

The smell of aftershave fills the bathroom. I'm glad my mother's new husband is such a nice man. I'm so glad that he is our new daddy.

The previous week I had had my tonsils removed. Pablo had brought a new doll, colouring pencils, and comic books to my bedside, and he had told the nurses to give me plenty of ice cream to soothe my sore throat.

But soon his attitude started to change, and slowly, he revealed a darker side. Maybe having stepchildren wasn't easy for him; maybe there were other problems. "Your damn brats are always in the way," I overheard him say to my mother. One night I woke up to screams. Mami was crying and telling Pablo that if he ever laid a finger on her, she would throw him out. She also called him a drunkard. I hid under my pillow. But the following morning everything and everybody seemed normal, and I assumed that I had had a nightmare.

The matadors on the posters around Plaza San Pedro looked gorgeous in their magnificent *trajes de luces*, or suits of lights. The men's strong leg muscles showed through their tight blue trousers and red stockings, their narrow waists accentuating their broad shoulders. All the men on our street, including my stepfather, had tickets to see three matadors perform at that afternoon's bullfight. Earlier that morning, while buying oranges and avocados from the vendor across the road, I had heard two boys talking about the bullfight: it was a fantastic event, they wanted to be matadors, and they couldn't wait for the show to start. It sounded really exciting and colourful. I asked my mother for permission to go, but she said no.

"Por favor, Mami," I begged.

"No. It's a horrible spectacle," she replied. I was in tears. She was so unfair and unreasonable.

That afternoon, while my mother was having her nap, I followed Pablo out of the house and pleaded with him to take me to the bullfight. He held my hand. "Come on, then." The circular stadium was two blocks up the hill from our house, but I had never been inside it. The bullring was full, and there were also people standing in every available space. A couple of Pablo's friends joined us. "Hola, niña," they said to me and patted me on the head.

"*Buenas tardes, señores*," I replied, feeling grown-up and important in the company of three big men. We pushed and shoved and managed to get seats with an excellent view.

The first matador entered the arena, wearing a blue-and-red traje de luces of shiny material and sequins, a red cape in his left hand, and a blue beret on his head. He bowed three times, and the public cheered and applauded. A woman next to me threw a red carnation onto the arena. "For you, my handsome," she shouted.

Pablo and his friends shouted, "*Vamos, macho! Vamos, macho!*"

A brass band was playing the strident music of the bullfight: "Ta-ra-ta-ta! Ta-ra-ra-ta-ta-ta-ra-ra!" Then, proud and erect, the picadors—horsemen with lances—entered, followed by the *banderilleros*, waving the *banderillas* (barbed darts) above their heads. After a tour of the arena, everyone left, apart from the matador.

And then, running as if possessed by a demon, a black bull entered, snorting through his nostrils, his horns glistening, his black coat wet with sweat. The ground trembled under his powerful legs, and thick strings of saliva sprayed from his mouth.

I wriggled in my seat; I'd never seen such a magnificent yet frightening animal. But I did not want to be scared—I loved the music, the loud trumpets, the drums, the *olés*! I loved the colourful clothes and the red capes.

The matador performed a sort of dance with the bull. "Olé! Olé!" I could feel my face burning in the afternoon sun. The matador teased the bull with his cape; the bull dug at the ground with his hooves, charged, and missed. "Olé! Olé!" This magnificent show was worth risking Mami's wrath.

But wait. What was happening now? Oh no! What were the banderilleros doing? Why were they sticking those nasty darts into the bull's neck?

The bull seemed angrier than ever and charged again. I feared for the matador, as I had heard that an enraged bull could gore a man to death. The bullfight didn't seem as much fun now as it had two minutes ago.

The excitement grew by the minute. The crowd wanted blood; they demanded blood; the olés grew louder. I wanted to hold Pablo's hand, but he was too busy shouting, gesticulating, and whistling. He had forgotten I was there. I became smaller and smaller and sank into my seat, wishing I had never come but still watching what was going on in the arena. Finally, after several banderillas and stabs to the side and belly, the matador applied a stroke of the sword into the bull's neck, and the beast collapsed. The sword was now sticking out of the bull's flesh; his big body twitched, and he emitted a piercing moan. Even then the animal defended himself with his horns, and the men had to wait until he was dead before they could approach him.

I was sick with horror. I covered my face with my hands.

From the corner of my eye, I saw the matador slice off one of the bull's ears, a trophy of victory over the beast. Loud cheers erupted from the stands. The attendants removed the carcass, leaving behind them a reddish-brown trail, and took it to the butcher's section, where it would be cut and quartered and its meat immediately sold to the public.

My ordeal was not over. There were still other bulls to be killed, but I shut my eyes and blocked out the rest.

Back at home I looked so ill and pitiful that my mother hugged me tightly, gave me a hot-chocolate drink, and put me to bed with a kiss. She sat beside me, held my hand and caressed my forehead. "You'll feel much better in the morning," she said. "Now close your eyes and get some rest." She left me to sleep without reprimanding me, but I knew she was annoyed with Pablo for taking me to see that bloody spectacle. I cried in my bed, feeling very sorry for the poor bulls and sorry for myself. I had got my just punishment for disobeying my mother. I promised I would never, ever go to another bullfight.

The adult world was becoming more and more perplexing. My mother and Pablo had been happy until a few months ago but now seemed to argue all the time; my grandmother had started praying even more fervently and more often than ever, begging God to forgive her; and Pablo had gone from being affectionate towards Carolina and me to speaking to us through clenched teeth.

One morning my mother and stepfather had another row in the dining-room. Carolina and I were on the first floor, standing by the banister, our fingers tight on the handrail, listening to the commotion below.

"You went with that common *frutilla* again," my mother cried.

"Oh, shut up! What do you know?"

I could not understand why my mother would compare anybody to a strawberry—frutilla, in South American Spanish.

Carolina asked me, "What's wrong with frutilla?"

I shrugged.

My mother was very agitated. "You'll never hit me again! Get out! Go to your frutilla!"

Pablo slammed the front door, and the whole house trembled. Carolina and I ran down to comfort our mother. We hugged her for a few seconds until Teresa started crying in her cot upstairs. I followed my mother up to the bedroom, and while she soothed my baby sister, I asked her what she meant by the word *frutilla*. She said that it wasn't that word but something that sounded like that. I asked her again, but again she would not tell me.

The following day I overheard my mother use that word once more while talking to Abuelita, but this time I heard correctly: *putilla*, a little whore. But who or what exactly was a whore? I guessed it was some sort of bad woman—it definitely was a woman—but I didn't know why she was bad or what she did. And why would Pablo have anything to do with one of them?

When my mother went out, I appealed to my grandmother. "*Abuelita, ¿qué es una puta?*"

"Sweet Lord Jesus!" Abuelita said. "Don't you say that again, or I'll wash your mouth with soap."

Why did the adults in my house refuse to enlighten me? I did not appreciate this enforced ignorance, and their attitude made me even more determined to find out. Help was at hand: there was a magical book, a marvellous tome that contained all the words in our language. My mother had recently bought the updated *Diccionario Español de la Real Academia de la Lengua* and had shown me how to use it. I removed the heavy dictionary from its place in the sitting-room and took it upstairs, where, sitting cross-legged in my bed, I opened it.

Puta (whore): a woman who sells her sexual services for money. An insult that can be applied to any woman of loose morals.

Sexual services? Loose morals? What on earth were they?

A Precious Element

Night-time arguments were the worst. Through the fog of sleep, I sometimes heard raised voices, slammed doors, and crying but was too tired and scared to find out what was happening. During the day things seemed normal. As usual, Mami, Carolina and I went to school while Pablo worked at the bank, and Abuelita and our maid, Pancha, looked after the house and little Teresa. Often I would see Mami in the mornings with bloodshot eyes and puffy eyelids. She would always say that everything was fine, but I suspected that was not the case. Pablo seemed to be in a bad mood most of the time and started coming home later and later at night—and occasionally not at all. I would usually be in bed by nine-thirty and would fall asleep immediately, soon to be woken up by angry sounds.

And then one night, well past midnight, I heard my mother sobbing and shrieking as she had never done before. I thought my heart was about to come out of my chest. My mouth felt dry, and I didn't dare move. I curled myself into a ball and hid under the blankets. Then I heard my grandmother going down the stairs to fetch our maid—her bedroom was next to the kitchen. Pancha and Abuelita then burst into my mother's bedroom to Pablo's loud swearing. The three women must have jostled with my stepfather, but I never enquired about the events of that night. Soon I heard the front door slam, and suddenly quiet descended upon the house. I tried hard to stay awake to go and see my mother, but my eyelids were too heavy with sleep. At breakfast the following morning, I learnt that Pablo would no longer be living with us. I was glad and relieved. Life was going to be so much better and more peaceful without him.

Two weeks after Pablo's expulsion, my mother and I came home one evening and found Abuelita crying inconsolably.

"Emma! What are we going to do? How will we wash Teresa's nappies and the rest of our clothes? How will we have a bath?"

"What's the matter, Mamá?" said my mother. "Calm down, calm down."

"How about flushing the toilet, washing dishes, and cooking? How will we manage?"

My mother was unable to get an explanation from Abuelita, who kept on crying. Finally, Pancha told us that a couple of workmen had knocked on our door that afternoon. They said that they had orders to cut off the water supply to our house. Abuelita and Pancha were unable to stop them.

"Don't anybody worry," my mother said. "We'll manage. You'll see."

And there we were: three adults, two girls, and an eight-month-old baby, suddenly living in a house with no running water. A precious element that we had always taken for granted was no longer available just by turning a tap.

Pablo went to see the landlord to try to evict us from the house. Desperately trying to resolve this situation, my mother tried to negotiate with both the landlord and Pablo, but they refused to refund the share of the deposit she had paid on the property and demanded she move out of the house immediately. She had no choice but to fight her corner and stay put. Despite working at two part-time jobs, she found it difficult to provide for all of us. Moving to another house was out of the question. She also took Pablo to court to force him to pay child maintenance. This was the start of lengthy lawsuits that went on for interminable years and sapped my mother's time, money and energy. She started speaking on the phone with her lawyer in a loud, agitated voice, and all of us could feel her anguish and her anger spilling over. My sisters and I would stay out of her way until she calmed down. For our sakes, she did her best to regain her composure as quickly as she could, though not always successfully. To her utter horror, once—or maybe twice—she pulled my hair when I disobeyed her. Immediately, she apologised and covered me with kisses. I was not happy about what had happened, but I knew I deserved it. Soon, however, we would hear her humming to herself in the kitchen, making a new batch of bread, pummelling the dough; after that she would start singing out loud, and we would join her in the singing and the baking, relieved to have our old Mami back.

I did not fully understand the ins and outs of the disagreement between my mother and Pablo. All I knew was that living without running water was not easy. Decades later, my mother would tell me a little about this particular time in her life and would answer some of my questions, but not all.

Carolina was six when she started carrying buckets of water home after school every day; I was eight. How could Pablo do this to my family, and how could the authorities allow it? In 1960s Bolivia, many outrageous things, many abuses, were possible, if you knew the right people or paid the right bribe.

And so for the next seven and a half years, we lived without running water. But my mother would not allow herself to feel defeated. She always said that if you fell down ten times, you had to get up eleven times.

We learnt to treat water with respect. We also learnt that, as the only family living without water in a modern city, we had become pariahs.

For a small sum, a neighbour let us use the tap in her courtyard. Every afternoon when we came back from school, Carolina and I helped Pancha collect water. The three of us made several journeys with the buckets until the tub in our bathroom upstairs was at least half full. We had to be careful not to walk too fast so as not to spill the liquid and wet our shoes. Pancha also collected additional buckets during the day, and I don't know how we would have managed without her. How did our mother do it? How did she keep us going to school with impeccable white uniforms? How did she manage with Teresa's cotton nappies?

Every drop counted. When we used the loo just to pee, we asked if anybody else needed to go, and only after two or three people had been would we flush the toilet. Handwashing was a different matter; our mother insisted we have clean hands at all times, especially before preparing food or eating. As far as washing clothes was concerned, we changed socks and underwear daily, but other clothes were worn several times.

Weekends were hard work. On Saturdays, Pancha and our mother washed by hand the bulk of the clothes, for which we needed to fill two or even three bathtubs. My mother paid a couple of Indian boys to help us carry the additional water; otherwise, we would not have had time to enjoy the weekend.

Apart from baby Teresa and Abuelita, we could not have baths at home anymore and started going once a week to the public showers near our home. These public baths were used by the poor and were not very clean, but we had no choice.

The first time we went there, we felt out of place and intimidated. Two older boys mocked Carolina and me.

"What you doing here, rich kid?" said one.

"You must have a dirty arse—that's for sure," said the other.

We ignored them and hurried away towards the showers. Luckily, two adjacent cubicles were free.

Carolina knocked on the thin wall that separated us. "Mariana, there are hairs in the drain and something that looks like green snot," she said.

"Yuck! Here too." I looked inside my bag and found a packet of paper tissues. From under the dividing door, I passed one to my sister. "Here. Wipe it off with this hanky. Don't touch it." Despite our revulsion at the condition of the place, it was wonderful to feel the warm water caress our skin.

When we came out, the boys had gone, but a couple of old men were sitting on the benches.

One of the men, staring blankly into space, said, "Are you sure the *pilas* won't come to get me? My comrades are dying of thirst…Maybe my turn to die is today…I want water, water…This Chaco is hell…The pilas are hiding behind those bushes."

The other man tried to reassure us. "Don't worry, señoritas. He's harmless. He's not well in the head. We're veterans from the Chaco War."

These men had fought for our country in the war against Paraguay from 1932 to 1935, which was a total disaster for Bolivia. I had learnt at school that Paraguayans—the pilas—and Bolivians, encouraged by the Standard Oil Company, had gone to war over supposed new oil fields in the hot and desolate Chaco region.

A friend of my mother's said that we could have a bath at her house occasionally. My first bath there was a luxurious experience, but after I had finished, I noticed a dark rim around the tub and had to scrub it hard with my towel to remove it, not very successfully. I was mortified. *Surely I'm not that dirty*, I thought. *What will she think of me? I bet she won't ask us to come back anymore.* But she did, a few times more.

One day Carolina had a little accident. We were nearly at the top of the stairs, laughing and chatting while carrying the water up to our bathroom, when she tripped and spilled the liquid all over herself. She started crying. How could she be so careless, so stupid? "Look what you've done, you idiot," I shouted. "Now we have to do it all over again!" Then I stopped. Maybe it was my fault, too, for giggling while working. The stairs and the hall were all wet as well, but at least they were not shivering like poor Carolina. It was the middle of winter, and we didn't want her to get ill. My mother put her to bed with a hot-water bottle.

When out with my bucket, I wondered what the children who stared at me thought. The Indians outside our house didn't seem to notice our new activity, but I was worried about my classmates who lived in San Pedro seeing me. Would they laugh at me? Would they think us dirty? Would they pity us?

I didn't want to invite any of my friends to play at my house anymore. When they turned the tap to wash their hands, they would know our secret, and when they flushed the toilet, that would be another bucket that needed fetching.

The following afternoon, as I was crossing the road with the water, two well-dressed boys followed me and said, "She's pretty, but look at those clothes."

"Yeah, and what's she doing working like an Indian?" And then they laughed.

I wanted to throw the water at them, hit them with the bucket and tell them to go to hell, but I hurried home instead, staring at the ground, my cheeks burning.

Little by little we adjusted to the new situation and carried on with our lives, always taking care of every single drop of water. Until our water was cut off, we had never considered what it would be like to live without this precious element. We knew that the Indians in El Alto and the Altiplano lived hard lives that lacked all modern conveniences, and although we felt sorry for them, their suffering had been something abstract to us. Now we knew the bitter taste of human unkindness and the reality of living without running water.

My mother did not waste time complaining about our circumstances. We just had to get on with our lives and make the most of a bad situation. Mami continued as before, singing while cooking, joking with us, dancing to the rhythm of the music our radio played. But our mother did get tired, very tired. Apart from working as a teacher in the mornings and at the Spanish embassy three evenings a week, she got a third part-time job as a clerk at an insurance company every afternoon after school. Each morning she would get up at six, and at seven-thirty we would all leave the house to go to school. When working at the embassy, she would arrive home at nearly nine-thirty at night. We were often asleep by the time she came home. I missed my mother terribly and regressed to my earlier childhood habit of crying myself to sleep while hugging her nightdress. After a sandwich and a cup of coffee in the evenings, my mother prepared her lessons, organised the house for the following morning, and went to bed just before midnight.

It was now August 1963, and Teresa's first birthday was approaching. While we were having breakfast on the morning of her big day, someone knocked at the front door. As I opened the door, a hand shoved a brightly coloured parcel inside. "For Teresita," a young messenger boy in blue overalls said before turning around and disappearing down the street. My mother quickly opened the parcel. It was a present from Pablo: a red corduroy dress with a white lace collar.

Pablo would not try to contact his daughter again for several years. After my mother had taken him to court, he'd started paying a derisory monthly sum towards Teresa's baby food, but apart from that he contributed nothing towards my sister's upbringing. I never saw Pablo again. He disappeared from our lives—from mine, anyway. No doubt our mother must have walked past him in the streets of La Paz, but she never mentioned any encounters. Except for one, several years later.

When Teresa was sixteen, she and my mother were walking back home from school one day along El Prado Avenue, arm-in-arm. Just before they reached the marble fountain with the statue of Christopher Columbus at the end of the avenue, our mother nudged my sister and whispered, "You see that man, Teresita? He's your father." My sister stopped in her tracks. A tall and elegant middle-aged man in a striped grey suit, silk scarf and bowler hat was approaching from the opposite direction. The man looked tired and pale and seemed lost in thought, staring at the ground. As he approached, he lifted his eyes and saw my mother and sister. He smiled at them and was about to remove his hat to greet them when Teresa let go of our mother's arm and stepped forwards to face the stranger.

"Mamá, I cannot believe you wasted your time on this piece of shit," she spat out at the stranger's face. She then took my mother's arm and led her away, her head held high, leaving the man speechless.

Teresa knew Pablo had spoken to the nuns at our school a few months earlier and had asked them to organise a meeting with his daughter. Teresa had refused, and the nuns had not insisted. It was far too late to start a relationship after sixteen years of neglect, and all my sister felt for him was contempt. What had possessed him to go and ask a favour at our school? He must have seen my sister, now a tall, slim, and pretty teenager, walking down El Prado with her friends, radiating health and self-assurance. Maybe he felt a twinge of regret; maybe he thought he could make amends. But Teresa would not change her mind.

As for my father, he neither contributed a peso to Carolina's and my upkeep nor showed any interest in seeing us—not even one time when we went on holiday to Tarija. He was just a name on our birth certificates. Our mother continued working as many hours as she could. A few times she tried starting her own business—a coffee shop, a bakery, a bed-and-breakfast, a ladies' fashion venture—but business success would prove as elusive as her ex-husbands.

To my sisters and me, she was both our mother and father. We didn't need anybody else; we didn't need a father; we were just fine as we were. In years to come, however, we would realise just how much the paternal abandonment had hurt us.

By the time little Tere's second birthday came, our mother was determined to celebrate it properly and said that we were going to invite a few friends. But what about the lack of water? Well, we had to put aside our embarrassment; it was time to enjoy life. Mami said we could tell people a little white lie, say that we didn't have water *that day*, if they asked. So she prepared our favourite birthday custard cake, with thin layers of light dough interleaved with lashings of custard, and Abuelita baked powdery, melt-in-the-mouth Arab-Spanish alfajor biscuits.

The sky was cloudless that afternoon when we went up to the roof terrace with our guests. I have a photograph of that celebration: Teresa is wearing a white taffeta dress with puffy sleeves; Carolina looks uncomfortable in one of my castoffs, a size too small for her; and I'm wearing an old grey-and-yellow chequered dress. We are beaming from ear to ear.

For nearly eight years we lived in the boat-shaped pink house with no water. We desperately wanted to put an end to the daily chore of fetching and carrying water, but moving to a different house was an expensive business, and my mother just couldn't afford it. Although I behaved like any other girl my age, my sense of duty increased tenfold: I had to make my mother happy; I had to help my family escape from our situation; I had to be top of the class. Always.

On a corner opposite our pink house lived an austere and bad-tempered Chilean man. Short and stocky in dark-green overalls, a grey apron, and thick black-rimmed spectacles on the tip of his nose, he ran a tiny grocery store no bigger than our kitchen, with shelves packed to the ceiling. Despite his severe nature, this man came to my family's rescue countless times by allowing my mother to purchase groceries on credit. "Here is what I owe you, Don Jorge. *Muchísimas gracias*," my mother would say to him. He would take the money without looking at her and whisper *bien* before turning his back and busying himself with his chores. All of this man's exchanges with my family were abrupt and monosyllabic. But he never refused us credit.

Carolina and I started attending catechism lessons at San Pedro Church in preparation for our first communion. One morning my sister and I were in a church room that gave way to a peaceful inner garden with long corridors, pillars and potted plants. We were praying with several local children under the supervision of two white-haired nuns. Suddenly, a priest burst in to tell us that John F. Kennedy, the president of the United States, had just been murdered. The priest told us to kneel and pray for the eternal rest of President Kennedy's soul and said that his murder was a catastrophe for the free world. We children dutifully obeyed his command and mumbled some prayers. The priest noticed our lack of enthusiasm and told us that we should be more concerned about this tragedy. But to us this was just an event that had happened in a faraway and strange land. That evening my mother commented that it was indeed a terrible thing for the United States, but it made no difference to the lives of ordinary Bolivians.

A few weeks later, Carolina and I had our first communion. Our mother stayed up all night sewing the veils and dresses, long and white and with blue ribbons along the borders. That day, my sister and I looked like younger versions of Mother Teresa and posed with angelic faces for the photos, after which we went back to our usual pranks.

Alone Again

December 1964

The last month of the year was always busy, what with my birthday, Christmas, Carolina's birthday and New Year's Eve.

A few days before Christmas, Mami was paid her monthly salary plus her teacher's Christmas bonus. At last we would be able to buy new underwear and shoes. But Mami had other plans, too.

"You deserve a nice treat, girls," she said. "What would you like for Christmas?"

A Christmas present! I knew Mami's salary wasn't enough to cover all our needs, but a small present would be wonderful.

After dinner, Carolina and I sat in our beds, pondering. Two-year-old Teresa was downstairs watching Abuelita bake biscuits.

"So what are we going to ask for?" Carolina said.

"It's no good saying we don't want anything," I replied. "Mami would be hurt."

"What if we choose just one special present to share among the three of us?"

"Good idea. How about the train set we saw at the toy shop in Miraflores?"

"No. It's far too expensive."

"A Monopoly set?"

"That wouldn't be fair to Teresa, would it?"

Suddenly, Carolina's face was full of excitement. "Do you remember that cute little bluebird we saw last Saturday?"

At the Indian market, we had seen men selling, in cages, exotic birds from the tropics. A little blue finch had stood out, the most wonderful bird ever. Yes, definitely, a bird was what we wanted. We were so excited about this and proceeded immediately to choose a name for our bird: it would be called Pípo.

"You're so clever, Carolina," I said.

That evening, when our mother came back from work, I ran to the front door to greet her. "Mami! Mami! I've had the best idea! We've chosen our present!"

Carolina gave me a dirty look.

"Well done, chicas," Mami said. "Come and tell me all about it."

Before my sister could utter a word, I said, "We'd like that pretty blue bird we saw last weekend. Remember?"

"Oh yes! What a lovely thing it is. Well chosen." Our mother looked at my sister and me. "But you'll be the ones responsible for its well-being. Is that clear?"

"Yes, Mami. Thank you, Mami!"

Carolina and I clapped our hands, delighted, and gave Mami a slobbery kiss.

The following Saturday morning, my two sisters, my mother and I went to the Camacho market. The place was buzzing. The better-off sellers had their own stalls with corrugated aluminium roofs and shelves full of goods. Bargaining and friendly banter were part of every transaction.

The Aymara and Quechua Indians had come from their villages in open-top trucks, bringing chickens and rabbits and huge sacks of potatoes, corn, quinoa and other products. The Indians could not afford to hire a stall, so they sat on the floor, cross-legged, displaying the food on low tables or on top of their thick, multi-coloured *awayo* cloths. Some stall-holders were also selling miniature straw huts and cribs for baby Jesus, having used fresh moss as grass for the floor of the nativity scenes. My mother's plan was to buy some fruit and vegetables first—they always disappeared very quickly—choose a pet bird and reserve it, and then go to the town centre to buy new pyjamas, underwear and shoes for us girls, and slippers for our grandmother.

After buying fruit and vegetables and half a kilo of meat, we went to see the bird sellers. Fantastic birds from the tropics were on display:

blue-and-red parrots with long tails and menacing beaks, little parakeets in green-and-yellow coats, delicate canaries, tiny finches. And then we saw it: the gorgeous little bird with electric-blue feathers and a beak as yellow as the sun—and it sang beautifully, too. We had to have it.

An acquaintance of my mother had just finished paying for her vegetables and came over to say hello. While Mami and her friend chatted, I asked the seller what sort of bird it was and how much it cost. The man said that the bird was a rare specimen from the Yungas, the semi-tropical area near La Paz in the foothills of the Andes, and gave us advice as to its diet and daily care.

The price seemed reasonable. My sisters and I looked at each other and nodded. Yes, this would be our Pípo.

Suddenly, our mother let out a cry. "Stop! Thief! Somebody catch her!"

I looked up and saw a short, plump woman dressed in black running and elbowing people out of her way before disappearing into the crowd. There was a commotion, and people came to comfort us. A woman in a red headscarf spoke to our mother. "I wanted to warn you but didn't dare," she said. "She had a knife. She cut the side of your bag and removed your purse in an instant. She's an expert!"

My sisters and I were numb with shock. I started crying.

Our mother said, "Be quiet, Mariana! Stop snivelling." She was trembling and very pale.

The woman with the headscarf said, "Why don't you report it to the police?"

A man replied, "What for? They'll do nothing, and if they ever find the thief, they'll share the money among themselves."

A policewoman who happened to be across the road was summoned. She came—not too willingly, it seemed to me—and asked my mother some stupid questions: "Do you know the thief? Do you know where she lives?"

It was clear that the money was gone for good.

Mami hugged me. "I'm sorry I shouted at you," she said. I could see bitter tears welling up in her eyes, but she controlled herself.

And that was it: December's salary and the end-of-year bonus gone. My mother, who had never been mugged, because she was always on the lookout, bit her lip.

As we had no money for the bus fare, we walked back home—the longest fifty minutes I could recall. We had bought some food for the coming days, but that was all. How were we going to celebrate Christmas now?

On Christmas Eve, Carolina and I took great care setting up the nativity scene on top of fresh moss: Mary, baby Jesus and Joseph inside the toy hut, with the animals and the three wise men watching from outside. I was in charge of displaying on the lounge windowsills the shiny red bubbles with white-and-yellow glitter from previous years.

Mami and Abuelita had asked my sisters and me not to come into the kitchen or the dining-room, as they were busy preparing spaghetti with shredded cheese. But when we came to the table, we found a surprise: roasted potatoes, a small stuffed chicken, and a chocolate Santa. How did our mother manage it? Two scented candles, the same electric-blue colour as the bird of our dreams, burned in the middle of the table. At midnight, when the clock struck twelve, we sang carols and wished one another a merry Christmas.

Mami then gave us our presents: a Walt Disney book for Carolina, a more grown-up *Patoruzú* magazine for me, and Play-Doh for Teresa. Wonderful! We had not expected anything at all.

"Here, Mami and Abuelita," Carolina said. "Mariana and I made these cards specially for you."

"And I made these." Little Teresa beamed as she gave everyone a painted pebble.

Abuelita wanted each one of us to sit on her lap. She had made her sweet lacayote empanadas with a covering of egg white and sugar, her especially luxurious recipe.

Our mother kissed us and pinched our cheeks. "Come here, mis amores. You are my treasures; don't you ever forget that."

The bedroom I shared with Carolina led to a small first-floor yard full of flowerpots. Beside the wall that separated us from our neighbours' home was the staircase that led to the roof terrace. The wall was not very high, and one could see into the neighbours' yard. One night when Carolina had gone to sleep in our mother's bed, I awoke to the sound of glass breaking. I opened my eyes and saw a stranger at my window removing the broken pieces of glass, his hand feeling for a knob or latch, trying to get into my room.

I was terrified but managed to scream, "Mami! Mami! There is a man at my window!"

From her bedroom my mother shouted at the top of her voice all the male names she could think of: "Manuel! Jorge! Francisco! Pedro! Miguel!"

The man fled. Mami, Abuelita and Carolina came to comfort me. "There, there, Marianita. I'm here now. He won't be coming back, tonight or any other time. I can assure you," my mother said. Abuelita and Carolina were also frightened, and my mother had to reassure them too. Mami then put a makeshift cardboard pane on the window. She and I slept in my bed that night, with the light on.

At breakfast the following morning, I heard her talking with Abuelita about our next-door neighbours. We had always limited our exchanges with them to basic politeness, as they had a sinister air about them. Mami suspected that it might have been one of their sons who had tried to rob us, but there was no way of proving this. Two days later Mami went to talk to several of our neighbours. "I'm sure you've heard what happened at our house the other night. I need to protect my family, so I've bought a gun, and I'm keeping it by my bedside," she told them. This was, of course, a lie, but we never had any more unwanted visitors.

To comfort us from the fright the failed burglar had given us, my mother took us to Helados Splendid for ice creams. After we had eaten our fill, we asked her to tell us again the legend of Illimani and Mururata, the two most impressive mountains around our city. That evening, when we were tucked up in bed, our wish was granted.

Dawn is about to break. A thin, luminous wedge appears behind the three-peaked mountain still shrouded in the deep purple of the dying night. A few pink clouds float over the city. As the golden orb rises above Illimani, orange and red tongues burst into the sky and engulf the mountain with fire. In an incessant chorus, the birds begin to sing and chirrup, welcoming the day.

It is still too early for the rocky giant. He is not ready yet to participate in this new day, so he shifts his weight from massive thigh to massive thigh, stretches his three peaks, yawns, and goes back to sleep for a while. Finally, he rises and sits on his throne, surveying his domain. With a jagged boulder, he combs his glacial snow and then looks at his reflection on nearby Lake Titicaca, the sacred lake of the Incas. He smiles to himself. He is handsome indeed—the most magnificent Andean mountain in the whole Cordillera Real—and he knows it. He is the prince of all the mountains and the sentinel of the capital of Bolivia, Our Lady of Peace, *Nuestra Señora de La Paz*. Like an experienced general, he ensures the safety of more than two million inhabitants (one million in La Paz and one million in El Alto), watching over the surrounding area, ordering the other peaks around and forbidding the two dormant volcanoes that lie not too far from the city from even thinking of erupting. He himself is an extinct furnace and cannot remember when—in which millennium before the start of history—he last spewed his infernal lava.

The other mountains remember that day, at the beginning of time, when Lord Wiracocha, the creator, put the Beautiful Mountain next to Illimani, only for Beautiful to annoy, bully, and insult him.

"The most handsome mountain is me," Beautiful would say, inflating his grey stone cheeks and frowning with anger.

"Please be quiet," the other mountains would plead. Nobody wanted to upset Illimani, the jewel of creation.

"No. I won't be quiet! I'm the best."

Illimani ignored him. But then Beautiful went too far: "You're nothing but a three-peaked muddy mess of muddy dirt!"

"Now, that's enough!" Mount Wayna Potosi intervened. "Show some respect to our prince."

But Beautiful would not be quiet and kept on insulting Illimani—until one morning, when, without a word, without a growl, the prince of mountains grabbed a huge flat stone and threw it across the skies, severing Beautiful's head. Now, silent and humble, Mururata, the Headless One, sits on the left side of Illimani, his head having travelled hundreds of miles to the Altiplano to give birth to another great mountain: Sajama.

Illimani's ancient eyes have witnessed so many events, seen so much history. Sometimes he thinks of the Aymara and Inca princesses who used to preside over lavish harvest festivals in the valley of Chokeyapu at his feet, where La Paz now nestles. Suddenly, there were no more festivals. The Spanish conquistadores had arrived, bringing fire-spitting arms and riding strange tall animals, subjugating the native empire and slitting the throats of anyone who did not submit to their will. They also brought horrible diseases that killed people in the thousands. Then the silver of Potosi, the richest silver vein in the world, was carried through the valley of La Paz on its way to Peru and then Spain. Much later, a nation was born, following a long and bloody war against the Spaniards. And then there were revolutions, carnage, and suffering. Illimani also remembers a handsome young foreigner with a funny name—Che, he thinks he was called—who only a few decades ago had tried to start a continent-wide revolution. He wonders what became of that young idealist.

Illimani sits there, regal, proud, and calm, presiding over our capital, enjoying the deep blue of the sky, scanning the horizon all the way to Lake Titicaca and the Altiplano, all the way to the beginning of the tropics in the Yungas. Watching, just in case.

He bathes in the love and admiration of the people and the respect of all the other peaks.

He is the prince of mountains.

During carnival time children and teenagers fought fierce battles through-out Bolivia, throwing small balloons filled with water at one another. Gerardo, Carolina and I hated getting wet, so we decided to stay indoors and make the most of the roof terrace.

On Saturday morning we were up on the roof terrace, planning our games and relishing the thought of soaking other children with impunity. Little Teresa was there as well but could not participate in the games, as she was too small.

The walls surrounding the terrace hid us from view. Standing on tip-toe, we could see the life below: street vendors, factory workers, house-wives carrying their purchases in big canvas bags, children walking home with their parents.

"Up, up," Teresa said, raising her plump little arms towards me. I lifted her into my arms, and stretching our necks, we looked down at the bus-tling street below.

"Look at that woman selling oranges and bananas on the corner," I said to Teresa.

"And those men in blue overalls," Carolina pointed out. "They work down the road in that grey factory, making Coca-Cola."

"And from here we'll be able to bombard everybody," Gerardo said with glee, his chapped cheeks redder than ever.

My mother called from downstairs, "Children, Granny has made cheese empanadas. Wash your hands!"

We rushed to the dining-room. Empanadas, our favourite treat!

Our mother reprimanded us for not wearing our hats. She had told us time and again that, because of the altitude, the sun's rays were much stronger here and that we would burn quickly.

"Don't be too hard on them," our grandmother said. "They're only children." She was always, always sticking up for us.

After lunch we started preparing for our water wars. We were allowed only two buckets filled with precious water. With the help of water guns, we inflated the balloons, and soon a dozen little bombs were shimmering in the afternoon sun: green, pink, yellow and red grenades ready to throw at the enemy.

Suddenly, my cousin said, "Some kids are coming down the road! Quick! Quick!"

We grabbed two balloons each and flung them at the unsuspecting children.

Splash! Splash! Boys and girls ran for cover, screaming and laughing.

Soon other children suffered the same fate. Gerardo and I were good at hitting our victims with these wet and glistening grenades—Carolina less so.

We soon ran out of filled balloons. While my sister and I were inflating some more, Gerardo shouted, "Hurry up. Here come two girls!"

Fast, I grabbed the two little watery packages we had in the bucket and handed the purple one to my cousin. The other balloon was a pretty pink colour, and it shone beautifully in my hand.

"Give me a balloon," Carolina said. "It's my turn now."

"No. I'll do it just once more, and then you can have two turns in a row," I replied as I hurled the rubbery thing onto the street.

"Damn and damnation!" an adult voice exclaimed.

Up on the roof terrace, we all froze and held our breath. If we had hit an adult, that person was sure to ring our doorbell to complain.

Quickly and silently we went down to the first floor to peer over the banister. Our mother was at the door talking to an irate, well-dressed woman, her elegant clothes all wet.

"Look what your children have done! This is outrageous!"

"I'm so sorry, señora," my mother replied. "Would you like to come in? I'll dry and iron your clothes."

"No. I'm late as it is."

"I promise you those rascals will be punished," my mother added as she closed the front door.

I exchanged anguished looks with my accomplices. How come Gerardo and I hadn't seen this woman? How could we have been so careless?

Trembling, we came downstairs to hear the verdict.

My mother looked at us with severe eyes. "I trusted you to behave yourselves," she said. "But you did not deserve my trust."

I wanted to apologise but was too ashamed to utter a word, and my legs felt as if they were about to melt.

What punishment awaited us? Not going to the circus next weekend? No comic books for a month? Cancelling the visit to the zoo?

No, none of that, but the worst punishment possible: no more water games that carnival.

My mother was not short of admirers. She longed for a companion, a friend who would bring stability into her life, but after two divorces she was cautious about starting a new relationship. She also worried about the impact a new man would have on our lives. Abuelita had relaxed her attitude towards men a little, and as long as they visited as friends of the family, she did not complain. But Mami also knew that my grandmother would view with hostility any serious suitor.

Ernesto, a wealthy man, cultured and refined, showered us with gifts and seemed keen to be a part of our family. My mother would have liked to marry this man—she would deal with Abuelita's opposition in due course—but the relationship was just too volatile. For three years he pursued my mother, declaring his never-ending love and promising her a brilliant future, while at the same time trying to control her every move. "I'm most disappointed, Emma," he would say with a stern face. "You were not in when I phoned. Where were you?"

His jealousy became obsessive, and he was even suspicious of her greeting any male acquaintance while walking home from school.

"Did you see the lascivious way he looked at you?" he would say.

"Don't be silly," my mother would protest. "He was just saying hello."

"And I didn't like the way he touched you!"

"What do you mean? He only gave me a hug."

But Ernesto would not let go of the matter until my mother was in tears. After several days of not speaking to my mother, he would come back with chocolates and flowers, promising to mend his ways. "I'm so sorry, dearest Emma. I don't know what got hold of me. You are the best thing in my life. Please forgive me." But soon the pattern would repeat itself.

Feeling anxious and harassed, my mother consulted her doctor, who told her that to keep her sanity she needed to end her relationship with this man. "He's poisoning your life, Emma. He'll never change," the doctor advised. But she would give Ernesto one more chance, again and again.

One day he forbade my mother to play rummy with her friends. Getting together once a month to play rummy with other señoras was one of her favourite pastimes. It was clear that nothing except the total control of my mother would satisfy Ernesto. Finally, she could not put up with this situation any longer. The breakup was painful but liberating.

"Let's go and celebrate my new freedom," she said a few days later as she filled a basket with fruit, sandwiches and a bottle of homemade lemonade. To our amazement, Abuelita agreed to go with us. She could not hide her delight that there would not be a new man in our lives. Saturday morning found us in Cota-Cota, a popular picnic spot with eucalyptus trees and a large pond, in the southern suburbs of La Paz. As my sisters and I sat on a bench by the pond, eating apples and watching the ducks swim past, I thought that I didn't want our mother to marry again. We had managed without a father figure. We would manage again.

Decades later, my mother said to me that ending her relationship with Ernesto was one of the best decisions of her life.

Other suitors reluctantly accepted that all my mother could offer them was her friendship. One of them was old Señor Schultz, a German Jew who had survived the Nazi horrors and had come to Bolivia in the late 1940s. Although I never saw it, I knew he had a concentration-camp number branded on his forearm. We all felt sorry for him.

I remember the first time he visited us. He arrived nearly fifteen minutes early and seemed disappointed not to find my mother there. He wore a ragged grey suit, scuffed brown shoes, and a grey hat that was a thousand years old. He was one of the thinnest men I had ever seen, with a gaunt face and receding, greying hairline. I thought his skin was incredibly white, incredibly pale, and wondered if all Europeans looked like that.

I invited him into our lounge and asked him to sit down. Instead of sitting down, he started inspecting our lounge: our discoloured green sofa and armchairs in a semicircle at the end of the living-room; the oval coffee table in the centre of the room with a lacy doily and the porcelain elephant, my mother's pride and joy, on top; our record player in the right-hand corner of the lounge; our bare floors. He kept on rubbing his hands, twisting his bony fingers, and smoothing imaginary wrinkles on his suit. Then he examined our music collection of twelve or so vinyl records, and when he saw that we had the waltzes of Strauss, he nodded approvingly. He also noticed two small bookshelves full of books and said, "Good, good."

When I offered him a cup of tea, he considered my offer for a couple of minutes before accepting. He seemed to be evaluating the cleanliness of our house, and was pleased to find that our furniture was well dusted. He sniffed the air and finally said approvingly, "It's nice, very nice and fresh." He wiped his forehead with a white handkerchief and then wiped the sofa before sitting down.

Señor Schultz sipped his cup of tea slowly. He was at least thirty years older than my mother, and the contrast between her vitality and his gloomy outlook on life couldn't have been greater. Maybe that was why he needed her friendship. That day he had brought a present for my mother: a box of chocolates, wrapped in brown paper.

The doorbell rang. Señor Schultz got up, excited, ready to greet my mother. Two little Aymara boys were at the door, their cupped hands joined together, asking for leftovers. My mother always gave them something to eat and, occasionally, old clothes as well.

"Wait a minute, children," I said and went into the kitchen to get some bread.

"Gracias, señorita." The children took the bread and left.

As I closed the door, Señor Schultz said, "Dirty, dirty Indians," and shook his head.

I didn't say anything but was surprised at his lack of compassion.

Mami arrived at last, laden with her teaching books and shopping. Señor Schultz got up to kiss her hand. I helped my mother with her parcels, hung her coat, and brought her a cup of milky tea and a biscuit. Mami opened the gift and beamed. "Muchas gracias, Señor Schultz. These are my favourite sweets."

A faint smile appeared on Señor Schultz's face. I wondered what horrors he had witnessed and what suffering he had endured. And now he was a sad old man, living alone in a foreign culture.

Abuelita was upstairs sitting in her bed, reading. When I took her a cup of tea, she complained about our visitor. Who did he think he was, pretending to win my mother's friendship? And didn't the Jews kill Jesus? Suddenly, she stamped both her feet hard on the floor. "I want that Jew to leave!"

"Abuelita! He's only a lonely old man." I held my grandmother's hand and asked her, "Won't you pray for him?"

Abuelita closed her Bible, looked at her age-spotted hands, and sighed. "Yes, I will." Tears appeared in her eyes. She crossed herself and said, "Sweet Lord Jesus, forgive my temper."

Then I went downstairs and apologised for the sudden noise, saying I had dropped a book.

Señor Schultz visited us dozens of times that year. Then, suddenly, he stopped coming. Worried, my mother enquired at the Austrian patisserie he used to frequent and was told that Señor Schultz had died recently.

He had died alone in his bedsit and been buried at the Jewish cemetery, wearing his ragged grey suit and scuffed shoes.

Everyone at school was excited about the main event of the year. On 21 September, the first day of spring, the prettiest girl in year six would be crowned queen, and all the children would play a role in the ceremony. The queen had a full court: dozens of princes and princesses, pageboys and attendants. Those who didn't want to take part in the coronation would help with setting up the stage and act as ushers. As most parents couldn't afford the paraphernalia required for this event, our school had a stock of coronation clothes and white shoes to lend.

That year, Carolina and I were lucky enough to be chosen as princesses. And even though Teresa was too young to participate, our mother made dresses for the three of us out of white tulle and taffeta, with red satin waistbands. Her sewing machine was in constant use for several days. A huge smile appeared on her lips, and her face shone with pride. On the morning of the big day, my sisters and I endured long minutes of energetic combing—and a few tears—while our hair was put in curlers and then set into elaborate hairdos.

Our mother decided that we would take a taxi to school that morning—expensive though it was—to ensure our clothes and hair were pristine.

Flowers and ribbons decorated the school hall, and an old red carpet for Her Majesty lay along the length of the corridor. As the excitement built up inside me, my knees became wobbly, and I found it difficult to talk.

Carolina seemed about to burst into tears. "I don't want to go," she said and grabbed our mother's skirt.

"Of course you do," Mami said. "You'll be princess for a day! And I'll be here, clapping all the time." She kissed us and sent us to join the other children inside the big classroom at the end of the hall.

I took my sister's hand and walked in. The pageboys were dazzling in their knee-length sky-blue capes, white tights, and ruffs and hats with feathers, and the girls seemed to have come out of a fairy tale, in their fluffy white or pink dresses.

"I need to pee," Carolina said. As soon as she said that, I too felt I needed to go. But wisely, Mami had persuaded us to visit the loo just before we'd left home.

"No. We don't want to ruin our dresses," I said. "And they'll be calling our names any minute now." I looked at my sister and at the other children. They were all twisting their fingers, fiddling with their hair, shifting from one foot to the other. And me? Well, I knew I was going to enjoy being the centre of attention for three minutes, but right now I had a lump in my throat and an even bigger knot in my stomach. I would be glad once this was over.

Señor Arias, our music teacher, peeked through the door. "Time to get ready, children," he said. We all smoothed down our dresses and tidied our hair. One by one, the names and titles of each child were announced.

"Cristina Márquez, *princesa de la Amistad*."

"Antonia Fernández, *dama de honor*."

As they entered, I sneaked a quick look through the half-open door and watched them as they proceeded towards the throne with delicate tiny steps, the ones we had practised for several afternoons after school to the sound of the "Triumphal March" from Verdi's *Aïda*.

It was now my turn to make my appearance, and I stepped into the hall, nervous but proud, and walked on the soft red carpet with my head held high, as my mother and Señor Arias had instructed, and went up a couple of steps to stand on the right-hand side of the throne.

Then Carolina entered, a timid and anxious smile on her lips, her walk hesitant, as if she were trying to disappear into the wallpaper, and positioned herself on the step below me, her head nearly touching my shoulder.

Finally, the trumpets announced the arrival of the queen. The kindergarten children, my mother's pupils, entered before her with little baskets of confetti and paper flowers that they dropped on the carpet as they walked. Her Majesty looked pretty in her long white dress and pale-blue jacket; her maids of honour stood by her side holding plump cushions with gifts and "jewels." She then sat on her throne with the sceptre of power in her left hand and was crowned by our headmistress as the last notes of the "Triumphal March" filled the air.

My mother later asked the photographer who had been hired for this occasion to take a picture of her three very own princesses sitting on a rug in the schoolyard, smiling for her on this brilliant September morning.

Our grandmother hit Gerardo, Carolina and me only once in our lives. And it was all our fault—or rather, my fault. One Saturday afternoon the three of us took part in a drawing-and-painting competition for children at the Monkeys' Park. This park was a zoo on top of Laikakota Hill in the Miraflores neighbourhood. It had yellowing grass verges and one or two frayed picnic tables, but the view was excellent. A few vicuñas and armadillos from the Andes and some monkeys and jaguars from our tropics were kept here.

The previous week Gerardo had brought home an advert for the competition. "Look! Look at these wonderful prizes," he'd said as he pointed to the ad. "Two tickets for the Argentinean circus that's coming next month! Two tickets to see *101 Dalmatians*! A big box of chocolates!"

Imagine! Going to the circus or the cinema! We had not been to either for ages. I knew I was good at drawing, especially people and animals. Gerardo and Carolina were good too. We definitely had to take part.

Mami was attending a teachers' conference that Saturday, so we begged her to allow us to go to the zoo by ourselves.

"Well, I don't know," my mother said. "I don't know…"

"But, Mami, I am nearly eleven," I said, "and very, very responsible."

"Hmm…" She stared at the three of us for a few seconds. "Well, I suppose you could go by yourselves. But you must promise to stay together at all times."

"Yes, yes! We promise," we shrieked with delight.

And then my mother added, "Mariana, you, as the oldest child, will be responsible for looking after your cousin and sister and for getting everyone home before five o'clock."

On Saturday morning our grandmother prepared a packed lunch and gave us a few coins for the entrance tickets.

"Promise to stay together and behave yourselves," she said.

"Yes, Abuelita. Don't worry."

"And you'll be here by five o'clock."

"Yes, Abue. Bye."

Dozens of children, accompanied by their parents or maids, were already queuing at the park's gate. Once the visitors were inside, pots of paint, crayons, paper, erasers and scissors were provided. One of the organisers, a thin man in a grey suit, came to greet us. "Children, open your eyes and take a good look," he said. "We are surrounded by beauty. We've got Illimani and the other mountains, with our city nestling in their lap; we have our animals in their cages and the plants and flowers in the park. The choice is yours."

Gerardo, Carolina and I were put in the same group in a shady part of the park with long wooden benches. I worked hard on a picture of two children picking flowers, Gerardo drew a condor flying near the mountains, and Carolina drew a baby llama and its mother. The results would be announced after lunch.

After handing in our pictures, we sat on the grass and ate our sandwiches. The view was magnificent: the wide valley of La Paz spread below us, and the peaks of the Cordillera Real hugged our city, touching the sky.

The results were ready by four o'clock. Gerardo, Carolina and I held our breath. To my great disappointment, I came in fifth place, with only a consolation prize of a bag of sweets. Neither cinema nor circus tickets for us, then. Carolina and Gerardo were equally disappointed. What had I done wrong? Everybody who had seen my sketches had always said I was good at drawing, but clearly I was not an accomplished artist yet.

To console ourselves, we ran to the swings and see-saws and paid another visit to the animals. We then played hide-and-seek, separating ourselves and breaking our promise. All of a sudden, I noticed that the sun was going down in the sky. "Oh my gosh! What time is it?" I shouted. A woman selling sweets told us it was six-thirty. "Oh no! Abuelita will be furious." We walked as fast as we could and made it home in thirty minutes.

Anxious and panting, we knocked on the door, our faces flushed red, our brows sticky with sweat.

Abuelita opened the door with a severe face. "Where the hell were you?" I couldn't believe my ears—our abuelita swearing! "I've been worried sick," she said, her face darkening. "Haven't you heard of the child kidnappers that prey on stupid children?"

Occasionally, stories had circulated about toddlers disappearing while playing unsupervised outside their homes and about little ones being raped or murdered, mainly in the poor neighbourhood of El Alto.

"We're sorry, Abuelita. We forgot."

"You broke your promise." She was breathing heavily and had trouble speaking. "I've been so worried." Tears came to her eyes as she picked up the broom, lifted it above her head, and hit us with it. Twice she struck the back of my legs, hard. Then she attacked the others.

"We're sorry, Abuelita," we pleaded. "Forgive us, please!"

I had never seen our grandmother so angry and distressed. She kept on hitting us until the broom broke in two. Then she stopped. She looked at what she had done and then, very, very slowly, gathered the broken pieces and dragged them to a corner behind her chair in the kitchen, where she shut herself to cry and pray.

"Our Father, who art in heaven, please forgive my temper and my anger."

I felt so sorry for Abuelita and so guilty for having failed her, especially since I was the oldest child and should have known better. Our gentle and affectionate grandmother had just broken a broom on our backs. However, none of us felt much pain. Shame was our overwhelming feeling. We went to bed without dinner that night, as Abuelita remained in the kitchen for the rest of the evening, crying, praying, and shivering. Mami got home after ten that night. Nobody said anything about our broken promise or the beating. The following day Abuelita called us to breakfast and addressed us as if nothing had happened. Then she started sweeping the floor as she did every day. But this time she was bent double, stooping over her broken broom.

"What happened to the broom?" my mother asked.

"I tried to kill a bug, and it broke."

"I'll buy you a new one tomorrow."

My negligence had badly damaged my grandmother's trust in me. I knew I would have to work extremely hard to make it up to her. I never wanted to fail her again.

One Sunday morning in November, during the school holidays, Aunt Alcira and Gerardo came to have lunch with us. While she ate her quinoa soup, my aunt told us an exciting piece of news: Eugenia—Mami and Aunt Alcira's youngest sister—was coming to La Paz with her five children. I was curious about this aunt, whose name I had heard mentioned during family conversations. Aunt Eugenia had not seen Abuelita for several years. Like her sisters, Eugenia had studied in Sucre, where she had met a dashing young lawyer, Marcelo. Soon they had married and gone to live in Santa Cruz, in the warm lowlands in the east of the country. Uncle Marcelo was rich and well connected, and they'd prospered rapidly; they had a house in the town and another in the countryside, as well as a farm. But why did Aunt Eugenia hardly write to my grandmother? Mami had said that as soon as Eugenia had got married, she'd devoted herself exclusively to her husband and children.

Abuelita couldn't wait to see Aunt Eugenia. "Dear Lord Jesus, thank you, thank you, for sending my darling girl to visit her old mother. Thank you for answering my prayers." Although she rarely talked about her absent daughter, my grandmother had included her in all her daily prayers. "I miss her so much," Abuelita continued. "I wonder what she looks like now. I'm sure she's still as pretty as when she got married."

The following Friday Alcira drove her blue VW minibus to the airport to welcome Aunt Eugenia and her children, and then she took them to her house, where they would be staying.

The following day, Saturday, Alcira, Eugenia, and all my cousins came to our house at noon. We were all excited about this visit, of course, but no one was as nervous as Abuelita, and I could see her plump body trembling slightly. As soon as Eugenia walked through the door, my grandmother rushed to greet her. She hugged my aunt tightly and held her for what seemed like several minutes. So many years without seeing her youngest daughter and with hardly any news, and now here she was, finally. "My darling, beautiful girl," she repeated over and over with tears in her eyes.

Aunt Eugenia kissed my grandmother on both cheeks. "Oh, Mamá, it's so good to see you. I have missed you terribly." For several days after this visit, my grandmother looked like a beatific Madonna from a Renaissance painting, a smile illuminating her face as she went about her household chores.

Eugenia was good-looking, with golden skin and short dark hair. Her children also had tanned complexions. My grandmother was enchanted with these new grandchildren: three boys, Marcelo, Andrés and Alberto; and two girls, Felicia and Rosalía. Abuelita hugged them and patted them on the head. The younger ones were shy and hardly said a word. Marcelo and his brother Andrés were the opposite and were soon chatting with Gerardo, Carolina and me.

To mark the occasion of my aunt's visit, a photographer was called. Soon after lunch we all went up to the roof terrace and posed with Mount Illimani and the blue sky in the background. In this photograph—the only one of my grandmother, her three daughters, and her eleven grandchildren together—our mixed-race heritage is apparent. Cecilia, Aunt Alcira's eldest daughter, has a pale complexion, while her younger sister, Silvia, is darker. Aunt Eugenia and her children are different shades of brown, while my sisters and I are pale. And Abuelita is the darkest of us all.

Aunt Eugenia stayed in La Paz for only ten days. All too soon she and her children had to return to Santa Cruz and Uncle Marcelo, and they would not to be heard of again for several months. It wasn't fair, no. But that was how it was, and my grandmother just had to accept it.

"Oh, my darling daughter," Abuelita said tearfully as she embraced my aunt, "please don't forget to write."

"I won't, Mamá. Don't worry."

And so Aunt Eugenia and her children departed as they had arrived, like a breeze that enters the house through one window and quickly exits through another.

I would next see my aunt two decades later, when I visited Bolivia with my British husband in 1985. Many years after that visit, I would find out that Alexander Seifert, who, together with his cousin Julius, my grandfather, had travelled from Germany to Bolivia in 1918, had one day knocked on Eugenia's door in Santa Cruz.

He had something of the utmost importance to tell her.

The Sacred Lake of the Incas

December 1965

After Eugenia and her children went back to Santa Cruz, Abuelita spent her days blowing her nose, wiping her eyes, and sighing deeply. I guessed she was wondering when she would see them again, thinking that it would be many years or maybe never. When anybody asked her what the matter was, she would reply that everything was fine. "I'm just a silly old woman," she would add.

To comfort her, my mother suggested that we all go to Copacabana, a pretty village and renowned pilgrimage site on the shores of Lake Titicaca. Mami told us that people came from the surrounding villages—and from Peru, just across the border—to do penance and to pray at the feet of the *Virgen Morena*, the Dark Virgin. To our great surprise and delight, Abuelita agreed to join us. "She's probably looking forward to asking the Virgen Morena to bless us," Mami said, smiling broadly.

On Friday the following week, at seven in the morning, we set off towards the lake. The bus climbed from the centre of La Paz up to El Alto, the town that sprawled over on one side of the rim of the valley, at the edge of the flat highland above our capital. Our mother started singing a lullaby, her voice sounding like the gurgling of fresh spring water. Carolina and I stretched our necks to admire the view, while Teresa slept on Mami's lap. The Andes appeared in all their splendour, revealing many mountains that were invisible from the centre of the city.

Soon our bus was travelling along the narrow unpaved road on the high plateau, the Altiplano, carefully keeping its distance from the lorry in front so as to avoid the cloud of dust churned up by the other vehicle. It was true what my mother had said: on these dirt roads people travelled chewing and spitting mud bricks. Even if you covered your mouth and nose with a handkerchief, you ended up with dust in your nostrils.

It seemed to me that we travelled for many hours, but it was probably no more than three. The sun shone strongly, and the sky was deep blue on this glorious summer day. The sparse vegetation was mainly sturdy yellow-grey grass, but it became greener as we approached the lake. A few Aymara peasants were tilling the land with their oxen; others were tending their flocks of sheep or llamas and the occasional pig or cow. Despite their colourful clothes, these Indians looked very poor. None of them had shoes; instead they wore *ojotas*, open-toed sandals made with bits of rubber from old tyres and pieces of string. The skin of their feet had a leathery look; their heels were cracked with deep grooves.

As the bus approached a hamlet of mud-brick houses with straw roofs, some children ran towards the bus to beg for bread.

"Please stop the bus," my mother said.

"No, señora," the driver said. "They are pests."

"Nonsense! These kids are hungry."

"It's just their bad habit. They like annoying the travellers."

"They need to eat every day, don't they?" my mother replied, staring at his fat belly.

Other travellers joined in: "Stop the bus! Stop the bus!"

"All right! All right!" The unsmiling driver stopped the bus.

Two passengers opened their windows. The children, their hands outstretched towards us, gathered beside the vehicle. An elderly man in a crumpled suit tried to give them some coins, but the children said that they wanted bread. A young woman gave them a bag of sweets.

Carolina, Teresa and I had each already eaten one of the cheese sandwiches our grandmother had prepared for the journey.

"Do you mind if we give these children the rest of your sandwiches?" our mother asked as she gave them our food before we could protest. "In future I'll buy a big bag of bread before we set off on our travels."

I didn't say anything, and neither did Abuelita or my sisters. We knew we would be having lunch at the next village.

Soon after we resumed our journey, Carolina shouted, "I can see the lake! I can see the lake!" After so many kilometres of grey and brown flat-land, a brush-stroke of glittering blue appeared in the distance.

A few minutes later, it was my turn to shout. "Look! Look!" A couple of Indians were in the lake, bobbing up and down in their yellow *totora* reed boats, their red-striped ponchos and multi-coloured, long-eared wool hats stark against the blue sky.

The peaks of the Andes could be seen in the background. The air felt icy. Smooth-looking golden fields of quinoa and patches of potatoes and *oca* tubers came into view next to a few thatched mud huts. I was won-dering what it would be like to live in one of those, when Carolina's voice interrupted my thoughts again.

"They look like balls of cotton wool." She pointed at a herd of llamas, pulling on Abuelita's sleeve. "Just like the toy ones we have at home."

Abuelita glanced up from her Bible. "Yes, child. They are indeed love-ly. Another work of beauty from our creator," she said before going back to her reading.

Why was my grandmother not looking at the view? She had spent most of the journey fingering her rosary beads, mumbling prayers, and reading her pocket Bible. I hoped she wasn't thinking of spending all her holiday praying.

At the village of Tiquina, all the passengers got off the bus and trans-ferred to a long open-top boat. Trucks, cars and buses would cross the lake separately on a barge. Mami went very pale. She hated boats and crossings.

On the other side, we joined a group of hungry travellers queuing at the only eating place in the village. This cafeteria didn't have walls—just a corrugated aluminium roof supported by concrete posts. The tables were long planks of wood with old fruit crates as seats. Under normal circumstances our mother would not have allowed us to eat the spicy food prepared by the local women, but this was a special occasion, the cooking smells were irresistible, and our stomachs were rumbling. Two chola women supervised their huge blackened cooking pots, shouting orders at their Indian servants and taking the money. They welcomed us with huge smiles, each showing off a gold tooth and wearing long silver earrings. Our palates were tempted by peanut sauce with shredded onions on top of boiled potatoes, dried meat with desiccated black *chuño* potatoes; and diced tomato, cucumber, lettuce and hot-chilli salad.

"You can eat any of the cooked foods," my mother said. "But don't touch the salads."

Abuelita refused to eat. "No, thanks," she said, turning away. "I'll wait until we get to Copacabana."

"But, Mamá, that'll be in two hours or more."

A stony expression appeared on Abuelita's face. "I'm not hungry."

"Will you have a hot drink at least?"

Abuelita shook her head.

My mother looked at me. "Oh well," she said and shrugged her shoulders.

I could not understand why Abuelita, whose copper skin was as dark as the Aymara's, felt so uncomfortable around the Indians.

My mother, my two sisters and I sat down at the coarse wooden benches next to fellow travellers and the local villagers and devoured a spicy vegetable stew. Abuelita went for a stroll just outside the cafeteria, squinting in the midday sun, taking careful little steps in her sensible flat shoes, her black shawl on top of her black coat.

After lunch we continued along a zigzagging mountain road. Soon the houses of Copacabana appeared below us; the richer homes had red-tiled roofs, while the corrugated tin roofs of the poorer ones glinted in the early-afternoon sun. Like tiny yellowing leaves, a few reed boats floated gently in the clear waters of the lake.

The bus left us at our hotel, an old building with peeling blue paint and guest-rooms around a central courtyard, where a woman was chopping onions for the evening meal. Our room had bare floors and whitewashed walls and faced the lake. Mami and Abuelita would sleep on rickety metal beds, and we girls would share a mattress on the floor.

"It's a bit cold, Mami," Carolina said, jumping on the mattress.

"We'll ask for extra blankets." Mami smiled at us. "Aren't you glad I made you bring your coats and tights?"

While we unpacked our belongings, Abuelita set up a small shrine in a windowsill corner. She lit a candle before a picture of Mary and baby Jesus and said, "Come now, girls. Let's pray to the Virgin and her Blessed Infant."

"Oh, Abuelita! Do we have to?" I complained. "We've just arrived."

"Precisely." She crossed herself and knelt in front of the holy image. "Let's give thanks to God for our safe journey."

"Girls, do as your grandmother says," our mother ordered, a look of resignation on her face. "We'll go to the village square as soon as we're finished."

Copacabana's old Spanish-colonial church had a thick sculpted wooden door and a wide tiled front courtyard that opened onto the square. Outside the church the villagers had set up stands on low tables covered with colourful striped awayo cloths and were selling big-kernel *pasankalla* popcorn, coca leaves for offerings, aniseed *confite* sweets and miniature tourist souvenirs.

"You can each choose a toy llama or alpaca," Mami said, "and a miniature reed boat."

Little Teresa became tearful. She couldn't decide whether to have a toy llama or an alpaca, so in the end she got both.

A woman with braided black hair was selling postcards with pictures of Jesus and the saints, as well as printed prayers and blessings, each card framed by a thin line of glitter.

"Emma, please buy me these postcards," Abuelita asked. "And also a bunch of those yellow daisies."

A few beggars sat by the church door. A blind man was singing and playing a mournful tune on his violin, asking the Virgin to ease his suffering, sounding as if his heart could not endure any more grief.

I could feel a lump growing in my throat. I dropped a coin into the beggar's bowl. Inside the church hundreds of candles shone in the darkness, illuminating the ornate gold-and-silver altar. A statue of the Virgen Morena, the dark-skinned Virgin, made by an Aymara artist, had pride of place at the altar. It was not time for Mass yet, but several people were already praying in side chapels. We pushed forwards and sat on a pew at the front. The air was heavy with the smell of incense, candle wax, fresh flowers and sweat.

Big heavy paintings hung on the walls depicting the crucified Christ, weeping virgins and martyred saints. I did not like all those open wounds, all that blood.

We knelt down, crossed ourselves, said a couple of prayers, gazed at the paintings and decorations, and after ten minutes were ready to go. Abuelita, however, seemed to be in a trance, her hands covering her face.

"Mamá, are you all right?" my mother asked.

A barely audible cry rose from my grandmother's throat. "Mother of God, have pity on me," she whispered.

My mother gave Abuelita a handkerchief. "Come on. Let's go. You need to come out and enjoy the sun." Gently, my mother helped Abuelita to her feet and, holding her hand, guided her out into the light.

What could be troubling my grandmother? We sat down on one of the benches in the plaza and, after she recovered her composure, walked back to our hotel for a short nap.

It was mid-afternoon when we went out for a stroll, and the air felt a little warmer. The waters of the lake were wonderfully blue; in the distance the Cordillera Real proudly showed off its snowy peaks. Abuelita smiled and said she had never seen such a wonderful sight in all her life. I was glad that, at last, she was enjoying herself. But a few minutes later, to my annoyance, she started reciting the Lord's Prayer.

Next to Copacabana rose Calvary Hill, where pilgrims followed the Stations of the Cross, or *Via Crucis*, up a steep stony path. Every year, a few devout Catholics attempted to climb fifty or so metres on their knees, and it was rumoured that one or two had done it all the way to the top. At each station people stopped to pray and leave small offerings to God. A shrine, three crosses—Christ and the two thieves—and a magnificent view awaited the pilgrims at the summit.

The following morning, after a good night's sleep, Abuelita asked to walk up to Calvary Hill. A black lace veil covered her hair; in her pocket she had her black rosary and her black leather-bound Bible with gold-encrusted letters on the cover.

Our mother insisted we bring our sun hats and sweaters. Here the sun's rays were stronger than at lower altitudes, and despite it being summer, as soon as the sun went down, the temperature plummeted. We started our ascent slowly, admiring the view and breathing the pure mountain air, Carolina and I leading the way, Mami, Abuelita and Tere following behind us.

A family of pilgrims was already walking up the cobblestone path ahead of us, carrying flowers and bags full of painted pebbles. We trod on freshly fallen eucalyptus leaves, their delicious smell filling our lungs.

Suddenly, a cry pierced the cool and calm afternoon.

I turned around. My grandmother was kneeling on the ground, her arms raised towards the sky, tears running down her cheeks. My mother, with an expression I had never seen before—a mixture of annoyance, pity and sorrow—was standing by my grandmother's side, trying to dissuade her from climbing the hill on her knees.

"I can't allow you to torture yourself," my mother said as she grasped Abuelita's elbow and helped her to her feet. "Anyway, what a thing to do in front of the children!"

"You're stopping me from seeking redemption," Abuelita said, hiccupping and sobbing. "I need to wash the stain."

My mother's eyes were wet, her face red. "God doesn't want you to hurt yourself," she said.

"You're a bad daughter," Abuelita said. "How can you do this to me? After all I've been through. After all that's happened…"

Mami hugged Abuelita and kissed her hand. "Come on, Mamá. We'll make other penances. We'll give more to the poor; we'll say more prayers."

I took out a clean handkerchief from my backpack and went to my grandmother. She looked so sad and defeated that I too felt like crying. What did she mean about "redemption"? What did she mean about "washing the stain"? Finally, she accepted my mother's proffered arm.

Carolina and I looked at each other, mystified. We then resumed our walk, Mami arm-in-arm with Abuelita and me holding her other hand. And again I wondered what my grandmother's secret could be. Why did she want to punish herself like that? What possible crime could she have committed? To me, she was the kindest of grandmothers, and if she could not go to heaven, then nobody could.

At each Station of the Cross, we stopped to pray and leave our handwritten notes to Jesus, plus one or two pebbles we had painted in bright colours. Abuelita also left the yellow daisies my mother had bought for her the previous day.

Soon after passing the seventh station, we came upon a strange ceremony. A group of Indians in their patterned red ponchos were burning coca leaves and alcohol on a makeshift stone altar. As the sweet smoke rose to the sky, one of the men said a few words in Aymara, while the other Indians, their heads bowed, repeated after him in a low murmur.

"Be very quiet, girls," our mother whispered.

"What are they doing, Mami?" Carolina wanted to know.

"They are praying to *Pachamama*, the Mother Earth."

On the ground, next to the stone altar, a small painting of the Virgin Mary and the infant Jesus lay propped against a rock.

Carolina pointed at the picture. "They're also praying to Jesus."

My mother nodded. "Yes, girls. That's what they do."

Abuelita sighed. "These are pagan ceremonies. How can they mix our sacred, true religion with their primitive customs?"

"Shh...Mamá. We don't want to offend them," my mother said. "Let them be."

At the top of the hill stood the three crosses and the shrine. Looking towards the horizon, it was difficult to tell where the lake finished and where the sky started; in the upside-down reflection, the snow-covered peaks sparkled like glacial diamonds. The trees swayed in the light, cool breeze, and again the smell of eucalyptus tickled my nostrils.

Our grandmother ordered us to kneel and pray. I repeated the prayers as instructed and added a personal plea of my own. While I begged God to give my grandmother some peace, my eyes were busy absorbing the contours and shadows of our white-and-blue mountains, the shimmering turquoise of our lake, and the immensity of the sky.

Part II

What Is the Truth?

All my life I have wondered about my grandparents and their tragic lives. From my earliest childhood until her last visit just before she died, my mother told me the same story about Julius and Filomena, her parents, adding bits of narrative here and there as the years went by and my curiosity grew. As a child, I accepted literally what I was told and did not notice the gaps in my mother's version of events. It was only when I myself became a mother that I started thinking more seriously about the tragic figure that had been my grandmother and about my grandfather's dark shadow.

But what, exactly, was the truth? My grandparents' tale had become incredibly tangled, and I sensed that Aunt Alcira and my mother were reluctant to tell me the full story. What is undeniably true—since all the accounts I have heard coincide—is that my maternal grandfather was a German immigrant, a medical doctor, and an adventurer. Nobody knows when exactly he arrived in Bolivia or why; we don't even know in which town in Bavaria he was born. True, too, that a terrible secret surrounded him, and neither my mother nor my aunts wanted me and my sisters to find out. It is also true that my grandmother stayed with him against her will; she never talked about him, and if his name was ever mentioned in her presence, an expression of disgust appeared on her face. True also that she was a religious woman who prayed all day long, constantly asking God to forgive her.

Here is one version of my grandparents' tale, inspired by various family accounts.

My Grandparents' Story

It was the end of the First World War. His country was humiliated, his home destroyed, and so many of his friends were dead. How did he ever survive the horror of the trenches? The young German doctor had had enough of mud, enough of death and suffering. There were days when he thought he'd go mad—too much greyness, too much filth, too much blood. Now Julius wanted to get away; he needed to forget.

His cousin Alexander, a baker, had seen an advert in the local paper and was now preparing to emigrate to a remote country in South America. "Why don't you come with me?" Alexander asked Julius. "As a doctor you'll have no problem finding employment."

"Hmm…I don't know," Julius replied. "I hadn't considered going as far away as that…"

"The New World. New opportunities."

"But we don't speak a word of Spanish."

"We'll learn it quickly," Alexander replied. "Anything will be better than this ruin of a country."

Julius nodded. He knew that his cousin was right.

The advertisement that Alexander had seen said that the mining industry in that Andean nation needed civil engineers, draughtsmen and accountants, as well as cooks and bakers. The mines were being modernised, the equipment was being updated, and the foreign personnel working there needed the basic comforts of home. Alexander had applied to work at the Ferrari-Ghezzi factory in the city of Oruro, Bolivia, where he would be handling industrial-size bread machines and ovens, baking for the many hundreds of people who worked at the mines. Desperate to leave as soon as possible, he sold his small cake shop at a loss and started packing his bags. Julius had just enough money to pay for his own voyage. His most precious possessions were his medical books and his knowledge. Soon the two young migrants bought one-way third-class tickets for the next transatlantic crossing to Argentina. Their big adventure was just beginning, and they were excited about it. They did not admit to each other—or even to themselves—that they hoped to return home one day.

Buenos Aires was a big city, clean with wide tree-lined avenues, tall buildings, and all modern facilities. You could almost think you were in Europe. At that time, Argentina was one of the richest countries in the Americas, and blond, blue-eyed European immigrants like Julius and Alexander were common in Buenos Aires. However, the cousins attracted some attention, mainly because of their long hair, thin bodies, dishevelled clothes, and dusty, worn-out shoes. As they had only a little money, they chose to spend some of it on Spanish-German dictionaries and teach-yourself-Spanish books rather than on new clothes. They were determined to master the language as soon as possible. Julius found learning Spanish not too difficult and took special care to pronounce the words correctly; unfortunately, his cousin was not as linguistically gifted as he, and his thick accent would be a hindrance for months to come.

From Buenos Aires they travelled by train and bus towards the northern border town of La Quiaca, from where they entered Villazón, in Bolivia. The cousins had noticed the contrast between the affluence of Buenos Aires and the poverty of the rural areas. Now that they were in Bolivia, it was clear that they had entered an even poorer country. The natives were intriguing. Julius and Alexander had never seen the likes of them, with their dark copper skin, high cheekbones, and melancholic eyes. The men wore ponchos, rough trousers, and hats with long ears, all made of coarse wool; the women were in wide skirts of different colours, wrapped in shawls against the icy wind, their shiny black hair in long plaits, many of them with babies strapped to their backs. Julius and Alexander soon realised that the indigenous Quechua and Aymara made up the bulk of the population.

The cousins were unable to find a bus to take them on their journey north, so they travelled first in horse-drawn carriages and then on a rickety truck full of farm produce. They were lucky to be allowed to sit in the cabin with the driver rather than travel on the open top with the peasants and their sacks of vegetables and chickens in cages. For more than three days, they voyaged over uneven terrain and dusty, winding paths, admiring the high Andean peaks, wide valleys, and deep ravines with fast-flowing rivers.

They arrived in Potosi, a legendary city heavy with history. At more than 4,000 metres above sea level, the silver mines of Potosi had been the main source of the fabulous wealth of the Spanish Empire from the sixteenth to the eighteenth century. The silver from Bolivia—called High Peru during the Spanish domination—paid for the Spanish Armada and still adorns glittering altars in thousands of churches in Spain and the Americas. Potosi was cold and windswept but full of impressive colonial buildings. The town was both beautiful and ugly; apart from the historic churches and palaces, the buildings were in a neglected state, with crumbling walls, peeling stucco and broken tiles. After centuries of exploitation, the silver was nearly exhausted, but the mines were now producing and exporting other minerals. The newly arrived young Germans wondered why Bolivia, with all its mineral wealth, was among the poorest nations on earth.

Julius did not like this cold and grey town, which reminded him too much of the greyness he had left behind, and the altitude affected him badly. European immigrants in the bars reserved for foreigners told him of a much warmer and charming place, Tarija, in the south of the country. "It really is a lovely town," a Yugoslavian engineer with a patch over one eye said one night. "Fruit and flowers all year round—and the women are beautiful. If I weren't going back to Europe, I'd definitely like to spend the rest of my life there." Julius decided to try his luck in this tantalising place. Alexander would soon continue on his way to Oruro—also cold and barren—where his employers were awaiting him. Unlike his cousin, Julius did not have a work contract; he was free to go and do as he pleased. So on a chilly, rainy day, the cousins parted company.

"May God bless and guide you," said Alexander.

"I wish you success in everything you do," replied Julius. Instead of just shaking hands, the two men hugged and patted each other on the back, promising to keep in touch. Alexander said it was funny that they had entered Bolivia from the north of Argentina and now Julius was going back towards the south, in a semicircle, the same direction they had come.

One warm and sunny February morning, a stagecoach from Potosi pulled into one of the squares of Tarija, bringing parcels and letters, travelling salesmen, and a slim stranger who towered above the short and swarthy local population. He had a radiant smile, and his blue eyes smiled, too. His head was covered in yellow hair; his eyebrows, lashes, and short beard were also blond; and his curls reached his shoulders. Although many exotic travellers had passed through Tarija, its inhabitants had never seen anyone as white, as blond, and as tall as this European gringo, who arrived with a big bag full of medical wonders and a trunk full of books. Unlike most other foreign travellers, whose Spanish was so broken that it was incomprehensible, this man made the effort to pronounce the words properly. The local people, not known for their reserve, asked him a few questions. The stranger seemed to enjoy the attention; he said he was from Bavaria and that he was a doctor and was interested in doing research on tropical diseases. Bavaria? The people of Tarija had never heard of such a place. The stranger then said that Bavaria was part of Germany. Ah, yes, several people knew where that was. They had heard about the awful war there.

"I need a cheap place to stay for a few days," he said, "and a good barber." So they took him to the town's inn, where he settled in a room above the bar, facing the main square.

The doctors of the town considered their situation. They held a meeting and decided that European medical knowledge would certainly be a great asset for Tarija, where the hospital lacked many facilities and the doctors were always overworked. Wouldn't it be wonderful if this man stayed and helped them? But they had to move fast, before the stranger continued on his journey elsewhere. That very afternoon the physicians went to the inn to speak to the foreigner. Smiling broadly, the new arrival came out of his room and sat with the other doctors in a corner of the courtyard. They ordered sweet almond cakes and wine, but the stranger drank only coffee. To the town doctors' great delight and despite the low pay, the handsome stranger accepted their job offer, provided he could make use of the hospital's lab and would be allowed to carry on with his research. "Our lab is at your disposal, Doctor Seifert," the head surgeon, Doctor Trigo, said. "We're very pleased to have you here in our humble town."

There was something about this man that made people like him and trust him, something warm and charming, and soon the folks of Tarija started noticing that his medical knowledge was indeed great. People were curious about the new doctor. In the evenings he would sit in the plaza and drink coffee or sweet peach juice—never wine—with them. In vain they tried to ask him about his life in Germany, whether his parents were still alive, whether he had a wife or a sweetheart, but he wouldn't talk about that, saying that he was looking forward to his new life in "this exquisite place."

Apart from drinking coffee and occasionally playing cards, the new doctor spent all his free time in the fields collecting samples of plants and insects or at the hospital reading medical texts, checking his petri dishes, and writing up his findings. He made it clear from the start that he was there to help and share his knowledge, as well as learn from his peers, and he was not interested in stealing their patients. And although he always treated his colleagues as equals and spoke to them with the greatest respect, the other doctors were in awe of him.

One day Doctor Seifert was called to the bedside of a seriously ill nine-year-old boy, sick with measles. None of the town's doctors had been able to cure this boy, and he was dying. The poor boy was as ugly as a monkey, his skin sallow, his eyes vacant. The German doctor felt a twinge of pity for this unattractive, helpless child and put all his knowledge and skill into saving him. This boy grew up to be one of the most important figures in the history of Bolivia: Victor Paz Estenssoro, a social reformer and four-time president of the country. In 2001 his obituary appeared in the *Times* of London and *The Economist*, naming him as a world-renowned statesman and visionary. But he would remain an ugly-looking man, nick-named *El Mono*, the Monkey.

One Sunday morning after Mass, a little girl said to her mother, "Mami, I hope Jesus stays in our town for a long time." Of course! That was who the newcomer looked like. He was gentle and kind and cured the sick, just like Christ. From then on Jesus would be his nickname.

Señora Castillo was at death's door with pneumonia. Of pure Spanish descent, she was a woman of delicate features—tall with green eyes and long chestnut hair. Her dark-skinned husband was a wealthy Quechua Indian. The whole of Tarija knew that Señora Castillo despised her husband and that she never ceased to remind him that she came from the aristocracy of Spain, while he was only a dirty Indian.

Many years before, after her father had lost all his money in the silver mines of Potosi, she had been forced to marry Señor Castillo, a rich mine owner who had saved her family from financial ruin. Filled with shame and hatred towards her parents for "selling" her into marriage, the beautiful señora left Potosi and came to Tarija with her husband to start a new life. She could not forgive her husband's shortcomings: his copper skin, his lack of education and refinement, his not being Spanish. She never kissed or hugged him, held his hand, or even smiled at him. As a devout Catholic, she fulfilled her wifely duties and produced six children—some pale, some dark-skinned. But the touch of her husband disgusted her, and she found it impossible to show him any kindness, let alone affection.

In Tarija she lived in one of the richest mansions of the town, with two courtyards filled with orange, almond and pomegranate trees; an orchard and chicken coop at the back; a cellar filled with the best wines and ciders from the region; a dining-room for sixteen people; and two additional reception rooms. The rooms were furnished with Spanish-style chests and tables of carved mahogany from the Bolivian tropics; the chairs, sofas and wallpaper were imported from France. On the walls hung reproductions of religious paintings by El Greco and Velázquez in dark wooden frames and original colonial paintings by Bolivian masters Pérez de Holguín and Flores. Señora Castillo ran the household with the help of several servants, and each of her six children had his or her own nanny.

Despite the efforts of Doctor Trigo and his team, Señora Castillo's health did not improve. Her pale face looked paler every day, and she became too weak to leave her bed.

Ever present at her bedside was her sixteen-year-old daughter, Filomena, the second youngest of her children. The older children were busy with their own families and hardly came to the house. A kind, gentle girl, Filomena was her father's favourite daughter. Señora Castillo felt ashamed of the dark-skinned half-castes her womb had produced and did not show them much affection. Filomena was one of the dark children, but because of her sweet nature, her mother grew to accept her and love her a little.

Before her mother became ill, Filomena had been attending a convent school. There she went dressed in a white tunic, her long black hair in plaits and white ribbons, a white rosary in her pocket, smelling of soap. Her days were spent praying, embroidering, reading the Bible and religious books, baking biscuits, going to Mass and confession, and practising the piano, followed by more prayers.

"You must keep yourselves pure, pure," Mother Superior used to say to the girls. "The world is full of temptation, of evil deeds, and Satan is just around the corner, ready to entice you into his net. Don't let any unclean thoughts enter your heads. Ever! That's the way sinful actions begin: in the mind. Chastise your flesh! Do penitence! Pray and ask God for forgiveness."

These words put fear into the heart of the shy and pious teenager. Since the world was so sinful and men so corrupt, she would have to protect herself by having as little contact with people as possible. She could see no better way to save her soul than to become a nun. She would marry Jesus and live a life of contemplation and purity.

"Pray, girls, pray, and repent of your sins. Pray to our Mother Mary to intercede on your behalf, and ask her son, Jesus, for mercy," Mother Superior's voice bellowed.

At break time, the convent teenagers played noisily in the schoolyard, teasing one another.

"Filomena! Filomena! They say the foreign doctor is very handsome. I bet you're dying to meet him!" one of her friends said.

Another girl added, "They say he's got lovely blue eyes. They say he looks like Jesus."

"Shh...shh...don't let Sister Angelina hear you," Filomena replied. "Then we'll all be in trouble."

"Aren't you wondering what it must be like to kiss him, Filomena?"

"No, I'm not. Leave me alone!"

"Let her be. All she ever wants to do is pray all day."

Señor Castillo had suggested to his wife that the foreign doctor treat her. She had refused, as she did not want a stranger to set foot in her home. Doctor Trigo and his excellent colleagues were already looking after her. No, she would not see the foreigner.

Soon Señora Castillo's condition deteriorated. Padre Alberto, who had known the family since they had arrived from Potosi, was called to hear her confession and give her the last rites. Filomena was inconsolable.

"Come to my study," her father said. "I need to speak to you in private."

"It's time for drastic measures," Señor Castillo said as Filomena shut the door. "I've decided to go against your mother's wishes. I'm calling the German doctor."

The first time Filomena saw Julius, she thought that a piece of the sky was embedded in his eyes. The rumours she had heard were true: he was a tall and handsome man. It was also true that he didn't care too much for his appearance: he was wearing cheap cotton trousers and a wrinkled chequered shirt, his hair reached his shoulders, and his shoes needed shining.

Filomena and her father waited in the dining-room while Doctor Seifert went to see the patient. After what seemed like years, Julius came out. "Señora Castillo is very ill, but we can still save her," he said. "I have left some of my pills from Germany to fight the disease and have written down the daily regimen she needs to follow."

"God bless you, Doctor," Señor Castillo said.

"But the next forty-eight hours are crucial," Julius added. "She'll need someone to be at her bedside night and day. Maybe one of the nurses from the hospital could help you."

Filomena immediately responded, "I will take care of my mother myself, Doctor."

"Excellent," Julius said and smiled.

Filomena blushed, looked at the floor, and twiddled her rosary beads.

She then accompanied the doctor to the front door. Julius looked into her eyes and said, "Don't hesitate to call me any time, day or night, señorita." Again, a wide smile appeared on his face.

As from the second visit, Filomena took more care of her appearance. The first time, he had come within an hour of being summoned, and Filomena, beside herself with worry, had not thought of dressing better. Today she wore her favourite white dress, combed her thick black tresses carefully, and put pink ribbons at the ends. She had never considered herself beautiful, but her classmates and relations were always complimenting her and saying that she was one of the prettiest girls in town. Her olive complexion was praised for its soft appearance, and her wide dark eyes and eyebrows were the envy of her friends.

Julius came to check on his patient daily, and daily he saw Filomena, always at her mother's side. At the end of every visit, she accompanied the doctor to the front door, where they said goodbye formally.

One afternoon, while saying *hasta luego*, he tried to shake her hand. She withdrew it, shocked. No strange man, especially one only known in a professional capacity, was going to touch her. The following afternoon he tried again, and this time Filomena thought that it would be rude not to shake his hand. Next time he not only shook her hand but also gently kissed it. His lips on the back of her hand felt cool and soft, and a delicious tingling went down her spine. She started looking forward to the doctor's visits.

Julius had noticed Filomena's devotion to her mother. She even slept on a cot next to Señora Castillo's bed. There she was, praying with her mother, caressing her hand, feeding her soup, wiping her forehead, singing softly to her, doing anything her mother needed.

"Señorita, I'd like to get to know you better," Julius said at the end of the first week. "May I be allowed to visit you? May I come to your home, not as your mother's physician but as your friend?"

"Thank you, Doctor, but that will not be possible."

"Why not?"

"I'm to enter a convent very soon."

"But you're not a nun yet, señorita."

"I'm afraid it's out of the question. Good afternoon."

That night Filomena dreamt that Julius not only kissed her hand but also held her face in his hands, caressed her hair, and softly kissed her lips. She woke up with a start. She had to put these silly thoughts out of her mind and do penitence. She felt too ashamed to admit even to herself that she had enjoyed the sensations that her dream had stirred. This dangerous situation could not be allowed to continue. So she decided to do penitence by saying more prayers, depriving herself of homemade delicacies, and helping the servants sweep and polish the floors—all to no avail; her mind kept going back to her dream. She still had to see the doctor while in her mother's room during the medical check-ups, but from now on she would ask one of the maids to walk him to the front door. However, that would be considered extremely rude. She would have to think of another solution.

The following afternoon she accompanied the doctor to the door, and when he kissed her hand, she had to contain the urge to hug him.

Suddenly, the shafts of soft light falling through the roof beams, the coolness of the stone slabs on the floor of the porch, the violets and tulips in their pots—they all seemed lovelier and more vibrant. She was amazed and horrified. This could not be happening to her!

The doctor asked her again if he could come to visit her. Pondering her answer, she glanced discreetly at his muscular forearms, covered thickly in soft yellow hair against his suntanned skin. She would have liked to touch those arms. His hands, big and square with thick long fingers, his wide shoulders and slender waist. How handsome he was, how manly. How he filled the room with his presence…Enough! Waking up from her reverie, she reminded herself that she was destined to be a bride of Christ and no man was going to divert her from her spiritual path. The sooner she entered the convent, the better.

Early one evening, at the beginning of the fifth week of intensive treatment, Julius came out of the sick woman's bedroom, beaming. "She is going to make it!"

Señor Castillo and Filomena hugged each other and praised the Lord.

"Thank you for saving my wife," Señor Castillo said, his hands trembling. It didn't matter that his wife treated him like a dog, hardly speaking to him or even looking in his direction. None of that mattered. What mattered was that his beloved was saved. How would he ever be able to thank the German doctor?

"God bless you, Doctor," Filomena said and looked directly into his eyes.

The following afternoon Julius came to the house to discuss his fees with Señor Castillo. They sat in the courtyard under an orange tree in blossom, drinking coffee and eating the biscuits Filomena had baked that morning.

"I don't require any payment," Julius said.

"Doctor Seifert, we are eternally grateful to you for saving my wife," Señor Castillo said, "and we must reward you accordingly."

Julius set his coffee cup on the table. "In that case, Señor Castillo, I would like to inform you that I have become very fond of your daughter. May I request permission to visit her? In due time, I would like to ask you for her hand."

"My daughter Filomena?" Señor Castillo nearly dropped his cup. "Well…she's still very young…"

The two men were silent for a few moments. Señor Castillo took a deep breath before continuing. "Doctor Seifert, we would be delighted to welcome you into our family. But first I need to speak to my wife."

"Thank you, Señor Castillo. I hope your wife will allow me to visit Filomena so that we can get to know each other."

"Yes, excellent idea."

"I know I don't have much to offer your daughter at the moment," Julius added, "but I'm a hard worker and am building a good career."

"Doctor Seifert, your reputation as a doctor is guarantee enough."

"Thank you, thank you very much. Can I see Filomena now?"

"It would be best if her mother and I spoke to her first." Señor Castillo beamed with pleasure. "Please come back tomorrow afternoon."

Filomena was horrified by the news. Didn't her father remember that she was planning to enter a convent? Why had her parents not consulted her?

"Dearest Father and Mother, you know I want to devote my life to Christ," she said as they sat together in her mother's bedroom.

"And bury yourself in the convent?" her mother said.

"With all respect, dear Mother, you never objected before."

"Now, now, my girl," Señora Castillo said. "I've noticed how your face glows in anticipation of his visits. I've seen the sparkle in your eyes."

"But Mother—"

"Don't lie now. You know that's against our Christian principles. Do you or don't you like the man?"

"I do like him. A little." Filomena raised her head and looked at both parents. "But that doesn't mean I want to marry him."

Filomena left the sitting-room in tears. For the first time in her life, she had the urge to scream and slam the door.

She flung herself on top of her bed. *Why are they doing this to me? Haven't I always been a dutiful daughter? What about my wishes? What will Mother Superior say? Yes, the man is attractive, but I don't want to spend my life with him. I've had a dream or two, a silly thought or two, but that's all there is to it.*

All of a sudden, the handsome foreigner became a threat to Filomena. Why did he have to come and disrupt her life? He had cured her mother, but that didn't mean it had to be repaid with her happiness. She shut herself in her room and didn't join her parents at the evening meal.

Señora Castillo had heard rumours that the German doctor was not a Christian, as he never went to Sunday Mass. Some people were saying that he was a Jew or, worse, an atheist. But her fears were allayed when the doctor was seen at church the following Sunday and the Sunday after. Now that the doctor's Christian credentials were confirmed, Señora Castillo was overjoyed with the proposal. Filomena marrying the most eligible bachelor in Tarija would compensate Señora Castillo for the shame she felt at having an Indian for a husband. However, she decided not to put too much pressure on Filomena. She wanted her daughter to be happy; she knew from personal experience that a forced marriage would end in sorrow. If Filomena wanted to be a nun, she would be a nun. However, if the girl got to know Doctor Seifert a little better, maybe she would grow to like him. Maybe.

The mores of the time dictated that girls from reputable families should stay at home as much as possible, only going out with their parents, older siblings, or another chaperone. Fiancés could visit the young women in their own homes, under the supervision of their parents. Señor Castillo advised Julius to visit Filomena three or four times a week; that way they would be able to get to know each other and talk about their lives, the books and music they liked, their plans for the future.

On Saturday afternoon Julius, wearing a suit and tie for the first time, came to visit Filomena. Tea and cakes were served in the living-room. Filomena's parents sat with them for the first few minutes as protocol demanded but then left the two young people alone.

"Dear Señorita Filomena," Julius began, "I'm sure you know why I'm here."

"Yes, Doctor."

"Please call me Julius." He played with his cuff links and adjusted his tie. "I would like to know all about you."

"There's not much to say, Doctor, other than that I'm destined for the religious life."

"How about books? What do you like reading?"

"The Bible...Ah, and *Don Quixote*, and also..."

As soon those words were uttered, Filomena's expression became even more solemn. Julius guessed that she wasn't yet ready to reveal much about herself.

A long silence followed.

"Shall I tell you about my life?" Julius asked.

"If you wish."

Julius told her about his studies and about his travels in Europe, but Filomena showed no interest in any of it, only occasionally saying "Aha."

Undeterred, Julius decided to declare his feelings. "I would be honoured if you accepted me as your fiancé. I know you are only sixteen and I am twenty-eight, but age is of no importance when two people understand and love each other. Apart from your beauty, you have enchanted me with the kindness you show everyone, even the servants."

"Thank you, Doctor. But my only wish in life is to enter the convent."

"That would be a mistake."

"Why?"

"Spend your life away from the joys and beauty of the world? What good would that do?"

"I want to serve Christ."

"You can serve him very well living a moral life, helping others."

Filomena smiled for the first time and looked at him with kindness. "You mean doing good like you are doing now?"

"Working in the community, yes."

"The religious life is my destiny, Doctor, and nothing will change my mind about that."

For several weeks Julius visited Filomena daily at her house. They drank sweet peach juice and ate lacayote cakes, but Filomena hardly said a word. There seemed to be no way of gaining her affection. Worried about his lack of progress in wooing the girl of his dreams, Julius met with Filomena's father to ask his advice. How could they convince her that it was possible to live a Christian life outside the convent?

"We have to give her time and be patient with her," Señor Castillo said. "With time she'll learn to love you."

One evening Señor Castillo had a private conversation with Filomena.

"My dear daughter," he said as he presented the girl with a brown leather chest with bronze feet in the shape of lion paws, "this chest contains your inheritance, your dowry. If the money I have for you in the bank disappears tomorrow, you'll still have what's in here." From an inner pocket in his waistcoat, Señor Castillo removed a silver key. "You must keep this key safe at all times. Never give it to anybody."

"Thank you, Papá."

"Go on, my daughter—open the chest."

The chest was full of gold and silver coins, doubloons, gold sovereigns, and pieces of eight from the *Casa de la Moneda*—the Royal Mint of Potosi.

After a few more visits, Julius asked Filomena's parents whether he could take their daughter on a picnic by the Guadalquivir River. "Excellent idea!" Señor Castillo said. "Yes, what she needs is to get out of this house. A change of scenery will be conducive to communication."

The following Friday, in the early afternoon, Julius and Filomena, chaperoned by one of the maids, were walking along the tree-lined Avenida Costanera, admiring the poplars and weeping willows and the shrubs and flowerbeds that lined the boulevard. The Guadalquivir River ran alongside the promenade, and they could hear the soothing sound of the water. Julius, whose extroverted personality and warmth had gained him many friends, once again found himself awkward and nervous in front of Filomena.

"How was school today, Señorita Filomena?"

"Fine."

"Did you enjoy your piano practice?"

"Yes."

"Isn't this a glorious day?"

"Indeed."

It was clear that Filomena did not feel like talking, but Julius still had one other card to play. From an inner pocket in his jacket, he produced a small purple velvet box and asked Filomena to open it. The box contained a gold ring.

"Filomena, please listen to me with an open mind. I promise to be a faithful friend and a devoted husband," he said. "Because of you, I will attend church regularly; because of you, I will pray at least twice a day."

Filomena smiled. "I am very honoured by your proposal, Doctor Seifert, but I cannot accept your ring," she said. "My life will be spent serving the Lord."

Filomena's rejection felt like a blow to the head. But Julius was not one to give up so easily, and for the next six months, his visits to the Castillos' home continued. He thought over and over of ways to win her heart or at least dissuade her from entering the convent. Slowly, an idea took shape in his brain. He would ask the Castillos for permission to take Filomena out on a second picnic. This time, he was certain, he would have better luck.

Permission was granted, and again Julius and Filomena, with her maid as chaperone, went on a picnic along the river. Again, Julius declared his love and begged Filomena to consider his offer of marriage. Again, she rejected him and repeated that she wanted to devote her life to Christ.

Despair took hold of Julius. What else could he do? He had been so patient and Filomena so stubborn.

The early afternoon was warm and peaceful—too peaceful, maybe, as apart from Julius, Filomena and the maid, nobody else was around. The few farm labourers who had sat by the riverside to eat their midday meal had all gone back to work, and the señores and señoritas who had strolled after lunch in their white linen suits and lace dresses had returned home to have a nap. No one else was around.

Suddenly, Julius whistled loudly and waved his right hand. Immediately, a man appeared from behind the weeping willows, leading a horse by the reins.

"Don't be afraid, dear Filomena," Julius said as he held her tightly. "No one will hurt you."

She kicked and screamed and kicked some more, while the maid, frozen with fear, stood by like a marble statue. It all happened very quickly; the man grabbed the maid's wrist and told her not to make a sound if she valued her life. He tied her hands with a rope and put a gag in her mouth. He then went to help Julius, who was having trouble controlling Filomena. "Be extremely careful with the young lady," Julius said to the man. "We don't want to injure her."

Julius mounted the horse, grabbed Filomena by her waist, lifted her onto the horse, and fled at full gallop. The man then untied the maid and undid the gag. "If you mention this to anybody outside the family, I'll cut your throat." The terrified woman fled home.

As the afternoon turned into evening and then dark night, Filomena's parents became frantic with worry. Where was Filomena? Where had Julius taken her? They were outraged that the German doctor had betrayed their trust. They knew they could not ask anybody for help; their daughter's dishonour would have to remain secret. Señor Castillo was hopeful, however, that Julius would return with his daughter. After all, Julius was a reputable physician, a respected member of the community. The Castillos did not sleep at all that night.

Very discreetly, before dawn the next morning, Julius brought Filomena to her home. The neighbours never saw or heard anything. Nobody, apart from the immediate family and their loyal servants, had noticed her absence.

Señor Castillo said to his daughter that now she had no alternative but to marry Julius to save her honour and avoid a scandal. The wedding was the talk of the town for several weeks, and the celebrations went on for days.

Shocking as this was, bride kidnapping was not unknown in several Asian, Latin American and eastern European countries at the beginning of the last century. Fortunately, the practice had virtually disappeared by the time I was a young woman.

I want to believe that my grandfather did not rape my grandmother. Why would he have done that? That would have earned the hatred and scorn of Filomena, and he wanted her to love him. I want to think that he kidnapped her so that she had no option but to accept his marriage proposal. I want to think that Filomena spent a chaste night with Julius. Later he must have been very sorry for what he'd done and begged Filomena to forgive him, to no avail. My grandfather's plan to win over the woman he loved misfired badly. She would despise him for the rest of her life. By spending a night alone with a man, her fate had been sealed and her freedom taken away. A scandal in a small town like Tarija would have been unbearable for her and her family. She had no choice but to marry this man.

I want to think well of my grandfather. At the same time, there will always be a hint of doubt in my mind. All those years ago, it was not uncommon for men to "seduce" women who rejected their advances. And when girls were forced against their will, the fault and shame was all theirs. Rape was a brutal, even lethal, affair committed by invading armies, bandits, or lunatics. Seduction was different: the seducer was always known to the woman, and although he did his best not to hurt her, he still applied force to get what he wanted. Was my grandmother "seduced"? If that is what happened, it must have been an unimaginable ordeal. She was a religious convent girl who believed angels brought babies into the world and that her body was a temple of the Holy Spirit that had to be kept pure.

I often thought of how angry and humiliated my grandmother must have been, how terrified and outraged. Julius was twenty-eight, experienced in the ways of the world, and a respected doctor in the town. Filomena was a naive convent-school girl. The balance of power had been on his side, and he had taken advantage of it. From that moment, she would feel a deep antipathy towards men, and sex would forever be something sinful and nauseating.

Emma's and Alcira's Accounts

As the years passed, my curiosity about my family's history was reawakened. I longed for a clearer picture of the events, and I also wanted my children to learn about their Bolivian roots. Not satisfied with the version I had been told since childhood, I decided to find out more about my grandparents. My mother and aunt could no longer dismiss my enquiries as just childish curiosity or say that they would tell me another time.

Here is what my mother told me one morning while we drank tea in my kitchen in England during her last visit in August 2003. She was pleased that I showed so much interest in our story and seemed eager to give me a fuller version.

"Soon after their wedding, your grandfather—my father, Julius—was offered a job in the town of Presidencia Roque Sáenz Peña—Sáenz Peña, for short—in the north of Argentina. It was an excellent opportunity for your grandfather's career, so he accepted the offer.

"Filomena and Julius bought a house in the town and settled into their married life. A year later, in 1926, their first child, your aunt Alcira, was born; two years later I came along, and Eugenia came two years after me. Three little girls for Filomena. A German nurse, Maria, came from Bavaria to help Filomena with the children. Your grandmother told me that when I was born, Maria told her that this new baby girl, me, would be her most devoted and loving daughter, her comfort and support. I wonder how she knew.

"In Sáenz Peña, Julius was again a successful and respected doctor. Unfortunately, one of his colleagues, Doctor Pugs, was jealous of his success. My father suspected Doctor Pugs of spreading malicious rumours about him, sabotaging his petri dishes, and misplacing his research papers. However, despite Doctor Pugs's best efforts to undermine him, my father's reputation remained untarnished. One day the hospital chose Julius to attend a scientific and medical conference in Córdoba as their representative. This was a great honour, and Julius felt very pleased with the way his professional life was progressing. Inside a black leather briefcase he packed his medical books and research papers carefully. He said goodbye to his family and told them he'd be back in a fortnight. Then he boarded the night train and settled into his private compartment to read before falling asleep. He would never see his wife and daughters again.

"The following morning, when the train pulled into Córdoba's station, the panicked shrieks of a train attendant pierced the tranquil morning air. Julius's lifeless body lay on the bloodied floor of his compartment, his throat slit. The contents of his suitcase were scattered on the floor, including his wallet, passport, silk scarf and gold watch. The police were at a loss as to why Doctor Seifert had been murdered. As far as they could tell, nothing of value had been stolen; much later, the organisers of the medical conference would ask the police for Doctor Seifert's research papers, which they believed he was bringing in his black briefcase. His killer was never caught and his research papers never found.

"Filomena knew about Julius's jealous colleague and wondered if it was him who had murdered her husband. But she had no proof of anything, and as she was a shy and weak woman, she did not dare speak to the authorities. She had no friends or family in Argentina, so she and her three little girls returned to Tarija as soon as your grandfather was buried. I don't remember anything about this terrible episode of our lives, as I was not yet three years of age. Alcira was barely five and Eugenia a baby in nappies."

And here is what Aunt Alcira told me about my grandparents when I interviewed her in her house in La Paz in October 2004.

"I remember the house in northern Argentina, in Roque Sáenz Peña. I must have been five or five and a half. Next to the house was a pond surrounded by willow trees, and our father sometimes took us there for a picnic on a little boat. I loved touching the surface of the water, feeling its coolness trickle through my fingers. After rain had fallen, I loved going out into the garden to jump and splash and spatter my skirt and apron with fresh mud. There were tall palm trees in our garden, and the cook would often split a coconut for us to eat. I remember the low branches of the willows caressing my face. I remember filling the pockets of my apron with sweet-smelling lilies.

"One day, when she was three, Emma, naughty as usual, climbed a tree and broke her arm." Unable not to criticise my mother, however mildly, my aunt added, "She was always a tomboy, your mother—always disobedient. And you know how she grew up to be so rebellious, so difficult."

My aunt coughed and blew her nose. Maybe she regretted saying what she had just said and expected me to reply, defending my mother. But I did not utter a word, as I wanted her to continue with her account.

She resumed her story. "Our father put Emma's arm in a sling, and she wore it for several weeks. Our German nurse, Maria, pampered her and took care of her.

"One day I came back home after playing in the garden for a couple of hours and noticed a queue of people with sad faces entering and leaving our house. My mother was wearing black, and so were all the visitors. Everybody was speaking in hushed voices and saying how sorry they were. I did not understand what was happening. When I asked when my papá was coming home, I was told not to disturb my mother, who was crying inconsolably. People said that all would be explained shortly. Soon I found myself in the cabin of a truck, travelling somewhere with my mother and sisters. Your grandmother seemed afraid of the people there, especially a woman who was seated next to us. She kept on pinching Emma's legs and mine so that we would not fall asleep and would be alert, just in case. When the truck stopped to refuel, little Emma said she needed to pee, and your grandmother, carrying baby Eugenia in her arms, took Emma behind a bush, leaving me in charge of our luggage. But I was afraid of all those strangers around me, so I got off the truck and joined my mother and sisters. When we returned to the lorry, we found that the woman who had been seated next to us had disappeared with all our luggage.

"We arrived in Tarija exhausted and nearly penniless. My father had put money for me and my sisters into savings accounts in a bank in Argentina, but the savings booklets were lost during the trip back to Bolivia. Luckily, in Tarija, Filomena still had the big leather chest with the inheritance her father had left her and was able to go back to live at her parents' house, where she shut herself away from the world. She refused to see anybody apart from her siblings and her two best friends. She even refused to go to church and begged Padre Alberto to come to see her once a week for confession and prayer.

"Your grandmother's older brothers were surprised by her return. They started visiting her several times a week, something they had never done before. During those visits, while one of them was chatting and entertaining Filomena, the other would give me some sweets and ask me to open the chest and remove one or two gold coins. They told me they were preparing a nice surprise for all of us and that I must not tell anybody what we were doing. After a few weeks, the chest was only half full. Your grandmother decided to keep the chest key inside a pouch and hide it under her corset at all times. My uncles then visited us less and less frequently, maybe once every three or four months.

"Your grandmother was too wrapped up in her sorrow and prayers to look after me and my sisters properly, so she hired a maid to take care of us. We grew up aware that we were the daughters of 'that funny recluse,' but as we belonged to one of the important families of the town, the high society of Tarija welcomed us back in their midst. Besides, we were the children of a European man, a German, and Germans were especially highly regarded."

Part III

New Relations

January 1966

After our short holiday in Lake Titicaca, my sisters and I spent the rest of the summer at home, reading our books and magazines and playing on the roof terrace. One Saturday afternoon, just before the start of the new school year, I went down to the kitchen for a glass of water. Carolina and Teresa were upstairs with their comic books, and my mother was having a nap. I was about to enter when a soft murmuring reached my ears from behind the half-closed door. I stopped and had a peek. Her head bowed, her black rosary held tightly against her chest, my grandmother was praying, sitting on her tiny kitchen stool. "Lord Jesus, hear my prayers. Forgive my insolence, but kneeling hurts too much," she said. "Please cleanse my soul. Protect my daughter Emma and her girls." She wiped her eyes and continued praying.

I wanted to go in to hug and comfort her but did not dare enter. If my mother ever caught Abuelita torturing herself like this, she would reprimand her: "Stop this nonsense, Mamá. You'll make yourself ill. Now, come out onto the terrace." Up on our roof terrace, Abuelita would cheer up quickly. She often thanked God for the blue skies of La Paz and the view of the Andes.

She was happy with us children, singing to us, telling us stories, cooking for us, hugging us. But then when the day's activities were finished, she would remember her past, her worries, her sins.

Abuelita, what had you done?

Aunt Alcira and Cousin Cecilia came to visit us the following Sunday. My aunt was in a cheerful mood and seemed very pleased with herself. After several years of hard work and judicious planning, she was at last the proud owner and headmistress of a newly built secondary school.

That afternoon Abuelita and Cecilia sat together, holding hands.

"What will you do now that you have finished secondary school, mi amor?" our grandmother asked.

"I want to be a doctor."

"A doctor! That's a very hard profession for a woman."

"Women these days can be anything they want," my aunt interrupted.

I looked at my cousin, at her long black hair reaching below her shoulders, at her wide dark eyes and her soft pale skin. She was gorgeous.

"Well, Emma, have you decided?" My aunt addressed my mother. "Is Mariana coming to my new school or what?"

"I'm not sure," my mother said. "I don't think I can afford the fees."

My aunt rolled her eyes. "Oh, for God's sake, Emma," she sighed. "If you need a reduction, all you have to do is ask."

"Thanks, Alcira." My mother was smiling, but I could tell she was annoyed. She hated asking favours from her sister. She and my aunt tried hard to be civil to each other, but their mutual dislike had deep and ancient roots.

In February I started the first year of secondary education at Colegio Integral, my aunt's new school. Because of my good grades, I had been allowed to skip the last year of primary school, which meant that, at eleven, I was a year younger than my classmates.

My aunt's school—what a change! What a shock. The school opened its doors with just over one hundred students. The buildings were half-finished; we had a dirt playground, dusty grey classrooms, and workmen and bricklayers in the courtyard. However, lessons took place, and discipline was strict. Aunt Alcira took care of that. My short-tempered, clever and ambitious aunt was feared by pupils and staff alike. The way she talked and the way she looked at you made your knees turn to jelly. She informed employees and students that she expected a lot from them.

"What do you think I pay you for?" Alcira would sometimes shout at her employees, or, "Get to work immediately!" at the terrified students.

Gerardo was also there, in the year below me. Changing schools was not so scary with him around. Luckily, I soon made a couple of friends. They both seemed as nervous as me and stood somewhat apart from the others. Edward, a tall and blond American, was in my year. Everyone called him Eduardo. There was something wrong with his upper lip, as if it had been split in two and some of the flesh removed. Although his Spanish grammar was perfect, he was unable to pronounce the words properly. Later, at home, my mother explained that Eduardo must have been born with a harelip and that was why he was unable to enunciate correctly. "Nowadays there's a simple operation for harelip babies, but maybe Eduardo's parents left it until it was too late," my mother said. Yes, it was a shame, but once I got to know him, his shyness evaporated, and a mischievous little smile started appearing on his face. My mother was concerned he would be bullied for being a gringo and having odd looks, but as far as I could tell, nobody pestered him. He did not have many friends, though.

My other new friend was Rosita, a cousin I had not met or even heard of before. She was three years older than me, and when talking to her, I had the impression of speaking to an adult. Her pale face was covered with freckles, her eyes and short hair were lighter than mine, and she had chapped red cheeks. We quickly became friends, discovered that we both loved reading, and started swapping books.

Rosita had some startling information about our family. She told me that her father and my mother were siblings. But how was that possible? As far I as knew, my mother and her sisters had no brother. At home that evening I asked for an explanation. "Rosita is your uncle Silvio's daughter," my mother said. "Silvio is my half-brother." I had never heard of this uncle or of my grandfather having a son. I also learnt that Rosita's mother was dead and that my uncle had remarried. Uncle Silvio had been away from Bolivia for a long time, and my mother hadn't heard from him in ages. "Still, he's back now, and it's good to see him," my mother said. Mami asked me never to mention Silvio in front of Abuelita, and I agreed to her request without giving it much thought. Maybe Abuelita did not like Silvio? Maybe he had somehow misbehaved? But I did not ponder these questions for too long.

One afternoon, walking back home with my mother, we came across my uncle in the street. My mother beamed at him. "Hello again, *hermano*. How nice to see you! Look, this is my eldest daughter, Mariana."

He didn't even look at me when he said, "Hola, niña." After that he ignored me. He seemed anxious, even a little angry, and his eyes kept on shifting from left to right. His grey suit was crumpled; his shoes were in need of shining. My mother offered to lend him a few pesos, but he declined. This encounter, which lasted less than five minutes, was the first of only two occasions when I saw my uncle.

When my grandmother heard that Rosita was at school with me, she said at once that she wanted to invite her to our house. I mentioned this to my cousin, and she became serious. "I don't think my dad will let me," she said. I wondered why but again did not ask. My mother pleaded and pleaded with my uncle until he agreed to Rosita visiting us the following weekend.

On Saturday afternoon I helped my mother bake some biscuits while Abuelita tidied the flowerpots and swept our little backyard. My grandmother wanted everything to be perfect for this important visit.

"Why has Uncle Silvio never come to see Abuelita?" I asked my mother. "And why do we never talk about him?"

My mother wiped the flour off her hands and added more water to the dough. "It's a very, very long story, which I'll tell you when we have more time. But tell me, how do you like your cousin Rosita?"

I smiled and showed my mother a book. "I like her a lot. Look—she's just lent me this story about a man who wakes up as a cockroach."

"I need to run some errands," my mother said. "I'll be back in an hour." She put the last baking tray inside the oven. "Switch the oven off in twelve minutes exactly, and remove the biscuits carefully. You can make the tea."

Abuelita could hardly contain her excitement. She had seen Rosita at Alcira's house once or twice but had not really had a chance to talk to her properly. Today she was wearing her Sunday clothes and had even put a bit of powder on her cheeks. I was surprised, even a little jealous. *Well, she never does that for us*, I thought.

And then the doorbell rang.

Abuelita rushed to the door. "How lovely to see you!" she said as she opened her arms wide and hugged my cousin. Then she took Rosita's hand. "Come, let's go and sit on the patio before the sun goes down. I want to hear all about you."

It wasn't every day that I witnessed joy in my grandmother's face. The last time I had seen her as happy and excited was when Aunt Eugenia and her children visited us.

Rosita told us that her father, a civil engineer, was working for the Ministry of Transport, building roads and schools in the countryside. Abuelita listened to this news with interest.

"My stepmother is pregnant again," Rosita said.

"Oh! How many brothers and sisters do you have?" Abuelita asked.

"This'll be her fourth child."

After twenty minutes in the afternoon sun, we went back inside. I had just served the tea and placed the biscuits on our prettiest dishes with paper doilies when the doorbell rang. I opened the door and saw my uncle Silvio standing two metres away from the door, looking gloomy.

"Won't you come in and have a cup of tea, Uncle?" I said.

"No. Rosita needs to come away right now." His eyes were hard, his brow knitted.

"Hi, Papi. I'll just say goodbye to Abuelita," my cousin said.

"That woman is not your granny!" he bellowed. "The only grandmother you have is Doña Juanita!"

I was taken aback by his fury. How dare he! Then I turned around and saw my grandmother cowering in a corner of the dining-room, looking at the floor, her face turned to the wall, her black shawl wrapped tightly around her shoulders like a shield against his angry words.

Rosita blushed. "Gracias," she whispered as she put on her coat. Silvio did not utter another word.

Sobbing, my grandmother ran to the bathroom and locked herself in, while I stood by the door, perplexed, sensing that there was nothing I could do to comfort her.

When Mami came back, I told her what had happened. I could still hear Abuelita's sobs in the bathroom.

"That man will not be coming here again," my mother said.

"Why is he so angry?" I asked.

"Never mind. Let's go and comfort Abuelita."

I knew that I could not ask any questions about what had just happened. I sensed that it was something too raw and maybe too big to discuss with a mere girl like myself. I would have to wait until I was in my fifties before I understood the reasons behind my uncle's cruel behaviour.

The Darker Side of Our Society

In 1952, two years before I was born, one of the most important revolutions in Latin America took place in Bolivia. The hero of the revolution was Victor Paz Estenssoro, four-time president of my country and a cousin of my father's. Nicknamed El Mono (the Monkey), he was also the ugly little boy whom my grandfather Julius had saved all those years ago. His government granted the vote to women and Indians, introduced land reform in favour of the exploited native peasants, legalised divorce, and nationalised the mines. Despite all these advances, however, the Indians and cholos would still be treated by the white middle-class society as third-class citizens for decades to come.

In all Latin American countries, having European blood was considered a good thing, something that set one well above the indigenous population. People would speak proudly of their pure Spanish ancestry or of their Italian grandparents. Germans were particularly well respected, their civilisation greatly admired, their pale skin and blue eyes highly valued—and the atrocities of the Holocaust conveniently ignored. No "decent" person that I remember ever wanted to admit to having a single drop of Quechua or Aymara blood, even though their Indian heritage could be seen in their faces. But my sisters and I never considered ourselves to be anything other than Bolivian and were brought up to be proud of our mixed heritage.

As a child I witnessed many scenes of abuse and discrimination against our native people. I felt outraged when this happened but also felt impotent and too shy to do anything about it.

Early one Saturday morning, I went to the Indian market with my mother. She chatted and bargained with the vendors while I listened. It was mainly the women who did the hard work, while the men "supervised" and then spent the rest of the day just hanging around. The sellers were friendly: "Niñita, look at my beautiful apples. Want to try some?"

A few of the cholas were fierce and proud, and you had to be careful not to annoy them: "You don't like my prices? Get lost, and don't come back!"

Shoppers would look for a *changador* porter to help them carry their purchases back to their homes if they lived nearby, or at least until they got a taxi. These changadors earned a pittance lifting and carrying heavy loads on their backs and heads. My mother, laden with sacks of vegetables and bags full of tinned food, hired a porter to help us carry the heavier items. The three of us headed home, my mother and I with heavy bags in each hand, the porter with a big bundle on his back.

After we'd unpacked, my mother suggested Carolina and I go buy some ice cream for dessert. On the way back from Helados Splendid, we heard a porter pleading with a well-dressed woman outside one of the houses in our street.

"Por favor, señora," the man said, "you have to pay me the full amount, por favor."

"How dare you, you shitty Indian!" the woman screamed. "You've made me late, late! You should've walked faster!"

"Only half is not fair, señora…"

"Piss off!" She then slammed the door in his face, and he meekly walked away, staring at the ground.

Carolina and I looked at each other. "Nasty witch," my sister said. *Yes, I hope she rots*, I thought, my stomach in a knot with anger.

At break time at school, I used to buy the meat- or chicken-filled spicy *salteña* pasties from a thin woman who came every day to our playground. She had a baby strapped to her back as well as a toddler who clung to her tatty skirt, and she told me that she had five other children. The woman's shoes and clothes seemed about to fall to pieces, so my grandmother gave me an old cardigan and a pair of slippers to give to the woman, which I handed to her discreetly inside a brown paper bag. Her salteñas were popular, and she usually sold the lot. One week I was broke; I had spent my lunch allowance on comic books, but the whole week the salteña seller allowed me to buy on credit. My mother knew nothing of my financial woes. At the weekend I persuaded my sister Carolina to lend me her savings. On Monday, at break time, I looked for the woman, but she wasn't there. On Tuesday she didn't come, either. In fact, she never came back. Eduardo later heard that she had ended up in hospital after a beating from her husband. My guilt was enormous. How would I ever be able to pay her what I owed her?

My mother was full of contradictions. She felt very sorry for the poor Indian children and old people begging in the streets and always gave them something. Those who knocked on our door were given a piece of fruit, a slice of bread, or whatever we had left over. She kept all our old clothes so as to give them away during the cold spells. And yet even though she believed that the Indians should be treated with respect, she did not think they were our equals. Emma was a product of the time and society in which we lived.

Although hardly any señoras went to work, having a maid was, and still is, part and parcel of Bolivian life. Traditionally, houses were built with a maid's bedroom and toilet, as no high-society señora would have allowed the servants to use the same facilities as her children. The maid's bedroom was usually the tiniest and coldest room of the house. Most maids slept on the floor on a straw mattress, often with no sheets or pillow. I remember touching one of those mattresses at the Indian market, an itchy and uncomfortable bundle of pressed straw with no covering. But my mother didn't think a straw mattress was good enough for any human being and provided our maid with a proper bed.

During the Friday afternoons when my mother and her friends got together to play rummy or canasta, I would sometimes hear the señoras say, "The only language these Indians understand is the whip. If you treat them nicely, they'll steal from you. Beat them, and they'll respect you." I did not agree with these comments and wanted to say so. But it would not have been possible for a young girl to speak up for the Indians, and the mere thought of confronting those ladies filled me with dread.

Our maid sat with us at mealtimes, unless we had guests, in which case she ate in the kitchen, as the dining-room table was not big enough. All of my mother's friends reproached her for allowing the maid to eat with us. At Christmas our maid received hugs and a present. "I don't know how you can allow an Aymara at your table, Emma," her friends would say. My mother didn't justify her actions or argue with her friends. She just smiled, changed the subject, and carried on doing what she wanted to do. My grandmother too grew used to having our maid at the table with us—it was the Indians outside our home who were not to be trusted.

Emma was not a saint, and her temper could occasionally be as fierce as Aunt Alcira's. "*Indio desgraciado!*" she'd sometimes shout at taxi drivers or porters who hadn't done exactly as she'd wanted, and on those occasions I wished the earth would swallow me, as I didn't want anyone thinking I had anything to do with that angry woman.

I never heard my mother argue with her friends about the rights of the Indians, but her actions spoke much louder than her words ever could. During a march in La Paz, when the miners walked for days from the mining centres to the capital to ask for better working conditions and to protest against the closure of the mines, my mother cooked a huge cauldron of stew and installed herself and her maid in the middle of El Prado to feed the hungry workers and their families. "How can I not help them?" she said. "They have walked hundreds of kilometres with their wives and babies."

Her friends were outraged. "Emma! What are you doing sitting here like a chola at the market? Why are you helping these troublemakers?"

"Because I have to," was her reply.

The "defenders of the people" sometimes behaved in ways that were anything but. I remember silver-haired seventy-year-old Señor Manuel Flores, an old family friend who came to our house occasionally to have tea and discuss politics with my mother. He was a founding member of the Movimiento Nacionalista Revolucionario, or MNR, the party that introduced major social and economic reforms and fought for the rights of workers and peasants following the 1952 revolution. One Friday afternoon, after finishing his cup of coffee and a slice of our homemade custard cake, Señor Flores asked my mother and me to go with him to the airport the following evening. "I would appreciate your help, Emma," he said, "as nobody else is available to come with me." His daughter was coming back from Italy, and he had hired a van plus a driver because his daughter was sure to bring a lot of luggage. He wanted everything to be perfect to welcome her.

The road to El Alto Airport was a long, steep slope rising nearly six hundred metres from the centre of the city. That evening, as usual, the traffic was moving slowly. On the road I could see people making their way up to their homes in the poor neighbourhoods around El Alto after a hard day's work in the centre of La Paz. At every bus stop, there were long queues; the buses came packed with people, some hanging out of the doors. We were soon caught in a traffic jam. At the next stop, a few metres ahead of us, factory workers in faded blue overalls, peasants in threadbare, dusty clothes, and street vendors with bags and boxes full of unsold merchandise were waiting resignedly, tiredness and hunger showing in their faces. A couple of young Indian men approached the car in front of ours and offered the driver a few pesos to give them a lift. This was refused. The men then approached our van. Señor Flores also refused.

An exhausted-looking Aymara mother with two little children and a baby strapped to her back signalled and begged us to take them.

"Manuel, let's give them a lift," my mother said.

"No," he replied and ordered the driver to carry on.

My mother protested, "But, Manuel, the van is more than half empty!"

Farther up the hill, an old man dressed in tatty clothes, bent double and leaning on a crutch, was walking beside a young boy. The boy pleaded with us to give them a lift.

"Please, Manuel, let's take them. He's a frail old man."

I also felt like protesting but said nothing.

"No. I don't want them dirtying the van. Let's hurry up!"

And so we did. My mother stopped complaining; it was Señor Flores's van, after all, and he hadn't hired it for charitable purposes. The driver did his best to make up for lost time, and we got to the airport with half an hour to spare. Señorita Flores arrived with several boxes and suitcases laden with the latest European fashions and presents for her friends and family.

Back at home, my mother said that it was a disgrace that Señor Flores, of all people, should have behaved in such a callous and hypocritical way. She was angry that our politicians' fine words about standing up for the rights of the dispossessed did not match their actions.

One Saturday afternoon I accompanied my mother to visit a friend of hers who had just come back from the United States. *Doctora* Pacheco, a lecturer at the state university in La Paz, had obtained a grant from an American university and spent two years studying for a doctorate in Latin American history. "When I spoke with her on the phone yesterday," my mother said, "I could tell that she was very proud of her achievements. She's a very capable woman, and our university is lucky to have her."

Doctora Pacheco, in her mid-forties, lived with her mother near San Pedro Square, a few blocks down from our house. The doctora and her mother were short and brown skinned, with high cheekbones and jet-black hair.

Their maid opened the door and showed us inside. Doctora Pacheco and her mother welcomed us into their sunny sitting-room on the first floor with comfortable cane armchairs and huge windows facing an inner courtyard with potted plants. On the opposite wall hung a silver crucifix and a picture of Jesus surrounded by ragged children and the words "May the peace and compassion of God always be present in this home" in a semicircle under his feet. Doctora Pacheco was eager to tell us about her years in America and about her well-received dissertation, "The Glories of the Inca Empire and the Mysteries of the Tiwanaku Civilisation that Flourished Near Lake Titicaca." She was proud of our historical heritage.

But all was not what it seemed. "You cannot imagine, Emma," the doctora said, her face darkening, "how hard it is to come back to this awful, godforsaken country."

"Yes, my poor daughter," her mother added, looking at us with pained eyes. "These ignorant Indians are holding all of us back. Don't you agree, Emma?"

My mother did not reply immediately. "It's not their fault that they're ignorant. They need education, but we're a poor country."

The doctora raised her eyes to the ceiling. "If only it were a matter of education…"

She then looked at her watch. Impatient, she shouted at the maid, "Is the tea ready yet?"

Short and brown with high cheekbones and plaited black hair, the young maid brought in a silver tray with cups and plates. "Buenas tardes, señora, señorita," she said. Nobody introduced her to us.

"Buenas tardes," my mother and I replied.

"Now go and finish your chores," the doctora said to the girl.

We drank the tea and ate a slice of walnut cake made from an American ready-mix packet. Doctora Pacheco then showed us some of the books she had brought back from America. They were heavy hardbacks with beautiful illustrations, and I wished I could stay the whole afternoon to have a good look at them.

But it was now time to go home. As we were leaving, the doctora asked my mother if I could accompany her to the market, and my mother said yes.

Soon I was in a taxi with Doctora Pacheco. Like every weekend, the market was crowded and chaotic. The footpaths were jam-packed with stalls; people crossed the roads at inconvenient places, darting in and out, slowing the traffic flow.

We sat in a traffic jam for a few minutes. The doctora became restless and started fidgeting with her shopping bags. "I came back to this," she said, "to traffic jams, incompetence and filth." A couple of porters, bent double under sacks full of vegetables, crossed the road in front of our stationary taxi. A look of anger appeared on Doctora Pacheco's face. She lowered the car window and shouted, "Get out of the way, you filthy dogs! Can't you see that decent people are trying to get through?"

Then she said to me, "The day all these vermin are eliminated will be the day we start making progress."

She continued haranguing the driver. I was speechless and dug my nails into the fake-leather seat. I had been brought up to respect my elders and wasn't in the habit of answering back. But oh, how I wished to tell the doctora, among other things, that if she looked at herself in the mirror, her Aymara features would stare back at her.

A Holiday in Tarija

December 1966

A few days after Christmas, my mother decided to send Carolina and me on holiday to Tarija. I was thrilled; nothing could be better than going there on vacation, as I well remembered from my previous visit four years before. Señora Aida, a friend of hers who was visiting La Paz, had suggested taking my sister and me back to Tarija with her, where she lived with her two young nieces. Teresa, being only four, would remain in La Paz with Mami and Abuelita.

The first part of the trip was by train from La Paz to Villazón, which was on the southern Bolivian border with Argentina, some thirteen hundred kilometres away. Our mother was a little tearful at the station, but Carolina and I could hardly contain our excitement. We settled into our compartment and soon were watching the Andean landscape rush past our window, the flat and vast Altiplano against the snowy peaks of the Cordillera Real, the limpid blue sky. Señora Aida, mostly immersed in her business papers or reading a book, spoke to us only occasionally.

As soon as the sun went down, the temperature plummeted. Luckily, my mother had insisted we bring coats and blankets. The poor Indians travelling in third class all shivered under their ponchos. Carolina and I went to the cafeteria and ordered a chicken sandwich and a hot chocolate. While the carriage swayed from side to side, the cook and waiter prepared the food, trying hard not to lose their balance or spill anything.

The train arrived in Villazón, an ugly, grey and windswept frontier town, in mid-afternoon the following day. We dragged our luggage to the nearest hotel and went to bed early, exhausted. The following morning Señora Aida suggested we cross the border into Argentina for a quick visit. After we showed our passports and proof that we were not intending to stay permanently—poor Bolivians were unwelcome immigrants to Argentina—we boarded a bus, which in a few minutes dropped us in the town of La Quiaca. What a different town this was! We were indeed in another country. The streets were paved; the footpaths were clean; the shops had pretty display windows. But the grey and barren landscape around us was still the same. For the first time in my life, I was aware of the painful contrast between my country's situation and that of one of our richer neighbours. I felt just a little jealous of the Argentineans and just a little ashamed of our poverty. And I was mortified for feeling like that, as my mother had brought us up to be proud of our country.

Señora Aida bought a handbag and some material to make dresses for her nieces. She told us that smugglers operated between La Quiaca and Villazón, with the goods' final destination being La Paz and other major Bolivian cities. We stopped at a cafeteria for tea and cakes and then went back to Villazón to catch the early-afternoon bus that would take us to Tupiza in the southwest of Bolivia.

The bus started its descent into the valleys, and the scenery around us changed gradually. The afternoon air was warm and smelled of crushed fresh grass. I was used to the brown-and-grey earth of the Altiplano, but here the soil was a rich and vibrant shade of red. We arrived in Tupiza at dusk and spent the night at the town's main hotel.

The following morning we found that the bus that was supposed to take us to Tarija had broken down and we would have to wait a few days for spare parts to arrive from La Paz. But Señora Aida was in a great hurry. Determined to arrive in Tarija as soon as possible, she decided we would continue our journey on the only transport available that day: an open-top Indian lorry full of farm produce. We were on our way that very afternoon, Señora Aida riding in the cabin with the driver and his assistant, and Carolina and I up on the top. The lorry was filled with sacks of vegetables and crates of fruit, chickens and rabbits in cages, and two dozen friendly Indians. The sweet aroma of ripe peaches and melons made my mouth water. We were a bit apprehensive at the beginning, as apart from talking to the Indians at the market, we had never really interacted with them. But we needn't have worried, as all of them made us feel welcome, the women especially. They addressed us as *niñita* and spoke to us with affection.

"Where is your mamá, niñita?" one of the women said.

"She's in La Paz with our other sister," Carolina replied.

"Oh, poor you, travelling without your mamá. Here, have a cheese empanada."

We went past fields of blond wheat fluttering in the warm breeze and rows of orange trees in blossom. When dusk came, the crickets started to sing; the sun hid behind the hills and finally disappeared, leaving a pinkish-purple sky. Fireflies flew up into the air, their bellies shining intermittently; frogs croaked and splashed in their ponds. The birds chirruped noisily, saying goodbye to the day.

I looked at Carolina; her eyes were moist. So were mine.

Carolina and I made friends with Señora Aida's nieces immediately. Tall and slender Lucinda was twelve, the same age as me, and was mischievous and giggly. Plump Marisol was two years older and was quieter and less extroverted than her younger sister. In the coming weeks, with these girls and their friends, Carolina and I would do things we could have never done in La Paz. In quiet cobbled streets we cycled without fear of traffic and ran free in the parks. We had picnics by the riverside and spent every evening in the plaza, eating ice cream and playing games with the neighbourhood children.

The pace of life here was slower than in La Paz. There was no need to hurry to do things today, as *mañana* was soon enough. I loved going to the market with Lucinda and Marisol to choose fresh fruit and flowers. I loved browsing in the high-ceilinged shops that smelled of leather and sold wide-brimmed hats and open-toe sandals for the campesinos and *mantas* and *mantillas* (ladies' shawls) for the fashion-conscious *cholitas* of Tarija.

And what a joy it was not to have to worry about water. Here we didn't need to collect bucket after bucket every day, and we could have baths or showers any time we wanted. We spent a relaxed, lazy summer just being girls, without a care in the world.

We also began discussing a fascinating new subject: sex. One afternoon, after coming back from the river, the four of us ran towards the bathroom, trying to be the first to have a bath. Instead of filling the tub, we started throwing water at one another, and soon there was a big puddle on the floor.

"Let's skate on our bottoms," Marisol said.

We removed our clothes down to our underpants and slid from one end of the room to the other. We were laughing and shrieking with delight when Lucinda said, "Did you know that the man puts it inside you?"

"He puts what inside you?" Carolina said.

"His willy. Don't you know?"

"Ugh! That's revolting," I said, throwing more water over Lucinda.

"Yes, it's true. My older cousin, who's seventeen, told me."

"Yeah. I heard it, too," Marisol said. "She read it in a book for married couples—how to do it."

"Tell us, tell us," we demanded.

"What will you give me if I tell you?" Lucinda said.

"If you don't, I'll do this," I said, squirting shampoo into my hands and rubbing it on her hair.

We all laughed. Carolina and I were spellbound with the details. However, I wasn't fully convinced. What we were hearing was incredible and disgusting. I'd have to ask my mother to confirm these stories.

We were told to inspect the room, especially the ceiling, every night before going to sleep, in case a *vinchuca* was hiding in a tiny crack in the paint or wood. Vinchucas are insects that live in the tropical and semi-tropical areas of South America. They hide during the day, mainly in straw or wooden ceilings, and come out at night to suck blood from their victims. The female vinchuca carries the Chagas parasite, which causes the disease of the same name. Although it often takes several years to manifest itself, this disease has no known cure. It affects the major organs of the body, mainly the heart. As the infection concerns few people in the developed world, not many resources have been devoted to research to find a cure.

One morning we went to visit some friends who lived on a farm. While the adults chatted and drank coffee, we girls went to explore the surroundings. Soon the smells of burning firewood and fresh bread reached our nostrils. In the clay oven, the maids had just baked *bollos*, brown rolls with wide strips of white dough. Carolina, Marisol and Lucinda were soon amusing themselves at the chicken coop, chasing poultry like idiots. I decided to go for a walk to explore the farm. As I approached an enclosed paddock, I heard a pitiful noise coming from behind the fence. It sounded as if something or someone was in agony. I opened the wooden gate carefully and had a peek. A horrible spectacle was in front of me: a man had just started killing a lamb and was cutting its throat with a serrated blade.

"You won't like this, niña. Go away," the farmhand said without stopping what he was doing. He was puffing and sweating, big drops running down his forehead.

My instinct was to run away, but, both horrified and fascinated, I stayed. "I'll be all right."

I entered the yard and shut the gate behind me. The lamb was bleating, its cry almost human, its body writhing in a paroxysm of pain. The man held the lamb firmly between his thighs. The animal's legs had been tied together, but it still struggled in jerky movements. The noise was awful, guttural.

Once the head was severed, the man made an incision down the entire body, splitting it in two. Then he slowly, and with great effort, peeled the skin off the carcass. I thought I would be sick, but I didn't move. The sight of that naked animal was worse than any of the horror films I had watched behind my mother's back. *So this is how we get the meat onto our plates*, I thought. *This is what the poor animal has to endure—an awful death so that we can enjoy its tender flesh.* That morning the reality of country life was brought home to me, the romantic and bucolic idea cancelled out by the facts of life—and death.

The carcass was cut and quartered, its bones broken, its innards removed, and the meat put in separate containers. The man's trousers were covered in blood. The soil on the ground was stained red.

"Girls, hurry up with the water," the farmhand shouted.

Two young women came in, carrying two buckets of water each, and proceeded to clean the place.

"I'll go get changed. Tell the master that the meat is ready for tonight's feast," the man said.

It was time for me to escape from that place. I desperately wanted to talk to somebody, but I knew I couldn't. The adults would be furious with me. And how could I describe what I had seen to the girls?

Put this out of your mind, I told myself. *It never happened.*

I needed to join my companions. I found them eating homemade ice cream in the orchard.

"Where have you been?" Carolina asked.

"Just walking. Can I have some water?"

"Don't you want some ice cream?"

I could not eat anything. My whole being felt disgusted. "Just some water, please, Carolina."

That evening everybody tucked into delicious lamb chops. Everybody except me.

This incident was the only blot on the magical landscape that was that holiday in Tarija. Although I didn't become a strict vegetarian, I took a profound dislike to mutton and beef.

When she heard of our arrival, Aunt Antonia, my father's older sister, invited Carolina and me to her house. She was a stranger to us, as we only knew her by name, but she greeted us with open arms and a huge smile. Her greying hair was gathered inside a lacy black net; her face was thick with pale powder. "It's so lovely to see you, my dear, dear girls," she said. "You're growing so beautiful and healthy. Just like your beloved father."

On the wall of the dining-room hung a photograph of my father wearing a brown double-breasted suit with matching waistcoat and bow tie, his double chin underneath a slight smile on his thin lips—a handsome man. I hardly remembered him; the last time I'd seen him was when he'd kidnapped me eight years before, when I was four.

My aunt asked Carolina and me to stand next to the portrait. "Mariana, you are his spitting image. The same nose and mouth. He'll be so proud of you when he sees you," she said. She then turned towards Carolina. "And you, my little one—his heart will just melt when he finally meets you." Our father had never seen my sister.

Aunt Antonia had prepared a feast. While we drank thick hot chocolate and ate fried *buñuelos* with honey, she told us that she had informed our father of our arrival and that he was desperate to see us.

My sister and I looked at each other. Seeing our father would be nice. I did not harbour any resentment towards him and wanted to experience what it was like to have a dad around.

"When is he coming, Aunt Antonia?" Carolina took the words out of my mouth.

"Very soon, mi niña. At the moment he's extremely busy at the farm. He's got so much to do, you know. He needs to supervise all his workers, manage all his lands. Very, very busy—you understand?"

I nodded. Yes, my father was a rich man with a farm, a bakery, and the ice cream parlour where we bought our lollies at the plaza. Why, then, did he never send any money for our maintenance? But I didn't say anything to my aunt.

"And did you know, Mariana, that my brother Aníbal came back from the USA to visit us a few years ago?" my aunt continued. "Well, he had some presents for Carolina and you, a couple of lovely pink handbags, but when he found out that your mother had divorced José, he was very upset. He gave the handbags to some other girls."

Carolina and I looked at each other. So we didn't deserve our uncle's present? And he punished us for the actions of adults? The unfairness of this seemed lost on Aunt Antonia.

Three days later our aunt invited us to her home again. "Auntie, when is Papá coming to see us?" I asked again.

"Don't you worry, mi amor," she said as she spooned thick caramel sauce onto vanilla ice cream. "He's such a busy man, such a hard worker. Such an excellent man, really. But he has no choice but to break his back working." She smiled at me. "Come now, eat up. He'll be here soon. I promise."

The following week Carolina and I were once more at our aunt's house. "Auntie, we're leaving in two days…Our Papá—"

"Of course he'll be here to see you. Have no doubt about that," my aunt said as she served us chopped peaches and sliced bananas.

Finally, the day to return home arrived. I cannot remember if my aunt came to see us before we departed, but it didn't much matter, as my sister and I had not had enough time to develop a close relationship with her. Carolina and I had enjoyed four weeks filled with new experiences and freedom. We went back home bursting to tell our friends all about our wonderful holiday.

As I grew up, I hardly gave my father a second thought. More than forty years later, one lazy Saturday morning in England, while telling my husband about this holiday in Tarija, I would hear my aunt's soft voice praising my father. As her voice grew louder, something inside me shattered, and a terrible pain broke free.

"He never came!" I said, shedding tears for my father for the first time in my life, finally letting go of the repressed anger and hurt of many years.

My Convent School

February 1967

One of the first things I did when I returned to La Paz was ask my mother to tell me about sex. What I had heard about the subject in Tarija was just too ludicrous to be true.

The day after our arrival, as my mother sat with me on my bed helping me fold my clothes, I asked her, "Mami, is it true that to make babies the man has to put his willy inside the woman?"

The blood drained from my mother's face. "Ehh...indeed...that's exactly how it happens," she said as she got up from the bed and left my bedroom. "I need to make an urgent phone call."

And that was all the sex education I got from her. School would be no better. I would have to learn about this fascinating subject the usual way teenagers learned at the time: from other teenagers.

A wonderful surprise awaited my sisters and me. Not happy with my aunt's school, my mother had enrolled us at Sagrados Corazones (Sacred Heart), a French convent school for girls.

Our mother had worried that the nuns wouldn't allow us in, since we were the children of a twice-divorced woman, but they accepted us without any reservations. Families in reduced financial circumstances and with more than one child at the school were offered a discount, but I was well aware that in order to pay our fees our mother would go without many basic things for herself. And as far as holidays were concerned, the only ones going on summer vacation for several years would be my sisters and me, while our mother worked through each school holiday in her part-time office jobs.

How smart we looked in our school uniform: a pleated grey skirt, white blouse and dark-blue sweater and jacket. Sagrados Corazones was situated in the centre of town on one of the main roads of La Paz, Avenida Mariscal Santa Cruz. Its grey stone building stood three storeys high, austere and elegant. The classrooms were spacious and full of light, with varnished wooden floors, and for the first time in my school life, I had access to a library and a chemistry lab.

Little Teresa attended kindergarten, Carolina joined year five of primary school, and I joined year two of secondary school. I was twelve, a year younger than the rest of the girls in my class, a nervous newcomer. Fortunately, Gloria, a plump girl with short dark hair and wide impish eyes soon came to talk to me.

Gloria invited me to her house within a few days of meeting me. She was the elder sister of three rowdy boys, whom she tried to keep at arm's length. They lived in a second-floor flat overlooking Plaza San Pedro, four blocks down from our house.

Soon my mother said that it was my turn to invite Gloria to our house.

I panicked. "Oh no, Mami! Could we not take her for an ice cream instead?"

"Of course we can go for ice cream as well, but Gloria needs to visit you at home. What will her parents think if you don't invite her back?"

My mother never said it in so many words, but I guessed she implied that a friend who would drop me because of our waterless situation wasn't a friend worth keeping. But I need not have worried, as Gloria pretended not to notice our disadvantage and never asked any questions about it.

From the start, she enjoyed ordering me around, but she didn't always get away with it. "Mariana, give me that book," she would say while twisting a strand of her hair with her fingers.

"No. I'm reading it."

"Well, hurry up, then. I want it."

She was a lazy student but made sure her work was up to date. "Oh, go on. Let me copy the maths homework, *please*," she would beg.

"You know you can do it by yourself if you try."

"Ooh, be a good friend. Come on."

She copied my work for several years. One time, during a history exam, she whispered to ask me something, and when I told her the answer, the teacher caught us and punished me! Gloria kept quiet and thought it funny. I didn't. But we continued being friends.

Gloria guarded our friendship jealously and felt that she should have exclusive rights to my time. "Why are you going to the cinema with her?" she complained one day while I got myself ready to go and watch a film with another girl, Jeannette.

"Because she invited me," I replied.

"Well, un-invite yourself and come with me. I'm your best friend."

"Yeah, but she's my friend, too."

She turned her back and walked out of the room. "Do what you want, then."

Jeannette and I had recently struck up a friendship, and I had been to her house for lunch a couple of times. She and her siblings were the only young people I knew who had reddish-blond hair and green eyes. My mother said that it was because they probably had Scottish or Irish blood. But I never asked Jeannette about it.

Although Gloria could be irritating and possessive, she was a loyal friend. "How dare you call Mariana a swot! Take it back, or I'll thump you, you idiot," she'd scream at anyone who dared mock me. I was in fact a studious child, my nose always inside a book, and I was always top of the class.

In this new school, I became timid and insecure. Gerardo still came to my house, but I missed not seeing him at school. My gringo friend Eduardo disappeared from my life completely, and I saw Rosita only a few times a year. At primary school I had been boisterous and mischievous; at my aunt's new school, I had had my cousins Gerardo and Rosita and my friend Eduardo to play and laugh with at break time. At both schools I had mixed with boys and girls from different social backgrounds. Now, in this nuns' school, most of the girls came from well-to-do white, conservative, and deeply religious families. Going for afternoon tea or Sunday lunch at one another's houses was part of every girl's life. But I didn't want anyone discovering my family's dirty, waterless secret or finding out that my mother struggled to pay the bills every month, so I preferred not to invite my classmates to my house. After school I walked home with the popular girls, often behind them, often on the outside, trying hard to keep pace with them, my voice drowned out by the loud chatter of the others. I did of course go for Sunday strolls in El Prado with my friends and to some parties, but nonetheless I spent my teens watching events from the side-lines.

Luckily, at home things were different, as my status as elder sister remained undiminished. I still enjoyed ordering Carolina about, expecting her to do as I said without too much fuss on her part, and most of the time I got away with it. Teresa was our baby girl, and she looked up to Carolina and me as the wise and knowledgeable big sisters. The bonds of affection between the three of us were strong and would survive petty childhood arguments as well as more serious adult disagreements.

Once a week we went to confession and then to Mass and communion. If we failed to receive the body of Christ, we were viewed with suspicion. Our confessor was Padre Francisco, a dour and white-haired Spaniard with a pipe between his lips. We used to kneel at the pews in total silence, making a list of our sins. When my turn came, I would tell the priest about my lying, my wasting of food, my arguing with my sisters, my occasional swearing when in a rage, and, most shameful of all, my impure thoughts, at which point Padre Francisco would ask, "Do you think these thoughts on purpose? Do you enjoy having them?" I would reply that I did my best not to think these thoughts but that they still came to my mind uninvited. Padre Francisco would say, "No sin there, my child. Say a whole rosary. You may go in peace."

Occasionally, we would hear our priest roar angrily at a girl, "What! You did what?" The unfortunate young woman kneeling at the confessional would weep with shame, while the rest of us tried to imagine her crime. Did Padre Francisco not realise that his shouting would encourage us to lie about our sins to avoid public humiliation? We were warned, however, that if we kept secrets from our confessor, God would punish us with eternal flames of damnation. Luckily for me, I stopped going to confession long before I had more substantial sins to report.

We had some interesting nuns at our school. Rotund and middle-aged, Mother Superior inspired fear in all of us. Her presence was enough to impose order and silence, as she stood erect, her arms folded across her ample bosom, staring straight ahead and talking loudly to us, as if we were idiot infants, in her thick French accent.

Sister Theresa taught maths, and throughout my school career I was her star pupil. She would sometimes say to the girls, "Why can't you work hard like Mariana?" and I hated her for saying it, because this made me look like the teacher's pet, which I did not want to be.

Sister Luisa was Gloria's aunt. She was petite, plump, and friendly. Every day she would tell us to keep our thoughts and actions pure—that even thinking sexy thoughts was sinful. But how could we escape sinning, since the more we wanted to avoid naughty thoughts, the more these thoughts came into our heads? She smiled so much and was so friendly that we felt we could tease her, push the boundaries a little, something we would not have dreamt of doing to another more solemn nun. One day, Ana Maria, the class tomboy, with the encouragement of the rest of the girls, asked Sister Luisa if making love with one's husband more than once in a blue moon, and other than for the purpose of reproduction, was a sin. Sister Luisa blushed deeply and replied that God would bless a Christian couple every time they made love. But how about, Ana Maria insisted, if they did it every day? Sister Luisa blushed again and said that Jesus would bless them. What if they did it twice a day? Three times a day? Five? Sister Luisa's cheeks were now crimson. "A married couple, joined eternally by Jesus, can never commit a sin, even if they do it ten times a day," she said. My friends and I were pinching ourselves, trying hard not to laugh. Imagine! What delights awaited us! Sex held such mystery for us, and we looked forward to the day when we would be in the arms of a handsome Prince Charming.

Sister Luisa also had the keys to the school library, and pupils could borrow books at any time. This was excellent news. A marvellous world of literature, history, philosophy and science—all specially written for children—opened up to me. Could I possibly borrow two books, please? Yes, of course. But what about those ones over there? Yes, take as many as you want. All you need to do is write down your name, the titles of the books, and the date on the register, and when you return them, you can borrow more. At last someone is making use of the library.

Old and crippled with arthritis, Sister Dolores taught us embroidery and sewing. A woman was not a proper woman unless she knew how to mend, darn, crochet and embroider. We could bring our own cloth, but she provided the colourful threads, strand by strand. Half-blind and half-deaf, Sister Dolores was usually in a bad mood, grumbling about us "disobedient and impudent girls." One afternoon we discovered that she kept chocolates in a small silvery box hidden under a bench in the corner. Gloria and Jeannette decided to steal some, and I helped them by keeping a lookout. Surely stealing sweets from a well-fed nun was not the same as stealing money from a beggar, we reasoned. So while Sister Dolores, her back turned away from us, showed a couple of girls how to cross-stitch, Gloria and Jeannette lifted the top of the box and carefully removed enough chocolates for all the girls in the sewing class. This was only discovered after several days, but it would have been impossible to ascertain which class had done it.

One morning I discovered a red stain on my underpants. I knew what it was because my mother had warned me about it. She didn't want me to think I was bleeding to death, as she had thought, due to my grandmother never mentioning anything about sex or bodily functions. What a nuisance this menstruation thing was, and how painful. The nuns never taught us anything about it, and although this was a girls' school, the subject was taboo even among ourselves.

Music played an important role in our lives. I learnt by heart the lyrics of the Argentinean tangos and Mexican *boleros* I heard on the radio. Pop songs by the Latin American heartthrobs Sandro, Los Iracundos, and Los Ángeles Negros were also played endlessly, to my great delight. But the tunes that touched my feelings like no others, sending a delicious shiver down my spine, were the haunting Andean melodies interpreted by Bolivian folk groups such as Los Jairas and Savia Andina.

Our radio brought the national and international news to our home. While doing her jobs, my mother would listen intently to the bulletins, often agreeing or disagreeing out loud with what was being said. We also bought a morning newspaper and sometimes an evening one. For my mother, it was important to be informed and listen to different opinions. It was also vital to read as many books as possible. Although men in general believed that women should be kept in their place, most of them treated my mother as their equal; she was not just a good-looking woman, accomplished cook, and good housekeeper but also an educated and intelligent professional who deserved their respect. She loved discussing politics and world affairs, and she analysed each subject in detail. She instilled in me a thirst for knowledge and a political consciousness.

Walking to school on bitterly cold winter mornings in July, my sisters and I would feel the ice on our cheeks and hands. We'd wrap up warmly with thick tights, knitted sweaters and woolly hats—oh, how I hated that hat! Nobody that I can recall had central heating at that time, and not everybody could afford to have more than one or two heaters in the house. We had one, which we kept by Abuelita's side and used mainly in the evenings. I often did my homework in bed, wearing my hat and coat under an itchy red blanket, shivering while I wrote.

For breakfast we had homemade bread with butter, washed down with thick hot chocolate. My mother's delicious wholemeal loaves containing milk and eggs could bring the dead back to life, but early in the morning my stomach turned at the thought of eating. When I was eight or nine, I had been a little chubby, but now that I was about to become a teenager, I wanted to be as skinny as possible. Skinny was what all the boys liked. Skinny was feminine. Skinny was the thing to be. The fashion magazines carried pictures of slim, glamorous models. There was a young English girl I admired with a funny name: Twiggy. I decided that from now on I would eat only once a day—fruit, if possible.

I knew what I had to do: when Mami was not looking, I would hide the bread in my pockets to dispose of it later, and I would discreetly empty the chocolate drink down the sink. I was aware of how hard my mother worked and felt guilty for doing it, but there was no other solution. Carolina knew of my wrong-doing, but I was certain that she would never betray me. Little Teresa never saw me disposing of the food, as she came down to breakfast a little later, and Abuelita had her breakfast in bed.

One lunchtime I ate the apple that our maid, Pancha, had put in my lunchbox but did not eat the sandwich, which I gave to a passing beggar later. After school I walked with my friends to Coliseo Cerrado, a sports ground near El Prado, to watch our school play in a volleyball competition. My stomach was rumbling, but I ignored it. Ana Maria, our star player, was performing brilliantly, scoring against the Santa Ana School. My stomach rumbled again. An Aymara boy came along selling crisps, nuts and sweets. I bought a packet containing two water biscuits; that would be the last food of the day.

My school won the volleyball tournament. Long live Ana Maria and the team!

Back at home, Abuelita had made thick vegetable soup and a spicy chicken stew, but I announced that I was not hungry.

"You have to eat something," my mother said.

"Only fruit, please. I ate a cheese sandwich at the Coliseo," I lied.

"Food bought outside is not good enough," she said. "Eat your dinner."

"No, thanks. I am not hungry."

"Eat it!"

"I don't want to…"

Suddenly, she grabbed my hair tightly and held my face next to hers. "You will eat everything that is put in front of you. I work my fingers to the bone so that you and your sisters do not grow up with rickets."

"Please, Mami…"

"Not another word! Look at you, getting thinner by the day. Do you actually eat the packed lunches we give you?"

I put a spoonful of soup to my lips and swallowed. For a minute I hated my mother. She was a horrible bully who insisted I eat that disgusting gunge. She didn't understand how I felt; she had no idea what it was like to be a teenager. No. I wanted to say all those things to her, but instead I choked back my anger and my pride while tears slid down my cheeks.

"There's no need to cry just because you're eating," she said.

What had started as an enjoyable day ended with me learning a hard lesson: I could not fool my mother all the time.

Anorexia and moody teenagers had not yet been invented. My sisters and I, although encouraged to be ourselves and express our ideas, were never allowed to throw tantrums—or to waste food.

The Storm

June 1967

My mother was lying on her bed having a little rest after lunch. Her arms were above her head, caressing the pillow. She had one leg bent and the other stretched, and she looked beautiful and relaxed. I wished this moment could last forever. She was wearing her cream-and-grey alpaca sweater and her brown cotton trousers—not very flattering, but comfortable. She had had a busy morning with her pupils, followed by a teachers' meeting, and had come back in a sombre mood. The headmistress had said that salaries needed to be readjusted—downwards, of course. Our mother made an effort, as she always did for us, and soon cheered up.

For lunch Abuelita had made thick vegetable soup with chick-peas, barley and spinach, and a poached egg floated in each bowl. I hated this soup, but there was no pleading or arguing with my mother about that. Luckily, Abuelita had also made cheese empanadas, lightly fried and dusted with sugar. But no soup meant no empanadas, so I swallowed the gooey concoction as quickly as I could. My sisters were having lunch at a friend's house, but at dinnertime they would have to endure what I was enduring. When lunch was over, I cleared the table and washed the dishes, while Abuelita retired to the sitting-room to read the Bible.

"Are you coming for a quick lie-down with me?" my mother asked.

In a flash, I jumped onto the bed with her, kicking off my shoes and grabbing a blanket to cover our legs. I put my head on her shoulder, and she caressed my hair. We sucked hard-boiled sweets and waited for the *radionovela* to begin. Each episode of this radio play was introduced by an excerpt from Grieg's Piano Concerto in A Minor. I loved this powerful, rousing music that transported me to thick dark European forests (always European in my imagination) full of mystery and dashing heroes. I closed my eyes and imagined a strapping and handsome young man with shoulder-length black hair and a red cape fluttering behind him, galloping on his black stallion towards his beloved, who was anxiously waiting in a castle deep in the countryside. My mother squeezed my hand. I could see she was enjoying the play. Good. For fifteen minutes she would forget about her worries.

All too soon it was time for my mother to leave for her afternoon job at the insurance company. She smiled and kissed my cheek, got up, yawned, and stretched her arms. In the bathroom she combed her hair and applied her pink lipstick. "Please remember to collect your sisters from the bus stop," she said.

While we had been eating lunch and listening to the radio, fat grey clouds had gathered above the city, darkening the afternoon sky. I didn't fancy the prospect of having to go out in the rain.

"Emma, don't forget the umbrella," Abuelita said to my mother as she left.

At four o'clock, as I got ready to collect Carolina and Teresa, I noticed that my mother had not taken the green umbrella so that my sisters and I could use it. She would now arrive home soaking wet, maybe with a cold, like last time.

Then the heavens opened. As I unlocked the front door, thick sheets of rain started lashing the trees and buildings on our street. I ran to the bus stop as fast as I could. The umbrella turned inside out in the furious wind; my shoes were soaking, my legs and ankles were spattered with mud. At the bus shelter, dripping and shivering, my sisters were waiting for me. I grabbed them by their hands, and the three of us ran back home, trying hard to avoid puddles and jets of spray from passing cars, only stopping to look both ways before crossing the streets.

At home Abuelita gave us warm towels to dry ourselves with and a lovely hot-chocolate drink. Then Carolina, Teresa, and I went upstairs to our bedroom. From our window we stared in amazement as the grey clouds disgorged their burden onto the streets below. Every few minutes, thunder shook our window-panes, and forked lightning pierced the sky.

Our mother had not arrived home, and we guessed that she would have trouble catching a bus or even a taxi—the whole public-transport system was in disarray. Abuelita was in the kitchen, mumbling her prayers to keep herself from panicking. It was up to me to pretend to be calm.

"Look!" Carolina said. "The street is a river now!"

Muddy greyish-brown water was coming down the hills fast, carrying stones and debris.

Carolina kept on fiddling with her belt. With a hint of panic in her voice, she wondered whether we would be safe.

"We'll be fine. Our house is on higher ground. Remember?" I said, only half believing what I was saying.

Last year a storm as fierce as this had wreaked havoc in Tembladerani and Villa Victoria, two of the poorest neighbourhoods of La Paz.

Little Teresa grabbed the end of my skirt and cried, "I want Mami. I'm scared."

I sat her on my knee and hugged her. "Don't worry, Tere. It'll soon pass."

That evening we heard on the radio that the severe storm had dislodged soil and rock from the mountains, bringing chaos to the slums on the outskirts of the city. Mud had destroyed the makeshift huts where the poor lived; the force of the murky water had overflowed the ancient drains, washing away market stalls, wrenching cobblestones from the road, and leaving hundreds of people homeless. The better-built neighbourhoods where the rich lived, on firmer ground and with better drains, were unaffected. We also were lucky: although ours was a lower middle-class area, the houses on our street did not suffer any damage, but the roads and footpaths remained muddy for several days.

Meanwhile, our mother had finished work. She had given up trying to catch a bus and had decided to walk—or rather, run—home. The centre of town was chaotic with traffic jams and flooded streets. As the storm was not abating, she decided to wait awhile and took shelter inside the entrance of an old building on a quiet street near El Prado. She hoped her girls were safe and dry at home; she hoped Abuelita was not panicking. After she had waited in this dark and lonely place for what seemed like hours, my mother's thoughts started running amok: *How will I pay all the bills? And the girls' school fees? It isn't even the middle of the month, and the money is all gone...And if they cut off the electricity, I don't know how we'll manage. What to do? What to do? And poor Mamá, with her tatty dress...God, that awful man—will he ever pay child maintenance? But look at the time! I've been here for ages...I have to get home.*

My mother decided to brave the storm and make a run for it. As she left her refuge and crossed the street, her eyes caught a glimpse of a tiny parcel the size of a bar of soap bobbing up and down in the floodwaters, heading towards the gutter at the kerbside. Quickly, she bent down and grabbed the mysterious bundle. The parcel was wrapped in thin see-through plastic and secured with an elastic band. My mother looked around her and, seeing not a soul, put the item in her handbag and ran back to her refuge under the doorway. There she removed the wrapping. Inside the parcel were two thousand pesos, a fortune in those days. Muddy shoes and soaking feet didn't matter anymore. She ran home as fast as her legs could carry her. She knew that if she handed in the money to the police, they would share it among themselves and have a good laugh at her foolishness. The following Saturday she bought new underwear for us girls and a new housecoat and slippers for our grandmother, and she paid the first instalment towards our first fridge.

We enjoyed this respite for a few weeks, unaware that a much worse storm was gathering.

I started paying more attention to the news, or at least to the headlines. I remember the Six-Day War between Israel and Egypt and the beginning of a bloody conflict between Biafra and Nigeria. Leafing through foreign magazines such as *Time* and *Newsweek*, I understood what my mother meant when she complained that they hardly ever mentioned Latin America, least of all Bolivia, unless the rich countries' interests were affected. We simply did not exist.

The local radio and newspapers started talking about a young foreign revolutionary named Che Guevara, who had infiltrated our country and was being sought by the government. President General Barrientos said that Che wanted to propagate communism and export the Cuban Revolution to Latin America; other people said that Che was fighting for a more just society. Liberation theology, a new Catholic movement, was sweeping Latin America. Praying for the poor wasn't enough, many progressive third-world priests were saying; the Church had to help the dispossessed have tolerable lives *before* death. Immediately, the government accused those priests of being communist sympathisers.

The miners, whose lives and working conditions were among the harshest in our country, had been discussing whether or not to support Che's guerrilla campaign. The government was determined to combat subversion and dispatched the army with machine guns and dynamite to teach the workers a lesson. On 24 June 1967, the miners of Catavi and Siglo XX, two of the most important mining centres in Bolivia, were massacred. There they were in the small hours of the morning, sitting around bonfires after celebrating the traditional San Juan Night with their friends and families. Their children and wives had gone to bed, but several men were still chatting and sipping *pisco*, the alcoholic firewater that they used to cope in this cold and barren mountainous mining area. Suddenly, bullets rained down upon them; sticks of dynamite were hurled towards the gathered men, catching them by surprise. Body parts soon landed near the embers of the bonfires; blood trickled down the wooden crates that the miners used as chairs; brains and guts lay splattered on the ground. The pitiful wailing of the wives and the screams of the children were heard for several minutes.

Then a terrible silence entered all the houses.

The soldiers wrecked and took over Radio del Minero, the miners' only means of communicating with the surrounding mines.

Twenty-seven dead and seventy-one seriously injured.

Bolivia, a country whose wealth depended on its mines, was killing its own children.

In October of that year, the Bolivian army, with the help of the CIA, captured and killed Che. His body was photographed lying in the laundry room of the small hospital in a village in the jungle, looking like a defeated and bloodied twentieth-century Christ. The CIA wanted to send a stern warning to all revolutionaries; instead, this image of the fallen Che, which exploded onto the international scene, stirred even more the sensitivities of the idealistic young.

On the cusp of adolescence, I was keen to be part of the popular crowd at school and worried about making a good impression on the boys who waited for us at the end of lessons every afternoon. I also worried about how hard my mother had to work to support us. National and international events were interesting, but they did not yet have too much relevance to my life. I could not at that time have guessed the tragic effect Che's ideals would have on the destiny of my family.

Cecilia and Néstor

One Saturday afternoon my mother came back home from the market with big news. "I've just seen your cousin Cecilia with her new boyfriend," she said. "Make me a cup of tea, and I'll tell you all about it."

Mami put on her slippers and sat in her armchair in the living-room, and we all gathered around her to listen to the news. Our mother told us that Néstor had been studying at religious seminaries, first in Argentina and then in Chile, but had given up his godly calling a few months before his ordination. He was now in La Paz and had recently enrolled in the Faculty of Medicine, where Cecilia was also studying. "The two of them have fallen in love and are seriously thinking of getting married," my mother said. "I wonder how your aunt Alcira is going to react when she hears that."

Aunt Alcira had big plans for her clever daughter: she wanted Cecilia to finish her studies before even thinking of marriage. And she hoped that a rich and well-established doctor would appear on the scene. Soon there were arguments, tears and slammed doors.

Early one evening Cecilia was helping her mother in the kitchen. But the meal preparation was not going well.

"It will be the end of both your careers if you marry now," Alcira said as she poured a little olive oil on the salad.

"Not at all, Mamá," Cecilia said. "We wouldn't be the first couple to get married while still at university."

"Don't talk such rubbish!" Alcira shouted. "Do you want to struggle to pay the rent? To buy food?"

"We don't want any luxuries. We'll have enough to support ourselves."

"Barely enough to get by."

"Please, Mamá."

"What's the rush, anyway? Are you pregnant?"

"Mother!"

"Well, don't go messing things up." After a short pause, Alcira added, "Of course, if both of you agree to live with me until you're financially secure, I might—just might—consider allowing you to marry."

"Begging your pardon, Mamá," Cecilia answered, "but we don't need your permission, only your blessing."

"A thousand times no! Finish your studies first!"

Cecilia removed her apron and threw it on the table. Her mother's intransigence had really exhausted her patience. "I don't want any dinner," she said as she wiped her eyes and left the kitchen. She spent the rest of the evening in her room, trying and failing to revise for her coming exams, her eyes red with crying and her head throbbing.

Alcira asked my mother for help. "When will this stubborn girl listen? Please talk to her, Emma."

My mother thought that Cecilia should decide her own future. She met up with Cecilia at a café in El Prado and asked her not to argue with her mother. "Bring the young man to our house," my mother said. "Abuelita would like to meet him."

Cecilia threw her arms around my mother. "Thank you, Auntie! I wish you were my mami."

Abuelita was indeed looking forward to meeting this young man, who had studied with priests, a fact that elevated him above other men. So one sunny July afternoon, Cecilia and Néstor came to our house. With his wavy black hair combed back, his thick dark eyebrows, and his wide eyes, he resembled the actor James Dean. Beaming from ear to ear, he gave each of us a hug and a kiss on the cheeks and presented our grandmother with a box of sweets. "For you, Abuelita." She was enchanted, and so were we.

Néstor and Cecilia sat together on the sofa, his arm around her shoulders. Surprisingly, Abuelita didn't object to this open display of affection.

"Our studies are going well, Abuelita." Cecilia smiled at our grandmother. "We'll soon start our probationary year at the Hospital Obrero."

"Oh! Poor you! That's a horrible hospital, so dirty and run-down," Abuelita replied.

"That's precisely why we need to work there."

"Couldn't you do your probation at a nice private clinic?"

"The rich don't need us," Néstor answered. "And then we're going to work in El Alto and the Altiplano, where the need is even greater."

"Señora Blanco's son finished his studies last year," Abuelita said. "He's a successful doctor and has just bought a house and a car."

The smell of freshly baked pastries wafted in. Cecilia smiled and changed the subject. "Where's that delicious cake, Abuelita?"

My mother called us to have tea with the melt-in-the-mouth cinnamon biscuits and the layered German custard cake she had just baked. Cecilia, always attentive and affectionate with our grandmother, helped her get up from her armchair. While savouring the pastries, I looked at my cousin and thought how pretty and intelligent she was. I wanted to grow up to be just like her. After tea we all went up to the roof terrace to admire Mount Illimani and the other Andean peaks.

As she was leaving with Néstor, Cecilia asked my mother whether she could take some biscuits. "There's a poor woman we know with a sick, bedridden husband and four little children," my cousin said.

"Of course, take all the biscuits, mi amor. I can bake more tomorrow."

After they left, Abuelita gave her verdict: Néstor was a true Christian man, good husband material.

Soon Aunt Alcira would complain that, when not studying, Cecilia and Néstor spent their spare time visiting and helping people in the poor areas of La Paz with food and medicines. Her "silly daughter and her fiancé" were "wasting their time and energy on those hopeless projects." We knew that Néstor and Cecilia actively supported the charitable work of the Catholic Church. Unknown to us, they had also become involved in other activities.

During Christmas the previous year, Aunt Alcira had started talking about the AFS—American Field Service—an exchange programme that aimed to promote understanding between the United States and the rest of the world. Teenagers from Bolivia could live for a year with an American family and attend high school, and gringo teenagers could come and stay here. Alcira wanted her youngest daughter, Silvia, to take part in this programme. "It's a wonderful opportunity, Emma," my aunt said to my mother. "Silvia will come back speaking fluent English." My sixteen-year-old cousin was keen to go, so she applied herself to studying for the selection exam, which she passed easily. In August 1967 Silvia flew to the United States, the first person in our family to embark on such an adventure.

Summer Job

November 1967

The summer holidays had just started. My sisters and I were enjoying lazy mornings in bed and wished our mother could also have a few lie-ins now that she was not teaching in the mornings, but she got up as early as always to get everything ready before going to her afternoon and evening jobs.

It was the end of the month, and money was tight. The night before, as I was going back to bed after fetching a glass of water from the kitchen, I'd overheard my grandmother say to my mother, "What are we going to do? We've only got a few eggs and some flour in the pantry. The shop-keeper says he's running out of patience."

To which my mother replied, "Don't worry, Mamá. I'll talk to him."

The stocky Chilean corner-shop owner tried his best to appear un-sympathetic, but my mother knew he had a good heart. Hiding behind his thick black-rimmed spectacles, he would mutter, "No more credit until you settle your bill." But somehow, week after week, we had enough in our larder to last us for a few days. I wonder how we would have managed without his help.

One afternoon during the first week of the holidays, Abuelita was in the kitchen chopping onions and chillies for dinner. My sisters and I had set the table and were now in the sitting-room reading our comic books and waiting for our mother to come back from work. Soon we heard her usual cheerful knock—five quick taps followed by two more—and ran to the front door to greet her. She seemed very excited, kissed us quickly, and called out to our grandmother while she removed her coat.

"Mamá! I've got some excellent news," she shouted, smiling broadly. "I've been offered a temporary job."

"That's good, Emma," Abuelita said as she came out of the kitchen and wiped her hands on her apron. "But I was hoping you'd have a little rest now that you are not teaching in the mornings."

"Well, we need the money more than I need a holiday."

"And what about your other jobs?"

"I've already asked for annual leave, and they've said yes."

This year our mother would not have any holidays at all.

The new post involved helping with the paperwork in one of the tin mines near Oruro, in the Altiplano. Abuelita was concerned about this. "A woman alone in the mines, surrounded by men…" she said.

My mother reassured us: she would be working in a nice office with polite and professional engineers, and there would be two or three other ladies there, too. But what worried Abuelita most was the unrest that had plagued the mines in the recent past. Mami reminded our grandmother that things had been peaceful in the country for several months now, and she didn't think the miners wanted any more suffering for themselves and their families. "Anyway, I wouldn't dream of putting myself at risk," our mother said.

"And how long will you be away?" I asked her.

"I'll be gone six weeks," she told us.

"Oh…we're going to miss you," Carolina said and put her head on Mami's shoulder.

"But I'll come back every weekend. I promise," our mother said and gave each of us a bear hug.

We all missed our mother terribly, so I tried hard to put on a brave face for my sisters. During the day I often heard Abuelita praying in the kitchen while she cooked or on the roof terrace while she hung out the laundry. Before we went to bed, she would make us kneel beside our beds to ask Jesus to protect and bless Mami and help the miners who worked down "in the bowels of the earth."

When Mami came back the first weekend, my sisters and I jumped into her arms and fought to be the first to kiss her. The strong sun had tanned her skin and tinted her dark hair a rich golden brown, which made her look younger and prettier. She had brought us some hard pink-and-white *confite* sweets made with sugar and aniseed. We all gathered around her in the dining-room, and while we sucked our sweets, she told us a little about the mine. We were all eager to hear her account, apart from little Teresa, who was only interested in our mother's hugs.

Mami sipped her milky tea. "The peaks surrounding the mines are just lovely, all snowy," she said, "but the pits are horribly grey and cold." She leaned back in her chair and continued, "Those poor miners—most of them won't reach their thirty-fifth birthday. Silicosis will take care of that."

"What's silicosis?" Carolina asked.

"Imagine the inside of a mine where the air is dusty and dirty. This dust gets into the miners' lungs, slowly poisoning and choking them. That's silicosis."

Carolina and I were shocked. "That's horrible," my sister said and made a face.

Abuelita crossed herself. "Oh, poor men. How they and their families suffer."

"You're right, Mamá. At the house where I'm staying, we have electric heaters, but the men in their shacks have nothing. And when there's an accident and the miners end up as amputees, all they can do is beg on the streets."

Our grandmother seemed to be thinking out loud. "Coca leaves," she said. "They chew them to dull their hunger and forget about the cold."

"Yes. And they drown their sorrows in alcohol, wasting the few pesos they earn." Our mother's expression was sad and weary. After a second cup of tea, she went on: "The men have to crawl down narrow passages and remain inside for up to twelve hours, breathing in the dust. The managers' lives are different—they have proper houses with hot running water and electricity. They don't risk their skins daily."

My mother was now tired and needed to lie down for a while. She went to her room for a quick nap and asked me to wake her up when dinner was ready.

"Will you tell us more about the mine, Mami?" I asked her.

"Yes, mi amor. But now I must sleep."

She slept for thirty minutes and had trouble waking up. Still groggy, she came downstairs to the dining-room for a bowl of thick chicken soup with chilli and onions, which warmed her right through. As it was getting late, my sisters went to bed. I made three mugs of hot chocolate with cinnamon and cloves, and Abuelita and I sat with my mother in the sitting-room to hear her account of a typical day at the mine.

She started by telling us how the blast of the sirens woke everybody at five o'clock, six days a week. Because of the altitude, the air felt like ice from sunset to early morning. Breakfast for the office workers was served at six o'clock: a mug of strong tea or black coffee and a crusty *marraqueta* bread roll with jam. From the window of the canteen, my mother could see the miners emerging from their mud-brick, aluminium-roof shacks, ready to go inside the cavernous mouth of the mountain, pit helmets on their heads and ropes and sticks of dynamite tied around their waists; the cold of the Altiplano slapped their copper-skinned faces, biting and penetrating their bodies despite their coarse woollen clothes.

Before entering the mine, the men first had a small ceremony with offerings to *El Tío*, the devil "uncle" that inhabits every mine, to befriend him and ask for his protection. A small painted clay statue of El Tío sat at the entrance of the mine, his eyes glowing like red-hot pokers, a smoking cigarette in his tiny mouth, coca leaves scattered around his feet, and wet patches on the earth where alcohol had been offered. The men needed his protection, as a rock-fall might kill them, a badly positioned stick of dynamite could blow their legs off, or toxic gases could poison them. The heat in the interior of the mine was suffocating and the clang, crash and boom deafening. "And their wives, the *palliris*," my mother said, "they work outside the mine sifting through the debris with their bare hands, looking for minerals. Often they have babies strapped to their backs, and their toddlers sit nearby in the rubble."

My mother told us that Bolivia produced and exported dozens of minerals and metals.

"Why is our country so poor, then, Mami?" I asked.

"There are many reasons, mi amor. Corruption here and corruption abroad. The gringos exploit us with unfair trade practices. The world is a ruthless place."

"Emma, you shouldn't say those things to Mariana. She's only a child," Abuelita said.

I protested, "No, Abuelita. I want to know."

I very much wanted to understand why we had so much wealth and yet were among the poorest countries on the planet. But neither my mother nor anybody else could explain our situation in simple sentences. To comprehend the complexity of the world, I would have to wait until I was much, much older and had read and studied dozens of books.

One Wednesday afternoon, three weeks after she had started her clerical job at the mine, a taxi brought my mother home. Why was she back before the weekend? She looked pale, and her usual big smile was absent from her face as she greeted us. I wanted to talk to her and find out, but she told me to go to my room to read, that she was tired and had a headache. My sisters, too, were dispatched upstairs to play with their dolls. We obeyed reluctantly and left her sipping a cup of tea and talking to Abuelita in the sitting-room. But I found reading a book impossible, as bad thought after bad thought bombarded my brain. After two minutes I came downstairs and listened behind the door.

"Look at those ugly big bruises on your calves," Abuelita said, "and your poor arm, all swollen."

"It's all right, Mamá. I'll wear trousers and long sleeves for a while."

"At least the makeup on your face covers the bruise on your cheek."

"Are you sure it doesn't show?"

"No. It's fine." And then Abuelita added, "I told you all men are evil."

"Please, Mamá, not now."

"Will they pay you compensation?"

"You must be joking!"

What had happened? Who had hurt Mami? I wanted to burst into the sitting-room and ask them, but I could not.

"Can you imagine if the jeep had been going faster?" said Abuelita.

"Let's not dwell on it anymore."

"School starts in a few weeks. That'll give you time to recover."

"Yes. I'm looking forward to that."

I worried about my mother for several days but did not dare ask her what had happened. For our sakes, she pretended everything was fine and carried on as normal. Soon we were all excited with Christmas preparations, and the incident faded from my mind. Many years later, when I was living in England and had my own children, my mother would finally tell me what had happened to her that day at the mine.

It was a bitterly cold morning in the high Andean plateau. The weak sun was barely visible, a pale stain against the thick grey clouds; a thin layer of frost covered the *paja brava*, the sturdy yellow grass. In the distance a lone shepherd was tending a few white llamas and brown guanacos. My mother and her boss, a civil engineer from Cochabamba, were travelling on a dusty road in the company's jeep. Señor Sánchez was a handsome man, tall and slim with dark hair and a thin moustache; his appearance reminded my mother of my stepfather. The jeep was filled with the aroma of the man's expensive cologne. The other two women in the office had said to my mother that Señor Sánchez was a womaniser and that she should keep him at arm's length. "Don't worry, girls. I know how to take care of myself," she had replied. However, she did not feel comfortable when he was around. He had been teasing her, harassing her, every day. "I'm here to work," she had said repeatedly. "I'm not looking for an affair."

That day, in the jeep, he told her, "If you keep on refusing me, you'll be putting your job in jeopardy."

She was outraged. "If that's the case, then I'd rather go back to La Paz."

He put his right hand on her thigh while steering the vehicle with his other hand. "You know you want me, Emma."

My mother removed his hand and told him to concentrate on his driving. He laughed and then grabbed her breasts, steering carelessly. As the car slowed down around a bend, my mother quickly glanced at the road ahead. She knew what she had to do. She opened the car door and threw herself onto the dirt road, her left side hitting the ground. Theirs was the only car, and they were the only people for miles around in that desolate highland.

Señor Sánchez stopped the car immediately. "Are you crazy, Emma?" He got out of the car and tried to help my mother to her feet.

"I want to go home to my children," was all she said, refusing to take his hand.

"Please get back in the car," Señor Sánchez pleaded. "I promise not to touch you." After a while he added, "I hope you're not thinking of complaining to the company."

Probably not. My mother knew that when a woman filed a complaint against a male colleague, the man nearly always declared that it was she who had tried to seduce him. She did not utter another word, and they travelled back to the mine in total silence.

Back at the mining camp, the management spoke first to Señor Sánchez while my mother, bruised and dishevelled, waited outside. After a few minutes, they called her in.

"What you did, Señora Emma, was extremely foolish," the chief engineer, Señor Ortiz, said. "You could have caused a fatal accident."

"But do you know why I did what I did?" my mother asked.

"We know all about it, señora. There's no need to go over it again."

"But you have not heard my side of the story!"

"That is enough, señora. What we need and demand from you is total discretion."

My mother understood perfectly that handsome Señor Sánchez was an experienced professional, an asset to the business, while she was just a temporary secretary who could easily be replaced.

"Since you are not interested in finding out the truth, I'm afraid I'll have to hand in my notice," my mother said.

"Señora! You cannot leave just like that. You have signed a contract. Remember?"

"Yes, I remember. But I'm afraid I must go."

"Your departure is most inconvenient for our company," Señor Ortiz said. "You are a very difficult woman."

After gathering her belongings, my mother went to the office to sign some papers and to collect her money. She was paid strictly for the days she had worked. The women looked at her with pity, the men with contempt.

My mother must have felt both angry at the way she had been treated and anxious at her loss of income, but she was determined not to burden our grandmother or us children with her worries. All I can remember of those days after the job at the mines is that until the school year started, to earn some much-needed cash, my mother and grandmother baked doughnuts and Christmas panettones, which our maid took to the nearby offices to sell.

Three decades later, in 1998, my mother, my two children, and I travelled to the historical city of Potosi. After visiting the imposing Casa de la Moneda, the sixteenth-century Royal Mint where the ingots of silver were kept during colonial times, we went to a little mining museum next door. There we looked at samples of the many minerals that dwell deep inside our mountains, saw some interesting ancient maps and photographs, and glanced at statistics concerning our mineral wealth, the advances made in technology and safety, and the meagre income generated by exporting these riches to the world. While I read an article displayed on the wall, bitterly thinking how much the world takes from Bolivia and how little we receive in exchange, my mother and the children went to look at a model of a working mine on the opposite corner from where I was standing. Suddenly, my eyes filled with tears. Seeing me cry, my mother started crying, too, and came to my side to comfort me. But it wasn't the statistics that had moved me to tears. A picture of a handsome copper-skinned young miner was smiling at me from its frame on the wall. He looked seventeen or eighteen, and I knew that, in a few years' time, well before his thirty-sixth birthday, silicosis would claim him.

1968: The Year I Was Thirteen

My aunt fought hard to stop Cecilia and Néstor from getting married, but they were determined. One Sunday afternoon Néstor rode his motorbike to my aunt's house to ask for Cecilia's hand and brought a bottle of French perfume for his future mother-in-law. Underneath his leather jacket, he wore a striped dark suit and a blue tie. Aunt Alcira, however, was unimpressed. There were tears and bitterness even on that day. "I hope we won't come to regret this decision," she said.

Cecilia and Néstor were married on Easter Sunday, 14 April 1968. She was twenty, he twenty-two. After the religious ceremony, we all went to the reception at the Círculo Militar Club in Plaza Murillo. I remember Cecilia beaming with happiness in her long bridal dress, dancing with her father, Uncle Eitel—who lived in Santa Cruz but had come to La Paz especially for the occasion—and Néstor looking at her, love-struck, a glass of wine in his hand. It was a small reception for family members and close friends only—not the grand event my aunt had wanted. Cecilia and Néstor had vowed to live a simple life, and although they didn't wish to live as austerely as Saint Francis of Assisi, they planned to dedicate their lives to helping others. So they decided that there should be no wedding feast but only some drinks and canapés. "The money saved will go towards our projects," they said.

As Cecilia and Néstor had been working hard on different projects and charities of the Catholic Church, the priests gave them two rooms and a tiny backyard in Sopocachi, where they would live for a few months.

Two weeks later I was helping my mother prepare lasagne for dinner. She was unusually quiet and wore a pensive expression. I wondered what was preoccupying her. She added herbs, salt and pepper to the minced meat and mixed the ingredients with a wooden spoon.

"What are you thinking of, Mami?" I asked her.

"Oh, nothing much."

"Come on—I know you are dying to tell me."

"Well...the thing is...I wish your aunt would stop arguing with Ceci so much."

I looked at her enquiringly. She continued, "Alcira wants Néstor and Cecilia to devote all their time to studying instead of spending so many hours on their church activities. Your aunt is always criticising Ceci's hair, her clothes, and the way she runs her home. I've told her she's behaving like the typical interfering mother-in-law and that all she's going to achieve is to alienate her daughter and make Néstor hate her. But she won't listen."

I finished layering the lasagne dish with strips of pasta. "I hope you'll listen to me when I'm married," I teased her, "and that you won't be too critical."

She smiled and winked at me. "I'll do my best."

It was a shame that my aunt and her daughter did not get along, especially now that Cecilia had just started her married life.

She was my best friend. She was sweet and kind but also shy and insecure—and had put up with my ordering her around from the moment she could walk. Carolina and I loved and supported each other, but as the older sister, I enjoyed having the final say in most things. Our arguments were inconsequential, and we never hit each other...until that day when, to my great surprise, she stood up to me.

"Carolina, fetch me my cardigan," I said to my sister. It was late afternoon on our roof terrace; the sun was about to set, and the temperature was quickly falling.

"I'm busy. Why don't you get it yourself?" Carolina replied, barely glancing up from her reading. "And you haven't even said please."

The cheeky monkey was answering back! It wasn't like her at all. I went down to my room and got my sweater. Back on the terrace, Carolina was still reading her comic book, enjoying the last of the sun's warmth. I'd had a bad day and was not in the best of moods. The girls from my class were planning a trip to Lake Titicaca, but I wouldn't be able to go, because of our eternal lack of money.

Carolina was sitting on the sunny side of the terrace on the only chair we had up there.

"It's my turn to sit down," I said.

"You can share the chair with me."

"No. It's too small."

"I'll get up in five minutes."

More cheekiness from her. It was unbelievable.

"I want the chair now!" I said as I pushed her off the seat.

Carolina got up from the floor and looked at me calmly. Then she came towards me and, without saying a word, slapped me across the face and returned to the chair. I was speechless. I ran down the two flights of stairs to the kitchen, looking for my mother.

"Mami! Mami! Carolina's just hit me."

My mother was baking wholemeal bread. She stopped kneading the dough and looked at me, her eyes wide open in amazement. "But that's so good. Well done, Carolina. What did you do to her?"

"Aren't you going to punish her?"

"No, I won't."

I flew to the bathroom. I could see a red mark on my left cheek. My younger sister had just stood up to me and let me know that I wasn't to boss her around any longer. That day she went up in my estimation considerably.

As I grew up and learnt about history, politics and economics, I re-alised that countries behave just like people. I realised the importance of standing up to bullies, whether they be other people, multinationals, or empires.

One morning Abuelita had just finished preparing salteñas in the kitchen and was washing and wiping every surface, fussy as always about cleanliness.

Suddenly, my grandmother screamed.

"What's the matter?" my mother asked.

"I've just seen a mouse." Abuelita pointed with her finger. "It...it ran under the table and disappeared into that corner."

Mami moved the table and chair carefully and peered into the corner.

"Look! That's where it came from: that hole behind those milk tins."

The mouse—or mice—had chewed through a bag of flour, which now had to be thrown away. "As if we had money to burn," my mother said.

Near the hole there were mouse droppings, which made Abuelita feel ill.

"That's it. We'll have to get a cat," my mother said.

At last! We had been asking Mami for a pet for an eternity. A dog was out of the question—nowhere for it to run around—but a cat would be ideal. Two days later, Kitty entered our lives. She was a two-year-old fluff with light-brown patches against her white coat, affectionate and house-trained, and she soon made herself at home. She proved to be an excellent hunter and killed several mice the first week. As an added measure, a bricklayer covered all the holes that he could find downstairs.

But the cat was not the only killer. One afternoon when I was preparing a cup of tea for my grandmother, I also murdered a mouse, a baby one.

"What a disgusting thing you are," I said as I hit the poor creature with the broom. "Here, take this!"

The blow wasn't hard enough to kill it, though. My stomach was in knots. I saw it writhing in agony on the floor, a thin crimson ribbon coming out of its nose. Intense pity and revulsion overwhelmed me when I realised what I had done. To put the wretch out of its misery, I struck at it again. As soon as the deed was done, I ran to the bathroom, shuddering, and buried my face in a towel, sobbing my eyes out. This would be the first and last time I killed a living being, other than insects.

Abuelita said that it was all right to caress the cat, but we had to wash our hands immediately afterwards. In the afternoons, while we did our homework, Kitty would sit on our laps, purring happily. We'd stroke her fur, and she'd purr even louder. For the next few months, life went on as normal, until my mother discovered Carolina's little secret. My sister had got into the habit of sleeping with the cat. Soon her scalp started itching and became red and sore. My mother took Carolina to a dermatologist, who said that my sister had caught a skin infection from the cat and prescribed a treatment of smelly ointments and bitter pills. Worse, poor Carolina had to have her head shaved. Children at school teased her. "Hi, baldie. Is it cold up there?" The doctor prescribed some drops for Kitty, too, but the medicine didn't agree with the animal, and poor Kitty died.

My sisters, my cousin Gerardo and I cried bitterly, and although we felt sorry for bald Carolina, we blamed her for the loss of our beloved pet.

We never had another cat.

At long last, I had permission to attend my first disco with boys. All my classmates had been going to *bailongos* for what seemed like years, but I had to wait until I was thirteen. Jeannette was celebrating her birthday with a disco at her home and had invited the whole class. The invitation was for eight in the evening, but I knew nobody would be there before nine. My mother, however, believed in punctuality.

It was a cold night, and my mother insisted that I wear my dark-blue winter coat, thick tights, and the brown woolly hat that I hated. It made me look stupid, and it ruined my hair, leaving it flat and limp. My stomach was in knots about meeting the boys, and the last thing I needed was to have to worry about my appearance. My party dress was nice enough, but it was the same old blue one with short sleeves and a white lacy collar I had worn to many other parties.

"Please, Mami. I don't need to wear it. I'm not cold."

"Wear the hat."

"Please, Mami."

"Wear it, or else we're not going."

"OK, Mami," I said. "But you know it's too early to go."

"It's rude to arrive late."

We set off on foot towards Jeannette's home. I felt that everyone was looking at me, laughing at the stupid monstrosity on top of my head, so I removed the hat and hoped that my mother wouldn't notice.

But of course she did. "Put the hat back on, or I'll start shouting in the middle of the street!"

We arrived at the house and found that Jeannette had not even changed into her party frock. Her parents were still preparing the food and rearranging the furniture in the lounge.

"Come in, come in," Jeannette's mother said.

"I'm sorry to be so early."

"Don't worry. You know what it's like. We invite people for eight so that they get here at nine."

Soon Jeannette came down the stairs wearing a white taffeta dress with a wide orange belt and orange trimming on the collar and sleeves, which went well with her reddish-blond hair and green eyes.

My classmates arrived after nine o'clock, and soon the record player was busy with the latest Latin American pop songs by Palito Ortega, Adamo, Sandro, Los Iracundos…I was also looking forward to listening to Los Beatles, from England, and contorting my body to the rock 'n' roll rhythms of "El Twist." I was talking to my friends when Jeannette tapped me on the shoulder. "Your mum is here." It was not even nine-thirty, and now I had to leave before the fun had begun.

As I was putting on my coat, the boys started arriving. The hated hat was placed firmly on my head, and my face went bright pink with anger and embarrassment.

"You don't want to catch a cold," my mother said, and I prayed nobody had heard her.

Why, oh why, did she have to be so loud and conspicuous and punctual?

Jeannette introduced Gloria and me to the boys of the Saint George Club. At last I was going to be part of the "in" crowd; at last I would have a normal teenage life, maybe even a boyfriend. I was shy in the company of boys, but I was determined to overcome my awkwardness.

Another group of boys, Los Jets—named after the gang in *West Side Story*—was also popular, and some of my classmates joined their ranks. There was rivalry between both groups, and if you were a Saint George girl, you were expected never to go to parties with Los Jets, and vice versa. However, rules were there to be broken, and I knew several girls who had friends in both clubs.

During one of the Saint George parties, one of the boys danced with me for most of the evening. Before I went home, he asked me to be his girlfriend, and I said yes. Emilio had a long, slightly hooked nose, and his nickname was Condorito (Little Condor), like the main character in the popular Chilean comic book. I was nicknamed Yayita, like Condorito's girlfriend. His eyes were small, and he was a little shorter than me, but I liked his light-brown hair and the blue sweaters he wore. Now that I had a boyfriend, I would be able to join my classmates in discussions about the mysterious kingdom of romance. Condorito, however, seemed as shy and insecure as me, or maybe more so. That night when he first asked me out, he didn't dare hold my hand, and when he talked to me, he did not look me in the eyes but instead stared straight past me. I forgave him all that, as I was thrilled to have a boyfriend at last.

At another gathering of the Saint George Club, I heard the two Tejada brothers, Juan Carlos and Roberto, talking about their cousin Raquel, an actress in Hollywood. Surely they didn't mean the famous Raquel Welch? Yes, they said. Raquel was their cousin. Her Bolivian father lived in the

United States and had married an American woman. Raquel's real surname was Tejada, but Hollywood had told her to keep her Latin identity secret.

Every Sunday my friends and I attended Mass at Maria Auxiliadora, a modern church in El Prado, full of light, with a wide pale stone staircase leading up to the main doors. After Mass we usually met up with the boys and had one or two spicy salteña pasties in one of the cafeterias on the pavement opposite the church—the most exclusive ones being those of Hotel Sucre and Hotel Copacabana, where the gringo tourists also congregated. La Paz was proud of El Prado, a long avenue in the heart of the city with flowerbeds and a tiled, patterned floor along the length of the boulevard. At one end of the avenue stood the statue of Simón Bolívar, proud on his magnificent horse, his sword pointing towards the freedom of half a continent. A statue of Christopher Columbus was farther down the road, and at the other end of El Prado, there was one of Antonio José de Sucre, another hero of the war of independence, also on horseback. Young people assembled around the marble fountain opposite the church; señoras, señores and señoritas followed the Spanish custom of Sunday paseo, circulating in a clockwise direction while others did it anticlockwise. Not many mixed-race cholos attended the Sunday stroll; it was mainly the middle-class white families who took part in this tradition.

On Sundays my mother would give me some coins to give to the beggars. "At least today they'll be able to buy some bread," she used to say. Sometimes I would see a peasant woman with babies, or a former miner with an amputated leg, sitting on the steps outside the church. As they came out after praying and singing to God, elegant ladies who had never done a day's work in their lives would shoo the beggars away. "Don't pester us. Why don't you get a job?" they would say. But who would employ a dusty peasant woman with babies? And what could the amputees do? Usually, these ragged people would just squat in narrow alleys. They were as brown as the surrounding mountains, as grey as the pavements.

During one of the Sunday strolls, the Saint George boys teased me, "Yayita, Yayita, when are you flying with Condorito?" I giggled nervously but didn't answer. So far Condorito hadn't even held my hand, and I wished that he'd be brave enough to put his arm around my shoulders.

My mother did not take the news of my having a boyfriend seriously enough. It was all part of growing up, she said, not at all like falling in love when you are in your twenties. I was a little insulted by her quick dismissal of my new status, but what else could I expect from my middle-aged mother?

The following week Condorito, wearing yet another of his blue sweaters, came to visit me at home. I was worried that he would need to use the bathroom and would then discover our water situation, causing me to die of shame. I quickly put this thought out of my mind and concentrated on preparing myself for my first kiss. We sat in the lounge, not knowing what to say to each other, I with my hands on my lap, feet together, like a proper señorita, and he beside me on the sofa, back straight like a soldier, looking at the pictures on the wall. My mother brought us lemonade and biscuits, but Condorito did not eat anything. I put on a Palito Ortega record, and then we talked about the San Juan bonfire party the following week. Ten minutes after his arrival, Condorito said that he had to leave. He hadn't even held my hand. What had I done wrong?

Condorito didn't telephone or come to see me the whole week. I wasn't in love, but I felt neglected all the same. And then bonfire night arrived. It had been exactly one year since the San Juan massacre, when government troops killed twenty-seven miners—suspecting them of being Che Guevara supporters—but we teenagers were not thinking about that outrage. Gloria's father brought Jeannette, Gloria and me to the party. It was bitterly cold, the middle of winter, but we soon warmed up with the excitement of the bonfire, which was held in the middle of a field. Dozens and dozens of teenagers were now arriving. A few parents hovered at the side of the field, making sure the fireworks were handled safely. The bonfire was huge, all yellow and red tongues crackling, leaping up into the air, spitting angry cinders like a dragon. Gloria and Jeannette were busy dancing. I chatted with a couple of girls from my school and tried to disguise my nervousness.

Condorito arrived, waved hello from a distance, and then went to talk to his friends. Well, was he going to ask me to dance? No, he stayed away the whole evening. That was it. We were finished.

I stood in line with the girls who didn't have dancing partners, my anxiety probably giving off a bad odour. I had joined the dreaded wallflower group and felt like a piece of merchandise.

My cousin Silvia had just returned from the United States after a year living with an American family and attending high school there. She had come back speaking fluent English, her mind full of travel and study ideas. One of the many interesting things she brought from America was a duvet, or eiderdown. How wonderful not to have to spend several minutes making the bed with sheets, blankets and bedcovers, as we did, but instead just throw the duvet on top, and the bed was made!

My mother was interested in what Silvia had to say about her experiences in the United States and said she wanted me to have the same opportunity as my cousin. But when my mother found out that she would have to contribute a percentage towards the cost of the scholarship, her face dropped. Going to America? Fabulous! But out of reach for the likes of us. Better not to dream impossible dreams.

Silvia would not remain in Bolivia for too long and would soon depart to study at the University of Geneva.

Cochabamba

December 1968

One Saturday morning a few days before my fourteenth birthday, Carolina, Teresa and I said goodbye to our mother at the bus terminus. That summer, she would again be working all through the holidays, while my sisters and I spent Christmas and New Year with relatives in Cochabamba. Our mother was a little tearful, but we girls couldn't wait for our adventure to start.

As our bus climbed up the side of the mountains, herds of llamas, alpacas and sheep appeared. Although it was the end of spring, a light blanket of snow had recently fallen in the high Andes, and the air was cold and crisp. Soon we left the mountains and started the descent into the valleys. The soil now had a reddish tint, a sign of its fertility. Before long we saw fields of sweet corn, their yellow heads appearing shyly at the ends of the stalks, their long green leaves gently swaying in the breeze.

Cochabamba, the "garden city" of Bolivia—streets lined with magnolia and jacaranda trees and filled with the sweet smell of jasmine and wide avenues and plazas with palm trees and bougainvillea. Aunt Amelia, a cousin of my father's, and her two daughters were waiting for us at the bus station. "Look at you, so pretty and healthy!" our aunt said as she hugged us and pinched our cheeks. We had met sixteen-year-old Victoria and her sister, Laurita, six, the year before when they had visited La Paz. We had got along well, but now I was a little nervous about spending four long weeks with them. I needn't have worried. Both girls kissed us on the cheeks.

"We're going to have such fun!"

"We were counting the days." They beamed.

My aunt hailed a taxi. At the house we met Uncle Roberto, my aunt's husband. He was short and dark-skinned, with a round, plump face and a serious expression, and he wore a brown suit almost permanently. Although he smiled and welcomed us when we arrived, he hardly uttered a word during our stay. He would spend his time working, reading, and keeping to himself. His main contribution to our holiday was taking a few photographs. My aunt said that a house full of women was enough to put any man off.

That afternoon, while we were having tea and cakes with the whole family, the conversation turned to the activities that my cousins had planned for the holiday. My aunt said that Victoria was in love with a nice young man who adored her.

"Tonight you'll be going out with Victoria and Eduardo," my aunt said to me. I shot my cousin a nervous look. I didn't fancy being in the way of two lovers.

"Don't worry. We've invited a friend of Eduardo's to come along as well," my cousin said. "He's a nice boy. I'm sure you'll like him."

That evening, Eduardo and his friend Chali came to collect us in Eduardo's red minivan. In those days very few young people had a car, so Victoria considered herself lucky to have a boyfriend who did. Chali, frizzy-haired with lovely dark eyes and thick eyebrows, owed his nickname to a silky red-and-blue scarf, a *chalina*, that was always around his neck.

We drove to a nightclub in the country, in Quillacollo, just outside Cochabamba. Tall palm trees and well-tended lawns surrounded the place—a two-storey white house with balconies.

"Don't tell my mother we've been here," Victoria said, flicking her long auburn hair away from her face. "She'd kill me." The nightclub was not supposed to admit people under eighteen, and the only one who qualified was Eduardo. Chali was seventeen, three years older than me. Nobody bothered to ask us for ID, and the darkness of the place helped disguise our ages. We sat at a table at the end of the room and ordered soft drinks. Dim red and blue lightbulbs burned in each corner of the room, creating a romantic atmosphere. My heart beat fast when Chali asked me to dance. It was a slow dance, and he pulled me towards him. *This is lovely*, I thought, feeling his cheek on mine, his hand holding mine, our feet gliding to the rhythm of an Argentinean love song. Yes, it felt nice to be in his arms, and he behaved like a perfect gentleman.

"I've had fun tonight, Mariana," he said later that evening, holding my hand. "I'd like to take you out again."

I was flattered. This handsome, curly-haired, dark-eyed boy who smelled of cologne wanted to see me again. "But we'll have to come with Victoria and Eduardo, too, won't we?"

"Of course, always with them," he laughed. "Otherwise your aunt won't allow it."

The days were warm and sunny. I loved walking along the sleepy avenues, my shoes crunching the freshly fallen blooms from the jacaranda and magnolia trees that had a mild and sweet perfume. Here I could wear sandals and light clothes instead of heavy sweaters and thick tights like in La Paz. And, blessing of blessings, I could have a shower any time I wanted.

All that summer, Victoria, Eduardo, Chali and I went out practically every day. My cousin and her boyfriend kissed and petted heavily in the dark, behind any door and in every available corner, any time my back was turned. If my aunt Amelia thought that my presence would deter Victoria and Eduardo from exploring each other's bodies, she was very much mistaken. Victoria was pretty, with long and silky light-brown hair and tanned skin. Short miniskirts and tight blouses were her favourite clothes—despite my aunt reprimanding her for it—and dreaming of Eduardo was her favourite pastime. She knew so much more about the world—and about boys—than I did. One day I'd be sweet sixteen, too; one day I, too, would be confident, sophisticated and sexy. I had a lot to learn from her.

Victoria and I spent hours listening to romantic Latin American records and to songs in Spanish by the French singer Charles Aznavour and each dreamt of our future *príncipe azul*, with whom we would live happily ever after. One morning the radio was playing songs from the famous Uruguayan group Los Iracundos—the Furious Ones—when Victoria said,

"I'm so glad you're here, Mariana. I wish you could stay forever." I beamed with delight. The two-year difference in age had suddenly disappeared.

Victoria and I slept head to foot in the same bed, being careful not to get a kick in the chin. I remember her caressing the sheets with her feet in a slow, sensuous way. Sometimes after we had said our good nights, she would sigh deeply and whimper a little. My aunt and uncle knew that Eduardo was excellent husband material and were hoping that soon he would ask for their daughter's hand. Aunt Amelia had told my cousin that if she ever found out that Victoria was doing anything inappropriate, she would have to stop seeing Eduardo immediately. A girl's virginity was her most precious jewel and a prerequisite for a successful marriage.

My aunt nagged Carolina and me to write to our mother. Telephone calls to another city were expensive, so unless it was an emergency, they were out of the question. We did, of course, get several letters from my mother, and I think I replied once or twice. Life in Cochabamba was so exciting, so busy, and La Paz was just a distant memory.

Most afternoons Victoria and I—and sometimes Carolina—were out at one of the ice cream parlours or cafés near the main plaza, where we'd meet up with our boyfriends. Chali seemed to like me a lot, and I him, but all we dared to do was hold hands.

One Saturday evening Victoria and I were drinking iced coffees at one of the benches outside the cafeteria, a few purple blooms from the jacaranda tree around our feet.

"The boys are late," Victoria said.

"Only by ten minutes," I replied.

I could tell that she was annoyed. What was keeping those boys? "Well, if he thinks I'm at his disposal—" Before she had finished her sentence, Eduardo and Chali arrived, each with a bunch of flowers.

"So sorry we're late," Eduardo said. "We wanted to get you girls some fresh flowers."

Victoria's annoyance evaporated instantly. Because we were in a public place, all she did was smile at her boyfriend, but I knew that what she really wanted to do was hug him tight and kiss him.

Chali presented me with a bunch of pink roses. He sat beside me and, for the first time since we had started going out, put his arm around my shoulders and gently kissed me on the cheek.

"Come inside, girls. It's time for dinner," Aunt Amelia called out to my sister Teresa, our cousin Laurita, and the two other girls with whom they were playing. They were a gang of four skinny six-year-olds, with long matchstick legs, short skirts, and straight black hair. The way they dressed and behaved, you would've thought they belonged to an exclusive club. They inhabited a world totally different from mine and Carolina's. Their days were filled with playing with dolls, plastic tea-sets, skipping ropes, and a pet dog belonging to one of the girls, a brown dachshund. Mealtimes were the only times we interacted with the little girls. If not eating at our place, they would walk to one or another of their houses and have a meal there.

Carolina was the one who didn't fit in with either of the two groups. She was too young, at twelve, to go to discos and too old to play with Teresa and her friends. Often she would join Victoria and me on outings during the day, but apart from that she had to find her own entertainment.

"Great news!" I said to Aunt Amelia as I hung up the phone. "Gloria, my best friend from school, has just arrived. She wants me to visit her at her uncle's house in Quillacollo. Can I go, Auntie, please, please?"

"Yes, of course you can. Your uncle Roberto will take you there."

The following Saturday I was at Gloria's place in the country. It was a wonderful old house, built in the 1800s, with furniture and paintings from that century. Long wooden beams crossed the ceiling; the inside walls were whitewashed, and the floors were covered with terracotta tiles. The outside was painted a pale pink.

"Let's go to the orchard," my friend said. "Pick any fruit you want. And take some home to your auntie."

Sweet-smelling peaches and apricots, juicy tangerines, big black grapes and dark-crimson figs tempted my senses. I was intoxicated with the smells and flavours of this mini-paradise.

"Tell me all about your Chali," Gloria said. "Has he kissed you yet?"

"Not yet, but I hope he does. Soon."

"I can't wait until I have a boyfriend," she said with a mischievous smile on her face. "I wonder what French kisses feel like."

We both giggled like idiots. Gloria made me promise to keep her informed of any developments in my love life.

A couple of women servants were sitting in the shade in a corner of the garden, one knitting and the other crocheting, their legs stretched out into the sunny part of the orchard, their long braided black hair reaching just below their shoulders.

"Buenas tardes, señoritas," they said.

I looked at the delicate little clothes they were making. "Who are these pretty things for?"

"I'm making bootees and cardigans for the maid's baby," one of the women said.

"And I'm knitting this blanket for my sister's child," said the other.

Love, babies, life. I definitely didn't want any babies, but I wanted to find out a little about love.

The following week Chali presented me with a pink rose and asked me to be his date at the coming New Year's Eve party.

I was excited about the biggest event of the year, but I had a problem: I had neither an evening party dress nor shoes, and no money to buy them.

"Not to worry," Auntie Amelia said. "You can borrow Victoria's blue dress and try on my black patent-leather shoes. You're size thirty-eight, aren't you?"

It seemed that half of the youth of Cochabamba were at this party. My feet hurt from so much dancing, and I had butterflies in my stomach, partly from too many fizzy drinks—but mainly in anticipation of the long-awaited first kiss.

Chali was polite and attentive. "When the clock strikes midnight, we'll have some champagne."

"I'll try, Chali." I wanted to please him even though I hated alcohol.

Timidly, he caressed my bare shoulders. This was a new experience for me; no boy had ever touched any part of my body apart from my hands. A delicious shiver went down my spine.

"Happy New Year!" A roar went up in the dance hall. Everyone cheered and started bursting balloons, throwing confetti, and toasting with bubbly wine. I could hardly contain my excitement; tonight I would finally know the taste of a kiss.

Chali grabbed a couple of glasses of champagne and pulled me out onto the balcony. The night was cool and full of stars. He took me in his arms and held my face in his hands. "You're so lovely, so pretty. Kiss me."

All of a sudden, my grandmother was talking to me: "Beware of sin. Men will lead you into temptation. Men will ruin your life. Keep yourself pure."

"No, no, Chali. I can't."

"Why not?"

"I just can't."

"Of course you can. You'll like it—you'll see," he said as he pressed himself against me and tried to part my lips with his tongue.

What was he doing? No, I could not let that happen. But I wanted him to kiss me...and yet...maybe not.

He held me fast. I panicked. I pushed him away, and as he tried to take me back in his arms, my hand flew to his face.

"Aii!" he gasped.

I ran inside and locked myself in the toilet. What had I done? Why did I scratch Chali's face? Didn't I want him to kiss me? Yes, I did. So what was the matter with me? Stupid, stupid! I came out of the toilet and looked for Chali to apologise, but before I could say anything, he put on his jacket.

"I'm so sorry, Chali," I mumbled, looking at the floor, my face burning.

"Victoria and Eduardo will take you home. Good night." He went out the door without speaking to anybody.

All of a sudden, on this warm night, I felt very cold, very tired, and a little sick to my stomach. I wanted to kick myself. How could I make it up to Chali? How could I win him back? But Chali would not give me that opportunity. He would not come to see me anymore. My first kiss was a total disaster, and my first proper boyfriend probably hated me.

The following day, before dinner, Aunt Amelia's landlady invited us to toast the New Year. We all went up to her flat on the first floor, where she offered us sweet cakes dusted with sugar and a little *copita* of cognac, which burned my throat.

"Happy New Year to us all," Uncle Roberto said, a rare smile on his usually dour face. "May our families get along well this coming year!"

The following day my sisters and I returned to La Paz in time to prepare ourselves for the new school year.

Two years later I'd return to Cochabamba for Victoria and Eduardo's wedding. Chali was there as well, as the best man. When we saw each other, we said a polite hello and quickly turned to talk to other people.

1969: The Year I Was Fourteen

February

No one was surprised when Aunt Alcira won a scholarship from the French government to further her teaching qualifications in Paris. She was extremely pleased, of course, but also worried about the many things she needed to do before travelling. All these months she had been trying hard to have a better relationship with her daughter and son-in-law, and now here was a golden opportunity to bring them all closer together. She asked Néstor and Cecilia to move into her house to look after Gerardo and to take care of the school while she was away. They were also eager to improve their relationship with Alcira and promptly agreed to her request. Cecilia would look after administrative matters, and Néstor would be in charge of religious education. Both of them would do this while continuing with their medical studies.

Cousin Rosita was now in year five of secondary education at my aunt's school. She and her classmates would soon learn to think critically about the harsh realities of life in Bolivia, thanks to the work of an extraordinary teacher.

Néstor was only a few years older than his pupils. The deputy head had introduced him to the class as Señor Paz, but he asked the students to simply call him Néstor. That first morning, he was not wearing a suit like all the other male teachers but a pair of jeans and a polo shirt. "Hola, chicos," he said as he opened his tatty briefcase, took out a pen and a notebook, sat on top of the desk, and faced the class.

Religious education was the most boring of subjects, and Rosita was not looking forward to lectures about the Bible or the lives of the saints.

Néstor's teaching, however, would be about something completely different. He started the lesson by asking for a definition of the word *love*.

The boys exchanged glances and sniggered. It would certainly be amusing to poke fun at this new young teacher.

Paco, the class clown, raised his hand. "Love…it's when someone is nuts about someone else." He grinned, revealing spiky metal braces on his upper teeth.

"*Lurve*…is when you blow kisses at a girl," another boy added.

The whole class was giggling; Paco and two other boys laughed out loud, others banged their desks, and others stamped their feet.

Why, oh why, were boys so immature? Rosita wanted to raise her hand and give her definition but remained quiet.

"Come on, you lot!" the teacher said firmly. "Do you want to spend the rest of the lesson repeating prayers as penitence?"

The teenagers calmed down, and Néstor proceeded. "You, young man, you who were laughing so loud, introduce yourself and give us your definition."

"Yes, sir. My name is Paco." He stood up. "Love…well, love is when you want to help someone just because you're friends." He scratched his head and added, "Or when you fancy someone and you feel warm inside…"

Néstor went to the blackboard, chalk in hand. "Let's look a bit deeper into this."

"Love is for your family and people you like," said Chela, Rosita's best friend.

Néstor asked, "Can love go beyond those close to us? Can we love and respect our Indians? Can we love the beggars?"

A look of disgust appeared on the teenagers' faces. Loving the Indians? Oh no! They were dirty and ignorant and smelly.

"Didn't Jesus die for them as well?" Néstor said and looked at each and every student in the class. They lowered their eyes.

"I'll be giving a combined RE and civics assignment every week," Néstor said as he wiped the blackboard. "This week I want you to write a short essay about what being a good citizen and neighbour means to you—about three hundred words."

Néstor encouraged his pupils to put themselves in other people's shoes, consider the deep inequalities and injustices that afflicted Bolivian society, and think of possible solutions to these problems.

A national census was taking place that year, so Néstor asked his students to work as volunteers gathering information for the census over the weekend. Rosita, Chela, Paco and three others volunteered to go to Garita de Lima, one of the poorest areas of La Paz. These middle-class teenagers had only a vague idea of the living conditions in the slums, having passed briefly along their outskirts when travelling by bus or car, but they had never been inside. Néstor wanted his students to observe the place with an open mind and talk to the people who lived there.

What they saw and heard that Saturday would shake them out of their ignorance about the reality of Bolivia. This was a face of La Paz they had never seen and a face nearly all middle-class people chose to ignore. Out of sight really was out of mind. During that memorable visit, the students became aware of the chasm that existed between their comfortable lives and those of the slum dwellers.

As in other parts of the world, the social and political reality of the country was of little relevance to most middle-class families. People wanted to live their lives without too much disruption. Parents worked hard to support their children and did their best not to become involved in politics. While young Latin Americans danced to the rhythms of Sandro and Los Iracundos, the militaries in our countries were busy oppressing, torturing and disappearing those who complained. The version of the events that would soon convulse my country would be shaped and reshaped until it fitted the mould that the regime in power preferred.

On Saturday Rosita got up early. Her father and all the other parents had agreed to their children visiting the slum, provided they were accompanied by adult supervisors. "I think it'll be good for you to see the other side of La Paz," her father had said. "Just promise me you'll be careful." She prepared a couple of cheese-and-ham sandwiches and a flask of milky tea. Armed with census forms, notebooks, pens and a little money, she walked towards El Prado, where she met up with her classmates. Split into groups of six students and one adult supervisor per group, the teenagers boarded blue-painted bus number two and bought tickets to the end of the line, virgin territory to them all.

The rickety bus shuddered up the steep slopes of La Paz. More and more people got on board, and soon Rosita felt as if she were about to suffocate. The air was heavy with the smell of so many bodies, mixed with the sweet aroma of the onions and oranges being carried by the house-wives in their canvas bags.

When an old peasant woman and two Indian mothers with babies strapped to their backs got on the bus, Rosita and her classmates gave up their seats. "Aii, niñita, gracias!" the old woman said, probably surprised that a señorita was showing her consideration.

"Plaza San Francisco! Villa Victoria!" The school-age boy conductor shouted at every stop, and also between stops, in a shrill and monoto-nous voice. These bus boys worked ten hours a day, collecting fares and announcing destinations along the route. Rosita hoped the boy at least went to night school, but who would have energy to study after a long day's hard work?

As the bus climbed up the hill and went deeper into the poorer areas, the houses became uglier and more dilapidated. At the final stop, every-body got off the bus. Rosita and her friends asked for directions to Garita de Lima and continued on foot.

The unpaved narrow street went up the side of the hill, winding among stones and debris. Foul-smelling brownish water ran along the pavement. After about five hundred metres, the road turned left and became an even narrower and dirtier passage, closed off at the end. Here were poorer houses still, grey-and-brown mud huts with sheets of corrugated alumin-ium or even pieces of cardboard as roofs. In the cul-de-sac four toddlers were playing in the dirt, their hands and faces caked with dry soil, their noses running, their clothes thin and ragged; the babies' bottoms were exposed to the air, no nappy or cloth to protect them. Rosita wondered where the children's mother was.

A dog defecated in a corner near one of the huts. A look of revulsion appeared on Paco's face. "This place is only fit for animals!"

Rosita shot him a reproachful look. "Be quiet. We don't want to offend them."

A front door opened, and an Indian woman appeared. She looked nervous, even scared, and quickly gathered the children.

"Buenos días, señora," Rosita said just before the woman disappeared back into her house.

The woman stopped and looked at the teenagers, surprised. Middle-class people did not usually address the Indians as señor or señora when talking to them.

The woman's reply was barely audible. "Buenos días, niñita."

Paco said, "We'd like to ask you a few questions, señora."

"Why?" the woman asked, worried.

"We're students. We want to write a report about the conditions in this place so that people are aware of your hardship."

"Aii, young man, the authorities know all about our lives," the woman said. "They promise to give us running water and sewage drains, but..."

"We'll try to help you!" Rosita said and smiled. "Are these your kids?"

"These two are mine," the woman replied. "I'm looking after these other two for my neighbour while she's working at the market." She told them her name was Yolanda and that she had other children, six in total. Two others had died in infancy.

Yolanda told her story tentatively. Her husband was a bricklayer, her two middle children worked shining shoes and cleaning the streets, and she took turns with her neighbour selling coffee at the market. The two older children had families of their own. Her husband was often unemployed. At times he would waste what little money he had getting drunk; occasionally he would beat her. As they listened to her story, the teenagers' faces dropped.

"My husband needs to forget his misery," Yolanda sighed.

"But how about you?" Rosita asked. "How do you forget your situation?"

"I go to church for some comfort."

"And what does the priest say?" Paco asked.

"The padre tells us to keep on praying and to stop sinning." Yolanda had a resigned look on her face. "He says that God knows why things are as they are—that we'll get our reward in heaven."

Paco rolled his eyes.

Rosita frowned. She did not think it was God's will that there should be poverty and injustice in the world.

It was now time to leave. The students promised Yolanda that they would contact the local authorities. Paco promised they would also write a letter to the newspapers. Maybe something would be done this time? At the front door, they tried to give Yolanda some money, but she refused politely. "There's someone at the top of the hill in a desperate situation. Please go and help her," she pleaded.

At the top of the hill stood the public oven. It was made of mud bricks, built in the traditional semi-spherical shape, and blackened by years of use. Here the residents of the slum baked their bread for a few pesos. The smell of burnt timber hung in the air; ashes were scattered around the oven, its open mouth deep and dark, its breath sour.

An icy wind was blowing from the mountains, and grey clouds were gathering in the sky. Suddenly, Rosita heard a baby cry but couldn't see anyone. The place was deserted; apart from the oven there was nothing up there. Again the baby cried. Where could those noises be coming from? The teenagers looked at one another. And now someone was coughing.

"This place is haunted! Let's get out of here!" Chela said.

"No. Wait! I think the noise is coming from the oven," said Paco.

They soon realised that the noises were indeed coming from inside the oven. "Be careful, now," Rosita warned. Cautiously, they approached. It was very dark inside, but the noises were definitely coming from there.

Rosita and her friends strained their eyes and watched attentively. A human shape, a woman, was moaning softly inside the oven, cold and hungry, maybe in pain.

Chela grabbed Rosita's hand. "I'm scared."

Paco approached the oven. "Can we help?"

The moans stopped immediately. Then the baby cried again. And another child whimpered.

"We want to help you," Rosita offered.

"No! Don't come any closer, or else I'll scream my head off!" a weak voice threatened. "Nobody is going to evict us!"

The awful truth hit the teenagers like a bolt of lightning.

Every night, after the oven had been used and cooled down, this woman, her toddler and her baby slept inside it.

Rosita looked at her companions. They all had serious expressions, and Chela seemed on the verge of tears.

"Señora, we're leaving you some money," Paco said. "Here, under a stone."

"And a sandwich," Chela added.

The three teenagers walked down the hill in silence. They caught the same blue bus, number two. It left them at El Prado, from where they caught other buses to their respective homes. Later that afternoon, while the impressions of the day were still vivid in their minds, they each wrote their report.

Later that term Néstor gave the year-five students other interesting homework. Rosita and her group went to the Ministry of Agriculture and Peasant Affairs, where they read articles and statistics about infant mortality, life expectancy, and the living conditions of the peasantry. "You'd think the agrarian reform had never happened," Paco said. "The llamas have better lives than our Indians."

The week before the end of term, they visited the Ministry of Mines and Petroleum to learn about the costs of producing and exporting our minerals, the pay and working conditions of the miners, the rock-bottom prices and low taxes the powerful multinationals paid for our raw materials, and the meagre net benefit to the Bolivian state. Rosita wondered how they could ever hope to better the country's situation under these conditions.

Bolivia was indeed incredibly rich and devastatingly poor at the same time. We were poor because we were underdeveloped, and we were underdeveloped because we were poor. And powerful forces had been and were still taking advantage of it all.

When Rosita finished studying all those documents, she felt sick to her stomach. A dark rage rose inside her.

Néstor's teaching had a profound impact on his students. On some, such as Rosita, the impact was life-transforming.

Two other events in 1969 made a deep impression on Rosita and on me. The first was the Bolivian film *Yawar Mallku* (*Blood of the Condor*), released in July of that year, and which UNESCO named as "one of the top hundred historically significant films."

Directed by Jorge Sanjinés, the film depicted the harsh lives and abject poverty of a group of Quechua Indians and the contempt and discrimination they endured daily. It was also a critique of the American aid programme, which, it was rumoured, had sterilised Indian women without their knowledge, among other things.

The nuns at my school wanted all the girls to see it, so one afternoon after lessons my whole class went to Cine 16 de Julio in El Prado. I came out of the cinema with red eyes and blowing my nose. "Excellent film!" I said to my classmates.

"I don't like sad films," said one of my friends.

"What are you wearing to tonight's party?" said another.

I was amazed. Although the film had touched some of my fellow students, it had meant little to many of them. The cruel reality of most Bolivians' lives was accepted as easily as the sun rising in the morning. The

Indians—inferior beings—had always been poor and downtrodden, and what could be done about it?

The other event was even more significant. In October, the American-owned Gulf Oil Company was nationalised. *El Día de la Dignidad Nacional*, or Day of National Dignity, was a happy day for many Bolivians. President Alfredo Ovando said that it was time to stop the bleeding of our natural resources. At home Mami opened a bottle of wine to celebrate, and even we girls had a sip. The complexities of the matter were beyond my understanding, but I knew it was unjust that a foreign company kept the biggest part of the cake, to the detriment of Bolivia.

During our fourth year of secondary school, my classmates started celebrating their fifteenth birthdays. My celebration would have to wait, since I was a year younger than the rest of the class, but I knew I couldn't expect my mother to incur such extravagant expenditure. This birthday (*quinceañera*) is an important milestone in a Latin American girl's life. According to tradition, the whole family and close friends attend Mass in the morning, and the priest blesses the girl and wishes her a healthy and happy future. In the evening there is a party to mark the passage to womanhood. The young woman wears a long evening dress made specially for the occasion. There are flowers, cake, champagne and music. Young men from other families are invited to the party, and this way the girl is introduced to a wider circle of society.

That same year three new girls joined our school. They were European-looking Argentinean girls, pale-skinned and fair-haired, and spoke Spanish with the thick sing-song typical of their country, which we found both charming and amusing. They also said "Che"[5] a lot. Rita joined our class, and her sister Marlene was in the year above. Margaretta, the third girl, also joined our year. The girls' fathers had been sent by their government

---

5 *Che* is an informal, non-Spanish word used mainly by Argentineans and Uruguayans. It means "mate" or "pal."

as military attachés to their embassy. These blue-eyed girls had German-sounding surnames. Their parents had chosen my school because it was run by nuns and most of the pupils came from white middle-class families. Although I didn't think anything of it at the time, I later wondered whether the fathers of these girls, who became my friends, might have been involved in some of the unpalatable activities of the Argentinean government of that time. Who were these men? And what were they doing in Bolivia?

Years later, the crimes of the Argentinean junta would come to the attention of the world. Bolivia, too, would be in the international news in 1983, when the Butcher of Lyon—the Nazi war criminal Klaus Barbie, who had been living in my country as an esteemed adviser to our military dictators—was extradited to France.[6]

The sisters Rita and Marlene soon found their place among us, participating in all the school activities. I was invited to their house for tea one afternoon. What a luxurious residence, what an enormous hi-fi music centre, what modern kitchen equipment—all shiny chrome and white tiles—and what elegant servants in starched navy uniforms they had. The girls could leave their dirty socks lying on the bedroom floor—something I could never do at home—and the maids would pick them up. Their mother was all smiles, very welcoming and affectionate. Soon Rita would be celebrating her birthday, and I was invited to her party.

The other new girl, Margaretta, was a different matter. An only child, she was reserved and quiet and had trouble making friends. Feeling sorry for her, I made attempts to break the ice. She was the palest of the new girls, with hair, eyelashes and eyebrows that were so blond they were nearly white. Her hair was tied tightly into a severe ponytail, which did not help her austere expression. Her fingernails were cut so short that I was afraid the tips of her fingers would bleed. "I must keep my hands and nails clean at all times," she'd say. "Bacteria are everywhere."

---

6 Barbie managed to evade prosecution for his crimes for more than four decades thanks to the help the CIA gave him in exchange for his anti-Marxist expertise. It is thought that he also helped the CIA capture Che Guevara.

While Rita and Marlene mixed with all of us, Margaretta spoke only to the white students in our class and avoided any contact with the darker ones.

"Are you going to the Alacitas fair this Sunday?" I asked her one afternoon.

"Oh no! My parents wouldn't allow it."

"Why not?"

"Not hygienic. Too many Indians."

How interesting it was that Margaretta despised our native people and avoided our darker-coloured classmates, and those same dark-skinned classmates of mine loathed their less-fortunate native compatriots.

At long last, television arrived in Bolivia in August 1969. The sets were expensive, but somehow my mother managed to buy one at a discount, in monthly payments.

The small black-and-white set came to our house early one morning and was installed in a corner of our sitting-room. That afternoon my sisters and I came back from school in a hurry and did our homework immediately in anticipation of the big event. Abuelita had no difficulty in making us eat our vegetables. Then we helped with the chores without being asked. At six o'clock the programmes started, and we gathered around the shiny black magic box. There was only one channel: Canal Uno, Televisión Boliviana. First they played the national anthem, and then the presenters, a handsome young man and a pretty woman, welcomed us to the first programmes: the flora and fauna in the Bolivian Altiplano, followed by the news and then Woody Woodpecker cartoons. The news showed us what was happening in Bolivia as well as in faraway countries. I had seen the New York skyscrapers in the movies, and now they were here in our lounge.

Soon there was a big commotion outside. About a dozen Indian children on the street, their eyes glued to the windows of our sitting-room, were pushing and shoving one another, trying to watch.

"Let me see! Let me see!"

"I was here first!"

"Move over, or I'll thump you!"

"Ow!"

My mother felt sorry for these ragamuffins and allowed them inside the house. "You can come in, children, but you must be quiet and behave yourselves."

"Sí, señora. Gracias, señora."

The children sat on the floor, cross-legged. Their behaviour was impeccable, and they didn't make a sound. But this would be the last time we invited them into our home. The smell was pungent—these were poor children who practically never washed. As soon as the programme was over, we switched off the set and told them that we needed to do our homework. From that day onwards, when watching television, we made sure the lounge curtains were open so that the children could watch from outside through the net curtains.

Winter seemed much harsher that year. A few days after the arrival of our treasured small screen, we sat in front of it on a cold and grey afternoon, drinking mugs of hot chocolate, and watched in awe the retransmission of the Apollo 11 landing, which had taken place only a few weeks before. We all agreed that it was an incredible achievement. A man on the moon! Science and technology were conquering another frontier, the mightiest country on earth pushing humankind forward. There he was—this man called Neil (we pronounced it *Nae-eel*) Armstrong—tentatively putting one foot in front of the other, breathing heavily, moving robot-like; and there it was—the lunar module—sending blurred yet amazing pictures of our planet and the moon. It was a magical moment, and my imagination took me into outer space…and then I heard a little scratching noise and turned around. The poor, undernourished wretches had also watched the landing from outside our window. Science, progress and wealth would not touch their lives.

A few months after the lunar landing, rocks from the moon toured the world, on loan from NASA. My sisters and I went to see them at the Centro Boliviano Americano, displayed under a big rotating plastic dome, a couple of soldiers guarding them.

"They look just like any other rocks," Carolina said, disappointed.

Later that winter our mother came home very excited.

"Mariana! Carolina! I've enrolled you at the Centro Boliviano Americano for English lessons on Monday afternoons after school. You start next week."

"But, Mami! We don't want to…" we protested.

Since Cousin Silvia's return from the United States, my mother had been talking about sending me there as well, with the American Field Service programme. The American organisation would choose the most capable and enthusiastic teenagers; there would be an exam and an interview. I had two years to prepare myself.

"And on Wednesday afternoons you are going to do French at the Alliance Française."

"Mami!"

"Now come here and give me a hug!"

This was typical of our mother. She never asked us whether or not we wanted to go to these activities; she just enrolled us. In my mother's mind, a woman had to stand on her own two feet and have a career. The way to achieve this was through education and hard work. The following term she announced, "You'll be learning typing at the Instituto de Secretarias, starting next Saturday."

Six-year-old Teresa was still too young to join Carolina and me. Lucky her.

We worked hard at school and at our extracurricular lessons and were usually top of the class. We would come home from school at three in the afternoon, have a snack and a rest, and then go to our classes. We walked everywhere, forty or more minutes each way, as the buses were usually packed. At the end of the day, before doing our homework, we would sit in the lounge and watch cartoons on TV for half an hour, with the Indian children watching from outside.

Hugs, kisses and encouragement were daily bread in our house. "You are clever. You can achieve anything you want." But our mother expected a lot from her girls, and if we failed to do our best, she would let us know it. "You were second in the class," she said to me with a long face once when I let my grades slip.

Our mother saved for several months to buy the *Larousse Children's Encyclopaedia*, thirty slim books with colourful illustrations. I caressed their glossy covers, their fresh inky smell tickling my nostrils. With these treasures in my house, I could never be bored.

One morning in late September, during first period, a nun came into my classroom and said Mother Superior wanted to see me in her office. My classmates looked at me, thin little smiles on some of their faces, relishing the thought that I was in trouble. What other reason could there be to be summoned to the dreaded office? But I hadn't done anything deserving a reprimand, so I worried that something was wrong. Maybe my mother hadn't paid the fees and my sisters and I would no longer be able to attend lessons? Maybe Abuelita was unwell?

I followed the nun to the headmistress's office, where I waited for interminable minutes at reception, fiddling with my belt and twisting my handkerchief.

Sitting high on her upholstered brown leather armchair, Mother Superior commanded me to enter.

"Good morning, *ma mère*," I said. My eyes were cast down, but I was aware that she was observing me.

When I looked up, the expression on Mother Superior's face was not the usual austere and menacing one. "Take a seat, my daughter," she said.

She then crossed herself and indicated to me to join my hands, ready for prayer. I became alarmed. What was she trying to tell me?

"I'm afraid I have some bad news, dear girl," she said. "As your sister Carolina is away today with the rest of her class, I'm sorry to have to say this to you alone."

I swallowed hard. "Is anything the matter, ma mère?"

"Yes, my poor girl. You and Carolina are orphans now."

The floor disappeared from under my feet. "Is my mother...?" My eyes started to well up with tears.

"No, no, it's not your mother, thank God." Mother Superior opened the top drawer of her desk and took out an envelope. "Look, my child. This morning we received a telegram from your aunt Antonia, in Tarija. Read it yourself."

Please inform Mariana Arce Seifert her father, José Arce, died yesterday stop Funeral tomorrow stop thank you stop signed Antonia Arce.

"There, there, my child. Let it all out." The headmistress offered me a paper tissue. I wiped my nose, relieved that my mother was well and alive.

"Let's pray for your poor father, my dear," Mother Superior said. "For his eternal rest in heaven."

The headmistress recited the Lord's Prayer, and I mumbled after her. She then told me not to be afraid to cry, that crying was good for relieving sorrow.

But I did not shed a single tear for you, Father—you, who didn't know me and didn't remember me. You, who had relinquished all responsibility for Carolina and me, your daughters. You, who had shown us not a smidgeon of affection, who had never written or telephoned us. Did you even recall the last time I saw you, that time when you kidnapped me to punish my mother? I was only four, and you dumped me in an ugly dark house and never came to see me. Often I have wondered what my life would have been like had my mother not rescued me.

Mother Superior, of course, did not know any of this.

Father, a marvellous word—a word of love, protection, guidance. But you, Father, you were absent from my life and Carolina's. You forgot we existed. Not a toy at Christmas; no caresses and stories at bedtime; no riding piggyback around the living-room; no warning us against unsuitable boyfriends. Neither a letter nor a birthday card, nor a present. Instead, a feeling of abandonment, of not being good enough. Instead, social stigma, emotional upheaval, the constant threat of poverty. And I yearned for you for so long, Father. I envied my friends whose dads pampered them, kissed them on the cheeks, called them the prettiest and cleverest girls of all. Carolina and I, daughters of a divorced woman, forever marked, set apart, pitied, fatherless.

How could I mourn you, Father, when I felt absolutely nothing—when I felt empty? You had not died yesterday but had been dead to us for over a decade.

"You know, of course," Mother Superior said, "that the death of a parent requires the wearing of mourning clothes for at least six months."

"Yes, ma mère."

As I said this, an uncomfortable feeling rose up inside my belly. It was not sorrow. It was rage. It was regret for our missed opportunities with you, Father, regret for our lost time and anger for your lack of love. No, I could not—would not—wear mourning clothes for you, Father.

I thanked Mother Superior for her kindness and went back to my classroom. When my classmates asked why our headmistress wanted to see me, I said that it was about some forms that my mother needed to sign.

That year, during the school holidays and while she was not teaching in the morning, my mother did as she had done for the past two summers. With the help of her two elder daughters, she made biscuits and doughnuts to sell in the nearby offices. She also made cakes for special occasions and dome-shaped golden panettones for Christmas.

Decades later, I can still picture her rising at five in the morning, pounding the dough on the rickety, dark wooden kitchen table, flour up to her elbows, tiredness weighing down on her shoulders. At seven o'clock, Carolina and I would take turns helping with the baking and the packaging. As soon as she saw us, a huge smile would appear on our mother's face, and she would greet us with a kiss. When the pastries were ready, the girl who had risen early would go back to bed while the other got up to deliver the goods, either on foot or by bus, accompanied by our maid. After lunch, as usual, our mother went to her part-time jobs at the insurance company and the Spanish embassy.

Carolina and I were glad that all this took place early in the morning. We didn't mind delivering our boxes to the offices just as their doors were opening. That way we could make a hasty retreat and discreetly go back home while our classmates were still asleep. Not one of our friends ever saw us. The celebration cakes and panettones were delivered later during the day, but Carolina and I did not mind if anyone saw us. To our teenage minds, bringing a birthday cake to a private house was somehow less embarrassing than bringing doughnuts for the office workers.

Gerardo had not come to see us for several weeks. Slowly, over the last few months, there had been a change in him. Now that he, Carolina and I were older, we no longer played the childish games that we had enjoyed not so long ago. Twice already, when my sister and I had seen him in the street with a group of boys, Gerardo had played cool in front of his friends and ignored us. Undeterred, I had approached him and said hello, and he'd had no option but to introduce us. The boys grinned, said hola quickly, and then carried on with what they were doing. *Fine*, I thought. *If that's the way he wants it to be, I will also give him the cold shoulder next time I see him.*

Gerardo was growing up, and it was time for him to leave behind the playmates of his childhood, his girl cousins. It was time to seek the company of other boys and do manly things. This was also a time of change for Carolina and me, as our friends had become more important in our lives than Gerardo. But what I didn't know then was that something else was worrying our cousin. His sister Cecilia and brother-in-law, Néstor, were becoming more and more involved with the liberation theology movement and, more worryingly, with an underground organisation. Cecilia and Néstor wanted Gerardo to remain outside their activities, but since he visited them frequently, he saw and heard what was going on in their house.

When Aunt Alcira came back from France at the beginning of 1970, Cecilia and Néstor moved out of her home and went to live near Plaza Andreu, not too far from my aunt's place. Abuelita noticed that my cousins were visiting us less frequently. "They are busy with their jobs and studies," my mother explained.

Néstor and Cecilia were about to embark on the most perilous journey of their lives.

The Violence of Hunger

A Meditation

A family tragedy that would reverberate around the whole country was about to befall us. Cecilia and Néstor would get involved in a new guerrilla uprising in Teoponte, and our families would enter a nightmarish place where only suffering and uncertainty existed. Néstor and Cecilia's story would unfold before our eyes and also behind our backs.

In 1960s Bolivia, abject poverty, social inequalities and racism were part of normal life. Most middle-class people were indifferent to the situation; as churchgoing Christians, they comforted themselves by believing it was God's will. Some were moved to give a piece of bread or a couple of coins to the beggars, but only a few "troublemakers" were thinking of changing the system. Cold War paranoia was at its height, and anyone who dared challenge the status quo was accused of being a communist.

Despite my family's precarious financial situation, I was aware that we enjoyed privileges that others did not have. My sisters and I attended a good school, had lots of books in the house, and wanted to go to university. In the slums of La Paz, especially in El Alto, just outside the airport, hardship and degradation were the daily diet of the inhabitants.

Néstor and Cecilia were devout Catholics committed to the aims of liberation theology, a religious movement that aimed to promote social justice. Many years later I would learn about other social campaigners with similar aims, such as the Brazilian archbishop Hélder Câmara—called a saint when giving food to the poor but a communist for daring to ask why there should be hunger—and the humanitarian Victorian reformers of nineteenth-century Britain. I realised that whether these campaigners were accepted or not was simply a matter of perspective and interpretation, and of whose privileges might be affected by the proposed changes.

I realised also that often when people in developing countries demanded what the richer countries had, they were deemed extremists, rabble-rousers, even terrorists.

Even before their wedding in 1968, my cousins had started attending masses and consciousness-raising meetings conducted by revolutionary priests, where they discussed "the violence of hunger," "the violence of exploitation," and "the violence of greed." Soon, the Vatican became worried about the Marxist overtones of this discourse, but it made little difference, as the number of the movement's supporters kept on growing. Unbeknown to their parents, my cousins had also joined another more militant organisation and had pledged to give their lives for its cause. Their deaths would plunge their families into a pit of pain and despair from which it would take them years to escape. Talking about this tragedy became taboo. For their parents and siblings, oblivion was preferable to reliving the trauma; silence, always a good companion, would help them forget. As a teenager, I was saddened by the terrible news but not excessively depressed by it—I had my own adolescent angst to deal with. For several years these tragic events were a nebulous memory at the back of my mind; as the years passed, however, I started thinking about the magnitude of what had happened and realised that it was time to break the silence.

Just as my grandparents' lives were a mystery to me, I hardly knew a thing about Néstor and Cecilia's story. As I grew up, my mother sometimes talked a little about my cousins if I asked her, but she never brought up the subject herself. Speaking with Aunt Alcira about this tragedy was, of course, out of the question. How could anyone ask a grieving mother what it was like to lose a daughter? After they had played such an important part in the history of my country, Néstor and Cecilia started to fade from memory. Although their involvement in the Teoponte guerrilla movement and their deaths had been mentioned for months in long articles in all the newspapers in Bolivia, soon other political and economic upheavals took their place.

Since I did not dare speak to my aunt about this most painful chapter in her life, I decided to ask Cecilia's younger sister, Silvia, once when she visited me in England, decades later. But it must have been too painful for her, as she quickly changed the subject.

Gerardo would tell me much later about the suffering his mother and mine had endured during those awful years and about what he'd seen and heard during the last weeks of my cousins' lives. He had been a fourteen-year-old boy when Néstor died, sixteen when he last saw his sister. "You know, Mariana," he said one day when I visited him in La Paz in 2008, "in all these years that I've gone with my mother to put flowers on Cecilia's grave, she's never once said a word to me about it. Not once." My aunt has kept all the horror and heartbreak buried deep inside herself. I wonder how she has managed to remain sane.

In 2006 a history book, *Teoponte*,[7] about the guerrilla insurgency of the same name, was published. The few hundred copies that were printed were sold immediately, and then the book became impossible to find. Luckily, my sister Teresa's eldest son had to study part of the book at school. So I begged the boy to lend me his copy, and ten years later, I still have not returned it. That book has helped me to make better sense of my cousins' ill-fated lives, their motives and ideals. Why did they join an insurgency group? Why did Néstor and his companions go into the jungle-covered mountains? How could they have conceived that they were going to bring down the government from there? It all seemed utterly naive. Yes, Castro and Che had started a guerrilla "focus"[8] in the thick-forested mountains in Cuba and had succeeded. But the conditions there were different, as they'd had the full support of the peasantry, better training and more weapons. Che's Bolivian campaign of 1967 was doomed from the start, as neither the Bolivian Communist Party nor the peasants supported him. Our campesinos were suspicious of the motives of this Argentinean foreigner who, in their eyes, was just another stranger who had come to take advantage of them; they also lived in fear of the military, who harassed them constantly. To the peasants, socialism, communism

---

7 Gustavo Rodríguez Ostria (2006), *Teoponte*, Cochabamba, Bolivia, Grupo Editorial Kipus.

8 The *foco* theory of guerrilla warfare claims that fast-moving paramilitary groups can provide a focus for insurrection—for example, by launching attacks from rural areas.

and capitalism were all forms of oppression. In their long experience since the arrival of the conquistadores, it didn't matter which system they lived under—at the end of the day, they were always downtrodden. In October 1967 the Bolivian army and the CIA hunted down and killed Che, crushing his dreams of a Latin America–wide revolution.

Che's death, however, did not deter the young idealists—many of them university students—from daydreaming. They would keep Che's legacy alive. They would go back to the mountains to fight for a better world. Where Che had failed, these new guerrillas would succeed—or so they hoped. But history would repeat itself. Teoponte would also end in disaster.

Che had founded the Ejército de Liberación Nacional (ELN), or National Liberation Army of Bolivia. By October 1968—the first anniversary of Che's death—the new ELN already had an impressive number of sympathisers. Néstor was among the first to join the group. Through him, other young people joined as well, such as students from the newly created Universidad Católica and pupils from San Calixto, a Jesuit secondary school. Two or three older girls from my school secretly supported the ELN, charmed by its romantic aura. Prince Charming was now a daring guerrilla fighter, a defender of the poor. It would be hard not to fall in love.

I remember a particularly intense conversation late one afternoon at my house, when Néstor brought his guitar. Before he had even had a sip of coffee, we had begged him to play folk songs by Los Jairas and Savia Andina. He sat on the arm of the sofa and strummed his guitar, his eyes dreamy, while Cecilia's soft voice accompanied him. We all joined in and were soon singing protest songs by the Argentineans Horacio Guaraní and Mercedes Sosa, until the smell of the alfajores our grandmother had baked filled the sitting-room and my mother called us to the table.

While we drank our tea and ate the pastries, my mother asked Néstor and Cecilia to tell us a little about their work with the church.

"I wish that Christians understood that their most important duty is to fight for justice," Cecilia said.

"I agree," said my mother. "But of course fighting for justice doesn't suit everybody. Look at how our politicians lie and steal while our people go hungry."

Abuelita never participated in these discussions; she just sat in her armchair, knitting and crocheting, nodding her head in agreement whenever Cecilia or Néstor said anything. My sisters were too young to be interested in these subjects, so they went to the roof terrace to play as soon as they finished their cakes. Although I didn't fully understand the intricacies of these topics, I wanted to learn about them, so I stayed. Néstor, Cecilia and my mother were soon deep in conversation.

My cousins said that what they wanted to achieve was a fairer society where abject poverty and political oppression would be a thing of the past, both in Bolivia and the rest of Latin America. They criticised the American government and its propaganda machine for their hypocrisy. "The gringos rightly condemn other people's wrong-doings but refuse to admit the crimes they themselves commit in the name of liberty," Néstor said.

"What Stalin has done to his people is criminal, Auntie Emma," Cecilia said. "But we mustn't confuse his murderous and totalitarian regime with what we want to achieve."

A crucial incident that occurred in November 1968 confirmed Néstor and Cecilia's commitment to their cause. The Ball of the Debutantes, a select affair for the elite of Bolivia, was to be held on a Saturday, the ninth day of that month, at the exclusive Club La Paz. Néstor and his companions considered the flaunting of excessive wealth an insult to the poverty of the masses. Cecilia and other young women in the group wanted to participate in the peaceful demonstration that Néstor was organising but were told that only the men would take part this time; the government was not known for respecting demonstrators' rights, and things could easily turn nasty.

On Saturday about fifty unarmed protesters, mainly from Catholic groups, gathered in Calle Camacho near the obelisk opposite the club, singing traditional Bolivian songs. The banners they carried read, "The life expectancy of our miners is thirty-two years," "Illiteracy is sixty-five percent," "Thousands survive on thirty cents per day." Inside, white-gloved, dark-skinned Aymara waiters in dark jackets served canapés and champagne while an orchestra played Viennese waltzes. The organisers called the police, and during a confrontation, a grenade exploded, killing two students and seriously injuring seven.

Néstor would later tell my mother how he had cradled in his arms one of the dying teenagers, a pupil at a state secondary school and the only child of a poor family. The following day the newspapers reported that the police had been called to disband a group of "agitators." Although the deaths were regrettable, illegal demonstrations would not be tolerated.

Rosita finished secondary school with top marks and then enrolled at the Universidad Mayor de San Andrés in La Paz. The major cities of Bolivia— La Paz, Cochabamba and Santa Cruz—were in the grip of revolutionary fervour. Idealistic young people talked about following the path of Jesus and the path of Che, giving up their material comfort in order to help the poor, and even taking up arms to fight for their cause. Discreetly, the ELN had infiltrated the classrooms and was now recruiting converts who could join their urban support section. The guerrillas who would soon be going to fight in a secret and remote rural location had already been selected after completing several months of intense jungle-survival training. But the ELN also needed fit and dedicated young people to work in the cities building makeshift radios, sewing uniforms, obtaining rucksacks and dry food, acting as spies and decoys in government ministries, and procuring arms and explosives.

The main political parties, from the left and the right, were also recruiting in the universities, holding question-and-answer sessions to explain their ideologies. One Friday afternoon, as Rosita left the campus and walked to the bus stop, she was approached by a tall, muscular man with a moustache.

"Hello, Rosita," he said. "You're at the Faculty of Medicine, aren't you?"

Rosita was suspicious and shy. "How do you know?"

"I've seen you in class," he said. "I always sit at the back. My name is Oscar."

He offered her a cigarette, which she refused. "Well, Rosita, is it true that Néstor and Cecilia are your cousins?"

She did not reply but flashed him a worried look.

The man continued, "Please don't be alarmed. I really admire them, especially Néstor. They are true Christians; they live as they preach."

Rosita nodded.

"I know that Néstor was your RE teacher," he said as he stroked his moustache.

"Yes. His lessons opened up our eyes to reality."

"That's wonderful. Now, there are a couple of things I'd like to discuss with you. May I treat you to a cup of coffee?"

Although Rosita felt a little nervous, her curiosity was stronger, and she accepted. They headed towards a cafeteria that was frequented mainly by older working-class people, two blocks away from the main campus. The place was busy with factory workers, but they managed to find a quiet corner. She put four spoonsful of sugar into her coffee, stirred and took a sip. Here she was drinking coffee with a man, feeling self-conscious and unattractive. He surely must have noticed her freckled face and chapped cheeks. The stranger looked much older than the rest of her classmates. He had sinewy forearms and square hands, which Rosita found appealing. But who was he, and what did he want? He started by talking about the situation in Bolivia and the desperate need for change. He also said that it was the duty of all good Christians to fight for justice.

"Are you from one of the political parties?" Rosita asked.

"I'm not at liberty to say at the moment," Oscar said. "But I'd like to give you something to remind you of our meeting." He put a sealed envelope in Rosita's hand. "We'll meet again."

"You are not really my classmate, are you?" she said.

"I'm at the University of Life," he replied. He got up, paid for the coffees and left.

Rosita did not dare open the envelope while at the cafeteria, so she walked back to the university and opened it inside a cubicle in the women's toilets. The envelope contained a colour photograph of Che on glossy paper and a page of liberation theology quotations. She smiled to herself and stuck the picture in her notebook.

When she arrived home, her father was pacing the lounge, reading the newspaper, and complaining loudly about the bad things that were happening in our country. As she was giving her father a kiss on the cheek, the photo fell from her notebook.

Uncle Silvio picked up the photo and held it by the tips of his fingers like a poisonous leaf. "What's this?" he bellowed.

"Er...it's a photo, Papi."

"I can see that!" he exploded. "How come you have it? Who gave it to you?"

"I cut it out from a magazine."

"And why did you do that? Don't you know that this man is a criminal?"

"Yes, Papi. I'm sorry." Trembling, she looked at the floor while her father tore up the picture and threw the pieces in the bin.

"Could it be that some of your classmates have been putting ideas in your head? Could it be that someone has given you that photo?"

"No, Papi, no."

"Are you sure? Can you give me your word?"

"Yes, Papi," she lied.

"Good. Because if I find out that you've been in contact with those troublemakers, I'll drag you by your hair out of the house—understand?"

"Yes, Papi."

"Néstor and Cecilia are involved with those idiots from the liberation theology." Uncle Silvio paced the room from end to end. "He's a naive and romantic failed priest, isn't he? But I feel sorry for Cecilia and for your aunt Alcira. I fear this will not end well."

Many years later, when I went back to my country in October 2010, I met the author of *Teoponte*. During our brief encounter late at night at a café in La Paz, Señor Gustavo Rodríguez answered my many questions about Cecilia's role in the guerrilla campaign and her untimely death. Days later I met a former guerrilla fighter, a woman, Cecilia's friend and comrade, and she, too, told me about my cousin's last days. The following week, at the public library, I read the newspapers from that terrible month, March 1972, when my cousin was murdered. There, splashed across the front page, was a photo of Cecilia's body covered by a sheet and surrounded by soldiers. All the Bolivian papers talked about the Teoponte debacle for several weeks, but soon the whole episode would be but a footnote in the narrative of my country.

Although I do not believe a guerrilla uprising was the way to solve Bolivia's problems—and I certainly do not approve of their violent methods—I nonetheless admire the guerrillas' ideals of social justice.

I wonder who, apart from my family, now remembers Cecilia. Homages have been paid to the members of the guerrilla group who went into the jungle, and a small monument to the men has been erected in a park in La Paz, inscribed with all their names. Néstor's name is of course there but not Cecilia's. Néstor's diary has been published and translated into English, and several tributes have been paid to him. But there has been nothing for Cecilia. This book is my way of keeping her memory alive.

The Beginning of the End

1970

Militants from other Latin American guerrilla groups started arriving from abroad. As accommodation was needed for these visitors, Néstor and Cecilia opened up their house.

One Sunday, Gerardo went to have lunch with Cecilia and Néstor. Three Uruguayan men, probably Tupamaros,[9] were staying at their house. The men were friendly and chatted and joked with the teenager. Gerardo had no idea who they were or what they were doing in La Paz; what caught his attention was their funny accent and their constant smoking. One of the men, burly with thick long black hair, had a pair of fine black boots.

"Look, Gerardo: this boot is called Che," he said, "and this other one Camilo."[10]

They all laughed. Another man started playing the guitar.

Cecilia added, "Gerardito, you mustn't tell anybody about our friends. Not even our family."

After lunch the grown-ups had a nap. While they slept, by accident Gerardo dropped his glass of lemonade on the kitchen floor. The noise was startling. Three dishevelled men burst out of their room with guns ready, their faces as white as the kitchen tiles. "It's nothing," the burly man said. "It's nothing."

During another visit Gerardo needed to use the toilet. The main bathroom was occupied, so he was told to use the one beside the main bedroom. As he crossed the room, he noticed that the top drawer of Néstor's bedside table was ajar. Being a curious adolescent, he had a look: a shiny

---

9 An urban guerrilla group from Uruguay.
10 Camilo Torres, a Colombian revolutionary priest and supporter of liberation theology.

black revolver, half wrapped in a lacy white handkerchief, lay on top of a black Bible with golden letters on the cover.

As the days passed, the house became more and more crowded, with sleeping bags in the tiny lounge and even the hall. In the evenings Néstor and the other men would play the guitar and sing protest songs, while the women sewed olive-green uniforms and prepared food. My aunt was of course unaware of all these goings-on. Her relationship with Cecilia was at an all-time low. Later, she would regret bitterly not having made peace with her daughter.

It must have been a Saturday in April or May when I went to the *tambo*, the traditional Aymara market, to do some shopping for my mother. The peasants sat on the floor, surrounded by sacks of black *chuño* potatoes and golden quinoa. Chickens and rabbits twitched nervously inside their cages.

I was about to pay for the *oca* tubers when a soft hand touched my cheek.

"Hola, Ceci," I said, turning. "Are you buying fruit for an army?"

Cecilia had two huge bags. "Néstor loves his fruit and eats it by the bucket-load, especially cherimoyas and mangos."

"Well, you've got a lot there. It looks heavy."

"Yes, but this kind young man is helping me," she said, pointing to an Aymara porter, who smiled shyly and then looked at the floor.

The porter's feet, shod in the usual open-toe sandals made of old car tyres, looked purple with cold.

"Señorita, you give me soup? You sure?" he asked timidly in his broken Spanish.

"Yes, of course," Cecilia answered, "and a pair of my husband's socks."

She then turned to me and asked, "Did Abuelita like the book I gave her last week?"

"She did, Ceci."

"Please tell her we love her and pray for her every day."

I kissed my cousin on the cheek. "'Bye, Ceci. Love to Néstor. Come and see us soon."

I watched as she and the porter left the tambo laden with shopping, until they disappeared among the crowd.

That was the last time I saw Cecilia.

¡Volveremos!

Saturday, 18 July 1970, the middle of winter. The sun had not yet risen, and the bitter cold felt like the blade of a knife. Sixty-seven young men, most of them Bolivian university students from middle-class families, as well as a few foreigners, were about to set off on a literacy campaign supported and sponsored by the government. Three days before, Alfredo Ovando, the president of Bolivia, had personally given them teaching materials and letters of accreditation. The young educators would go deep into the Teoponte jungle to the north of La Paz, near Beni, to teach adults and children the basics of reading and writing. Sixty-seven young men eager to help others less fortunate than themselves.

But all was not as it seemed. These literacy campaigners were embarking on a dangerous, clandestine mission of their own, fully aware that some of them might not return. Like Christ's apostles, they had given away their possessions. Some of the men had never met the others; some were surprised—and glad—to recognise familiar faces. They were all very nervous. They were also more than two hours behind schedule. If needed, they would call the whole thing off and regroup later. They could not afford to endanger their mission. But soon the caravan started, at eight-thirty, from a street near Plaza Villaroel. Leading the convoy was a pickup truck, then a VW van driven by Francisco—Néstor Paz in his previous life—followed by two trucks. Each young teacher was wearing the armband of the Alfabetizadores literacy campaign, a blue A against a white background. They were all singing and telling jokes; the voice of the popular singer Benjo Cruz, now called Casiano, rose clear above the other voices. Protruding from a corner of each vehicle was a white flag with a big blue A in the centre, fluttering in the wind. Hidden underneath innocent-looking suitcases and teaching materials lay rucksacks containing olive-green uniforms, cases of grenades, bullets and firearms. Beneath their ordinary clothes, on a chain around each man's neck, was an identity tag: his blood group and his *nombre de guerra*, his new warrior identity.

Two years before, in July 1968, the ELN had announced in the press that it would launch another guerrilla campaign in the mountains: *"¡Volveremos a las montañas!"* And today Chato Peredo, the new *comandante* of the ELN, whose two brothers had fought alongside Che, was fulfilling that promise. The violence of hunger and oppression had to be stopped.

The previous morning, Pedro Basiana, a Jesuit priest, had celebrated Mass in a tiny chapel in the poor working-class neighbourhood of Pura-Pura. Only two people—a young man and his wife—attended this Mass, which was said especially to ask God to protect the young man and his companions. Their arms around each other's shoulders, Cecilia and Néstor took communion. *"Vaya con Dios*, my son," Father Basiana said and sprinkled them with holy water. "Bless you, my daughter," he continued as he put his hands on her head. Cecilia bit her lip to stop the tears. But her husband never noticed this. What he saw on his wife's face was a calm expression and the hint of a smile.

"Thank you, Father. Pray for all of us," Néstor said.

"I will. Every day."

Now it was time for Cecilia to say goodbye to her husband. He enveloped her in his arms.

"Take good care, my princess," he said and kissed her lightly on the cheek.

She rushed towards the bus stop without looking back, tears coursing down her face. Néstor's companions and all the things he needed for his coming enterprise were waiting at a secret address.

The early-morning sun set the Andean peaks on fire. As the convoy entered the lonely road, the men's songs changed. No longer were they singing folk and pop songs. Now they were smoking, patting one another hard on the back, and chanting, "*¡Victoria o muerte! ¡Victoria o muerte!*" All of them were prepared to lay down their lives for their cause.

During Che's Ñancahuazú campaign, a woman, Tania, had fought alongside men. This time women would not participate in the fighting. Their role, however, was invaluable. They would provide domestic, emotional, and practical support. Their sewing machines would work nonstop, making uniforms and rucksacks. They would find hiding places for ammunition and prepare homemade explosives. Those who worked in the Ministry of the Interior would spy and steal information. Those working in private clinics stole medical supplies and those in offices stationery.

19 July–2 November 1970

The newspaper headlines read, "Government Determined to Hunt Down Guerrillas. The National Liberation Army Will Be Eliminated." Three years after the death of Che Guevara, a new guerrilla war had erupted in the Teoponte jungle. Among the guerrillas were three survivors of Che's failed 1967 Ñancahuazú campaign. Some guerrillas had spent several months in Cuba training for this new adventure. Back in Bolivia, they had all gone on training marches in the countryside around La Paz by the Muela del Diablo Mountain, the Devil's Tooth. They had also had long sessions of shooting practice and learnt how to manufacture explosives.

My mother would soon hear on the radio a communiqué from the National Liberation Army explaining why they wanted to fight the government and the Yankee *imperialistas*. Cecilia and Néstor's names were among those read out.

My aunt and my mother were very secretive. Only years later, my mother would tell me what she and Alcira had had to endure and the measures they'd taken to protect us and Abuelita. As a teenager, I was worried about my looks, my studies, our lack of money, and finding a boyfriend. I had a vague idea that something was not right in my country and my family but was not unduly troubled by it. And I was of course unaware of the conversations going on between my mother and my aunt.

Cecilia had disappeared. "I wish I hadn't argued with her," Alcira had cried. "Emma, please help me find her."

Getting in touch with my cousin and her companions was not easy. After several weeks of uncertainty, Cecilia contacted my mother via a third party.

"They have enough food at the moment, but they need cigarettes, soap, toilet paper and sanitary towels," my mother said.

Soon shoes and clothes would be needed, too. But where was Cecilia? The contact from the ELN would not say. All my mother knew was that while Néstor had gone with other men into the jungle near Teoponte, Cecilia and others were working for their cause and hiding in a safe house in Cochabamba.

Cuba and other countries had been supporting the ELN, but now Castro no longer thought this kind of guerrilla warfare was viable and withdrew his support.

Chato Peredo, the new comandante, and his men started by attacking the installations of SAPI, an American gold-mining company on the banks of the Teoponte River; they blew up the dredger. The American government became alarmed. The CIA could not allow Marxism to flourish in Latin America.

The United States had been training the Bolivian military in the Pentagon's School of the Americas since 1946. There the Latin American soldiers learnt counterinsurgency and interrogation techniques that did not care much for human rights, and they used their skills to wage war against their own people. Teachers, religious workers, student leaders and others who spoke up for the rights of the poor were tortured and disappeared by those trained at the so-called School of Assassins. US-trained Bolivian troops were sent into the Teoponte jungle under strict instructions not to take prisoners. "They hunted us like rabbits," one of the survivors would later say.

The jungle was a dense, unbroken sea of green. Progressing on foot was difficult and slow, and finding food was a major problem. Occasionally the guerrillas would catch a monkey, a macaw, or a wild pig. Soon they started dreaming of all the delicious little dishes their wives and mothers used to prepare at home: the spicy chicken stew, the salteñas, the fried sweet empanadas dusted with sugar, the hot-chilli pork with onions and potatoes...When a couple of men stole two tins of sardines, Chato ordered that they be shot. As the author of *Teoponte* says, "They were killed by the same friendly hands that only yesterday had patted them on the back and offered them a mug of hot coffee." Discipline had to be maintained.

The men's voices and laughter resonated in the sweltering afternoon while the insects hummed around them, and the macaws flew screeching above their heads, flashing green and yellow, glinting red and blue. There was no breath of air in this thick lushness, and the sun scorched the men's skin. Night-time brought some relief to their suffering. The moon and the stars shone brightly while the guerrillas dreamt their revolutionary dreams in the coolness of the dark.

The military threatened the peasants, whose support was vital for the success of the campaign: "If you collaborate with the insurgents, your communities will suffer." As the days passed, the guerrillas became more desperate and disillusioned. Chato and his lieutenants started wondering whether the arduous training by the Muela del Diablo in La Paz had been enough preparation for this gruelling campaign.

The jungle, mighty and unforgiving, started devouring the men: insect bites got infected, maggots appeared in their open wounds, dysentery was rife, their feet began to fester inside their rotting boots, and they were starving. A primeval fear took hold of them. They were about to start on a journey to their darkest fears.

When eight men asked Chato to be allowed to leave, their wish was granted after much soul-searching and heated discussion. Wearing civilian clothes, the eight walked through the forest in search of a village where they could give themselves up. Captured by government troops, they were tied to trees and machine-gunned. No prisoners were to be taken. The government would not allow the families of the dead men to see the bodies. Cochabamba, Oruro, La Paz, and other cities erupted in mass demonstrations and hunger strikes, demanding justice. The government relented.

Uncle Silvio

Rosita's father died in a road-traffic accident on his way to build a school in a village in the foothills of the Andes, in the Yungas, near La Paz. The road to Yungas was a narrow, unpaved one-lane track that hugged the side of the mountain. As the truck turned a corner on the infamous Carretera de la Muerte, Death Road, one of the most treacherous roads in our country, it met another vehicle coming from the opposite direction. The driver was unable to avoid a collision, and the truck fell with a mighty roar into the abyss. The driver and his assistant, although seriously injured, survived the accident. Uncle Silvio died instantly.

My mother wept for her brother. He had had a sad, hard life and had spent many years feeling bitter and full of resentment. And now he had died in this senseless way. Before going to the wake at his house, she said to me that we were lucky at least to have a body to bury, as sometimes the rescue operations were too dangerous and the dead were left where they had fallen. My uncle left a young widow scarcely older than Rosita, plus four younger children. I remember the tall white candles by his coffin, their tiny flames slowly melting the wax while mournful black-clad relatives silently sat around the coffin, sighing quietly, wiping their eyes, sipping coffee; the widow's pinched expression and knotted hands; Rosita's swollen eyes. My cousin had lost her mother when she was little; now her father was gone, too, and living with her stressed-out young stepmother would not be easy.

My grandmother, of course, did not hear a word about Silvio's death.

The Move

Soon before my fifteenth birthday, my mother started looking with feverish urgency for a house to move into. I wondered how she could afford it. Had my stepfather and the landlord come to an arrangement with her? All I knew was that we'd had enough of living without water for more than seven years. We had managed—my mother especially—to keep up our spirits and energies most of the time, but there were occasions when we felt tired and dejected. It really was time to go.

I accompanied my mother to view a few houses to rent, but they were all unsuitable. Finally, we found a three-bedroom house in Sopocachi, the same neighbourhood where we had lived until I was six, and a date was set for the move. The landlord had said that he would have all the relevant documents ready on the day of the move. The prospect of having warm showers filled me with delight—and the thought of not having to carry heavy buckets every day, even more so. Our excitement grew by the hour, and even eight-year-old Teresa started packing her dolls and comic books. The week before the intended move, the landlord telephoned my mother to tell her that the deal was off—he had decided not to let his house after all. And that was that. All our dreams came crashing down. We had to unpack our stuff and resign ourselves to living in the dreary, waterless house once again. "How stupid I've been," my mother said. "A deal is not a deal unless it's signed."

Soon we went to see three other houses, nicer than the one we had just missed. But they were just a bit too expensive. My mother reworked her sums, but even if we went without Christmas presents, she just couldn't afford any of them.

We were back where we had started, until one day when my mother found a three-storey, six-bedroom house, also in Sopocachi.

"But, Mami, how can we afford to live in that enormous house?" I asked. "And do we need six bedrooms?"

"Well, I've spoken to the landlord," she said wearily. "He doesn't mind if I sublet a couple of rooms. All he wants is his rent money at the end of the month."

"Will you do that, then?"

"Yes. And I'll serve breakfast and dinner." She looked exhausted.

This time my mother signed the tenancy contract immediately. One warm Saturday in October 1970, we moved into the big house, two blocks up from Plaza España. Calle Mendez Arcos was a peaceful street, unlike the hustle and bustle of San Pedro. It was also not far from the centre of town.

The minivan came at seven in the morning. My mother and I spent most of that day at the San Pedro house loading the van, while the rest of the family and our maid went to the new house. As my mother was not present to insist the men carry the heavier furniture to the two floors above, the items were left downstairs in a mess.

Dusk caught us in San Pedro when we were putting our last belongings in the van, and we realised our stomachs were grumbling. Carolina and the maid had joined us by this time. We hadn't eaten or drunk anything since breakfast, and we hadn't had a rest, either. The Aymara woman who sold meat kebabs on the corner outside our house was there as always, preparing food on her wobbly little table and stand. We had never considered buying anything from her; we thought the food was probably unhygienic—lethal, even. But that night her roasted potatoes and spicy skewered meat with onions and peppers smelled like heavenly food. We each ate a kebab and drank lukewarm, milky tea from her chipped enamel-covered mugs, the same metal mugs used daily by the labourers who bought from her. We had never tasted such a delicious meal.

We slept soundly that night in our day clothes, since we couldn't find our pyjamas. The following morning we girls got up to go to school, and our mother went to her three part-time jobs. It would take us several weeks to unpack.

The first warm shower in the new house was a sensuous, luxurious experience. It seemed that all the water and electricity we hadn't used in those seven and a half years in San Pedro were used in the first showers my sisters and I had. I remember letting the warm water caress my face, back and legs long after I had finished rinsing off all the soap. I used up all the hot water in the huge tank just for this one shower, and Carolina and Teresa had to wait fifty minutes for the water to heat up again.

We were intoxicated. This was liberation! This was freedom! No more daily fetching and carrying heavy buckets. No more spilling water on our legs, no more wet shoes. No more embarrassing moments with visitors. No more nasty remarks from other children. No more smelly pee in the toilet. No more disgusting public showers with other people's hair and snot in the drains. No more!

My mother told us that two new young lodgers would be moving in soon.

"Who are they, Mami?" Carolina enquired.

"Two gringo boys from Utah, Mormon missionaries."

"Mormons? What's that?"

My mother said that the Church of Jesus Christ of Latter-day Saints was trying to establish itself in Bolivia.

Abuelita was worried. "Will they try to convert us, Emma?"

"Don't worry, Mamá. I've told them we're devout Catholics. I'm here to provide food and lodging; that's all."

Little by little we installed our furniture and made the house our home. Our old furniture had never looked so attractive in the other house; the music coming from the record player had not been as sweet; even the news coming from the ancient radio seemed more interesting.

"We're so happy, Mami," Carolina said and put her arms around our mother's neck. "Muchas gracias!"

"Come here, my sweeties." Our mother pinched our cheeks and planted loud kisses on our foreheads.

"I'm so pleased with the kitchen," Abuelita said. "It's twice as big as the other one. And there's running water!"

The porcelain elephant that had kept us company in all the houses we lived in—Aunt Alcira's house in Pasaje Alborta, the San Pedro house, and now our lovely home in Calle Mendez Arcos—once again had pride of place on the central coffee table in our lounge, its proud, vigorous greyness cheering us while we unpacked the many crates and cleaned up the place.

The three bedrooms on the first floor were for our tenants. The two Mormons would each have a bedroom, and the third room would be rented to a university student or young office worker. Our lodgers would also have breakfast and dinner at our house. In months to come, and thanks to this new source of income, my mother was able to furnish the entrance hall with a dark wooden coat stand and a framed mirror in the Spanish-colonial style she loved so much; she also purchased two small rugs with Andean motifs for the lounge and dining-room. We had never known such luxury.

We occupied the top floor. My sisters shared a room, and I had one to myself. "I feel like a princess in a castle," Teresa said. My mother and grandmother shared the third bedroom.

The only thing we missed from the other house was the roof terrace. Here we had a small courtyard outside the kitchen, where we put our potted plants and hung the washing, but there was no room for cycling or other games.

Soon three new lodgers moved in with us: a young woman who was studying journalism at the Catholic University and two shy American farm boys from Utah, barely out of their teens. These Mormons had never been abroad or even travelled much outside their own communities. Their Spanish was not up to scratch, and we helped them with their pronunciation. They went everywhere as a pair, dressed in their distinct uniform: a suit, tie and white shirt with a name badge on each boy's lapel: "Elder So-and-So." They carried briefcases, but the Book of Mormon was always in their hands. They never tried to convert us, however, our mother having put them off doing it. They worked extremely hard on preaching, proselytising, and organising fun activities to welcome new people into their church. Their meetings, held at a hall next to the Church of the Carmelites, offended the many Catholics going to religious services there. But there was nothing anybody could do, as there was freedom of religion in Bolivia.

"Why don't they help us with literacy or feeding programmes instead of yet more superstition?" my mother complained. I agreed with her.

During the years we stayed in this house, several Mormon missionaries lived with us, some more memorable than others. My mother made them all feel welcome, and they considered us their surrogate family. I remember blond and blue-eyed Elder Randall, nineteen, playing his guitar in the kitchen and singing Simon & Garfunkel's "I am a Rock," his eyes misting up. He would have a break, wipe his forehead and nose, drink half a litre of milk in one go, and eat a dozen of Abuelita's biscuits before telling us that drinking tea and coffee was bad for the body and the soul. Then he would play another country ballad, always on the verge of tears.

While still working at her part-time jobs, my mother now spent nearly all her spare time cooking, cleaning, washing, and ironing for the lodgers. The maid helped her with these chores, as did Carolina and I, but there was always a lot to do. Often we ate our meals with the lodgers, and I would watch as my mother got up repeatedly from her chair to serve one or the other of them. Carolina and I pleaded with her to sit down and enjoy her food.

"Mami, I will bring the salad."

"Sit down, Mami. I will pour the coffee."

All to no avail. Our mother had to do everything herself. Carolina and I set the table, and the maid cleared the dishes away, but the food had to be served by the *ama de casa*, the lady of the house. In my eyes, she was far too servile, and my stomach tightened with humiliation and anger. Why couldn't she behave like the lady she was? Why didn't she accept our offers of help? And then, exhausted by her daily exertions, she would run out of energy by mid-afternoon and, too tired to talk to us in the evening, be in bed by nine o'clock.

The Debacle-1

Despite his mysticism, which some of his comrades said interfered with his efficiency as a fighter, Néstor was a popular and active member of the guerrilla group. Most of them were atheists; all were committed Marxists. In his diary, Néstor wrote to Cecilia often. "My beloved little princess, I miss you terribly and pray for your well-being. I am totally confident that God will reunite us soon. I know he supports and blesses our cause. Be strong, my darling."

In another entry, he wrote, "If I die, I want my death to be full of meaning, to have a ripple effect and influence other, like-minded people who will also struggle to bring happiness to mankind."

Soon the guerrilla group was forced to split. Several men got lost and were shot by the troops, some while surrendering. Néstor and two others became separated from the main group. They were weak with hunger. "Three days ago we ate a spoonful of lard and a pinch of salt each," he wrote. "Yesterday we were luckier: we caught a baby monkey."

After several days without food, Néstor wrote to God, "My dear Lord, today I really feel the need of you and your presence. Maybe it's because of the nearness of death or the relative failure of our struggle...I left what I had, and I came. Today may be my Holy Thursday and tomorrow my Good Friday."

The government sent more and more troops to the jungle, until, in the end, twelve hundred soldiers were hunting just fourteen emaciated and exhausted rebels.

The sun is now at its zenith. Three famished guerrillas, Quirito, Alberto and Néstor, drag themselves through the forest. Their breath is fetid, their shabby uniforms are caked in mud and sweat, and their rifles and rucksacks weigh a ton. Ahead they can see a small clearing. The sound of running water reaches their ears, refreshing, inviting. Néstor says he cannot go on, so he lies down and refuses to move.

"Please just leave me here. I'll be all right," he says.

Quirito and Alberto encourage him, "Come on, brother, just a few more steps."

"No. I can't. You carry on, please."

Quirito and Alberto plead again in vain. So they decide to carry Néstor.

Quirito teases him. "Up you get, you bloody priest," he says as he lifts him.

Néstor replies, "Be quiet, you Chilean, and give us back our coast."[11] They all laugh.

Néstor's arms are now resting on the shoulders of his friends, his body too heavy for his weakened comrades, his legs trailing on the ground.

They set him under the cool shade of a tree. "Are you OK, amigo?" Alberto asks him.

Néstor's eyes are half-closed; his chin is nearly touching his chest. "Hmm…yes…"

"You'd better stay here with Néstor while I fetch some water," Alberto says to Quirito.

Quirito becomes distraught. "I don't want to die," he cries. "Not like this."

"Don't give up hope, brother," Alberto says. "We'll all feel better after we've had a drink."

The air feels like molten lead. Alberto walks towards the stream, wiping his forehead constantly so that he can see where he's stepping.

When he returns from the stream, he finds Quirito sobbing. Néstor is dead.

Three years to the day after Che's death, and one day short of his twenty-fifth birthday, Néstor Paz has died of hunger.

Alberto bursts into tears. The two surviving guerrillas hug each other, read a passage from the Bible, and say a prayer for their dead friend. Then

---

11 Bolivia lost access to the Pacific Ocean during a war with Chile in 1879.

they drag his body and leave it beside the stream before continuing with their search for their comrades. Soon they will meet up with Omar's group.

On the last page of Néstor's journal, Néstor's cousin Omar writes,

Néstor Paz Zamora, "Francisco"
Died on October 8, 1970, at twelve noon.
Cousin: You have given me the greatest example of love for mankind.
Thank you.
Omar.

As a Marxist and a Christian, Néstor would become one of the heroes of the Latin American revolutionary movement and would inspire many people, young and old alike. His guerrilla journal, *My Life for My Friends*,[12] was translated into English and published by an American Catholic organisation, the Maryknoll. Later, the renowned Argentinean writer Julio Cortázar would also pay homage to Néstor in his book *Libro de Manuel*, portraying him as the committed guerrilla fighter who died of hunger.

Of the sixty-seven guerrillas that entered Teoponte, only nine survived, thanks to some villagers who hid them and sent a message to the newspapers in La Paz. Their fight had lasted less than three months. Comandante Chato and Alberto were two of the survivors.

It was several weeks now since Cecilia's disappearance. A few months before, my mother had decided to ban newspapers from our home and to replace the radio with a cassette player. My grandmother was not going to find out the awful truth.

---

12 Néstor Paz (1975), *My Life for My Friends*, New York, Orbis Books.

"Please don't talk about your cousins in front of Abuelita," my mother pleaded with me. "And your sisters mustn't hear about this, either."

Cecilia had again sent my mother a message via a contact from the ELN, asking for a few clothes and some money. She also asked for absolute secrecy. My mother, relieved to hear confirmation that my cousin was still hiding in a safe house in Cochabamba, was eager to help.

Abuelita's high blood pressure and the hardening of her arteries—atherosclerosis—made her life a misery. She spent most of her time in her room, either in bed or sitting on a chair, praying and reading the Bible, her mind becoming more and more confused.

She kept on asking, "Why haven't Cecilia and Néstor come to see me?"

"They were here only last week," my mother would say. "Don't you remember, Mamá?"

"Ah, yes, of course." And after a pause, "And what did they say? My memory...I can't remember much..."

One evening after I came back from my English lessons, I went downstairs to help with dinner. The sweet smell of empanadas filled the air. My mother was writing something and quickly hid what she was doing when I entered the kitchen. She then asked me to prepare a salad of olives, green apples and tomatoes.

After the meal Abuelita asked again, "Emma, when was the last time we heard from Cecilia? I'm getting worried."

"I have a surprise for you, Mamá," my mother said. "I wanted to give you this after you've had your medicines." She then took a letter from her pocket and read it aloud:

Dearest Abuelita:
Néstor and I are in Santiago, Chile. The scholarships for our postgraduate studies finally came through.
They're working us hard, these Chileans, but we love it.
Santiago is a very nice city, much bigger than La Paz and

much noisier. We've found accommodation in the centre of town, near the teaching hospital.
Will write some more soon. Néstor sends his love.
Hugs and kisses,
Cecilia

I couldn't believe my ears. My mother—a letter forger.

"Oh, that's lovely," Abuelita said. "But why didn't they come to say goodbye?"

My mother didn't lose her composure. "They had to leave in a hurry. Their course started right away."

"Oh!"

Abuelita fingered the black beads of her rosary and said, "I want to keep Cecilia's letters in my special tin."

The letter was put inside the round tin chocolate box with pink carnations on the lid, which Cecilia had given her and which she kept under her bed.

This would be the first of many letters to Abuelita.

I remember my mother trying hard to contain her tears when we saw the newspaper headlines in the street. Néstor and nearly all his companions were dead. I put my arm around her and gave her a handkerchief to dry her eyes. And we still had no news of Cecilia.

"Your grandmother mustn't hear a word about this," my mother said, blowing her nose.

I hugged her. I wanted to say something to comfort her, but the right words refused to come to my lips. Why did bad things have to happen to good people?

Life went on. I felt sick with worry about Cecilia's whereabouts but did not want anyone asking me anything about it. What we were going through was too painful, too embarrassing, too awful. I wanted to talk to Gloria and Jeanette about new lipsticks and eye shadow and the coming parties with the Saint George boys. I wanted to hear school gossip. Thank God neither the nuns nor any of my friends ever said anything about our ordeal.

April brought fantastic news: I had been accepted to go to America as an exchange student with the American Field Service! To celebrate, my mother gave me some money to take Gloria and Carolina for an ice cream in El Prado.

Back home, after kissing my mother and grandmother, I went up to my room to change. There a surprise awaited me.

"Mami! Mami!" I called. "Where have my clothes gone?"

My mother rushed upstairs. "Shh...don't let Abuelita hear you."

"What's going on?"

"I've had to give some of your clothes away. I'm sorry."

"You could've asked me first."

"There was no time."

"Who did you give them to?"

"I can't tell you."

I looked straight into my mother's eyes. "Is Cecilia in any trouble? What's going on?"

"Please, child, don't ask."

"I'm not a child! I'm sixteen!" I fought hard to contain my anger. "Mami, please. You can trust me."

"No, Mariana," my mother said firmly. "Don't ask any more. And don't let Abuelita worry about any of this. You'll get some new clothes soon, mi amor," she finished as she went downstairs.

But we didn't have any money for new clothes. I bit my lip and wiped away a few angry tears. I opened again the flowery cotton curtain of my makeshift wardrobe: three sweaters, two pairs of trousers, a skirt and a pair of shoes were missing. Thank God my only party dress had not disappeared.

Then I went and sat at my desk by the window and looked at the snow-capped mountains and our neighbour's small garden. The sun was about to set. The sky was tinted pink and purple. In a few weeks, I'd get on a plane with other Bolivian teenagers and travel to America.

California

August 1971–July 1972

Early in May a letter from my American host family, the Scharfs, arrived. Two teenage girls and a nine-year-old boy, the father a doctor, the mother an occupational therapist. Oh, and they lived in Pasadena, a rich suburb of Los Angeles. The elder girl, Jenny, sixteen like me, wrote that over there people used deodorants and shampoo.

Really.

I didn't know how to reply to that. I wanted us to have a good start. Maybe I would send them a photo of my family in our "civilized" clothes.

Abuelita and Mami had started crocheting the most beautiful pink suit for me, a skirt and jacket. I loved it, and everyone who saw it admired it. But I wondered whether it would be a bit too warm for California.

Three other Bolivian teenagers had also been chosen by the American Field Service to go to the United States: a girl from Tarija, a boy from Sucre, and a miner's son from Catavi, one of our most important mining centres. I was glad a boy from a humble family had been given this opportunity.

The week before my departure, I became a bag of nerves and was unable to concentrate on the simplest tasks. Luckily, Carolina helped me pack. I also caught a cold—the last thing I needed just before travelling. Two sweaters, two skirts, a dress, a pair of trousers, two blouses, pyjamas and underwear, as well as my toothbrush and a comb, plus photos and postcards from Bolivia, all went inside my tiny suitcase.

At El Alto Airport, I met my adventure companions. The boy from Sucre introduced himself as Marcelo Antonio Trigo Ramírez, sports journalist. His lips were thick and very red, his skin very pale. He was talkative and a bit nervous. He wanted to sit with me on the plane. When I told him I was born in Tarija, he said that he loved that town; he said he also loved La Paz; he said I looked like an intelligent and sweet girl; he talked nonstop. I did not dislike him, but I also wanted to speak to the other two.

"*Hola. Soy Mariana,*" I said to the boy from the mines.

"I'm Armando, but I've already been re-baptised Catavi," he replied. He had high Aymara cheekbones and copper skin. And a lovely smile.

"*Hola, me llamo Carmen,*" said the girl from Tarija. She was tall and pretty and had long wavy dark hair that reached to the middle of her back.

"Right, let's have a group photo," said one of the AFS organisers. *Click.* Four smiling, excited teenagers—unlike the parents, who were all tearful.

My mother and grandmother wiped their eyes. "Be careful. Be good. God bless you." My sisters hugged me hard; our maid squeezed my hand.

The plane took off. The scenery was spectacular: the snow-covered Andes against the blue sky and Lake Titicaca shimmering in the sun.

I still had the cold I had caught the week before. It had been just a common cold, and it was nearly gone, or so I thought. Now my throat was on fire, and my muscles ached. I was glad Marcelo Antonio Trigo Ramírez was doing most of the talking. As the plane climbed higher into the sky, my ears started to hurt. A lot. I called the stewardess and asked for a couple of aspirins but was told that they were not allowed to give out medicines. I fell asleep. Then a terrible pain woke me. Someone had stuck a needle inside my ear. I needed to see a doctor—soon.

We landed in Lima, the capital of Peru. The local AFS representatives, friendly and cheerful, were waiting for us. They bought me a packet of aspirins, and I swallowed a couple immediately. The centre of Lima was an attractive mixture of colonial and modern buildings but, as in La Paz, poor *barrios* clustered around the outskirts. In the afternoon we watched the changing of the guard in front of the presidential palace at the Plaza de Armas, the main square of the old town. For dinner we ordered *ceviche*, a typical Peruvian dish of raw fish marinated in lemon juice with boiled potatoes and chopped onions, at a cafeteria by the seaside. Raw fish! I didn't think I could swallow such a disgusting thing, but encouraged by the Peruvian guide, I tried some and found it delicious: the lemon, parsley, and onion flavours complemented the white flesh. We sat outside watching the Pacific Ocean roar and foam, big waves crashing hard against the rocks, the sunlight creating rainbows in the fine spray. I wished we still had a coastline; I wished Chile hadn't taken it away from us. It hurt to be landlocked.

The following day we flew to New York. During the flight the pain in my ear seemed worse than ever, and I was dizzy. As we disembarked, a blast of hot, humid summer air hit us, and I felt as if I were boiling in my crocheted pink cotton suit. The air was heavy, laden with traffic fumes. A bus drove us across town. I had seen plenty of tall buildings in La Paz but nothing like these sleek, elegant skyscrapers; and there were so many cars, so many people. We stayed at a university campus, empty of students now that it was summer. The college was as big as a small town, and we were given maps of the place. At dinnertime I was appalled by the hundreds of plastic cups, cutlery and plates that were used once and thrown in the bins. Why could they not have ordinary plates and reuse them? Cartons of milk and juice, snack boxes and fizzy-drink cans all went into the garbage. I had never seen such waste.

AFS students from all over the world had arrived at the college, each and every one of us excited about the big adventure ahead. That evening there was a party to wish us good luck before we embarked on flights to our different destinations. The girl from Tarija, Carmen, would be staying in Oregon, not too far from California. Marcelo Antonio and Catavi were staying with families on the East Coast. We said goodbye and promised to write to the others at least once a month, an unrealistic promise that none of us would keep.

On the flight to LA, the throbbing in my ear was agony. Maybe a vein had burst inside my head? I took a couple of aspirins and tried to sleep. I put the embroidered pink handkerchief my grandmother had given me to my left ear and dozed off. Soon a piercing pain woke me; the handkerchief was moist with a thin yellowish discharge.

I can't remember much about my arrival in Los Angeles or how my host family greeted me. The father, being a doctor, must have given me antibiotics and done his best to help me. But it was too late. My left eardrum had burst, and I could not hear a thing on that side. My host father said there was a small chance that my hearing might not return.

Two or three days after my arrival, I felt as if I were still flying, the buzz of the aeroplane loud inside my head, making me dizzy and nauseated. When I looked at the floor, it swayed like a boat on choppy waters. My stomach heaved. The ringing in my ears went away after a while, but the sick feeling stayed with me for several days. And I still could not hear anything in my left ear.

At night, in the darkness, the enormity of the metropolis of Los Angeles weighed on me. In La Paz I could visualise the whole of my city; I knew where I belonged. In California I was just an insignificant speck amid a huge mass of millions of people, millions of cars. How would I cope?

"Don't forget your tablets," Brenda, my host mother, said and smiled. She made a real effort to be kind and welcoming, and I will always be grateful to her for that. She wanted me to call her Mom, but I wasn't too sure about that, so I called her Brenda. Jenny, sixteen, smiled and laughed a lot, and I hoped we would become good friends. Unfortunately, she soon had to pack her bags to go to college, and I was left with her younger sister, Louise, who didn't seem to like me at all.

The smells here were different. Outside there was the fumes-laden brownish-grey smog and the oppressive, humid heat. Indoors the smell was sugary and soapy. The spout on the cold-water tap was like a mini-shower, the water coming out in hundreds and hundreds of bubbles. Brenda told me we didn't need to open the windows—that the air conditioning took care of everything. Inside they all wore summer clothes and walked barefoot, something I had never done before.

Louise made her dislike of me very obvious; among other things, she forbade me to wear my slippers in the house because they made a swishing sound against the linoleum. I felt intimidated and diminished in her presence but didn't stand up to her. How could I? I didn't want to argue with anybody; I wanted to be a good guest.

The family members were all tanned, especially the parents, whose skin had become leathery after so many years in the sun. They were all talkative and outgoing. The girls, especially Louise, often argued with their mother and answered back. Louise was particularly rude: "I hate you! I hate you!" This behaviour was shocking to me, as I could never dream of talking to an adult like that. Although I often felt my mother didn't understand me, as teenagers all over the world do, I did not openly defy her until much later. My mother had her feet firmly on the ground and had no time for my sentimentality and angst. I did lie to her, of course, and grumbled behind her back, but I could never contemplate screaming at her or slamming doors. Instead, I would go up to the roof terrace to vent my anger by punching the air and screaming abuse at passing birds.

The whole family seemed concerned that this girl from a third-world country might not be acquainted with the most basic hygiene. "This is a toilet. You must flush it every time you use it, like this," Brenda said. *Yes, Brenda, we have one of those at home,* I wanted to tell her, but said nothing. Later, Jenny informed me that they showered every day and that each person had his or her own towel. Did I need any deodorant? Any toothpaste? Did I know how to floss?

"And you look very nice, very American, in that dress," Brenda said.

I appreciated her buying me that summer dress, but I had similar ones back home.

And I was not American. I was Bolivian.

California was a culture shock, but not because I was awestruck by the wealth of America. What disturbed me was the way society functioned there. Apart from being rude to their parents, some teenagers talked openly about free love and contraception, and most seemed to do as they pleased. Coming from a convent school, for me, this was another planet—which didn't mean I was not curious about sex.

Several things made an indelible impression on my mind: the suffocating heat, the hum and coolness of the air conditioning, the smell of petrol fumes in the air, the thin blanket of smog visible on the horizon, the mountains of plastic garbage at the end of each school meal. At home in Pasadena, Mrs. Scharf cooked delicious dishes but rarely kept any leftovers. When I saw perfectly edible food discarded every day, I couldn't help thinking of the hungry children who sometimes fought with stray dogs for a piece of bread in the rubbish dumps near El Alto.

At school there were nearly two thousand students, compared with the few hundred in my convent school. People changed rooms at the end of every lesson. Back home, my thirty or so classmates and I had had our very own classroom, and it was the teachers who came to us—except when we went to chemistry and foreign-language classes. Suddenly, I was confronted by hordes of loud, pushy teenagers. There was no room in this environment for shy or nervous adolescents, who instantly became outsiders and were labelled as geeks and weirdos. I had never stammered in my life, but now I found myself unable to say what I wanted easily, and my English still needed developing. So there I was: timid, stuttering, blushing. Also, because my sense of balance had been affected by the burst eardrum, dizziness became a constant companion during those months, which seemed interminable. I didn't know it then, but as a consequence of that infection, I would remain deaf in my left ear for the rest of my life.

Who would have time for someone like me? Well, a soft-spoken American boy tried to befriend me, but it didn't work out, as I did not really like him. I made friends with a few other rejects and tried hard to see them outside lessons, but it was not easy. The school was too big, there were three different lunch-break slots, and I kept on getting lost. Lunchtimes were torture, and most of the time I sat by myself, shut out of the close-knit teenage cliques. As my English improved, I tried hard to participate during lessons; once or twice I was the only one who knew the answer or had done the homework, but, terrified of calling attention to myself, I kept quiet. On the odd occasion when I plucked up the courage to speak, my contribution to the debate passed unnoticed. But despite these difficulties, I kept on trying to make friends and kept smiling.

What was happening to me? I had come to America eager to experience a new culture and enjoy myself. Instead, my shyness and insecurity increased tenfold, and I retreated more and more into my shell. I worried that I might have some terrible mental illness and checked my host father's medical books several times when I was by myself in the house. Paranoia, schizophrenia, neurasthenia, lunacy—I seemed to have one or more symptoms of those terrible ailments. It never occurred to me that what I was going through was an exacerbated case of teenage angst and homesickness.

At home Louise continued her campaign against me, and although I felt furious with her and wanted to answer back, I never dared. I suspected her parents knew how badly she behaved, but neither they nor I said anything about it. Anyway, how could I come to America as a guest and then become a source of tension for my host family? The AFS understood that sometimes teenagers and their host families did not get along, in which case it was perfectly acceptable for the young person to continue the year with another family. But I did not want to do that. It would have meant admitting my failure, as I blamed myself totally for my predicament, and besides, I did not want to disappoint my mother. I also feared that my nervousness and insecurity would be incomprehensible to many of my family members, who took their importance for granted. To them, I would have deserved everything that had happened to me. Why was I such a wimp? Why did I not shout back? Why did I put up with the bullying?

Slowly, things improved at school, and I managed to make friends with a few girls as well as other AFS students from neighbouring areas. When the school year came to an end, several classmates wrote nice things about me in my yearbook, wished me good luck, and said that they'd miss me.

AFS wanted the exchange students to participate in as many school activities as possible, and I was encouraged to join the cheerleaders. There I was in the school gym, wearing a short green-and-yellow outfit, shaking pompoms, practising steps, jumping and shouting encouragement to the school's football players, and lining up to hug and kiss the sweaty players at the end of every football match. But I felt totally ridiculous, and after four months of this, I decided I'd had enough and informed the sports coach that I didn't want to do it anymore.

Latin Americans, especially Mexicans, were derided at school. All countries south of the border were, apparently, full of corrupt, lazy, ignorant, and dirty people. Opinions like this were bandied about openly, and the Mexican kids who happened to be around pretended they hadn't heard—but not always, and arguments erupted occasionally.

It must have been hard for my host parents, who, despite their best efforts, didn't know what to make of me—and I didn't know what to make of myself, either. I felt tense and self-conscious most of the time and also angry with myself for not being cool. I put on weight—six or seven kilos—and sought solace in chocolates and biscuits. I started writing my most private, anguished thoughts in a diary, such as how much I resented Louise and how nasty she was. As luck would have it, when the time came to return to La Paz, despite carefully packing everything else, I left my diary in Pasadena. A few months after returning to Bolivia, the letters from America stopped coming. I wonder if, after some time, my host family had begun to understand the awkward teenager who had lived at their house for nearly a year. I know they did their best and am grateful for all they gave me. In California I learnt a lot about the world and about myself. In time, I came to understand the Scharfs' younger daughter, her anger at having her world invaded by a strange girl, having to share her home and her parents, and having nothing in common to talk about.

During my year in America, I learnt that my country—like most developing countries—was invisible. "Bolivia? Never heard of it." "Is Bolivian a difficult language to learn?" "Does your family live in a mud hut?" "Do you have cars in Bolivia?" "Do you have electricity?" Apparently not. Outside the United States, the world was a jungle.

Sometimes I had to bite my tongue and contain my anger, such as during a civics lesson when a tall muscular boy wearing the school's green-and-yellow football sweatshirt said, "If those dirty wetbacks nationalise our companies, we should just burn the whole damn thing!" What did these kids know about the realities of life outside America? Not much, I suspected. I learnt that whether you are a person or a country, if you are not rich and powerful, you are a nobody. Might is right, and only the fittest survive. If you are small and quiet, the world treats you as insignificant, and if you get in the way, they brush you aside.

I was shocked at how arrogant and ignorant dominant cultures can be. One day my host parents took me to visit one of the big museums in Los Angeles—the history museum, perhaps? I was enjoying the exhibits when, to my disbelief, I saw, against a wall, a four-by-six-metre photograph of the Gate of the Sun in Tiwanaku, one of Bolivia's most precious and mysterious ruins from a civilisation that lived near Lake Titicaca centuries before the Incas. In big letters, the caption beside the exhibit said, "Tiwanaku, Peru."

"It's not in Peru!" I protested to my host father.

"Are you sure?" he said.

Of course I was sure. I had been to Tiwanaku several times with my family and on school excursions. Doctor Scharf suggested I write a letter to the museum, but I never did. Would they have listened to a girl from God knows what non-existent, backward country? Probably not. Years later, in England, the BBC refused to listen to my mature self when I wrote to complain that Potosi was in Bolivia, not Peru. Big countries are never wrong.

At the end of July, all the AFS students met in New York before flying back to our respective countries. The other three Bolivians, Catavi, Carmen and Marcelo Antonio Trigo Ramírez—the talkative one—and I were happy to see one another again. We all had incredibly exciting stories to tell, and all of us said that we'd had a fantastic year, but I wonder whether, like me, they were embellishing the truth. After arriving in La Paz, I never saw them again, as they all lived in other cities. I don't recall having a debriefing session with the local AFS—maybe there was one, but I cannot remember it.

I kept in touch by letter for about a year with several young people I had met in California—pen pals from Norway, Brazil, France and

Indonesia—but slowly, the letters became fewer and fewer as each one of us got on with our lives. My American adventure was well and truly over.

Although my year in California was not a happy one, it was useful. Good things came out of this challenging year abroad, and the difficult situations I encountered there made me stronger. I returned home speaking fluent English, with a better idea of what I wanted to do with my life and a determination to overcome my shyness. I also realised that although abroad was good and exciting, there were plenty of things that were wrong with it, and that made me appreciate my country even more.

The Debacle-2

W hile I was in California, Aunt Alcira trudged up and down the streets of La Paz every day, hoping to see her daughter. Where was Cecilia? Was she safe? How could they contact her? Alcira looked inside every window, peered behind every half-open door. Two or three times she even tapped a slim, long-haired girl on the shoulder. "Oh, sorry. I thought you were someone else," she would say.

Once, at the Aymara market, while Gerardo was loading ears of corn and potatoes into a basket, Alcira shouted, "There she is! There she is!" She had caught a glimpse of a fleeting figure that disappeared underneath a counter. She dropped her shopping bag and rushed to look behind the counter, but nobody was there.

"Come on, Mami. Let's go home," Gerardo said. "I'll make you a nice cup of tea."

Alcira was trembling, her gaze lost in the distance, her face as pale as the ghost she'd just seen.

As the situation was so delicate and Alcira wanted total privacy, the maid had been dispatched to work for a few months at a friend's house. When they got home, Gerardo warmed a tin of tomato soup and cut up some *Kollana* cheese and a loaf of wholemeal bread. "Mami, please eat something," he pleaded. This time Alcira ate everything that was put in front of her. She then went to bed and slept for two hours in the middle of the afternoon.

My aunt moved heaven and earth to contact the ELN. She wanted to talk to the urban section of the guerrilla movement to beg them to allow Cecilia to leave the organisation. Finally, one of their men agreed to a late-night meeting, and Alcira invited him to her house. A plump, short man with a thick Argentinean accent, a black felt hat pulled tightly on his head, came the following week.

"Don't switch on the courtyard lights," Alcira told Gerardo. "Our visitor will have to walk carefully. The kitchen light should be enough." As soon as the man entered the house, she closed the curtains.

Alcira greeted him and forced a smile. "Gerardo, get a cold drink from the fridge for this gentleman. If anyone comes looking for me, say I'm not in," she said.

"Hello there," the man said. Gerardo nodded. He brought the soft drink on a little tray, offered it to the stranger, set the tray on the coffee table, turned around, closed the sitting-room door, and went to his bedroom to listen to pop music and read his magazines. His mother had told him she needed to be alone with the man. She hadn't said who the man was, but Gerardo was no fool.

I really, really hope they let my sister go, Gerardo thought. One hour later Gerardo heard the man leave the house. "How did the meeting go, Mami?" he asked.

"You'll find out all in good time," my aunt replied.

Gerardo wished his mother were not so secretive; he knew she would feel much better if she confided in him and shared her worries. Alcira hardly slept or ate. But why did she have to shout at him all the time? He had to be extra patient with his mother. The tension in the house was palpable, and soon he started spending a lot of time in his room or at friends' houses.

The following Friday, his black felt hat tight on his head, the man came back at midnight. Gerardo waited in his room, listening to his records.

When he heard the sound of a car driving away, he rushed to the kitchen and asked, "Is my sister coming home?"

Alcira beamed at him. "They are letting her go, thank God."

Gerardo hugged his mother.

"She'll be home next week—next week!"

A dilapidated safe house in the Muyurina district of Cochabamba, at three in the morning, during the fourth week of March 1972.

Stucco peeling off the outside walls, overgrown grass and weeds on the lawn, a solitary skeletal black dog whimpering and sniffing around. Inside the apparently deserted house live six ELN supporters, three men and three women. Tonight only one of the men, Javier, is there, along with two of the women, Cecilia, and an Argentinean girl, Sol. It is Cecilia's turn to be the lookout. Javier and Sol are asleep.

A thin, pale slice of moon is in the sky. Cecilia has just entered the darkened kitchen at the back of the house to get a glass of water. She likes being by herself, which is difficult under the present cramped circumstances, but she tries to steal a few minutes' solitude as often as she can. She fills her glass and drinks the liquid eagerly. When she finishes, she caresses the rim of the glass while the memories of her life with Néstor fill her mind. It has been nearly eighteen months since his death, but his absence will always be a raw wound. Often she wishes death would claim her, but she has promised her husband to keep on fighting to the bitter end and cannot afford to feel sorry for herself. She misses his touch, his kisses, his words of encouragement; she misses the prayers they said together, the plans they used to make for their future; she misses singing with him while he played the guitar. His mind and hers had been so perfectly synchronised, and he had known her so intimately that she found it was not necessary to tell him what she wanted—he guessed her wishes even before she herself became aware of them. He had told her that if he died, he didn't want her to mourn him for too long, and he had made her promise not to spend the rest of her life alone. She has kept her promise, and now there is a new man in her life, an ELN comrade. But how could Néstor have thought that he could be replaced so easily? It is madness; it is impossible. Life without him is empty and meaningless. Her new companion is a nice, decent man, but she will never feel for him what she felt for her husband.

She hardly cries these days. But earlier this evening she cried bitterly, as did Sol, after one of the men reprimanded them severely for a minor error. She opens the tap and fills her glass again. As she drinks, she becomes aware of a strange sound like the rustling and crunching of leaves. But there are no fallen leaves on the ground at the moment. Carefully, silently, she opens the cupboard where she keeps her gun in a corner of the kitchen. She enters the yard and hides behind the laundry sink. Someone or something is trying to climb over the yard wall; someone is breathing heavily, pushing and shoving against the wall. In an instant Cecilia realises she and her comrades have been betrayed. She knows the soldiers are just outside the yard. She knows they have come to take her. But she will not allow them to take her alive. She ducks down and runs along the length of the wall, brandishing her gun. She opens fire.

Javier and Sol are there now, with their guns. Dazzling red-and-orange fireworks streak the night shadows. The smell and noise of the explosions fill the air. A cry is heard. Cecilia has been shot dead. The soldiers quickly overpower the other two guerrillas.

I am grateful Cecilia died quickly. I am grateful she did not have to endure torture as her companions did. After a year of torment, Javier managed to escape, only to die a few weeks later at the hands of his pursuers. The Argentinean woman, Sol, was savagely tortured, her naked body pierced by needles and tied to a block of ice until her heart stopped. Cecilia was lucky to escape that brutality.

The criminals who committed these evil acts were never punished.

During the last days of March 1972, while I was in California, the following events were taking place in La Paz:

Aunt Alcira told my mother about her successful meeting with the ELN contact. The sisters cried and laughed nervously, and for the first time in many years, they hugged each other. It didn't much matter now that they didn't like each other so much; what mattered was that Cecilia was coming back.

My mother thought it was quite safe to allow the daily news into the house again. Every morning she would bring a breakfast tray and the newspaper to Abuelita. One morning, my mother was in the kitchen when the phone rang.

Our next-door neighbour said, "Emma, have you seen the front page of the paper?"

"What is it?" my mother asked.

"Cecilia has been murdered!"

My mother dropped the receiver and shot upstairs to Abuelita's room on the third floor. Abuelita was about to start her breakfast and hadn't opened the newspaper yet. My mother grabbed the paper and fled the room.

"What are you doing, Emma?" Abuelita protested.

"Just a minute, Mamá. I want to cut out a voucher," she replied as she went downstairs, wiping her tears.

Once again, newspapers were not allowed in our home. Once again, the radio set disappeared and was replaced by a cassette player.

I returned to Bolivia from California in July 1972. From the plane I caught a glimpse of the serene blue waters of Lake Titicaca and the peaks of the Andes. My younger sister Carolina had made a banner that said, "*Bienvenida*, Marianita." But who was that tall, skinny young girl with long black hair waving her hands frantically? It was Teresa, my baby sister, now nearly ten. My mother looked ill, which worried me, but she said she was feeling just fine. Abuelita had not come to the airport because of her health.

A couple of days later, my mother called me to the kitchen to tell me that she had bad news, just as I had guessed. She was not herself: her smile was gone, she was pale, and she kept on sighing loudly. I made my mother a cup of tea, and she sipped her drink slowly before she spoke.

"Cecilia has been murdered," she said as a tear rolled down her cheek.

I sucked in my breath, not believing what I was hearing.

"Your grandmother knows nothing about this," she continued, "and we must carry on with the pretence."

I was devastated. My lovely, sweet cousin. Murdered.

I wanted to find out how and why it had happened, but my mother was unable to speak any more about it that day. She went to bed for a lie-down and asked me to bring her a glass of water and a couple of aspirins. The following morning, however, her need to unburden herself was too great, and she continued with her account.

Cecilia's body was brought back to La Paz in a small military-transport plane, and my mother and Aunt Alcira went to El Alto Airport to receive her. Uncle Eitel—Alcira's first husband and Cecilia's father—arrived from Santa Cruz.

Uncle Fernando—my aunt's second husband—and Néstor's brother Mario identified Cecilia's body before it was transported to the cemetery. After that things happened very quickly.

"It was an icy morning, with big dark clouds," my mother said. "Cecilia's body arrived in El Alto in a cheap coarse pine coffin. The newspapers had sent photographers and reporters, but they were not allowed in. 'She's a common criminal,' one of the government agents said to the press. 'No photos.' I felt my insides burning and wanted to slap that man's face but had to control myself."

After a short pause, my mother continued. "Your aunt Alcira was like a zombie. I don't know how she was able to walk. She signed some papers and gave them to an arrogant general who had a look of disgust on his face. Then the agents put the coffin inside your aunt's van, and everybody headed towards the cemetery. Your aunt and I got in her car. Alcira drove the van herself. Can you believe it, Mariana? She drove the van with her daughter's dead body inside it."

My mother blew her nose. "At the cemetery we were surrounded by government agents. Apart from the immediate family, nobody else was allowed to be present. We all had bloodshot eyes from so much crying.

Eitel, Fernando and Alcira seemed to have aged twenty years. Remember what an acrimonious divorce Eitel and Alcira had? Well, here they leaned on each other's arms and wiped each other's tears. My heart was breaking, but compared with your aunt's suffering, my pain was nothing. And then I thought bitterly how things had not changed, how the poor peasants were still poor peasants, Bánzer was an even harsher dictator, and Cecilia and Néstor had sacrificed their lives in vain. A couple of agents pushed the coffin inside the *nicho*[13] and then sealed it with wet cement. No flowers, no prayers for our girl."

My mother's lips and hands were trembling as she finished her account. "The agents then said, 'Everybody leave! It's over! Move! Move!' and signalled us towards the exit. Alcira's knees gave way. Eitel and Fernando had to support her to stop her from falling, but they themselves looked as if they would faint at any minute. 'No!,' I shouted, 'this girl has a name!' and, pushing the agent aside with my elbow, I wrote on the moist surface with the tip of an old pencil, 'Cecilia.'"

Too many things reminded us of my cousins' terrible deaths and their short young lives. My mother even stopped baking the empanadas and alfajores that Cecilia and Néstor loved. It was hard for my mother, but I could not begin to imagine what it must have been like for my aunt. After shutting herself in her house for a week, Alcira buried herself in work and refused to talk about her feelings with anyone. Immediately after Cecilia's burial, Gerardo went to stay with a relation of his father's for a while.

My mother spent her days wiping her tears. While she went about her domestic chores, loud sighs like the moans of an animal in pain would come from deep within her body. I felt extremely sorry for her, but her constant sighing irritated me. My irritation soon turned into guilt and self-disgust. Maybe I was an unfeeling, selfish girl; maybe my heart was made of stone.

---

13 Hispanic cemeteries have a system where a coffin is inserted in a recess, or niche (*nicho*), rather than buried in the ground.

Dictators

I remember being caught in a demonstration, my eyes streaming, my lungs stinging. I remember the nausea, the acrid taste. I remember bursting into a cake shop and slamming the door shut and the lady at the counter offering me a soaked handkerchief against the tear gas.

I remember rushing home as fast as my legs could carry me, wondering if my sisters and mother were safe. I remember later hearing about the water cannons and the injured students and the following day seeing the cobblestones and pavement slabs near the university torn from the ground to make barricades against the army.

I remember General Miranda overthrowing the government of General Ovando, only to be overthrown a few days later by General Tórres. I remember jets flying over the city, their machine guns spitting fire, and my mother telling us to quickly, quickly put our mattresses against the windows and lie flat under the beds. I remember the accelerated pulse, the cold sweat, the dry tongue.

And when it was all over, all of us citizens of La Paz picked ourselves up and carried on.

Bigger evil was let loose in August 1971, when General Bánzer came to power in his bloody coup. But I do not remember that. Away in California, I was unaware of what was happening in my country.

General Bánzer's seven years of butchery and suffering—we all remember that.

My Last Years in Bolivia

August 1972

And so I resumed my life in La Paz. My year in California soon seemed like a dream, and the shyness and insecurity I had felt there quickly disappeared and gave way to a more confident me. I went back to my pre-California weight without much effort—now that I was happier, I didn't need food to comfort me. While in California I had not attended church much. Now that I was back in La Paz, I decided to skip Sunday Mass altogether and instead just met up with my friends in El Prado for salteñas and the usual promenade. Slowly, God was becoming less and less important in my life. Try as I might, I could not understand how he could allow all those terrible things to happen in the world.

I had five months of freedom before the start of the academic year, in January. I liked both humanities and science, but now I had to make a choice. Wouldn't it be wonderful if I became a respected scientist, like Marie Curie? After much consideration I decided to study chemical engineering. My mother, as usual, brimmed with pride at my decision to study hard science.

While waiting for university to start, I read books and did a secretarial course. Early one November morning, I found myself queuing with hundreds of young people at the enrolment offices of Universidad Mayor de San Andrés, the state university of La Paz. Until the 1960s, when new office and apartment blocks began sprouting all over the city, the San Andrés skyscraper had been the tallest building in our capital. At that time, apart from a small enrolment fee, university was free to all Bolivians. Most of the students were white and middle-class, from private schools. There were also some cholos from state schools and, surprisingly, a few Aymara and Quechua Indians.

That morning the air was heavy with the smells of sweaty armpits, greasy hair and stale socks. Three young white men standing behind me stuck their noses up in the air and, looking with disdain at the two Indian students queuing in front of me, sniggered and commented out loud, "What a pong!"

"Why do *they* want to come here, anyway?"

"Don't worry—they won't last a month."

"Don't they know university is for clever people?"

From the corner of my eye, I glanced at the copper-skinned youths. Dressed in cheap hand-knitted sweaters, polyester trousers and threadbare jackets, they stood erect, their faces like stone, their fists on their chests clutching their documents, deaf to the insults. I don't know if other students were as embarrassed as I was, but nobody said anything. I was glad that our Indians were at last attending university. They would face much greater challenges in their studies than the rest of us and would enjoy none of the advantages we had, like a proper roof over our heads and a hot meal at least once a day. Silently, I wished them good luck. A few years later, some of those Indians would graduate as lawyers, doctors and architects, but they would still face discrimination for decades to come.

Lectures took place in huge ground-floor classrooms that held two or three hundred seats. The acoustics were bad, so nobody dared even cough while the lectures took place. Smaller groups were taught in classrooms on the tenth or twelfth floor. Often the lifts were broken and we had to clamber up stairwells, our legs aching. The toilets stank, so I went without soft drinks or coffee while on campus. But despite these minor inconveniences, I loved being there and worked hard to keep up with the demands of our teachers.

There were only three female students—two other girls and me—in a class of ninety-four in the first year of engineering studies. The boys did not seem to object to us being there, and they treated us well. After lectures I hung out with my classmates, often going for salteñas and Cokes in the cafeterias in El Prado. My mother, full of contradictions as ever, worried that I was spending too much time with the cholo students. Although she was glad that our native people were at long last allowed into our universities, she did not want me socialising with them. "Be careful, Marianita," she would say. "These cholos are not like us. They envy what we have and will take advantage of you as soon as they can." I would listen to my mother's refrain and nod in agreement, but I had no intention of dropping my new friends.

My country was still under military rule and still recovering from the trauma of the guerrilla insurrections of recent years. An unstable political situation meant unstable universities, which were among the first places the dictatorship sent its troops to repress dissent. My family was also struggling to survive. In California I had enjoyed a break from my mother's worries and laments. Since my return, she was again speaking in hushed tones to my grandmother about our precarious finances. Again she was wondering how we would reach the end of the month. And I started questioning whether becoming a top scientist under the present circumstances was a realistic possibility. Tense and unhappy, she would jump out of her skin at the slightest noise. I couldn't remember the last time she had bought herself a good pair of shoes or warm trousers. She wore her shabbiest clothes at home, with a blanket wrapped around her hips, two or three pairs of thick socks, and an old woolly hat on her head. In autumn and winter, we all shivered but never as much as our mother. She had been wanting to buy a second electric heater, but other, more pressing necessities had taken priority. The one heater we had was always kept by Abuelita's side; otherwise, we wore several layers of clothing.

On two or three occasions during my first year at university, the students staged protests against the government. Their requests were ignored, so they removed the paving stones from the road, causing major disruption. Soon we had soldiers, barricades, tear gas, violence. The threat of closure hung over the universities once more, and then classes were suspended for several weeks. It had been this way for years. While the military fought for power, we Bolivians endured suffering and disruption.

One afternoon, after I came back from my lectures at San Andrés, my mother called me to sit with her in the kitchen. We were drinking hot chocolate when, out of the blue, she asked me, "Did I tell you that your cousin Rosita also got into trouble?"

Rosita, Uncle Silvio's daughter, her chapped cheeks full of freckles, serious and studious, playing cards with me at my aunt's school. I hadn't seen her or even thought of her for years.

"She's in the Achocalla prison," my mother said, "accused of being a left-wing dissenter."

Achocalla was a name that brought back pleasant childhood memories. Achocalla, where I'd had many picnics and adventures with my primary-school friends; where the air smelled of fresh grass and burnt wood from the barbecues our teachers used to prepare; where I once "rescued" a little fish from a drying pond, filled one of my shoes with water and put the fish inside it—with disastrous results for both fish and shoe. Achocalla was now a place of infamy, a place of fear and pain, where prisoners were raped and beaten; where, during a never-ending night, Rosita heard the horrific cries of agony of a comrade tortured to death in the cell next door; and where a new-born baby was taken from its ELN-supporting mother and given to a military couple.

"The father of one of the girls at your school, a colonel in the army, is responsible for several of the disappearances and murders," my mother said.

"What's going to happen to Rosita, Mami?"

"Your aunt Alcira and I will get her out of there. I promise you that."

The day was cold and overcast. Aunt Alcira, my mother and I were at the departures lounge of El Alto Airport. Rosita had been freed after my mother and Aunt Alcira had begged a government minister, on their knees, to release her from prison. Their wish was granted but under the condition that Rosita go as far away from Bolivia as possible. Luckily, an acquaintance of Aunt Alcira's was living in Canada, and this person agreed to provide Rosita with food and lodging for the first few months. Imprisoned in appalling conditions for being a left-wing student, my cousin had witnessed and endured unspeakable abuse and was now being expelled like a common criminal. Others were not so lucky, as some of her companions would be tortured to death, while others would remain in prison for many more months.

When we saw Rosita, my mother and I tried hard to disguise our shock. After so many months in Achocalla, she looked like a ghost, her body thin and malnourished, her face pale and unsmiling, her eyes empty, her hair lank. My mother tried to hug her, but Rosita was unresponsive and stood there like a statue, tightly holding on to the pockets of an old cardigan my aunt had given her, saying nothing. She had been taken directly from her cell to the airport, in an unmarked police van, with only the clothes she was wearing. After much bargaining and pleading, the government agents had allowed her to change her clothes inside the van. Aunt Alcira had been allowed to enter the vehicle and had tried to give as much advice as she could to Rosita. "Make sure you dress warm. Canada is a freezing place. Wear thick boots, furry hats, earmuffs, long woollen tights." In her confusion, Rosita refused to believe that anyone could live in such glacial conditions and looked at Aunt Alcira as if she were crazy.

It was now time to go. Rosita, her face expressionless, boarded the plane, carrying the small suitcase that Aunt Alcira had prepared for her, and which contained only a few old clothes and a toiletries bag. Her destination was an alien place thousands of miles away. Another planet. But Rosita's story is not mine to tell. She has written a few pages about her life; maybe one day she'll write more.

No, it's not fair that Rosita is forced to leave our country, I thought. She was only nineteen, two years older than me. What would become of her? How would she cope? I smiled stupidly and, searching for the right words to comfort my cousin, only managed, "Don't worry; everything will be fine." She did not reply, and I was unable to read her blank face.

After Rosita was put on that plane bound for Quebec, I lost touch with her. I heard that she lived with Aunt Alcira for a while (my aunt and Gerardo would soon leave Bolivia and stay in Canada for several years) and that later she moved out to study and live independently. Slowly, my memory of her receded to the back of my mind. As the years passed, I sometimes asked my mother for news of Rosita, and she would tell me that my cousin was living with a partner, had two daughters, and was working as a lecturer at Montreal University. All good news, but of her emotional well-being I knew nothing. Several times I thought of asking Aunt Alcira for Rosita's address and writing to her, but I never did.

In years to come, I sometimes wondered whether I too would have joined the fight for justice if I had been just a little older and had not gone to California. In years to come, especially when my daughter, Olivia, was in her late teens, I would think of Rosita with extreme sadness and remember how she once was subjected to horror, degradation and exile at such a young age.

One of our most repressive right-wing dictators, General Hugo Bánzer, came to power via a bloody coup in 1971, bent on purging Bolivia of troublemakers. Liberation theology priests who had supported the ELN were expelled from the country. Aunt Alcira, who had never been involved in politics but happened to be related to two of these troublemakers, was made to pay for their crimes. Bánzer soon decreed that she could no longer work as a teacher, and she wasn't allowed to write any more academic books. Alcira then decided to leave Bolivia for good.

Alcira and Gerardo came to my house to say goodbye. She no longer looked like the proud, competent and forbidding professional woman of yesteryear. The farewell was a restrained affair, with only a few hugs and no tears. My aunt had said that none of us should give *them* the satisfaction of our crying, so we didn't, although my mother would later weep alone in the bathroom.

"We're *never* coming back," Gerardo said, grinding his teeth.

The words stuck in my throat. "Good luck" was all I managed to mumble.

"Take care of yourselves and write soon," my mother said as she waved from the front door, her lips quivering, her throat tight.

Several years later, when Bánzer was no longer in power, Alcira and Gerardo returned to Bolivia. "This is where we belong," my aunt said. "This is where we're staying." She went back to teaching and writing. And she bought herself another school.

Gerardo and I did not talk about our family's ordeal for many years, pretending that it had never happened. Finally, in our fifties, we spoke about it for the first time.

But I never dared speak to my aunt about her most dreadful loss.

Every morning we woke up to the sound of birds chirruping and celebrating life. Spring was in the air, the sky outside my grandmother's window was deep blue, and the white and red carnations on her window ledge were blossoming in their pots.

September of 1973 was a shameful month in the history of Latin America. General Pinochet, with the help of the CIA, had just deposed the democratically-elected socialist president of Chile, Salvador Allende, unleashing a period of state terror and murder. Pinochet was good news for our own dictator, Bánzer, and the two of them would collaborate in getting rid of "troublemakers."

The situation in Bolivia was also tense. Political opponents were still being imprisoned, held without trial, tortured and disappeared under the auspices of Plan Condor, a campaign of political repression and terror developed by the CIA to eradicate Marxism in Latin America. In years to come, we would learn that tens of thousands in Uruguay, Paraguay, Brazil, Bolivia, Chile and Argentina had paid with their lives for their political views, the repression being especially vicious in the latter two countries.

My grandmother's mind was more confused than ever, and her heart and atherosclerosis seemed to be worsening by the day. My mother insisted on sleeping in the same room as Abuelita, even though this meant that her own sleep was disrupted most nights.

My sisters, my mother and I took turns looking after Abuelita, but there were a few hours during the day when the only person available to look after her was Pancha, our maid, who could not always reach my grandmother in time. Abuelita would by then be in tears; she had probably wet or soiled herself, spilt her beaker of juice on her clothes, or lost her reading glasses under the bed. Or her bones were aching. It was humiliating enough to be fed and dressed by other people, but having to wait for someone to alleviate her pain must have been intolerable. "Dear Lord, don't abandon me in my final hour," she often said.

As for me, I had not set foot inside a church for at least a year.

My mother was struggling to pay the doctor's fees. Anyway, he had said there wasn't much he could do for my grandmother. When the money ran out, my mother borrowed from her friends, determined to fight the illness to the end. She hired a nurse to give Abuelita her daily injections and help us with her care.

"How can you afford this, Mami?" I asked. "You are two months behind with my sisters' school fees…the doctor has told you there's nothing he can do, and—"

"Let me worry about that," she replied bluntly.

Nurse Catalina came highly recommended. The plump, grey-haired woman with a starched cream uniform soon made herself at home and set up a care routine. My mother could only afford two hours of the nurse's time in the morning and one in the evening.

Having this stranger in her life greatly exacerbated my grandmother's confusion. "I don't want that prostitute poking and prodding me."

"Abuelita!" I held my grandmother's hand, looked into her eyes, and, just as my mother had done two years before, lied, "Don't you know that she's a nun?"

"A nun, you say?"

"Yes. She's one of those who go out into the community to help others."

"Oh! I'm sorry. Where's her convent?"

I didn't lose my cool. "In Sopocachi."

My grandmother smiled and squeezed my hand.

One afternoon, after having tea with Gloria, I came home and found my mother crying inconsolably in the kitchen. "Why can't she find peace?" she said. "She fears God will never forgive her."

Once again, I wondered what my grandmother's terrible secret might be. Once again, I cursed fate for making her suffer like this.

I went upstairs to my grandmother's room, kissed her, sat by her bed, and started reading her a short story from one of the many books that Cecilia had given her.

After a few minutes, she interrupted me. "It must be three years since we last saw Cecilia and Néstor."

"No, Abuelita, it's only a year," I lied again.

"Are they still studying in Chile?"

"Yes, Abuelita."

"Ah...I miss them. Can you please read me Cecilia's last letter?"

I reached under her bed and pulled out her round chocolate box with pink carnations on the lid, in which she kept her precious things. Inside, dozens of letters from Cecilia—my mother's forgeries—were neatly folded.

"Gracias," she said when I finished reading. Then she clutched her black rosary to her chest and added, "I'm very tired."

She closed her eyes and went to sleep. I kissed her forehead softly.

"Buenas noches, Abuelita."

I looked out of the window and saw Mount Illimani, its glacial snow glinting and shimmering, majestic; and it seemed for a moment that this silent, ancient witness to our history was spreading wide open its three peaks, embracing my city.

Later, my mother's anguished howls would be heard from across the street.

My grandmother died without receiving the last rites, with no priest to comfort her and absolve her of the sins she thought she had committed. But I knew her faults had been forgiven long ago and that she was now, at last, resting in peace.

To keep "agitators" out, the government kept on closing the universities, reopening them, and closing them again. Continuing with my engineering studies at San Andrés University became difficult. I was angry and disappointed. What would I do with my life now? All this time, apart from working at her part-time jobs, my mother had continued baking cakes and biscuits for the nearby offices. She had also recently started, with some success, a small business selling knitted alpaca shawls and sweaters for ladies, but the economic situation at home was still difficult. I couldn't bear to see her so anxious and exhausted. So I decided to leave university, for the time being, and looked for a job. However, I was determined not to abandon learning altogether and promised myself to study and read as much as possible at home, during the evenings. As I was fluent in English and had secretarial qualifications, I soon found employment at the Foreign Transactions Department of Banco Mercantil.

The bank was housed in one of the elegant buildings in the city centre, with high columns, elongated windows, and a wide stone staircase leading up to its thick front doors with brass knockers. The working day was long, from eight-thirty in the morning to six-thirty in the evening, with a two-hour break for lunch—far too long for my liking. At four o'clock every afternoon, a teenage boy brought sweet tea with bread and jam to our desks—afternoon tea, Bolivian-style. My colleagues treated me well from the beginning, and soon I felt as if I had always worked at the bank. Receiving my first pay packet was wonderful, and giving the entire amount to my mother was even better. I was nineteen and felt on top of the world.

My mother and I had again been invited to have Sunday lunch with her new friends, the Loperas, an Ecuadorian couple she had met a few months before. Señora Lopera, especially, seemed to adore my mother, and the two of them had developed a strong friendship.

I didn't fancy spending yet another boring Sunday afternoon in the company of middle-aged people. The Loperas were kind enough, but I didn't have much to say to them, so I told my mother I didn't want to go.

"But this is going to be a special occasion," my mother said. "Their son has just arrived from Italy, and he'd like to meet you. It'd be rude not to come."

I moaned and complained some more, but my mother was having none of it. "Don't be so stubborn," she added. "I'm sure you'll find plenty to talk about with the young man. Swap stories about California and Italy, for a start."

Unable to object any longer, I resigned myself to spending an afternoon making small talk with a nervous, socially inept and ugly boy.

The following Sunday I found myself sitting in the Loperas' living-room, drinking iced Coca-Cola and nibbling crisps before lunch. The Loperas were wealthy businesspeople and lived in one of the most exclusive residential areas of La Paz, Calacoto. Unlike most houses in Bolivia, theirs had central heating, deep-pile carpets in every room, en-suite bathrooms and walk-in wardrobes.

From their brown skin, it was obvious that the Loperas had Quechua blood. They were educated, articulate and rich. And they were foreign. Which was why, despite their looks, they had been accepted into the high society of Bolivia—unlike our own Quechua and Aymara Indians, who found it nearly impossible to climb the social ladder.

I was sitting by the French windows admiring the azaleas in the garden, the midday sun warming my legs, when an olive-skinned young Adonis with high cheekbones and dark eyes walked in. He was just as I had always imagined an Inca prince would look.

First he kissed his parents and paid his respects to my mother. Then he turned his attention to me.

"Nice to meet you, Mariana," he said and kissed my cheek.

I was so glad my mother had persuaded me to attend this Sunday lunch.

Once the meal was over, Javier took me on a tour of the garden. He told me a little about himself, and I learnt that he had just finished his accountancy studies in Milan and was now thinking of helping his father run their business in La Paz. "I would very much like to see you again," he said, which was exactly what I was hoping he would say.

And so we started dating, to my mother's—and his parents'—great joy. Three or four times a week, he would come to my house to collect me in his royal-blue Mercedes to go to the cinema, a discotheque, or a restaurant. Never in my life had I gone out so much, and I found it quite exhausting. Being with him was the best thing in my life, but I didn't want to neglect my studies. I was determined to go back to university as soon as I could and did my best to read and revise late in the evenings. We also spent many hours at his house listening to the latest British and American pop songs. I know it sounds odd, but Paul McCartney and Wings' "Band on the Run" will always remind me of La Paz.

Despite being a little shorter than me, Javier's physical presence was imposing. I loved his sinewy forearms, big hands and long fingers. I spent hours just looking at his beautiful face, slowly running the tips of my fingers along his slender lips and thick dark eyebrows. He was six years older than me and so much more worldly-wise. He wore Italian-designed clothes that matched his skin tone. Brown was not a colour I liked, but he looked gorgeous in his stylish russet suits.

One afternoon when I returned home after watching a film with Javier, I found my mother with a serious face. "Señora Lopera has just told me that Javier has a girlfriend in Italy. Did you know about that?"

No, of course I didn't. So the next time he came to see me, I asked him about the girl.

"Don't worry about that, my little princess," he said. "She's just a girl I used to go out with in Milan, very clingy and very needy. She still thinks we're together."

"And are you?" I asked him.

"No. I'm finished with her. The only girl for me now is you. Don't you ever doubt it."

If he said I was his everything, I had to believe it.

I remember standing in front of one of the new skyscrapers in El Prado, a dark, emerald-green one, and raising my eyes to the eleventh floor, where Javier worked. "I hope you're having a lovely day, Javier," I said to myself and sighed, before continuing on my way to my job at the bank.

The weekend before, he and I had had dinner by ourselves at his house. A couple of logs had crackled in the fireplace in his lounge, the red embers glowing in the semi-darkness, the air sweet with the smell of eucalyptus smoke. Javier had held a crystal tumbler full of whisky and soda, two ice cubes floating in the liquid, clinking against the glass. "Won't you try even a little?" he asked. I hated alcohol, so he poured me a fizzy drink instead. "You are the best girl in the world," he said. "I want to be with you forever." How sweet his words were and how innocent and silly I was.

Javier and I dated for several months. His parents and my mother were pleased and probably hoped that, sooner rather than later, Javier and I would get married. But I had many other things I wanted to do with my life before marrying anyone. The thought of ending up surrounded by children, devoting my life to looking after my husband, and spending long afternoons playing cards with other señoras filled me with dread. Books and learning were important to me, and so was travelling. No, I didn't want to get married, not for several years. And yet if Javier proposed, I suspected I would probably say yes. When I was with him, I felt happy, but I also sensed that he wanted to dominate me. As soon as I was alone, my desire to be free of any ties returned. Javier said he was a modern man and respected women, but he had hinted that as a husband he expected to have the final say in all matters. To him, my studies and ambitions were nice hobbies that helped me pass the time. What was the use of learning history, philosophy and science? He would much rather I learnt practical things like accountancy and the running of a business, which I found dreadfully boring. Still, infatuated with each other, we chose not to discuss these things too deeply. And I also chose to ignore the warning signs.

I had been working at the bank for about fourteen months when, one evening, as I arrived home from work, my mother greeted me with a bigger smile than usual. "I've a proposal for you, Marianita," she said, "something wonderful for your future."

I looked at her, wondering what new far-fetched plan she had hatched.

"How would you like to go to Switzerland to study?" she asked me.

Here we go again, I thought. More impossible dreams.

"Don't open your eyes so big. You look like a baby cow," my mother said. "Let me explain. Your cousin Silvia is suggesting you study in Geneva. She says you can live with her for the first few months, and then she'll help you find cheap student accommodation."

My cousin Silvia was intelligent and ambitious, and she had itchy feet. She had not remained long in Bolivia after her return from the United States and had gone to Geneva to study at the School of Interpreters. She had finished her studies and was now living in Switzerland and working as an interpreter at the United Nations. Two weeks earlier she had arrived in La Paz on holiday, and I had seen her a couple of times at family meals. Without my knowing it—so as not to raise my hopes in vain—she had suggested to my mother that I, too, should study languages at the School of Interpreters.

What a wonderful and generous suggestion, I thought. But...how could I contemplate leaving my mother to struggle alone? Studying in Europe? Preposterous!

"I haven't told you how well my alpaca fashion business is doing, have I?" my mother continued. "I have been putting some money aside for several months now."

I was amazed. And extremely pleased. At long last, things were starting to go well for my mother. But why the secrecy? Before I could ask her, she read the enquiry in my eyes.

"I want my daughters to go to university, to have careers. I don't want them to depend on men…You, as the eldest child, will be the first to succeed. Then your sisters will follow." She had tears in her eyes when she finished.

I put my arms around her shoulders. I was amazed. My mother—secretly saving for months, making sacrifices for me. "No, Mami," I said as I handed her a handkerchief. "It's too much to ask of you." And indeed it was a crazy thing to contemplate. How could she think I would agree to such an enormous expense? "I can always go back to studying at San Andrés; you know that."

She became annoyed. "Don't talk nonsense. You *are* going, and that's that. We cannot waste this opportunity."

My cousin's kind offer was indeed hard to ignore. A new life, a wonderful and exciting opportunity, lay ahead. Europe, its old civilisation, and its ancient seats of learning were opening their doors to me. But that meant leaving my mother and sisters, leaving my country, and leaving Javier. What on earth should I do?

"But what about my French?" I said. "It's not good enough."

"You are good at languages. You were fluent in English after just two months in the United States, weren't you? This afternoon you can go with Carolina and enrol at the Alliance Française for advanced intensive lessons."

And so we started making plans for my departure. My brave, resourceful, entrepreneurial mother was determined to give me, her eldest daughter, a better future, no matter what the cost to herself. She now confessed to me that, without my knowing it, she had taken out a bank loan to pay for my first year of studies and the air ticket to Switzerland, a fortune for a single parent from a developing country. Later she would find a way of paying for the other three years of studies. For the time being, she was desperate to grab this wonderful opportunity.

I fully believed her when she said that the money she had been saving would be enough to pay for my course and that she had the means to repay the bank loan without too much trouble. How could I have been so naive? My only excuse is that I was young and extremely excited at the prospect of going to study in Europe.

My mother, wisely, had kept an open mind about Javier. Having a good-looking boyfriend was fine, but studying in Europe was more important, especially if the said boyfriend was so indecisive. Soon she heard from Javier's own parents that his Italian girlfriend was coming to La Paz. Of course he had not mentioned this important news to me. I was furious. He was a liar and a cheat. Maybe going to study abroad was the best thing for me.

But the next time Javier and I went to the Montículo Park to look at the views of La Paz, my anger evaporated. Javier parked his car just outside the park's *mirador*, an open balcony on the crest of the hill. We stood by the pretty pink brick wall, our elbows on the edge. Below me, at the bottom of the hill, were the modern houses of the affluent neighbourhood of Sopocachi, and farther down still were the roads leading to Obrajes and Calacoto, two of the richest areas of La Paz. From here we admired the wide valley hugged by the Andes; Mounts Illimani and Mururata dominating the view; the jagged reddish-brown peak of Muela del Diablo, the Devil's Tooth, reaching out to touch the blue sky.

I was sure Javier would have a perfectly good explanation concerning the Italian girl and that he would ask me to stay with him. When I told him of my plans to go and study in Geneva, he was upset.

"How can you go away and leave me?" he said.

I squeezed his hand and kissed him. "Do you want me to stay, then?"

"Of course I do."

"And what about your fiancée? I hear she's coming."

He opened his eyes in surprise. "Who told you that?" He scratched his head and continued, "Yeah…she's coming, but I don't want her here."

"Are you going to marry her?"

"That's what she thinks, but…it's you and only you I love. Please, let's not talk about this any longer."

We were silent for several minutes. He put his arms around me and kissed me. Finding the right words for what we both wanted to say was impossible. After a few minutes, he suggested he take me home. "Everything will turn out for the best; you'll see," he added.

Adiós, Bolivia

February 1975

My departure for Switzerland was imminent. In ten days I would board a plane bound for Geneva and my new life. Javier hadn't phoned me to say goodbye or wish me good luck, probably out of embarrassment or even shame. Yes, he ought to have been ashamed, the rat. But now he was busy with his newly arrived Italian fiancée. He knew what he was doing; he knew he was going to marry this girl, and still he had played with my feelings. "I'll never give you up, Mariana," he had said so many times. "I just have to sort out this mess." He had known my mother was planning to send me to Europe and had begged me to stay, over and over, even though he had no intention of breaking up with the other girl.

The last time I saw him had been about a month earlier, late one evening. He had parked his car a hundred metres from my house and away from the street lamp that cast a dim shadow over the pavement. He'd kissed and caressed me eagerly in the semi-darkness. "I'll never let you go, my gorgeous girl," he'd repeated. The street had been deserted, so I'd foolishly responded to his caresses. It would have been so upsetting if one of the neighbours had seen us. He had been gently stroking my cheek when I'd said it was time for me to go home. "I'll call you tomorrow," he'd said. "I love you." That night, however, he did not walk me to my front door, like other times. As soon as I stepped out of the car, he started the engine and drove off without looking back or waving. As I walked down the wide cement steps to my house, I sensed the words I had just heard were not sincere. I wiped my eyes and blew my nose before I took out my key. My mother and sisters had gone to bed, thank God, and I didn't have to pretend that everything was fine.

Although she never said anything to me, I knew my mother thought Javier was good husband material. She had always been suspicious of other boyfriends and watched me and them like a hawk. I had always arrived home before curfew time, eleven o'clock, as I knew she would wait until I was safely back before she went to bed, but she never worried about Javier. On the other hand, she was making plans for my immediate departure. For my wise and prudent mother, studying in Europe was a safer bet than a marriage proposal that was slow in coming.

My mother's sacrifice and commitment were enormous; taking out a bank loan to send a daughter to live and study abroad meant depriving herself of even basic necessities. She would ensure my sisters never went without, of course, but her own needs would go unattended for several years. "I want you to have a much better life than the one I've had," she would say. "You'll have a career; you'll be successful." I wonder what sacrifices she made to repay the loan. In the fevered excitement before my departure, not knowing if Javier would propose and looking forward to independence and university life, I thought about my mother's sacrifice only a little. I did appreciate everything she was doing for me, of course, and it saddened me to leave her and my sisters, but a new life was beckoning. If only Javier would make up his mind...

Meanwhile, there was so much to do and organise: health checks and vaccinations, a new passport and visa, and documents for the university. I knew that the separation from my family and friends would be hard. I also had to say goodbye to my city, to my beloved Illimani, to the blue sky of my childhood. Choosing what to take with me and what to leave behind was also difficult. The airline allowed only one suitcase per passenger. How could my whole life fit in a single bag? My books and other treasured things had to stay behind and would be lost in the many house moves and changes that still awaited my family. My mother put a dozen family photos in an envelope beside my passport and fifty Swiss francs in an old blue wallet. A few days before my departure, I carefully washed and ironed my better-looking clothes and started putting them inside the suitcase. There was no money for new outfits. Once packed, until my departure, I borrowed clothes from Carolina.

I waited in vain for Javier to phone me. Instead, my mother heard from his parents that his Italian fiancée was arriving the following week and they were all making plans for the wedding. Alone in my room, I felt bitter tears well up in my eyes. *He never meant what he said…he doesn't love me… he was just playing with me…*

My mother and my sisters did not mention Javier at all in our conversations. I was grateful for that. I hid my tears, dejection and embarrassment from my family and tried to pull myself together and get on with the preparations for my departure.

Weightlessness. The absence of a body. Only my eyes.

I'm floating on air. A fierce storm is gathering above my head; menacing dark clouds surround me. The sky is deep purple. The cold is penetrating, biting. Two icy hands hold my face in their grip. My head is about to explode. Then something inside me starts to burn, my flesh turns to jelly, and my body smoulders. I shiver with fear and feel as if I'm leaving earth, towards danger, towards a sweltering fire. Its blinding red flames leap and twirl in the emptiness that surrounds me, sucking in the air…and I wheel… and I roll…and I am carried by the wind like a feather towards nothingness…towards oblivion…and darkness.

And silence. And emptiness.

"Oh, look—she's waking up!"

"Poor Marianita. How are you feeling?"

"Here, have a sip of water."

"Careful, don't overwhelm her. Let her wake up slowly."

My mother's cool and comforting hand touched my sore forehead. Where was I? Was this my bedroom? Yes, it was. My temples were throbbing, my head hurt, and my mouth was dry. The room was spinning around me. And I needed to pee.

"I don't feel well."

My mother smiled and held my hand. "You've been asleep for the past three days, mi amor. You had a high fever."

"What happened?"

"Carolina was helping you pack when, out of the blue, you just slumped on top of the suitcase, mumbling nonsense."

"I—I don't remember..."

"You gave us a good fright. Doctor Ramírez came immediately; he said it was all due to emotional tension because of your trip—but I blame that boy, too, for playing with your feelings."

I didn't say anything. Despite his ardent declarations of love, Javier had never proposed marriage to me. He'd never promised me anything.

"We were worried that..." my mother said. She burst into tears. "That you'd gone into a coma. But Doctor Ramírez was confident that you'd wake up by yourself. He gave you an injection that brought the fever down."

Carolina smiled and said, "We all took turns to be by your side. We never left you alone."

"Oh, Mami, Caro, Tere." I squeezed my mother's hand. Then I added, "I have to pee. I'm desperate."

As I raised myself from the bed, dizziness forced me to lie down again.

"Slowly, my girl. Here, let me help you."

I was a healthy twenty-year-old, but I had to accept their help. I leaned on Carolina's arm as she guided me to the bathroom.

Thanks to my family's care, after a couple of days I recovered my strength and started getting ready for the biggest journey of my life.

To this day, I have no recollection of that three-day episode—the fever, as my mother called it—and have reconstructed it from what my family has told me. Apart from the pink and purple blobs, the wind and the fire, I remember nothing. Several days of my life were lost, erased forever from my memory.

As a four-year-old, I had hallucinated after eating a whole jar of mustard. And now, for the second time in my life, I was encountering monsters that rose from beyond my consciousness. I didn't know it then, but eighteen years later these beasts would haunt me again a third time with renewed viciousness, after a near-fatal traffic accident in England.

And so I left my country on a bright and glorious February morning. I hoped to return one day as a useful professional. Europe and its ancient culture awaited me—university life, independence. But my excitement was mixed with sadness and apprehension. My self-esteem was not too high. I wished I was like my mother, who exuded confidence. She waltzed into banks and government offices as if she owned the place. She was articulate; she knew the intricacies of bureaucracy, knew how to talk to lawyers and civil servants and never felt intimidated by any of them. But I was the opposite of her; I blushed easily and was occasionally tongue-tied. And this was the anxious girl Emma was sending to study abroad! How would I cope? How? Panic invaded me. A sick feeling in my stomach and a knot in my throat made me feel as if I was about to faint. But I didn't want to dwell too long on those thoughts. I reminded myself that I was not only a bag of nerves. There was the other me who knew I was intelligent, and pretty, and ambitious. The other me that wanted to make the most of my life.

My mother and sisters were crammed in the back seat of the taxi; they had graciously allowed me to sit in front so I could enjoy the better view. The cab started the arduous crawl up to El Alto Airport, and I watched intently, absorbing every building along the road, engraving each Andean peak in my mind, memorising every street. I said *adiós* to Mounts Illimani and Mururata. I said *hasta pronto* to the Sopocachi of my childhood; I waved *hasta luego* to El Montículo and its amazing views over the city. As the taxi drove along El Prado, with its wide tiled central walkway, I saw myself as a thin and shy fifteen-year-old at the Sunday paseo with my friends, nervously talking to the boys of the Saint George Club, eating salteñas after Sunday Mass. Soon we were travelling along Avenida Mariscal Santa Cruz, and I waved goodbye to San Francisco Church—one of the baroque jewels of our colonial past—and to the bustling Witches Market, with its miniature ceramic handicrafts and toy alpacas for the tourists and llama foetuses for our native traditional ceremonies.

The taxi reached the rim of El Alto, and the huge wide bowl that was La Paz appeared in all its glory. The lump in my throat became bigger and harder, and I was barely able to talk.

I was excited about the big adventure that awaited me in Europe. I was eager to go. But I was also heartbroken. A part of me would forever remain in Bolivia; a part of me would always want to return.

And then I was at the Lufthansa check-in desk, handing in my ticket and suitcase. Everything proceeded smoothly. They'd soon be asking the passengers to go to passport control.

Carolina, my confidante and best friend, whose long letters would comfort me during times of sorrow, put her arm around my shoulders; young Teresa clung to my coat. My mother's eyes were glistening; she squeezed my hand and forced a smile.

It was time to board the plane. One last hug now and one final kiss for my mother and sisters. We all bit our lips to contain our tears.

They waved from the aisle. "¡Buena suerte! ¡Te amo! ¡Cuídate!" And then I was gone.

In years to come, I would often think of my mother on that February morning at the airport, sending me—her precious eldest child—away to another continent, letting me go, probably forever, so I would have a better future. She had no idea when we would meet again—nearly four years would pass before I was able to return on a short holiday—and she would have to wait several months for a phone call, as intercontinental calls were expensive. Weekly letters would be our only consolation.

I wonder what she felt as the taxi brought her and my sisters back to the house. She must have put on her happy face for my sisters' sake, but inside she would always carry a dull ache that refused to go away.

Part IV

After Bolivia

What happened to me after I left Bolivia is of little relevance to this story, and a brief account of only the most significant events is all that is needed.

Life does not always turn out the way we imagine it will; the best plans often go awry, and sometimes we have to give up our dreams. In Geneva I lived with my cousin Silvia and her fiancé for the first six months and then moved out to a student residence. I cried for Javier for a few weeks, pathetically calling out his name, but after a while more pressing concerns occupied my mind, and I devoted my energies to getting ready for university. By the time lectures started, I was fluent in French, thanks to intensive lessons and having been blessed with an ear for languages.

Although my mother knew Geneva was expensive, the reality of living there was much more costly than she had imagined. I lived on the cheap, buying clothes and shoes in discount supermarkets and hardly ever going out to cinemas or restaurants. Participating in the students' social life was costly, so I did very little of that. To supplement my mother's remittances, I worked in different jobs for a few hours after lessons and full-time during most holidays.

Homesickness plagued me from the start, but I had to content myself with my mother's weekly letters, as phoning home was out of the question. Carolina's long letters were a great source of comfort. As I didn't want to worry my mother unduly, I confided my most private thoughts to my younger sister, and she understood me as no one else could. But what I really needed was to see my family again, so for three years I saved every available centime to go back home during the summer holidays.

Arrivals and Departures-1

In July 1978, after three and a half years of absence, I was finally able to return to Bolivia. In the days before my departure, excitement and anticipation overwhelmed me. I had trouble eating and sleeping, I felt sick to my stomach, and my voice became barely audible. Maybe something was seriously wrong with me! I was worried about seeing a doctor when money was so tight. "Don't fret too much about it," said Graciela, the Argentinean girl who lived in the room next to mine at the students' residence. "It's just nerves." She was right, of course.

The Lufthansa plane left Geneva for Munich, from where it crossed the Atlantic towards South America. Overcome with exhaustion, I slept for most of the journey. We changed planes in Rio de Janeiro and continued towards Santa Cruz, in Bolivia. We were already flying over Bolivian territory when I stretched my arms and legs, pulled up the flap that covered my window, and was greeted by a spectacular view: a thick dark-green carpet covered the ground below, crisscrossed by dozens of meandering rivers like silver threads. The Amazon rainforest: mighty, exuberant, life-giving.

Not long afterwards, the stewardess instructed the passengers to buckle their safety belts. This time, when I looked out of the window, my eyes filled with tears. We were now flying over the Andes, powerful rock-and-ice giants, crowned by sharp, serrated peaks. These were the mountains of my childhood; these were the landscapes of my dreams. Soon we approached the vast deep bowl of La Paz, the highest capital in the world, its buildings hugging the sides of the mountains, the sky deep blue, Mount Illimani watching over the city as it had done for aeons. I held my breath, feeling the intensity of the scenery around me.

The aircraft circled the city before landing at El Alto Airport. As I descended the steps of the plane, I noticed a lone figure, a young man standing a few metres away from the plane, wearing a furry hat and wrapped in a long, thick, camel-coloured coat. He didn't look like someone from the airport maintenance crew or a pilot. What was he doing here? And how did he get permission to enter the landing area? My feet had hardly touched the ground when the stranger approached me and said, "Bienvenida, Marianita," and hugged me. I burst into tears. I knew immediately who he was: my sister Carolina's husband, Hernando, who worked at the Ministry of Foreign Affairs.

As my brother-in-law and I walked towards the entrance, a cold wind blew from the mountains, a purifying and energising force. The light around the peaks was brilliant, nearly white. The snow of Mount Mururata, the headless one, and of cone-shaped Huayna Potosi glittered in the morning sun. I was home.

My mother and two sisters were waving frantically from behind the glass doors of the arrivals lounge. I knew that my mother was nervous about the freezing winter temperature and my readapting to the altitude. I knew that, overprotective as always, she would have brought a thermos flask with hot coca tea, altitude-sickness tablets, extra cardigans, a thick coat, and even a blanket for me. I knew I would willingly go along with her wishes.

Then the airport doors opened to welcome the new arrivals, and I fell into my mother's and my sisters' arms and was enveloped by their warmth.

In August I flew back to Geneva, ready to start my last year of studies—provided I successfully resat a couple of exams. In the meantime, my mother had encountered new and bigger financial problems, and it became increasingly difficult for her to support me. Apart from continuing with her baking business and providing board and lodging to different tenants, she had also tried her hand at exporting her knitted alpaca ponchos and sweaters to Europe and had set up a restaurant with a partner. Unfortunately, she became a victim of fraud and lost nearly all her money. My part-time jobs provided me with a little income, but without my mother's monthly remittances, I had no option but to leave university. Soon I found secretarial work in an office and moved out of the students' residence.

Earlier that year, at a party, some friends had introduced me to a young man from Northern Ireland. Jim had also been studying languages, in Belfast, and had come to Geneva for his year abroad and to improve his French. He also improved his Spanish with me. We soon became inseparable. When the time came for Jim to return to the United Kingdom to finish his degree, we found it too hard to be apart. So on an icy-cold December night in 1981, I arrived in England, twenty-seven years of my life packed tightly in a single suitcase, my hopes for the future inside one of its pockets and no souvenirs other than a few photographs. Never in my wildest dreams would I have imagined that one day I would share my life with a boy from Belfast and live in England. In September the following year, Jim and I were married. Our first child, Christopher, was born three years later, in 1986, followed by Olivia in 1988.

With each passing year, Bolivia became more distant and unattainable, a dream, a fantasy. Even going back there on holiday was difficult. In forty-one years of absence, I have returned to my country of birth only eight times.

Britain is where my husband and my children live, and it is now my country, too. But Bolivia is the land of my sweetest dreams.

Arrivals and Departures-2

I remember vividly the first time my mother came to England, in September 1982, for my wedding. At that time, Teresa and her new husband, Christian, were living in the United Kingdom but would soon go back to live in La Paz. One warm sunny morning, Jim drove Teresa and me to Heathrow. As we waited impatiently at the arrivals gate, Teresa and I were unable to stand still. Soon after the arrival of our mother's flight was announced, the passengers started appearing, bleary-eyed and dishevelled. My sister and I examined everyone who came through the gate. Was that lady in the blue coat our mami? No. That one in the flowery dress? No. That one over there? No. I hadn't seen my mother in four years and couldn't wait another minute. Suddenly, peering into the dim light of the wide passage, I saw her emerge from its mouth, walking towards the exit in her black trousers, red jacket and polka-dotted red-and-white scarf. I was brought up to obey the rules, but as she came through the gate I could contain myself no longer and jumped over the barrier. "What are you doing, Mariana?" Jim protested. But I was deaf to his admonition and ran towards my mother to envelop her in a bear hug, giggling like a silly girl. Teresa, brandishing a bouquet of red roses, followed my bad example and jumped over the barrier to hug and kiss our mother. We walked towards the exit holding hands, surrounded by dozens of smiling faces of the waiting public. No immigration or airport official came to reprimand us. In the next twenty-one years, Mami Emma would come to see me five more times.

Meanwhile, in Santa Cruz

The blue flies whirred in the scorching Santa Cruz afternoon; the lizards hid in the cracks of the cooler rocks. The air felt dry; the rains were late. A thin blue-eyed old man stood in front of an elegant house, Aunt Eugenia's house. He was hot and thirsty. He looked at his watch, checked his fingernails, straightened his tie, adjusted his panama hat, smoothed his light cotton jacket, and cleared his throat. He looked at his watch once more and then knocked on the door.

A maid wearing a starched white apron appeared.

"Buenas tardes," the old man said. "I need to see Señora Eugenia." With his left hand, he brushed away his white hair from his forehead.

"Who should I say wants her?" the maid asked.

"My name is Alexander Seifert. I am her father's cousin."

"Please enter, señor."

The old man was ushered into the sitting-room. The furniture was of rich dark mahogany; every corner was adorned with glazed terracotta pots with exotic plants and flowers. From the hanging photographs on the walls, his distant relatives smiled at him. They did indeed resemble the Seiferts of long ago, the ones he'd left in 1918, except that those in Germany had golden hair and blue eyes. He thought, *Ah, that must be the husband. He does look different from the rest. But the children—they all have the thin elegant noses and delicate lips of our family. Yes. And Eugenia is her father's daughter.*

The old man sat down and removed his hat. He would be ready to welcome death once he had spoken to Eugenia. He was tired. His journey had been too long and too painful; there had been too many lies. He wanted to be free of his burden. He'd forgiven Julius a long time ago; he had also forgiven himself. He hoped Eugenia would also be able to forgive her father—or to understand him, at least.

The maid came back with a glass of iced lemonade. "Señora Eugenia wants to know exactly what it is you'd like to discuss with her."

Señor Alexander gulped down the lemonade. "Gracias," he said and wiped his mouth with the back of his hand. "I need to tell Señora Eugenia about her father. He and I arrived in Bolivia together from Germany."

The maid went back inside to inform her mistress. Five minutes later she was back.

"Señora Eugenia is very sorry, but she cannot see you."

"But...but why?" Alexander Seifert became pale. "I've waited all these years...and now I'm very, very ill and may not have long in this world. I must—I must see her," he pleaded.

The maid went back inside. Several minutes passed, but to Señor Seifert they seemed like hours. Fat drops of sweat, cold and slimy like snails, appeared on his forehead. He started to shiver.

The maid was back. "I'm sorry, señor. My mistress says she regrets it very much, but she cannot see you."

Alexander Seifert looked at his hands and noticed that they were trembling. He tried to stand up, but his legs turned to jelly, and he dropped back onto his seat. After all these years, unburdening himself of those heavy, awful secrets was not going to be easy.

"Are you all right?" the maid said.

Señor Seifert's face was as white as the linen doilies on the coffee table. "I'm OK," he said. "Please, please go back and tell Señora Eugenia that I'm begging her to see me. I don't have much time left on this earth. Please, I beg of you."

But Aunt Eugenia, probably frightened of what the stranger might reveal, refused to see him. Instead, she asked the maid to phone for a taxi to take Señor Seifert back to wherever he'd come from.

Alexander Seifert left my aunt's home, his limp hat in one hand, his wrinkled jacket in the other, dragging his feet. Tears prickled his eyes;

despair and anger rose inside him; his heart was beating fast; his stomach was in a knot. A few days later, he died without writing down or telling anybody what he knew.

What Alexander Seifert knew concerns me personally. Now I will never find out who my grandfather Julius really was. I will not understand what happened to my grandmother. Bits of stories from here and there, speculation, family myths and folklore are all I'm left with.

Abuelo, I am your granddaughter, and yet I know so little about you. Maybe one day I'll travel to Germany—with an interpreter—to look you up in the archives. There must be lists of passengers who left in transatlantic ships bound for Buenos Aires soon after the First World War. Lists of medical doctors and other professionals, of people who went to South America in search of better opportunities or who ran away from unbearable lives.

Going to Germany to search the archives…an extremely difficult and expensive enterprise. In the meantime, I dream, and I wonder. And I write down my family's story, keeping to the facts wherever possible but also imagining what I can never know.

Rosita's Revelations

One Saturday in March 2000, Jim and I found out that our eleven-year-old daughter, Olivia, had a malignant tumour. Within a few hours, we had entered a twilight zone of fear and panic. Like a forest fire, the terrible news spread through our extended family. Chemotherapy, operations and unpleasant treatments—Olivia would endure all these for a whole year.

A month after the start of her treatment, while I was sitting by Olivia's hospital bed reading her a story, Jim brought me a letter that had arrived that morning from Canada. I knew immediately who it was from. I tore open the envelope and read my cousin's letter three or four times, savouring each word. It was a long letter, full of friendship and affection, in which Rosita tried to give me courage and strength, plus shared news about her daughters and her life in general. She also gave me her phone number. So the next time Jim stayed at the hospital with Olivia, I telephoned my cousin and heard her voice for the first time in nearly three decades.

Thankfully, Olivia got better and now leads a full and busy life.

After that initial contact, Rosita and I emailed each other and spoke on the phone several times, sometimes for hours. In 2005, five years after receiving her first letter, I phoned her for a brief chat, unaware that this would be one of the most important conversations of my life.

"I don't think you know the whole truth about our family," Rosita said.

"Well, I know what my mother told me, but I know she kept a lot from me," I replied. "I'd like to learn more."

On this phone call, I would hear of painful events that I could never have imagined. Did I know, for instance, that when our grandfather fell in love with our grandmother, he was already married to Señora Sara L., a beautiful woman from the high society of Tarija? No, of course I didn't.

If I had been confused before by my grandparents' intricate story, I was now dumbfounded.

"And do you know what happened to my father?" Rosita continued.

As a child I had been told that Silvio was my mother's half-brother, my grandfather's son; when I was an adult, my mother admitted that Silvio was in fact Filomena and Julius's first child, her full brother. I also knew that somehow the mother-son relationship had gone sour, but I had no idea why. I sensed that this was too delicate a subject to discuss with my mother, that talking about it would bring tears to her eyes. So I kept my curiosity to myself.

This is what Rosita revealed during those long conversations: Señora L. and Julius were not a happy couple. My grandfather wanted to leave her, but in those days divorce was not allowed. Señora L. had always longed for a baby, but she was unable to have children. When she found out that Julius had not only been unfaithful but had also had a child with another woman, she was overwhelmed with anger and humiliation. Julius had broken his sacred marriage vows; he had committed a mortal sin. He had to pay for the pain he was causing. Señora L. threatened to make Julius's adultery public.

I can imagine my grandfather begging her to forgive him and keep quiet, for everyone's sake, as the scandal would ruin his reputation and his career, and she, as the wronged wife, would become an object of pity. But Señora L. could not forgive. She cried and cursed Julius and her barrenness for several days. No, she would not be made a fool of any longer. Those two sinners had to pay, and she would demand the highest retribution from them. What she wanted in exchange for her silence was utterly cruel: Filomena had to give up her baby so that he could be brought up as Señora L.'s own child.

I wonder how my grandmother kept her pregnancy and the birth of her son a secret. Did her parents send her away to the countryside to stay with relatives? How did they explain Filomena's absence to their friends? What did they do once she came back with her infant? So many questions will remain forever unanswered.

I imagine my grandmother sobbing and pleading with Julius: "Please let me keep my baby, please. He's only little; he needs me." She had suckled her child, sung lullabies to him, fallen asleep with him on her chest. She could not possibly give him up.

From beyond her laments, I can also hear my grandfather's loud voice, adamant: "You have to surrender the child. We'll have others. How can I provide for you if a scandal ruins us?"

So one morning at dawn, a servant left Filomena's house carrying a little bundle wrapped in fine white cotton and walked surreptitiously towards the house of the other woman, the wife, while my grandmother, on her knees on her kitchen floor, wept. "No! No! Noooo!" she wailed, tightly clinging to the soft blue cardigan she had knitted for her infant—the only thing she had left of him.

Standing beside her, not daring to touch her to comfort her, Julius, too, cried silently.

Filomena would never forgive Julius for ruining her life and forcing her to give up her baby. She had borne a child out of wedlock with a married man; she was a fallen woman, a sinner.

Soon after surrendering their baby, Filomena and Julius left for Argentina. It is possible that, despite their best efforts, their secret had been discovered. They had no option but to run away from scandal, as living in Tarija as outcasts would have been intolerable. It is also possible that Julius had been offered a better job there. What is beyond doubt—from all the years that I knew my grandmother—is that she did not follow him willingly. In Argentina they would have three more children, all girls: first Alcira, then Emma two years later, and Eugenia two years after Emma. For Filomena, sex would forever be something dirty and terrible.

It was only when my grandfather was murdered that Filomena returned to Bolivia to face up to her shame and live like a recluse.

In the meantime, the little boy, Silvio, found out that the woman who had brought him up was not his real mother and that Filomena had given him away when he was a baby. Who told him this and why? The pain and anger inside the boy's heart must have been enormous. He would never understand that Filomena was forced to surrender him. His hatred for his birth mother would become a permanent part of his being. Somehow, he could accept his father's motives, but in his eyes, his mother's actions were unforgivable.

Just before she died, when Silvio was eighteen, Señora L. told him that his dead father had left an inheritance for him and his sisters. At once, he went to see the girls to demand his share. When he found out that most of what their father had bequeathed them had been lost during the exodus back to Tarija in 1930, he was furious. His sisters gave him what little remained of the inheritance, but not happy with that, he asked them to loan him enough money to help him go away. Then he left for Argentina, where he stayed for many years, squandering all his money, trying to forget all that had happened to him since his birth. My mother often wondered whether he was still alive and would only see him again decades later, in La Paz, after Aunt Alcira saw his wedding announcement in a local newspaper and contacted him.

I was unprepared for what Rosita revealed to me that afternoon. I had wanted to know the truth for so long, and now the truth was crushing me. Finally, the pieces of the puzzle fitted together. Finally, I understood why my grandmother had spent her life asking God for forgiveness. She'd had no choice but to stay with a man she loathed; she'd given birth to four illegitimate children; she'd had to give up her beloved firstborn against her will.

I finished my conversation with my cousin, hung up the phone, and burst into tears. I carried on crying until the next day. I cried for my grandmother and for my mother and aunts, who had told us lies to protect their mother's secret. I cried for Uncle Silvio, too.

Did Filomena's daughters fear that we, her grandchildren, would think less of her if we knew the truth? But my overwhelming feelings for my grandmother were love and compassion. And I was angry, very angry, with my grandfather. He'd been a professional man, a doctor, and much older than Filomena; she'd been just a naive convent girl. It is clear he abused his higher status and took advantage of her vulnerability.

In future conversations, Rosita and I would wonder whether Julius had in fact kidnapped Filomena. If he had, had he forced himself on her? We would like to think not, as why would he ruin his chances of happiness with the woman he loved? But maybe the truth was simpler than that. Maybe the kidnapping incident was just a tale Filomena's family had concocted to protect her good name. It is possible that she'd become infatuated with the handsome foreign doctor and, because she was ignorant of the facts of life, fell into his arms, unaware that her actions would have consequences. Pregnant and unmarried, her life ruined, she'd had no choice but to stay with him.

Julius and Filomena had lived in an oppressive society in conservative times. "Poor grandparents," Rosita said. "Their lives were harder and sadder than they should have been. If our grandfather had been allowed to divorce his wife, maybe all our destinies would have been different."

And so my grandfather's ghost came back to haunt me. As did Néstor and Cecilia's story. Thirty years ago I had left Bolivia. I was a married woman now, and the mother of two children. But my country of birth and the stories of my Bolivian family, although relegated to the back of my mind, had never left me. Now more than ever, after Rosita's revelation, I was determined to break open my family's chest of secrets.

Adiós, Amada Mami

Monday, 8 September 2003, is a date I will never forget. At that time I was working in the mornings as an assistant to an economist in a big old house on a hill just above Wargrave, in Berkshire, surrounded by beautiful gardens with goldfish in a pond and woods inhabited by hares, pheasants and peacocks, which we sometimes saw from our office window. That day I finished work at one o'clock and drove back to my home in Wokingham to change clothes and then catch a train to London, where I was to attend a party. The late-summer sun was shining; there were only a few cars on the winding country road and not a cloud in the open sky.

The night before, I had thought of phoning my mother, who had recently gone back to Bolivia after enjoying a holiday with me and my family. She had been here last in 2000, when she'd come to help us when Olivia was ill in hospital. Although she was only seventy-five, my vivacious mother had become a fragile old lady, unsteady on her feet, stopping every few steps to catch her breath, her back hunched. What had happened to her? Time, which does not forgive and does not make allowances for anybody, had wrought its changes on her. Her movements had become slow and stiff, so I had coaxed her into doing daily exercises, and after a few days she had been able to put on her tights without too much effort. "I forbid you to think of yourself as old," I had told her. "You've always been a fighter. You can't just give up."

It had been wonderful to have her again all to myself, and we had stayed up talking every night. But things between mothers and daughters are not always idyllic, and we sometimes got on each other's nerves. I did not appreciate her occasional comments on my clothes or my very short hair. She had developed some irritating new habits, like chewing her food with her front teeth. "Oh, Mami, you look like a rabbit when you do that," I would say.

Instead of complaining about my unkind remarks, she advised me to be more tolerant and patient with my husband and children. "I know you have a lot on your shoulders, but life is too short and precious to waste by being upset," she would say. "Try to see things from Jim's point of view. And remember, kids misbehave because they are kids."

I listened to her words and knew that she was right. She had been—like nearly all the women in our family, me included—passionate, impulsive, and highly strung. But age and experience had given her wisdom and acceptance.

As a special treat, we had taken her to the Canary Islands, where she had loved the sea, the charming little villages, the warm climate and the food.

During her stay I had made a point of asking her a few questions about our family's past, questions I had wanted to ask all my life. But the past was uncomfortable territory, and she preferred talking about the present. "I'll tell you some more another time," she would say.

All too soon it was time for her to go back to Bolivia. The farewell at Heathrow was unusually stressful. She was nervous and seemed more scared than ever of flying. We requested a wheelchair for her, as she found walking along those interminable airport corridors difficult and exhausting.

"You'll be fine, Mami. Don't worry. You'll be fine," I said as I hugged and kissed her goodbye. "Come back soon. We love you!"

She wiped a tear and waved as an attendant pushed her chair through the passport-control gate; she looked elegant in her black trousers and grey chequered coat, her short greying hair combed back, a pink scarf round her neck.

Adiós, querida Mami. Adiós.

This farewell was much worse than others. My stomach was in knots, and a tight lump lodged in my throat.

My mother had lived most of her life in the highest capital of the world. However, as she got older, she had found returning to the altitude a little harder each time. A couple of days after her arrival, she was admitted to hospital with heart and lung trouble. Teresa had phoned me from La Paz to reassure me: "Don't worry, Mariana. Mami is in good hands. Our doctor says she'll be able to go home at the weekend." But the weekend came and went, and our mother remained in hospital. Anxious, I telephoned her every evening at the hospital. She chatted animatedly despite sounding a little tired, and we usually finished our conversations with jokes and giggles.

That Sunday evening I was feeling rather exhausted and wanted to go to bed early, as I knew Monday was going to be a long day; after working in the morning, I had to travel to London and would be back home late in the evening. *I'll call you tomorrow, Mami,* I said to myself. *Won't phone you just now, but I'll definitely call you tomorrow. Sleep well. Buenas noches.*

After work the following day, I went home to change my clothes. From Wokingham I caught a train to London and arrived at Wimbledon Station at four-thirty. Armed with my London map, I found my way to the party. Some Bolivian ladies had invited me to this get-together, held in honour of one of our friends, Carmen. Just outside the house where the party was taking place, I phoned my daughter to make sure that everything was fine at home. Things were far from all right. Teresa had telephoned saying that she needed to speak to me as a matter of urgency and that I should return her call immediately.

Still standing outside my friend's door, I tried hard to remember my sister's long number in La Paz, twenty-four digits in total. But the number would not come to me. I concentrated hard. I had to remember. And then the numbers came: 0844286464...

Teresa answered in a calm voice and asked me how I was. I ignored her and enquired about our mother instead.

"Mami passed away this morning," Teresa said. "She had a heart attack."

A boot kicked me in the gut. Tears overwhelmed me, and I screamed in the middle of the street, unaware of anything or anybody around me. I was forty-eight, a wife and a mother of two, but right now I was just a little lost girl. How would I manage without my mother? I would never again be able to hear her comforting, wise words over the phone. I would never again enjoy her company or laughter. But how could she be dead? She was part of me. How could she not *be* anymore?

It was now time to ring the bell and join the party. A dim orange light was coming through the net curtains of the Wimbledon house. I could see the silhouettes of people inside the sitting-room. I wiped my tears and composed myself. When the hostess opened the door, I whispered in her ear, "I've just found out that my mother has died. I need to make some phone calls, so could I please go somewhere private?" Shocked, she guided me to her bedroom, and I asked her not to tell the other ladies, as I did not want to ruin Carmen's party.

First I telephoned Jim at his office to ask him to find me a flight to La Paz for the following morning. Then I called my daughter.

"Olivia, please sit down. I have bad news."

I could sense her apprehension. "What is it, Mami?"

"Abuelita died. This morning."

She gasped.

"Olivia, you have to be strong. Start packing a suitcase for me. Make a list of the things I'll need to take. And a list of people we need to phone. Cancel your maths lesson for tomorrow. Find my passport. Send an email to my boss. Prepare some sandwiches for dinner, please, Olivia."

I hope my daughter has forgiven me for talking to her in such a commanding way, but everything had to be ready that evening. Inevitably, some ladies heard the news and came to give me their condolences and offer their support.

"My son says he'll phone the airlines for you."

"Here's a glass of water."

"She was such a lovely lady, your mami."

Then I joined the party and had a cup of tea—no cakes, as I found it impossible to eat anything—and, for Carmen's sake, pretended everything was fine. After half an hour, I made my excuses and said goodbye.

My thoughts were in turmoil during the journey home. Sorrow, anguish, and more sorrow kept me company on the underground and then the train. Guilt and regret overwhelmed me. Why hadn't I telephoned Mami the night before as I had been doing most nights? How could I have thought we had all the time in the world? The nice things I had wanted to say to her only a few hours before would now remain forever unsaid. I felt responsible for her death. She had died because she had flown across the world to see me. She had died because she'd wanted to say goodbye.

All the years I had been living in England, I had known that one day I would have to get on a plane to go bury my mother. Now that dreaded time had arrived. The following morning I was on a plane to La Paz, where my sisters were waiting for me to proceed with our mother's funeral.

Carolina and Teresa met me at El Alto Airport. At Teresa's home I changed into fresh clothes before going with my sisters to the chapel where Mami was resting. Friends had been coming throughout the day to pay their respects; flowers and cards surrounded her coffin. A few people were now sitting in the pews, praying for her. My sisters nodded and smiled at those present, but I was too distressed to even look at anybody.

My mother had passed away early on Monday morning, a few minutes after waking in her hospital room. She had asked the nurse to help her go to the bathroom to have a wash, and as the nurse was guiding her to the wash-basin, our mother had collapsed. The nurse had called for help, and when other members of the staff had come, our mother was already dead. How cruel it was that Emma, who had devoted her life to her children and grandchildren, had died without any of her daughters there to hold her hand.

I wanted to see her lovely face once more before she was taken away from us. I lifted the lid of the coffin and saw her sleeping, a serene expression on her face, as if all the suffering she had endured, all the hurt and humiliation of those hard years, had never happened. As if her ears had never heard any harsh words or insults; as if her eyes had never shed bitter tears; as if her heart had never been broken. She was at peace at last. But she was gone from me. A terrible sorrow invaded me, and I broke down. Why did she have to die and leave us? Why could she not make an effort to wake up? But silence was her only answer. Where had her warm personality, her laughter, her smiles gone? Where was her essence? Where was her soul? Where was the radiant woman she used to be? I spent several minutes just looking at her, memorising each and every one of her features, each of her wrinkles and freckles.

The funeral took place the day after my arrival. The little church was packed, as not only had her close friends and family come but also some of my school friends, her maids from forty years ago, and a couple of bricklayers who had helped build her small house in the countryside.

My sisters put her knitting needles and a scarf she had been making, plus a tomato plant from her garden, inside our mother's coffin. Photos and drawings made by all her grandchildren and letters from my sisters and me also went in.

When the time came for us to say a few words in her honour, Teresa and Carolina could not contain their tears and were unable to read out their messages. I was the last to speak and was determined not to cry. I, Emma's eldest daughter, would show death that I could honour my mother.

And then it was time to lower her coffin down into the earth, the final farewell. I looked at her once more before she went down and thought, stupidly, that it was too cold and too lonely down there and that she needed a blanket.

She had always loved nature, our mountains, our blue sky. She was buried in a garden cemetery, her tomb next to pine and eucalyptus trees, facing her beloved Illimani.

After the funeral the immediate family went back to her house in the country, built with so many years of hard work, the walls full of photographs of her three daughters and eight grandchildren. Aunt Alcira gathered everyone around the table and asked me to say a few words. After that we said a prayer, had a glass of lemonade, chatted a bit more, and went home.

Dark thoughts had been tormenting me all this time: Had I caused my mother's death by making her come to England to see me? I knew she'd needed to keep an eye on her blood pressure, and I knew she was growing old and fragile, but nevertheless I had wanted to see her. I'd wanted my children to see her. I'd wanted to give her a good holiday away from her worries. Also, her doctor had said that she was fit enough to travel. So she'd come. But who knows—maybe she would have died anyway without seeing us. The problems and worries she had endured for so many years might have contributed to her untimely death. I shall never know.

The last time she'd come to England, my mother had brought several photos from her own youth and from my childhood. She'd known I wanted to learn about her life and piece together the history of our family. During this—her last visit—she'd told me many things I did not know, but there were still things she chose not to tell me. I'd respected her wishes and not persisted. I'd known the questions I'd had in mind would be painful for her and would open up old wounds.

Looking back at all we'd shared during her last weeks in England, it seemed to me as if my mother had been preparing her final departure, saying her farewell to me.

Teresa, Carolina and I spent many hours together every day, sometimes until the early hours of the morning, in Teresa's kitchen, drinking cup after cup of coffee to stay awake. We rediscovered how strong our sisterly bonds were, despite each being so different from the others. We remembered our mother as she had been, with her qualities and her defects. We talked about the mistakes she'd made, not judging her but admitting that, under the circumstances, we could not have done better. The three of us were glad that our mother had also had joy in her senior years. She had been proud, for instance, that my sisters and I had much better lives than hers and that all three of us had stable marriages. Teresa had insisted that she move in with her and her family, and my mother had truly enjoyed living there, being loved and pampered daily. Her last months had been filled with affection and laughter, or at least she'd given the impression of not being unduly worried.

Five days after my mother's funeral, I boarded a plane for England. I had to make an enormous effort to breathe normally and stay calm. I did not want people to see me cry; I did not want them to ask me awkward questions or pity me. I was leaving my country, my place of birth. I was leaving my sisters and the rest of the family—and my mother, buried deep in the cold, hard earth, sleeping for eternity. The woman in the seat next to me tried to engage me in conversation, but I was unable to respond. The plane flew above the capital, and I saw once again the raw beauty of my native country.

And I thought of my mother, lying in her wooden coffin with her tomato plant, her knitting needles, and her half-finished scarf, beside the letters we had written her and the photographs from her daughters and grandchildren. There she rested, swaddled by our hugs and kisses, facing the landscape she had loved so much. Adiós, amada Mami. Adiós! You are one with the mountains now.

1998

Five years before my mother's death, I had returned to Bolivia on holiday with my children, in August 1998.

One sunny afternoon, while my children visited their cousins, I asked my mother if we could go to the General Cemetery to pay our respects before the tombs of my grandmother and my cousin Cecilia.

The cemetery, a small city of dusty walled streets the colour of bleached bones, was made of thousands upon thousands of niche alcoves. The walls of the necropolis were several metres high; the alcoves, tightly packed one on top of the other like a beehive, each contained a single coffin. Although she had been here many times before, my mother had trouble finding our loved ones' niches in this labyrinth. With the help of a map, we found Abuelita's after a few minutes. My mother opened the glass door with her key and put a bunch of violets inside. Then we reached Cecilia's resting place and were silent for a few minutes. Here was a young, beautiful, intelligent woman, her future stolen at the age of twenty-five, murdered. My mother wiped her eyes. "At least your abuelita had the chance to live her life and died of old age," she said. I thought of the babies my cousin could have had. Cecilia, a childless pachamama, had died searching for a more just society.

I asked my mother for a pen and a piece of paper, and I wrote:

Dearest Ceci:

I was lucky to have had you in my life even for a few short years. You set an example of love and generosity.

Your sacrifice and courage were not in vain. They are your legacy to us. I promise to honour your memory.
With love and gratitude,
Mariana

My mother did not have a key to Cecilia's niche, but I managed to slip the letter through a tiny gap at the bottom of the glass door. Inside, dried roses that had nearly disintegrated lay in a thick layer of dust, and I wondered how long it had been since anyone had visited.

Every time I returned to Bolivia after that 1998 visit, I noticed a remarkable change in my aunt's attitude towards me. Although she had always treated me well, she now showed her affection more openly. My letter to Cecilia has never been mentioned to this day, but I know my aunt has read it. We have never, in all these years, spoken about her daughter. And Gerardo has told me that, in the forty years since his sister's death, he and his mother have never talked about it, either.

Ten years later, in 2008, Olivia and I returned to La Paz on a four-week holiday and stayed at Teresa's house. Apart from visiting our friends and relatives, one of the objectives of this trip was to find out more about my grandparents' lives. One afternoon Teresa came home with news that might help with my enquiries: a new relation had recently contacted Aunt Alcira saying he was the grandson of Alexander Seifert, my grandfather's cousin. This was exciting news; I had to meet that man.

Two days later, at a cafeteria in Calacoto, Teresa and I met our brand-new cousin. Armando was about fifteen years older than me, with a thin beard, greying hair, thick spectacles and a paunch. As soon as he saw us, he stood up to greet us. He kissed us on both cheeks and smiled broadly as he helped us remove our coats. "So nice to meet you at last, cousins," he said. We exchanged pleasantries and talked about our lives and families. But I was dying to hear what he knew about my grandfather, so I started asking him questions as soon as was decently possible. Armando was patient with me and answered my enquiries as well as he could, allowing time for me to make notes. I would later use this new information to write about Alexander and Julius's arrival in South America and about Alexander's first and only visit to Aunt Eugenia.

The following week I had afternoon tea with Aunt Alcira. On her dining table lay a couple of plates full of pastries from the patisserie shop she had owned for the past few years. My aunt was eighty-two, but still she worked both as headmistress of her school and manager of her bakery. Age had softened her temper, but her employees were still a little nervous around her. My daughter, who was then twenty, was terrified of her. I was not. I had stopped fearing my aunt a long time ago, and she had treated me with affection for as long as I could remember. Now that my mother was no longer with us, Alcira had assumed a slightly maternal role towards my sisters and me. Once again I noticed how much she and my mother resembled each other physically—so much that when my friends saw a photo of my aunt, they invariably thought it was of my mother. She had put on a few kilos but still looked attractive, with her dyed light-brown hair and her intelligent dark eyes. She would stop working when she left this earth; she said that work kept her young and clever. Like my mother, she would not simply sit and wait for old age to run its course.

Aunt Alcira knew I wanted to ask her about our family's past, and I knew she was not keen to say much. For the past few years, she had been especially attentive towards me. She greeted me warmly and called me *hijita* and Marianita—terms of affection more suitable for a little girl. I didn't feel patronised, as I understood she could not help addressing me in this manner; on the contrary, I enjoyed her pampering, which reminded me of the way my mother used to talk to me.

She hugged me tightly and kissed me on both cheeks. "Mi amor, I want to hear all about you and your family. But first things first. My maid has prepared a tray full of your favourite pastries: alfajores, empanadas de lacayote, *ojarazcas*. If there's anything else you want, just say the word, and we'll get it from the shop."

We sat in her lounge, furnished with the same cream-coloured uphol-stered armchairs and mahogany coffee table of my childhood, adorned with the porcelain figures and dark-green glass ashtrays I remembered so well. My aunt's black-and-white portrait of herself as a young woman, in semi-profile, a trick of the camera showing smoke coming out of her left eye, was still on the wall, beautiful and alluring.

My aunt poured tea into gold-rimmed china cups and told me to help myself. While we savoured the pastries, her face became serious. "I don't know why you want to dig up the past," she said. "Anyway, our story is riddled with lies, and I don't feel like talking about it."

I had come here prepared for exactly this type of reaction. When Teresa had told Aunt Alcira that I was writing our family's story and wanted to ask her some questions about Julius and Filomena, she had replied that it had cost her many bitter tears and years of struggle to achieve what she had and she didn't want any more suffering. Clearly, she was still trauma-tised by all she had gone through and feared that our family's past would bring ruin and disgrace upon all of us. I understood her apprehension but did not share her anxiety. Who on this planet could say that their ancestors lived wholly exemplary lives? And why should anyone be held responsible for what their relations did decades ago?

"Dear aunt, please don't be afraid to confide in me," I said as I helped myself to an ojarazca. "I'm writing our story because we need to know who we are. I know there are things that will remain a mystery, and I prom-ise to make it clear that what I'm writing is only a probable account."

Aunt Alcira smiled. "That is good."

I told my aunt that there were many episodes in our story that made me feel extremely proud. I told her that ours was a story that needed to be told and that my main reason for writing was to pay homage to our family's bravery. As I said this, I took out two parcels from my bag. "Here you are, Tía. A couple of presents for you."

She unwrapped the smaller box, a special gift from my husband, Jim, a piece of Belleek porcelain from Ulster, a delicate white vase decorated with tiny green flowers. The other present was a blue pashmina, which she immediately wrapped around her shoulders. "Oh, this is so beautiful, so soft," she said and smiled.

I sensed that, after opening her presents and listening to my reasons for writing our story, she was better disposed to telling me what she knew. I had not told her that I was also writing about Néstor and Cecilia. I dared not mention this to her, as I could imagine what a painful subject it must be. However, both my cousins Gerardo and Rosita wanted me to finish writing this book. They both believed my aunt would be glad that Cecilia's sacrifice was at last acknowledged. As far as Alcira knew, I was writing only about my grandparents. I felt bad about not confessing what I was doing, but Néstor and Cecilia's story was not my aunt's alone. Their story belonged to everyone in my family. It belonged to Bolivia.

During that visit Aunt Alcira confirmed what Rosita had told me: my grandfather was already married when he started a relationship with Filomena. Their firstborn, Silvio, was given to Julius's wife when he was only a few days old. My grandparents had never actually married.

I also learnt about my grandmother's return to Tarija after Julius's death. When Filomena arrived from Argentina, although her parents and siblings reproached her for bringing dishonour upon their family, they nevertheless welcomed her back into their home. Full of guilt and shame, she became a recluse. To avoid further disgrace, her family asked a friend of theirs, a grandee of the town, to obtain baptism certificates—birth certificates did not exist at the time—for the three girls, in which they appeared as legitimate daughters of Filomena and Doctor Seifert—one of the lies my aunt was referring to.

Alcira was unable to explain how the narrow and conservative Tarija society had accepted Filomena's girls without much fuss. Maybe it was because my grandmother had come from one of the richest and most respected families in the town; maybe it was because my grandfather was German and European foreigners at that time were highly regarded.

"Muchas gracias, Tía," I said as I kissed my aunt on the cheeks. I left her home with a sketch-pad full of notes about my grandparents' lives and my head still full of questions.

In January 2006, for the first time since the arrival of the Spaniards, a native Bolivian, an Aymara Indian, was elected president of my country. Evo Morales was invested in a traditional ceremony in Tiwanaku, at the pre-Incan ruins near Lake Titicaca.

What a different country this was from the Bolivia of my childhood, where no Indian was ever allowed inside the cafeterias my family and friends frequented and where Quechuas and Aymaras were treated with contempt because of their brown skin and were even blamed for their poverty and illiteracy.

What a long way we have come. What a long way we still have to travel.

Change is slow and often painful. In a country where the overwhelming majority of the population is of Amerindian origin, Evo had to happen sooner or later.

Finding Out

October–November 2010

Two years after my last visit, I returned once again to the city of my childhood and adolescence and stayed for six weeks at my sister Teresa's house. My baby sister was now a successful businesswoman and the director of her own company. She was the only person in our family who called me Mári, a name she gave me when she was a toddler. Tall, slim and sure of herself, she left the house in the mornings dressed in smart business suits, a silk scarf around her shoulders, and just the faintest scent of Chanel No.5. I was very proud of her.

During this holiday I wanted to publish a few articles in the local papers, interview the historian who wrote *Teoponte*, and travel to Tarija to learn more about my grandparents. I was worried that six weeks wouldn't be enough time to accomplish even half of what I wanted to do.

I also wanted to spend time just walking around the city by myself, absorbing its sights, sounds and smells. Apart from when I came for my mother's funeral, I had usually returned to Bolivia with either my children or my husband and had needed to attend to them. On this holiday I was free to do as I pleased.

As I ambled through the streets of La Paz, enjoying the scenery and observing people, a peaceful feeling entered me, and soon I sensed my mother's presence. Her ghost followed me through the bustling avenues. She was with me in every shop, building, and park that I visited—the same places that she and I used to frequent. The sky was clear, deep blue, the warm air caressed my skin, and soon childhood memories flooded my mind. I raised my gaze towards the tall buildings, towards Illimani and the other Andean peaks, and I found my mother in every place I went.

I walked up Avenida Villazón, trying to find my primary school, Colegio Bancario, where she had worked as a kindergarten teacher and where I spent five happy years. I believed it was there, in that narrow passage grandiosely named Calle del Aviador. I entered the passage and at the end I saw a two-storey greyish-green building and a sign above the door: Instituto Bancario. My heart beat fast. I was sure the door must be closed—but no, it was open. There was nobody at reception—only a few teenagers chatting in groups. It was four o'clock; lessons were over. The central hall, which had seemed enormous when I was a girl—with a green-and-white-tiled floor where all the school ceremonies took place and where we sang the national anthem daily—seemed to have shrunk. I stepped into my old classroom, where I'd learnt to read and write, and everything was as it had been nearly fifty years ago: the long wooden planks on the floors, the old desks with names and drawings engraved deep into the wood, the dusty greyish blackboards. I left my classroom and walked towards the preschool area, my mother's room, and I saw her again, as I had seen her so many times, smiling, surrounded by her little ones, handing out Play-Doh and coloured chalk. The children sat cross-legged on the floor, their eyes on their teacher, listening to her every word. They all wanted to be her favourite. I heard their giggles, their voices: "Me, me, Miss Emma!" She patted the boys and girls on the head, sang with them, clapped hands with them, and hugged the ones who were feeling shy. Her laughter filled the room with joy. I wanted to engrave this picture in my mind, but my eyes became cloudy, and her image melted away like mist.

I left the school, continued towards Plaza del Estudiante, and crossed the street towards El Prado. My mother's spirit came with me, and together we ascended the pale stone staircase that led to the main door of Maria Auxiliadora Church. After saying a short prayer, we left the church and continued up towards the end of El Prado and the statue of Simón Bolívar. I walked up to Plaza Murillo, the presidential palace, the cathedral and the Museo Nacional de Arte...and Emma came with me, my constant companion.

I was tired and thirsty. The sun was at its zenith; people started to leave their offices in search of lunch. At a cafeteria near Plaza Murillo, I ordered a coffee and two savoury salteña pastries filled with spicy chicken and diced potatoes. They were delicious but not as good as the ones my mother used to make.

Her image was vivid in my mind, and my thoughts took me back to the events of the previous day. The day before, I had visited my mother's house, the humble house in the country just outside La Paz, where she spent her last years and endured long days of solitude, her three daughters in faraway places. Somehow, she found ways of shaking away all negative thoughts, dusted herself off, and got up. What a comfort it was to think that at the end she was not alone, thanks to Carolina and Teresa, who came back to Bolivia to provide her with companionship and affection in her final days. I, living on another continent and tied to my British family, was able to give her only a little of the love and support I so much wanted to give her.

The day before, I had crossed the threshold of her old house in Achumani, a lovely semi-rural suburb on the outskirts of La Paz, which Teresa had kept exactly as it was the day our mother died. Emma was there waiting for me, looking at me with her sweet big eyes from every photograph. Her ghost was hiding behind each potted plant, behind each object that I touched, smelled and caressed. She was there sitting on the stool by the little telephone table of carved dark wood, made by a master Bolivian wood-carver. She was there like a noble Spanish *maja* beside the chest of drawers, also of carved wood, her pride and glory and testimony to her exquisite taste. The ravages of time and the many blows that life had struck her had taken away some of her beauty, but her spirit remained indomitable. Until the very end, she maintained that everything would be all right, that soon her problems would be over...but it saddened me to think that her twilight years were maybe full of worries.

I then saw her standing in her kitchen, kneading bread on the table, wearing her long white apron and with flour up to her elbows, pounding the dough, her hair tied in a bun.

The ghosts of my childhood and adolescence were also waiting for me at my mother's house: on the coffee table, the porcelain elephant that had followed us from house to house; on a wall, the photo of her three princesses, who, wearing fluffy dresses of white tulle and red ribbons, would enter the school hall to the music of Verdi's *Aïda* to celebrate the coronation of the school queen on the first day of spring. Three little girls made of candyfloss, smiling for their mother on a brilliant, sunny day.

And then that ancient thick red blanket with thin white stripes—one on each side—reminded me of her bed with the metal frame, and I saw myself as a child, covered by that same itchy blanket, shivering during the cruel winters of La Paz.

I entered the bedroom that she shared with my son, Christopher, when we came to see her in 1998. On top of the bedside table was a photograph of Christopher and my husband, Jim, in our home in England. Hidden among her other papers, I discovered also a photo of Olivia, aged eight or nine. Our past lives, countries and cultures—all mixed together.

Tears pricked my eyes. I opened the doors and drawers of her wardrobe, and I found her there, too. Her clothes made a profound impact on me. I caressed, touched, and smelled her blouses, wishing their scent and texture to remain with me for hours. Her grey suit, of English cloth and English style; her pleated red skirt; her white shirt and the green one.

Where have her spirit, her laughter, and her joy gone? All I have left are my memories of her and the good example she set, her photographs, a few letters.

And then it was time for her to return to the ghostly home she had inhabited for the past seven years. But I knew she'd come back; I knew that tomorrow she'd follow me through the streets of La Paz and that I'd again find her in every object that she touched, in the magnificent three-peaked Mount Illimani that she so loved, in the clear sky of our city, in our country.

Teresa, Gerardo and Aunt Alcira organised family gatherings and parties in my honour and made a fuss of me. My sister pampered me, always smiling, always eager to satisfy my wishes. She asked her maid to cook the

Bolivian dishes that I loved so much but that she herself was not too keen on; she made sure the radio was tuned in to the stations that played our music rather than the latest American hits; she enveloped me with affection. I often thought of Jim and the children but didn't really miss them.

It was a race against time, so I crammed as much as possible into every day. By the middle of November, the newspaper *Los Tiempos de Cochabamba* had published three of my articles; I also wrote a story about my mother, which would be published later. I met up with Señor Gustavo Rodríguez, the author of *Teoponte*, and he told me about Cecilia's last days. At the public library, I read the newspapers of that terrible month, March 1972, when my cousin was murdered. All the things I wanted to achieve were done, except one. I needed to see for myself what I already believed was a truthful account of my grandparents' story. It was time to go to Tarija.

Teresa and I packed our bags and boarded a plane to Sucre, our colonial jewel of a city, where we stayed for a couple of days before continuing on our journey to the town where I was born. We arrived in Tarija on a warm Wednesday afternoon and lodged at a hotel near the main square, Plaza Luis de Fuentes. After a good night's sleep, we got up early and started the day in haste. First, we walked to the civil-registry offices to obtain documents that would help Teresa navigate the complexities of the small inheritance our mother had left us. We then visited the German consulate, hoping that they would be able to help us find information about our grandfather; unfortunately, the consul was on holiday, and I was told that if I wrote a detailed note about what I needed, the consul would deal with my request as soon as she returned. The receptionist gave me two sheets of paper, and I composed a long, polite letter explaining the nature of my enquiries. I wrote Teresa's address and telephone number in La Paz as well as my email address. (Six years later, in 2016, I have finally finished writing this book, but I have still not heard from the German consul.)

After lunch my sister and I went back to our hotel for a quick nap. We were exhausted after our intense morning. Thirty minutes of sleep should have been enough to recover our strength, but when the alarm rang, neither Teresa nor I could wake up, so I pressed the snooze button. Ten minutes later the alarm went off again, and again we did not move. Our legs felt like lead; our eyelids weighed a ton. We lay in bed for another half hour. It was nearly five o'clock when we finally got up, still groggy. "It must be our age," Teresa joked. Yes, and the sheer intensity of our enquiries and the knowledge that we only had two days to find out all we needed to know.

Teresa suggested we go for a walk around the town. "Good idea," I said. I wanted to show her my father's home, only a couple of blocks from the main plaza.

The late-afternoon sun was warm. The air smelled of jasmine. We walked up Calle General Trigo, the street where my father and mother had lived until she left for La Paz. I had trouble identifying the house. (A few old buildings had been demolished and new ones built in their place; others had been renovated.) Time had erased so many aspects of our lives. I knew that my father's house had been converted into a shoe shop, but I saw no sign of that. "I think it was here," I said and pointed to a two-storey building that lacked the traditional red tiles and heavy wooden doors. This new house looked clean and bright and modern, but it was soulless.

We headed towards the market, the same market where my mother had eaten lunch with her school friends more than seventy years earlier. The cholas were busy dispensing hot drinks and homemade cakes. The smells of cinnamon, cloves and vanilla brought back many memories. "Look, those empanadas," I said to Teresa. "Just like Mami's." We bought four cinnamon buns plus four empanadas de lacayote iced with sugar and egg white. Although our hotel provided breakfast, the following morning my sister and I would eat what we had purchased at the market, the food of our childhood. Sitting on long benches, people were eating and drinking from the same enamel mugs and plates that I remembered so well. Thank God the market had not changed; thank God the cholas still wore their wide, colourful skirts and puffy, short-sleeved blouses, their long hair in plaits, each with a flower behind her ear.

We paid for our cakes and set off towards a shop near the market. The smells of leather and freshly ironed cloth hung in the air. For decades this shop had been selling the rough sandals and shoes the cholos and campesinos wore to work in the fields; it also sold wide-brimmed hats and silky mantilla shawls with tassels and embroidered flowers—all the things any self-respecting *chapaco* needed. I breathed in deeply; I wanted these smells to remain inside my lungs for as long as possible.

We climbed up the hill towards Iglesia de San Roque, the church where I was baptised. Unfortunately, it was closed, and we would not have time to return for another visit. To console ourselves we walked to the edge of the hill to admire the view. The town appeared beneath us, with its red-tiled roofs and trees in bloom. There wasn't a cloud in the sky; the birds were singing, and a soft breeze gently touched our hair. I wished Jim and the children could live here with me in this blessed corner of our planet. I looked down at the street we had just climbed and imagined the procession and celebrations of Holy Week. I pictured dozens of flower arches straddling both sides of the street, men carrying the statues of the saints on wooden beams, women wearing lace veils on their heads, incense smoke rising to the sky, pomegranates, wine for the adults, peach juice for the children. I saw a pretty sixteen-year-old girl, Filomena, dressed in white from head to toe, her face covered by a see-through veil, deep in prayer, fingering her white rosary, her face serene, virginal.

"It's just lovely!" Teresa said, and my Easter vision disappeared.

It was nearly time for dinner, so we headed towards the plaza to eat chicken pasta and salad at the Gato Pardo, one of the oldest and most popular cafeterias in town. After dinner we sat on a bench in the plaza to enjoy the evening and watch people go by. The statue of the founder of Tarija, the conquistador Luis de Fuentes, was still here, as was the statue of my distinguished ancestor, Aniceto Arce, with the same proud and severe expression on his face. And I thought of my mother as a young Emma sitting on these same benches, strolling around the plaza, chatting and laughing with her friends. I saw her walking arm-in-arm with her girlfriends while the young men in the plaza blew them kisses and flirted with them.

Emma's friends were a little shy and didn't look the men in the eye. She, however, addressed them, her head held high. "Hola. Buenas tardes." On a late afternoon like this, she had smelled the scent of the orange trees in bloom and looked up at the tall date palms—just as I was doing then—and watched as the sun started its descent towards the horizon. On an afternoon like this, she had been here, full of energy and joy, her future ahead of her. I didn't share these thoughts with Teresa—I didn't want to make her cry. Seven years after our mother's death, my sister still found it hard to accept her absence.

Back at our hotel that evening, we telephoned an old lady who had known our grandmother, a relation of hers. "Buenas noches, Señora Castillo," I said and introduced myself. I told her that I was sorry to disturb her and that my cousin Silvia, whom she knew well, had given me her number. I told her that I, too, was Filomena's granddaughter and that I wanted to ask her a few questions about my grandmother. Immediately I sensed the tension at the other end of the line.

"Oh no, señora," the old woman said, "I cannot see you. I'm too exhausted. I don't feel well at all."

"I'm sorry to hear that," I said, "but I promise I won't stay long."

"No, no. It's not possible. I suffer from bad headaches."

"Por favor, señora," I pleaded, "I don't live in Bolivia, and tomorrow afternoon I'm going back to La Paz. I would love to learn just a little about my grandmother, please."

"That is a pity, a real pity," she said, "but I cannot see you. I am very sorry."

And that was it. The last person alive who had known my grandmother as a young woman had just refused to see me, and there was nothing I could do about it.

Friday—our last day. Teresa and I got up early and had a breakfast of coffee and the empanadas we had bought at the market. An important day—maybe the most important of all—was ahead of us. That morning we were going to the cathedral to see our mother's baptismal certificate.

When my mother and aunts were born, birth certificates did not yet exist. As practically everyone in Bolivia was a Catholic, certificates of baptism were the only documents people needed. I wondered how Jews or atheists managed. We left the hotel in good time to be the first at the cathedral's office, but when we arrived, we found that there was already a queue of about eight waiting at reception. Soon a young clerk arrived, dressed casually in jeans and a green-striped T-shirt. He said, "Buenos días," and, leaving the door open behind him, went into his office. From where Teresa and I were sitting, we could see what he was doing. After putting pens and sheets of paper on top of his desk, he pulled up a chair, called the first person in, and shut the door. Teresa and I waited for about forty minutes. I had a lump in my stomach and imagined my sister did, too. We leafed through the magazines on the side table, sat down, got up again, twiddled our thumbs, combed our hair, applied makeup, checked our mobiles. Finally, our turn came.

"You go in, Mári," Teresa said, her expression tense. "I'll wait here."

I was surprised. My sister, a strong, determined professional who didn't suffer fools gladly, had for the moment lost her nerve.

The clerk offered me a seat and asked me how he could help. "I'd like to see the baptism certificates of my mother and aunts, please," I said. I gave him names and dates. He opened a file on his computer to find out exactly where the relevant books were. He could not find anything under S for Seifert, so he looked under C for Castillo. "Ah, yes. Here they are." He got up and turned to the back wall, filled from floor to ceiling with shelves full of thick books of entries. He removed one from a shelf near the floor and brought it to his desk.

Dark and leather-bound, the weighty tome occupied nearly half the surface of the desk. The clerk opened the book and started turning the thick pages, handwritten in black ink. "Here," he said and pointed with his finger. My mother's baptism entry was in front of me, and I saw that the infant Emma Castillo, daughter of Filomena Castillo and Julius Seifert, born in Argentina, had been baptised in Tarija in 1930; her status was given as *hija natural*, illegitimate daughter. In black-and-white, my grandmother's secret stared out at me. My aunts' certificates said the same: they were all illegitimate children. Of course, I had been expecting to see exactly what I was then seeing, but maybe at the back of my mind I was hoping that things would turn out differently.

What Rosita had told me was now confirmed, but I was still dumb-founded. A quiet sadness invaded me, and I wanted to cry, but I was also relieved that the truth had at last come out. All those years believing that my grandparents were married, that he had kidnapped her to force her to accept him...All those years witnessing my grandmother's torment and wondering why she had to suffer so...All those years of my questions not being answered, of my mother getting angry at my hinting at any impro-priety on my grandfather's part...Years of silence and lies.

And yet what else could my mother and aunts have done? My grand-mother had been consumed by guilt and shame, believing she didn't de-serve redemption, and my mother had tried to protect her own mother from more suffering, from probing and questioning that would again cut her like a sword. My mother and her sisters *had* to go along with the lies and the silence. I understood all that. And I understood even more the reasons for not saying a word about their brother, Silvio. I was filled with compassion for all of them, for their long decades of suffering. I also wondered, when did the three girls find out the truth? I suspected that it must have been Uncle Silvio who told them, when he came back from his years of self-imposed exile, still full of resentment towards his mother and sisters. Yes, it must have been him, as who else could have revealed such momentous facts? Alcira, Emma and Eugenia must have been young adults when Silvio reappeared in their lives, and as grown-ups the shock of learning the truth must have been even worse than if they had been children. Silvio, too, had suffered, his mind consumed by anger, never understanding the reasons behind the facts.

Teresa had to see this with her own eyes; she needed to come in and give me strength, so I asked the clerk to call her in. My sister entered, read the entry, held her breath for a few seconds, and let out a sigh. Our eyes met, and we held each other's gaze for a moment without smiling; then she reached for my hand, and I put my other arm around her. With the clerk's permission, I took a photograph of the entry. I also requested a printed copy of my mother's certificate. When he handed me the printed version, I was surprised by something: it was different from the original record. It said that Emma Seifert was the legitimate daughter of Filomena Castillo and Julius Seifert. How was that possible? And then I remembered what Gerardo had told me: Filomena's parents had paid to have the certificates altered to protect the girls.

My love, respect and admiration for my mother and grandmother were unchanged. Who was I to judge them? What would I have done in their place?

"Is there anything else I can do for you, señora?" the clerk said. Professional and polite, his face was inscrutable. I was sure he'd witnessed this type of emotional scene before.

There was nothing more to do here, so we thanked him and got up to leave. It was time to collect our suitcases and go to the airport. Teresa and I walked back to the hotel in silence. I knew that later we would talk about this morning's events, but at the moment words and feelings didn't seem to match.

I had finally reached the end of my quest. Writing this book had helped me to understand a little better two big family tragedies and allowed me to rescue from oblivion Filomena, Néstor, Cecilia and Emma, whose lives shaped the destinies of so many people. This book was my way of keeping their fire alive.

Throughout my journey I learnt a great deal about my family and about myself, and although not all the mysteries were solved, the search for the truth gave me solace. I had long ago accepted that I would probably never know my grandparents' real story, as the only people who could tell me what actually happened were Julius and Filomena themselves. All

I could do was tell our tale based on family stories that had been hidden behind locked doors.

Emma and Filomena, two great pachamamas, taught me about finding courage to survive amid terrible circumstances. I hope I have inherited some of their wisdom and strength.

Postscript

The Poignancy of All Our Lives

Soon after my sixtieth birthday, when I thought my book was finished and ready to be published, life brought me yet another surprise. In an unexpected turn, a true story that resembles a magic-realism tale from García Márquez started to unfold before my eyes. After nearly six decades of absence, my father—or rather, his ghost—reappeared in my life.

One Thursday in April 2015, my sister Carolina sent me an intriguing email. "An unbelievable thing" was the title of her message. As I read it, I could hardly believe what she was telling me. A few days before, a stranger, a woman who lived in Argentina, had contacted her via her Facebook page. The woman, called Sandra, was wondering whether Carolina was the same Carolina Arce Seifert[14] from La Paz, daughter of José Arce Ortiz from Tarija. Sandra said her father was also called José Arce Ortiz and that she was hoping to get in contact with his daughters from a previous marriage, two girls called Mariana and Carolina. Sandra knew that our mother's surname was Seifert and many other details that only a child of José's could have known. Carolina was wondering whether she should reply to this message and whether she should accept her request of Facebook friendship.

---

14 In Spain and Latin America, every newborn baby is given two surnames: first the father's surname (Arce, in this case), followed by the mother's surname (Seifert). This can be confusing for English-speaking persons.

I telephoned my sister immediately. "I think both of us should contact her," I told her. "All the information she's given us is one hundred percent correct. I don't think she's a fake. Tell her I want to contact her, too. Give her my email address." Within a few hours, the three of us were exchanging messages. Sandra had been able to find Carolina on Facebook because my sister had kept her maiden name—in Spanish-speaking countries, when a woman marries, she doesn't change her surname but simply adds her husband's at the end. Sandra could not find me, as I'd become Mariana Swann when I'd married Jim.

I learnt that Sandra had a younger brother, a man called José, like my father. Sandra was fifty-two, eight years younger than me, and José was fifty. Sandra said that our father had had a serious relationship with her mother, Olga. He had married Olga a few months before his death so that the children would not be disadvantaged. "My father was a loving dad, very affectionate with me," Sandra said. "He used to sit me on his knee and tell me that little José and I were not alone, that we had two other sisters, Mariana and Carolina. Every time he said this, his eyes would fill up with tears. I was only six when he died, but I remember well his pain when thinking of his other daughters."

That weekend Carolina, Sandra and I corresponded feverishly. In my first message to Sandra and José Junior, I told them that our memories of our father were very different. To them, he had been a loving dad. To Carolina and me, he'd just been a name on our birth certificates, a total stranger. He'd died when I was fourteen, and unsurprisingly, I'd felt nothing when I'd heard about his death.

It was difficult to read what we each had to say. Sandra's portrait of our father was that of an affectionate man but also a victim. According to Sandra, he had lost his house as well as his happiness when my mother, Emma, had left him and gone away to live in La Paz. Apparently, our father had always maintained that Emma was the woman he had loved all his life and also the one who had hurt him the most by taking away his little daughter Mariana. (My mother was pregnant with Carolina when she left Tarija and gave birth to my sister in La Paz a few months later.)

Carolina and I could not believe our ears. We were also more than a little annoyed, as we were not about to have our mother's name blackened like that by someone we hardly knew! But we didn't want to argue with Sandra. Now that we had found one another, all three of us wanted to learn about our past. I wrote a long letter to Sandra and her brother, José, telling them about Carolina's and my experiences of growing up without a father. Did they know that our father had never sent my mother any money to support us? Did they know that one of the reasons she'd left him was because he was a womaniser? Did they know that when I was barely four my mother went back to Tarija to sort out her affairs and he took this opportunity to kidnap me? God knows what sort of life I would have had if she hadn't found and rescued me. And it was not true that he had lost his big house, because ten years after our parents' divorce, when Carolina and I had gone to Tarija on holiday, we'd found our father's older sister, Aunt Antonia, living comfortably in that very same house.

I remember that holiday in Tarija very well and have devoted a whole chapter to it in this book. That summer, in December 1966, Carolina had celebrated her tenth birthday and I my twelfth. We'd had a wonderful time marred only by our disappointment in our father not coming to see us.

The hurt of that rejection had stayed deep inside me, finally bursting out one sunny Saturday morning more than forty years later, when I'd sobbed for my father for the first and only time in my life, in my husband's arms. "He never came; he never came!" The pain and anger I had carried for decades had flowed out of me like a torrent that could not be contained.

Knowing what I now know of my aunt's behaviour, it is highly likely that she'd lied to us. Telling José that his pretty young daughters were looking forward to seeing him could have been detrimental to her plans. What if, in a sudden burst of love for us, he'd decided to set up a fund towards our education? What if he'd given us too many presents, depriving Aunt Antonia of what she considered to be rightfully hers? She couldn't have risked losing everything to some skinny little girls after all the hard work she had put in. It is possible that she had never told our father that we were in Tarija and had made sure that he'd stayed on his farm during the two months of our visit.

My newfound siblings knew nothing of this, of course. Sandra said that she didn't want to hurt or offend us but insisted that our father had suffered because of losing his wife and daughters. I was disturbed by this suggestion, as I could not imagine him ever having any feelings for me or Carolina. From what I had heard as a child, my father did not seem to have been an assertive man. His older sister, Antonia, had run his house and financial affairs. However, despite his weakness of character, he had not been a helpless victim but a grown man who had known what he was doing. His neglect of Carolina and me could not be laid at my mother's feet.

Carolina and I spoke at length over the weekend. She worried that maybe we had opened Pandora's Box. I hoped not. It was clear that Sandra and her mother and brother had also suffered, and she was just telling us her version of events. She seemed kind and sincere in her desire to get to know us. My husband was also concerned that these new revelations would open up old wounds. "I don't want you getting hurt, Mariana. Be careful, be suspicious," Jim said. Sandra's husband, in Buenos Aires, had uttered similar words. However, despite our reservations, we persevered in our efforts to learn about our past.

In one of her messages, Sandra said that in a marriage there are always two people. On the Monday following that intense weekend, Karen, a friend of mine, came to see me. I had not planned on telling her anything about my newly discovered siblings, but, as this was a momentous piece of news, I told her everything. "I'm upset by the suggestion that my mum is fifty percent guilty for the collapse of her marriage," I said. Karen sipped her coffee slowly, her expression serious as she gathered her thoughts.

"Your new sister is right," she said after a short pause. "From what I've read about your mother, she was completely unsuitable to be José's wife. She was a free spirit, impossible to control."

Suddenly, a window opened inside my brain. Of course my mother and father had been incompatible. She had been an independent, intellectually ambitious young woman who could not tolerate any restraints. José had needed a submissive little wife who'd treat him as her master and allow him to do as he pleased, extramarital affairs included. Besides, two other factors, apart from his unfaithfulness, had contributed to the collapse of their marriage: José had wanted to live on his farm, a two-day journey on horseback, deep in the country, without electricity or running water. Emma had refused to live there. The other reason had been Antonia, looming over the newlyweds, controlling everything and trying to control my mother. Who could put up with such interference?

After Karen left, I emailed Sandra and suggested that we speak on the phone. I telephoned her in Buenos Aires that very evening, determined to listen to her with an open mind.

It was surreal speaking to a stranger who shared fifty percent of my genes and a big chunk of my early history. During that conversation I learnt about Sandra's life and her family's suffering. Her mother, Olga, had been a humble servant in our father's house. Meek and insecure, her relationship with José had been "odd," as Sandra put it. "My mother neither asked for anything nor expected anything from our father. She did as she was told and never contradicted him," Sandra said. "Of course, Aunt Antonia hated all of us and called us dirty Indians. Whenever I visited Antonia's house—our father's house in Tarija—wearing my best dress, my hair braided and tied with pretty bows, she would always have me remove my clothes for disinfecting and force me to take a bath. In her eyes, I would always be dirty. Most of the time, we lived in the country, as Dad loved his farm. What I remember most about him is his kindness and tenderness towards me and his tears when he thought of his other daughters. According to my mum, your mother, Emma, was the only woman he ever loved."

Slowly, a different portrait of my father started to form in my mind. Maybe he hadn't been the cold and uncaring man I believed he had been? He had loved us—me, in any case, as he had never seen Carolina.

Sandra remembered him once rolling a wad of banknotes to send to La Paz—maybe for Carolina and me, but she couldn't be sure. She remembered him anxiously asking people who had been to the capital for news of his little girls. Sandra also said that our father had once gone to La Paz to have an eye operation and had wanted to see us but somehow had not been able to.

"The suggestion that my mother stopped our father from seeing us or that she didn't tell us about any money, or other things, she received from him is abhorrent to Carolina and me," I told Sandra. "I hope you understand how distressing and offensive that is." Sandra said that it was not her intention to offend us or to judge our mother. All she was doing was repeating what she had heard and observed as a child. Conversely, she found hearing the bad things I told her about our father upsetting, too.

Sandra and I agreed that what a child remembers is not always accurate and that a child's interpretation of what she witnesses can also be erroneous. False memories, distortions of the facts, prejudice, even outright lies may have become part of what we each remembered.

For instance, the roll of banknotes that our father had said was being sent to La Paz could have been intended for one of his business contacts there. It is also possible that the money never reached its destination. Bank transfers, although difficult and expensive, were possible at that time, so why did my father not send the money that way, if his intention was to help my mother? That she'd hidden something like this from us would not make much sense. Often throughout this book I have described overhearing my mother and grandmother talking in our kitchen about our lack of funds. Emma worked at three part-time jobs, leaving the house at seven-thirty in the morning and returning after nine on the evenings when she worked at the Spanish embassy. If my father had sent us money, then Emma would not have had to work so hard and would have had more time to spend at home with her children.

The more I thought about it, the more I realised that this whole episode about my father was full of inconsistencies. If he really had cared for Carolina and me, why hadn't he helped our mother support us? Why hadn't he made a determined effort to contact us? He'd known we attended a Catholic convent school in La Paz, because Antonia sent a telegram to the school announcing his death. It would not have been difficult to find us. Why had he kidnapped me? Why hadn't he come to see Carolina and me during our holiday in Tarija? So many questions without answers...

In this book I have not mentioned that my father had had two children out of wedlock twelve years before he'd married my mother: a boy called Pedro and a girl called Beatriz. I have not mentioned them, because they do not play any role in my family story—that is, until now. Aunt Antonia, Pedro and Beatriz had hated any woman who came between them and José. When my father had married Olga, Sandra's mother, they'd done all they could to make her life—and her children's lives—a misery. "They were especially angry when our father married my mother, as this meant we'd inherit at least a part of his estate," Sandra said. "Our father's last days were very difficult. He had a bad fall while riding his horse, and soon after that he had a stroke. He was weak and in constant pain."

According to Sandra, our father wanted to leave his affairs in order, so he made Pedro promise over and over that all his children would be looked after financially after his death. "I'll do as you say, Papá, but stop asking me the same thing every time!" Pedro would complain. Our father's health deteriorated by the day. One morning little Sandra heard on the local radio that her dad, José Arce, had passed away. She didn't really understand what that meant, and only much later did she realise that she would never see him again.

Immediately after our father's death, Antonia and Pedro entered Olga's house, opened every drawer, and removed everything of value they could find. Olga had been too scared to say anything, and she'd let them do as they pleased. They'd threatened her: "You'll end up in jail, and your children will be taken away unless you go away from Tarija." As Olga had been a timid and uneducated woman, she'd had no idea that, as José's wife, the law was on her side. Terrified of losing her children, she'd packed her bags and left for Argentina with hardly a peso in her pocket.

And so Carolina, Sandra, little José and I were deprived of our rightful inheritance. But dishonesty hasn't brought much happiness. Aunt Antonia is long dead, having spent her life hating and despising others. I believe

Beatriz and Pedro now live in Cuzco, Peru, in reduced circumstances, having squandered nearly all their ill-gotten loot.

My telephone conversation with Sandra lasted one and a half hours. When I hung up, I felt weak in the knees and was ready to go to bed.

Carolina soon started to recall other events, such as overhearing conversations between rich and beautiful aunt Angelica Arce—our father's cousin—and our mother. Aunt Angelica had been one of the most attractive women in Tarija. After she'd moved to La Paz, her health had deteriorated. She'd spent her days sitting at home, her beauty gone, afflicted with cancer in one of her eyes—I can still picture her white eye patch. Aunt Angelica loved my mother and had agreed with her decision to leave her marriage. Carolina said Angelica and our mother used to talk about the harsh conditions Emma would have to accept before my father let her go. My mother had been allowed to leave Tarija only after signing a document releasing him from any financial obligations towards her. (After all, in those Catholic, macho times, she was the one breaking up her marriage.) That my mother had accepted these conditions can only mean that her relationship with my father and his bullying sister Antonia had been utterly unbearable.

Carolina also remembered us receiving a huge round cheese from our father's farm—the only time we recall ever having received anything from him—when she was about eight and I was ten. Our mother had immediately made us write letters thanking him for his present; each of us had also sent him a photograph, which we'd signed on the back. We never received a reply. If he'd loved us so much, why hadn't he pursued this little window of opportunity? Could it have been because Antonia had got in the way again?

Sandra said her mother had a few photos of our father and there was even one of him holding me as a baby. I stopped breathing for a few seconds. My father had held me in his arms. I had never imagined such a scene. I only have one sepia photo of him, looking serious in his three-piece suit. "I would love to see that photo. Please, please make a copy and send it to me," I begged Sandra. A few days later, I received several photos via my Facebook page. There he was, my father, looking tired and old and fat, wearing a suit, as always. His expression was sad and his eyes were droopy. I scrolled down the page and came across a tender image: my dad with me in his arms. I must have been four or five months old, a plump baby dressed in hand-knitted baby clothes and bootees.

But even more surprising was seeing a photo of Carolina, aged eight, wearing a hand-knitted polka-dot sweater, with short hair, smiling timidly, the same photo I have at home in my family album. On the back of the photo, Carolina had written, "*Para mi amado papito* (To my beloved daddy)," and signed it Carola Arce. To my beloved daddy! The only explanation for such a salutation is that my mother must have dictated it to Carolina. This has to be the photograph Carolina had sent (I sent a similar one), together with a thank-you letter, after we'd received the big cheese wheel from his farm.

During other email exchanges, Sandra told us that in the past few months she had started thinking more and more about her childhood and our father. She found this odd, as she didn't usually think about these subjects and also had terrible trouble remembering events from her past, to the great annoyance of her family. "I'd been sleeping badly, dreaming about my dad, and waking up during the night. I felt that he wasn't at peace, that he was still looking for his other daughters and that maybe he wanted me to find you. So I started searching for you. I kept on seeing him, in my mind's eye, sitting with me on his knee, fat as he was, with his double chin and big stomach, calling me *hijita*, so tender and affectionate. Then he'd become sad and tearful, thinking of what he had lost. These dreams disturbed me. I had no choice but to keep on looking for his little girls, Mariana and Carolina. That's how I found you. I was afraid you wouldn't want to reply to my message, that you'd be angry and suspicious. I'm so glad to speak to you two at last. I feel Dad is a little happier now."

It was as if a voice from our distant past had awakened and stirred our souls. Even mine. I am an agnostic. I do not believe in angels or spirits. I believe that after death there's only oblivion, a big emptiness. And still, despite my lack of faith, I found myself deeply moved by the events of those few days.

In the 1950s, Bolivia had been one of the few Latin American countries that allowed divorce. My mother had left my father in 1956, barely four years after divorce had become legal, and had been obliged to accept the tough conditions imposed by my father. She'd lived in a male-dominated, conservative and Catholic society where leaving one's husband was scandalous. Who knows—maybe that's also why she'd chosen to leave Tarija: to escape the malicious gossip. Or maybe she'd simply wanted a fresh start.

It is of course possible that she'd kept part of the truth from us. She had been a divorced woman, struggling against the odds to support her three daughters and her own old mother. It is possible that she'd remained angry and resentful for a long time—and who can blame her? Whatever happened after she divorced my father can never alter my respect and love for her.

Listening to what Sandra had to say about our father filled me with peace as well as with compassion for him. I am glad that Sandra and her brother enjoyed having a dad, even if it was for only a few years. I am glad he was a kind and loving father to them.

"He was a peaceful man and used to spend his time listening to music and reading books," Sandra said. That image was the opposite of how I had imagined him.

Learning about the other aspects of his personality has given me comfort. I have lived for sixty years hardly thinking of him and being angry with him the few times I did. I'd spent my life convinced that he had never cared for me or my sister. It is good to know that he had cared a little, even if his way of caring was so feeble. I am sad for his suffering, and I hope that now he can rest in peace.

About the Author

Mariana Swann grew up in Bolivia during times of profound social and political upheaval. When she was twenty, she left for Switzerland to study translation at Geneva University. There, she met her future husband and moved to England to marry him in 1982.

After university, she worked as a part-time translator and teacher of foreign languages for many years. In 2010, she went on to receive a master of arts in creative and life writing from Goldsmiths College, University of London.

Raised with a keen sense of social justice and in a politically active family, Mariana appreciates her culture and her beloved homeland. She has published short stories and newspaper articles. She resides in Wokingham, England. *Pachamama* is her first novel.

18953671R00205

Printed in Great Britain
by Amazon